STARS LIKE GASOLINE

JESSIKA GREWE GLOVER

STARS
LIKE
GASOLINE

JESSIKA GREWE GLOVER

For Mommy
&
Heidi
My Geminis who
Love this story as much as I do

And for Damian. For Always.
You'll always be the future I want.
And you're always the most beautiful thing in the room.

CONTENT WARNING

While *Stars Like Gasoline* is overall a fun and romantic romp, it contains content which may be considered sensitive. Some of this includes:

Racism and slurs, homophobia, domestic abuse, violence, and stalking.

Preface

I grew up in a "strict" Catholic household in sweaty, bug-ridden South Florida. Like Celia, I was never really one to subscribe to the religion but rather the cultural aspects of being in a traditional Catholic family. As a self-proclaimed amateur historian and anthropologist, I am fascinated by the strings of religion which tie so many parts of our histories together, creating a global ancestral quilt. One of the most fascinating parts of Catholicism (and many other religions, however, I'm trying to stay focused here!), is how everything about it is so mystical. From saints and the Holy Spirit, to First Communions and Last Rites, to drinking. The. Blood. Of. Christ. Yet, one must not color outside the lines of Catholic woo-woo, lest that be seen as pagan, demonic, etc.

In *Stars Like Gasoline*, I wanted Celia and Oscar's family to be a middle ground between deep Roman Catholic roots and the fact that Celia is legitimately being haunted in her modern life. I wanted the love of their family to be a sanctuary and sounding board for them, even if the echo from the sounding board came back as a bit archaic and, well, fanatical in its religious depths. Enjoy the romp through this book that has occupied a large portion of my heart for quite some time now.

—Jessika

Chapter 1

Celia

I was the only one left at the Vero Beach Museum of Art. A computer tab was open for each file on the Emil Cesar collection we had acquired the week prior, and I set about closing each to wind down my workday. The last I hadn't titled, and I sighed aloud, knowing I was going to have to head back to the crates where the collection was stored, awaiting its exhibition at the end of summer. Against the concrete wall at the back of the storage area was the painting I sought. I was normally thorough in my record keeping, so the unnamed piece was a curiosity.

Each click of my heels echoed as I moved closer, doing nothing to assuage my anxiety over the oncoming summer storm. Every low-pressure system brought with it unwelcome visitors. Oppressive shadows that mimicked my movements and ran nails down my spine. Those who seemed to think the fact that I had what the Cisneros side of my family referred to as *un pie en el otro lado*, or one foot on the other side, was an invitation for them to reach out from the beyond. I was six years old the day I told my abuela I had met her mother. My long-dead grandmother. The one whose sepia-toned photo was wedged under a thin sheet of glass on my abuelos' dresser, next to their water-damaged wedding photo and a lone collection stub from the Catholic church in Fellsmere. Abuela had turned to me, silver rosary in hand.

"Es eso la verdad, Celia?" she asked me, pulling the Virgin Mary shaped holy water bottle from behind her perfume. Oscar always called it Abuela's action figure, and Abuelo would scold him then chuckle, whispering that he too thought the shape of the bottle was bizarre.

"Si, Abuela," I answered her, fiddling with the floral bedspread. Una bruja—a witch—to some. To my family, it was simply who I was. Just as much a part of me as my dark hair or strong legs. My strange husky voice and my love of art, which ran deep enough that I made it my career.

Flipping on an additional light in the back room of the museum, I moved to the Cesar painting, trying to get a better look at the brushed seascape.

My phone buzzed from the pocket of my slacks, but I didn't bother to check it as I knew it was my brother, Oscar, wondering why I was late for dinner at our mom's house. Oscar was the reason I made the move back home to Vero Beach from Boston after the death of Nate, my brother's fiancé. We spoke daily while I lived away, and after Nate's death, I could hear in his voice that there were more bad days than good. When Nate's mother's beachside bungalow went on the market, I jumped at the opportunity to make the move home and into the house of my brother's dead fiancé's mother.

When it buzzed again, I shot him a text saying they should eat without me, as I'd been held up at work, and then squatted down to inspect the art. As soon as my rear end touched my heels, the lights in the room flickered. I started at the strobe effect and put a hand to my pocket, as though the technology within were a talisman. A pregnant pause in the room's atmosphere kicked off a waltz of uneven beats in my chest. I stood to walk out, happy at that point to close the file, sans name, when the room fell black. In my peripheral vision stood a shadow, somehow darker than the room itself. It vibrated with the rumble of thunder from beyond the museum walls. Abuela had always warned me to never look apparitions in the eye. "Move slow, m'ija, and treat them like perros callejeros"— rabid dogs. With my first footfall, frigid hands shoved me from behind. I ran for the door, squealing like a pig in slaughter when it slammed into my face. After fumbling for the handle, I pulled it open and took off at a raceworthy sprint, calling my brother as I fled.

A dim light shone on the chandelier in the foyer of the museum, giving me a stroke of hope to make it outside. Our security guard stood on the front steps talking to a man who looked about my age. Once outside and in company, I heaved a breath and realized I couldn't tell them what had happened. No one would believe me. Oscar was still yelling into my phone, which I clutched to my ear. The guard kept asking what happened and should he call the cops.

I shook my head, saying I was spooked, and the other man smiled at me, pushing a fall of hair from his forehead. I laughed, pretending to go along with the girl-afraid-of-the-dark charade. Both men offered to escort me back to my office and fetch my handbag, an offer which, I admit, I accepted.

"I'm Jacob. Wentworth," the man offered. He held out his hand as we walked the length of the museum. Jacob had the sort of blue eyes that looked haunted and perpetually on the verge of tears, which I was quite sure worked to his advantage.

"Celia Sullivan," I introduced myself and took his hand.

"The new curator. I heard mention of you. My dad is on the board here."

I nodded, checking my phone for the time. I'd missed dinner. Again. I really did feel bad. I made it out to Tía's house

3

in Fellsmere more than I saw my mom who lived five minutes from me.

"So, you've overseen the Emil Cesar collection here? All sorts of mystery surrounding that one, huh?" Jacob asked. I thought for a second before I answered, my heart still on a treadmill.

"A bit of mystery, I guess. Only in the anonymity of the benefactor," I said as I switched off the lights and grabbed my things.

Once I had my bag in hand, and the workday officially behind me, I heard Jacob starting to ask if he could take me for a drink, his slight southern accent turning the *i* in drink to an *a*. I was opening my mouth to answer when my brother pulled up to the front of the museum. Oscar waggled his eyebrows at me, moving the raised scar on his cheek.

"I'd love to get a look at the collection sometime. If for no other reason than to tell my dad I met you." Jacob winked at me with those Caribbean-blue eyes. Security made certain I was fine before calling this Wentworth character over toward the sculpture garden.

I thanked Jacob, deliberately pretending I didn't hear his offer for a drink, and left.

Oscar followed me home in the rain, though I insisted I was fine. I raced to my door and waved to him through the storm from under the bougainvillea-curtained overhang at my porch.

POWER WAS OUT COMPLETELY across my neighborhood. I stripped out of my wet clothes and put on some cozy shorts and a sweatshirt before retreating to my bedroom with a glass of cabernet and a book. It was only six in the evening, but the house was dark. The curtains allowed enough light in for me to read, while corners of the room remained swathed in darkness. Soft shadows danced on the freshly painted, white walls. Reflections of rain dotted the paint, bouncing from the mirror. Darker pockets moved in the suspension of breath between lightning flash and thunder. I looked up, but saw nothing, and jumped when the thunder came. All day I'd been twitchy, just waiting for the building weather to manifest into something *other*. As frightening as the occurrence in the museum had been, this storm felt like that had been just the beginning.

Seeing Oscar had texted me, I opened my phone.

The room turned from night to day in the space of the next flash, and a scarf-like trail of deep black drifted toward the bed. A sick sort of transfixed paralysis held me in place, staring at the trail. It spread wider, like smoke released from a chimney. My feet pulled higher on the bed in an instinctive retreat from the sludge. Though its initial appearance was shapeless, the longer I watched it, the more it formed. Within the next flash of lightning, inky hands reached for me. I flung myself from the mattress, out the door, into the living room.

I hadn't had the time to finish remodeling the living and dining rooms yet, so tools, paint, boxes, and sheets covered the entirety. Shades drawn, it was fully dark. My bare foot caught a drill left on the ground, and I stumbled into the couch with a curse.

Lightning flashed, and I swallowed. A void of brightness spilled from the hall into the living room. I'd backed myself into a corner and wanted to slap myself. Stupid, stupid girl. I called Oscar, watching the void move toward me.

"There's something here," I said, just above a whisper. "Help me."

Darkness moved closer, hovering a couple feet away. I banked right and threw myself at the door, feeling cold fingers touch my feet. Outside was mercifully absent of that void, but I stood in the street—in the middle of the street—looking at my house, the rain matting my hair and clothes for the second time in an hour.

Within minutes, there were police cars coming from both ends of my street, my brother's car trailing them. Closing my eyes, I shook my head. Oscar ran to me along with the officers. I gave them permission to look in the house, though I knew there was nothing there. Nothing they would be able to find anyway.

I felt like a tool. Knowing my face was about twenty shades of red, I took a deep breath and looked at my brother. He stood next to an officer, each holding an umbrella over my head, yet somehow the rain was sliding between the two directly onto me.

"Celia?" Oscar asked. I met his eyes. I couldn't tell him what'd happened in front of an officer. So, I glossed over the truth and felt like a criminal. The story I gave the officer was a mishmash of what I did when I got home. When it came to the part with the shadows attacking me, I gave a cursory explanation.

"There was a noise," I said, thinking really it was a lack of noise. "And movement in the house. I don't know how else to describe it. I wasn't alone, and there were shadows and noises, and I sound like I'm telling you there were monsters under my bed, don't I?"

To his credit, the officer smiled warmly but didn't laugh.

"If they are under your bed, then we will find them. Could it have been someone lurking outside? Maybe you saw shadows? On the window? Not to discredit you," he amended, cheeks turning pink. "It's just as sketchy if someone had been outside your window in this weather." It hadn't occurred to me until he said it, that the lightning had stopped. He sounded vaguely familiar, but I couldn't place him. I'd probably dealt with him on the phone before. We've had to call the cops on a bunch of drunkards who loiter in the museum lot after dark. "Want me to keep someone outside tonight?"

"It's not—"

"Couldn't *you*?" Oscar asked the officer.

"I . . . could," he answered carefully, dark eyes narrowed at my brother. I told them it wasn't necessary, though in my head I was downright terrified to go back inside alone. Oscar asked him again.

"Oscar, come on. It's no big deal. I'm sure this officer—"

"Kikumoto," he said. "Sergeant Kikumoto."

"He's a sergeant, Os. He's doesn't need to be on babysitting duty. You could stay with me."

"Oh, I will. Adrian?" He turned to the sergeant. Ah, he *knew* him. I looked at Sergeant Kikumoto now. Tall. I wasn't terribly tall, but he towered over both Oscar and me. Six foot? Maybe taller. Dark, straight hair, tanned in a way that told me his skin was a divine gift of genetics and the Sunshine State. He looked at us with nearly black, almond-shaped eyes, sighed, and agreed, before leaving to speak to other officers. Oscar then bombarded me with questions. I told him what happened, and he paled.

"I didn't make it up, Os. And I'd had maybe a sip of wine at that point. Honestly. Something *was* in there. Twice today I've been . . . bothered by one of *them*."

Growing up, spending half of our time with the Mexican side of our family out in Fellsmere, we heard all the old tales of spirits and restless dead from our abuela and tía. Never had I felt uncomfortable in my own place. As a child, I knew when spirits were around. Oscar too. The parts of me I kept under wraps with the Sullivan side of the family were given a warm welcome by the Cisneros side. None of my family in Fellsmere batted an eye when I acknowledged a passing specter during dinnertime or shut the bathroom door harder than necessary and yelled "Mind your own business" to dead air. Those were all harmless entities. Every once in a while, I crossed paths with one who wasn't simply curious. Every once in a while, my skin pricked in warning.

Every hair on my arms stood on end as I told Oscar what had happened. In all the encounters I'd had in the past, I had never quite felt how I did just moments ago. What I felt deep in the part of me that recognized the song of the dead was that the one in my house this evening was what Abuela warned me about. Malevolence and spite.

EVERY NOOK, cranny, and corner of the house was checked. Once the officers left, Oscar and I smudged it, put holy water out, even pulled out our Tía Teresita's rosary that I kept tucked away. We must have looked a sight, dancing around the bungalow with bundles of sage and palo santo smoking from our hands. Not to mention the blue-and-white Virgin Mary bottle of holy water, which I splashed like it was gasoline and I was covering up a crime. It was properly evening by the time we crawled under the covers. I hadn't made up a guest room, so Oscar bunked in with me for the night. My eyes couldn't stay away from the corner where I'd first noticed the shadow. Though the room was clear and calm now, my nerves were still at level ten. Oscar fell asleep instantly. He always could nod off when and where he wanted. I, on the other hand, lay awake for hours watching the time tick by. Around two I got up and walked to the kitchen. Sleeping was useless, so coffee was made. Percolating sounds bubbled merrily from the pot. With the air conditioner cranked up inside, the windows were fogged over from the humidity outside. Soft knocking sounded at the front door, and I nearly peed myself. Sergeant Kikumoto stood on the other side.

"I saw the light come on and stay on, and I wanted to check in," he said. "Sorry to disturb you."

"Couldn't sleep. I'm making coffee if you'd like some." I slapped at a mosquito on my exposed leg. That was why I'd moved away. The damned bugs. I also noticed I was barely dressed, wearing only short sleep shorts and a cami. He said he'd love a cup and followed me through the house.

"Kikumoto," I said abruptly as we sat at the kitchen counter.

He nodded.

"Japanese?" Obviously. God, Celia.

"My grandparents."

"That far back?"

"Most people assume I'm Cuban here in Florida."

"Do you know of the artist? Taiko Kikumoto?"

He shook his head no.

"Your name means 'book of chrysanthemums.' I'm sure you know that. Taiko Kikumoto used to hide a small chrysanthemum or a book in his paintings. We could find the series or year he painted it based on which he hid. In later years it was both. I've always liked working with his stuff."

"What did he paint?" Sergeant Kikumoto sipped from his black coffee.

"Lots of water." I laughed. "Oceans, rivers, waterfalls. There is always water with levels of hidden quirks. It's never just a landscape. Social commentary, political thumb biting, sexual references; he had little subthemes to each painting."

The sergeant was quiet for a long stretch of time. I poured more coffee and pulled my hair into a ponytail.

"I'll have to look him up. I don't know much about art. Took art history in college but nothing beyond that. I've never even been to the museum here. Where you work?"

He smiled, and I thought he was quite handsome. And it wasn't just the uniform. He and Oscar would look good together.

"Come to the museum when I'm working. I'll show you around," I told him. "As thanks."

"I'd like that. Can you tell me what really happened here tonight?"

My cup slipped from my hands and clattered to the counter. I grabbed a tea towel and mopped up the mess. There was absolutely no way I would tell him what happened. Oscar ran in, looking like a wild dog with his hair in a mad tangle, T-shirt askew. When he saw us in the kitchen, he blew out a breath and slumped into the counter stool I'd vacated. In the low kitchen lighting, my brother's scar was more pronounced, his face showing a hint of violence in his past. The events he had lived through that dimmed his smile for a time. Losing Nate dimmed it again, but I was seeing it brighten, day by day, since I'd moved back home. My gaze moved from my brother to the officer in my kitchen. The sergeant didn't ask me again what had occurred, but I felt him sizing me up. Good God, Almighty, he had that stare-into-your-soul way about him.

"Adrian, would you reach the coffee for me?" My brother yawned, rubbing where his eyes met the raised tissue of his cheek.

"Okay, so you two . . ." Rather than ask, I left it open for them to explain. I didn't think Oscar had been with anyone since Nate's death over a year ago, but I also didn't pry.

"We?" the sergeant asked. "Oh. Oh! No, we aren't . . ."

"Adrian and Nate were best friends," Oscar said, stifling another yawn. "Christ, what ungodly hour is it?"

"We were in the navy together. Found out we were both from here. I did my tour, got out, have been a cop ever since. Nate went career." I felt once again like I had missed so much, living away from my brother for so many years. "I need to get home, guys. There should be another unit outside."

"Are you off duty?" I asked him.

"I was off when I knocked on the door. Was about to head out when I saw your light on. Thanks for the coffee. Here's my card." He took a gold pen from his breast pocket and wrote on the card. "Oscar has my number, but you should have it too. Call if you need anything."

CHAPTER 2

CELIA

THE FOLLOWING WEEKEND, OSCAR AND I DROVE OUT on Highway 60 to Fellsmere to see our aunt and grandparents. Years before, when we were children, Fellsmere didn't have the newer communities that have been more recently developed; it was nearly all rural and farming. Our family had a small two-bedroom house that they shared. When our father was alive, he lived there for a time as well. The weekends we spent in Fellsmere growing up were cramped but always fun. At least after Papi died.

Oscar turned his car onto the street and pulled over in front of the chain link fence outside Tía's house. Onions, cumin, pasilla peppers, and tomatoes assaulted my senses before I had a chance to open the gate. We unlatched the metal security door, then pushed into the front door of the house. Our grandparents stood from their wood-armed recliners and shuffled to us.

"You don't have to get up, Abuela," I said, kissing her cheek. She smelled of baby powder and Chanel N° 5, which I had gifted her for Christmas three years ago.

"Ja, hija. We're just happy you're here. Teresita is making your favorite."

"Si, Celia," Teresita called from the kitchen just on the other side of the living room wall. "Sopes con pollo y mole!" she yelled over the sound of the radio playing her favorite pop station.

"Tía, you never make my favorite when I come to visit," Oscar yelled.

"Sí, pero, Oscar, you come out more now that Celia is home."

Home. Though we lived with our mother full-time in our childhood, once Papi died, Mom let us come stay with Tía, Mom's sister, and our grandparents. Our house in Vero was always perfectly put together. Too perfect. Our mother was an interior designer for clients all over the Treasure Coast. Somehow, though, Oscar and I secretly preferred staying out here. We would throw the blankets over our heads and talk all night in our fort. Tía Teresita was the best cook I'd encountered, leaving our bellies always full and happy. I know it broke their hearts when I moved away for school ten years ago. I had never felt like I belonged in Florida. But here I was, back again.

ANOTHER SERVING of sopes made its way onto my plate, and I tried to protest, but Abuela said to eat and that I was too skinny. While my mouth was full of the thick, spiced chocolate-based sauce with chicken and masa harina, Oscar said I had a ghost in my house. I nearly spat the mouthful out. Tía shrieked and made us tell her exactly what had happened. Once we finished the brief tale, the three elder members of our family looked to one another. At once, they started speaking, everyone selling a different course of action.

"I am not rubbing a raw egg all over my body," I told Abuela. She threw her hands in the air.

"Aye, Dios mío," she exclaimed. "I will call Padre Ignacio. He will come over."

"Abuela," I tried to reason. "I really don't think a priest will come out when I have just seen shadows.

"Shadows! Es un fantasma, Celia. You need to be blessed."

Tía left and came back to the room to put a necklace around me. It was a thin gold Cuban-link chain with an onyx evil eye hanging from it. By the time we left, I had a Publix bag filled with trinkets and leftovers. In the car, I lifted a bottle of mango wine from the bag and showed Oscar.

He laughed. "I think we laid it on too thick about liking it."

"Can't you give it to a client or something?" I asked, turning the bottle in my hands while he drove. The side eye he gave me told me enough.

"Speaking of clients, I need to head down to Boca on Monday for a meeting with our finance managers. I'll be gone until Thursday. Why don't you stay at my place?" he offered.

It was time I stay alone, and I told him as much. Besides, I thought, I had all these amulets to keep me safe.

THE MUSEUM WAS WINDING down for summer hours and getting ready for the art camp it hosted each year. Vero Beach was quiet in the hotter months, as it was a hub for snowbirds who escaped the northern winters. The anonymously gifted new collection monopolized my time. Cataloging and putting together a small opening for the collection became my top priority.

Rembrandt-like darkness and vignette took up the outer edges of each piece, bar the sculpture. In the center of each, however, was an almost whimsically bright seascape. Each shore or open ocean was different. From tropical, to what looked to be Nova Scotia, though the title of that one was simply *The Final Cycle*, so we had no confirmation on the location. I held up my iPad, filming the collection, stopping in front of each piece so I could go back later and screenshot it. A text message from the ticket booth buzzed on my phone.

Visitor for you. Cute enough that he might know your brother. That was a bit presumptive on her part.

Thanks, Barbara. I'll be right there.

I turned off the iPad and locked the room. Picking at a piece of packing material caught on my camisole, I realized I'd left my blazer in the storeroom. A small gathering of older ladies stood around the entrance, a taller male figure fortifying the back of their crescent. His face was tipped up toward the eight-foot-tall chandelier suspended from the ceiling. I walked up to them.

"It's always seemed like something out of place here," I said by way of greeting. "A little darker and mysteriously beautiful."

He turned to me as though he had been lost in the glittering black glass beads hanging from copper.

"Sergeant Kikumoto. What can I do for you?"

"Adrian, please," he said, holding his hand out to shake. "I was off and thought I'd see if you had time to give me the tour." I smiled and led him around the other side of the elaborate light piece.

"Fred Wilson was the artist for this. It's on loan from the Pace Gallery in New York." I motioned to the glass leaves and flowers. "The ceiling here actually had to be reinforced to hold the weight. Fitting, I think, given the name of the piece."

"You're going to make me ask. I can feel it."

"*The Way the Moon's in Love with the Dark.*"

"I may have to file that away for later."

"Please do." I walked him on but caught him looking back

at the black chandelier, his shoulders shifting under his pressed, olive-green T-shirt. We wandered through different galleries, talking about the pieces he questioned and ones I'd curated (not too many as I'd only been there less than a year). He stopped in front of a colorful glass chair and looked at it quizzically.

"Anya Sturm," I said. "Like it?"

"I . . . don't think so. No." I laughed a bit too loud, clapping a hand over my mouth. His dark eyes twinkled, and I felt a little tingle in my toes I wasn't expecting.

"Neither do I," I whispered and moved on. "Come, I want to show you a Kikumoto. Which sounds really dumb when saying it to you."

A tempest hung behind hunter-green partitions, framed in gold. Within the storm, a ship was marooned on a jagged rock made of words written in Japanese characters. Looking closer, one saw fish skeletons made of characters as well, a human heart pierced on the sail.

What They've Done to Her, Kikumoto, Taiko. 2006.

"It's a darker one," I explained quietly. The gallery was mostly empty, but still I spoke in soft tones. He moved closer to listen. "Most of his, I can show you another time, are more satirical in nature. This one is a statement on the subservience of many women in Japan. His mother was abused by his father. Taiko himself was abused. Kicked out of his home for being gay. His mother committed suicide. Look here." I pointed to a small icon of an open book with a chrysanthemum flower blooming from its open spine. I explained that this was the first in his last series of paintings. Taiko Kikumoto dropped off the radar for nearly ten years after his mother's suicide.

"Where is he now if he isn't painting?" Adrian asked.

"No one knows, really. Either he's dead or just off the grid. It was quite a score for this museum."

Adrian shoved his hands into his shorts pockets. He stared at the painting.

"Oscar told me. About the"—he waved his hand—"thing that happened at your house."

"He shouldn't have." I turned on a four-inch heel and led us from the gallery down a hallway. "Come. Let me show you the latest." I gave him a pretty smile that I knew wouldn't fool him. He sniffed a laugh, no doubt knowing when someone was being obtuse. The keypad clicked open the lock.

We squinted in the dimly lit room. Twelve assorted-sized paintings and one sculpture lined the walls.

"Emil Cesar. Gifted to the museum last week. I'm working on an exhibition night to showcase them."

"I feel like I've seen this somewhere," he said, standing before a tropical beachscape. It looked like a scene from *Peter Pan*. As though you were looking through the porthole of a ship onto the beach; an alligator winked at you. Dreamlike in its whimsy, the piece was as skilled as any master in the precision of the brushstrokes. The hairs on my arms rose, and I noticed him shiver. I'd only cataloged half of the pieces. The uninventoried pieces were still in their crates as we just didn't have the room at the moment to open them.

"Oscar is better now that you're back," he said. "After Nate was killed . . ."

I faced him fully.

"I tried. I did, and a few other friends. Even your mom. He was a ghost. Not to be insensitive about your experience," he said with a lopsided smile.

I rolled my eyes to keep the emotion from showing.

"I mean, every time Nate left, we all knew there was a chance. Occupational hazard. He was getting ready to retire, after the wedding. I never told Oscar. He was redoing the house—your house—to sell, so they could move to the place in Spain he'd bought. It just . . . I guess you never know. But he's better now that you're here."

I was nodding, and the damned tears fell regardless of my internal pleas for them to stay the hell put and not wreck my mascara. "Thank you. I wish I'd had time to know Nate better. I hate that I didn't. I guess I would have met you sooner too, huh?" I asked with a forced laugh.

He chuckled back.

"Well, Sergeant," I said, straightening my stance. "How was your tour?"

"Well worth the money. The tour guide was exceptional."

I saw him out and even walked him through the sculpture garden in front of the building.

"Call if you need anything."

Returning to work was a bit of a buzzkill. My emotions were running at NASCAR speeds, and I was exhausted. I hadn't talked that much since my days volunteering in institutions in New Haven and Boston. When a text came in to meet a couple of old friends for drinks, I was glad of it.

SWEATING glasses sat on the high table I shared with Darcy. Each time the door opened, her head whipped to it, and I guessed that at least one of the other people we were waiting on was a romantic interest. Darcy's serial monogamy had been a constant since third grade. She had a prom queen look, with her curled blonde hair and petite, tanned body. I knew she was more of a mathlete than cheerleader though. Whatever she did careerwise had to do with writing corporate loans for billion-dollar properties.

A waitress came by and took the glasses away, bringing us a

second round of mezcal with soda and lime. Two young children ran up and down along the wooden deck, throwing french fries into the water, watching the catfish fight over them. The scene was so repetitious, I shook my head, thinking the alcohol had hit quicker than it should. Smoked fish dip, tuna nachos, and chili fries quickly filled our table. Luckily the rest of our party arrived to help us eat it all. It took me a minute to recognize Jacob Wentworth in the small group. He slung an arm around me like we were old friends and tugged on a wave in my hair. Two other men stood behind him with a girl wearing the cutest lace-up gladiator sandals. I immediately complimented her on them, and she held out her leg, saying she got them at the outlets the previous week.

"I'm Sarah," she said, holding out her hand. "This is Adrian." She stepped sideways, and one of the two men with Jacob was the same Adrian to whom I'd given a tour hours earlier. Sarah's polite southern accent, which I guessed was South Carolinian, slipped out as she ordered the same drinks as us. Just before the sun started to set, the outside deck of the restaurant became almost unbearably hot. I had to pull all my hair up on top of my head and secure it with a pen I fished from my bag.

"Impressive," Adrian said, pointing to the impaled bun. Jacob turned to me and flicked the bun. I flicked him back.

"She's always done that. Stabbed her hair up with whatever was lying around. Chopsticks, pencils, you name it," Darcy said. I laughed and sipped my drink. The heat, and alcohol, was going to my head.

"So y'all knew each other in high school?" Sarah asked.

"Celia and I met as kids. We were inseparable until she left for Boston. Broke my damned heart."

"Oh, you recovered fine," I said with a scoff, throwing a pickle spear at her.

"Where's Oscar tonight?" Adrian asked, looking down over his drink.

"Mm," I mumbled, swallowing a bite of ahi. "Out of town for a few days."

He narrowed his eyes and looked at his phone as though I hadn't spoken. My own phone buzzed.

Didn't want to say it out loud, but call if anything creepy happens. I'm off today and tomorrow, but we can have a car outside if you want one.

I should be fine, I texted back. *The Catholic side of the family supplied me with everything short of an exorcism. Gracias a Dios.*

He laughed quietly, and Sarah looked at him. He smiled at her while slipping the phone into his pocket. Funny, I thought. I'd gone from thinking he and Oscar may have been into each other, to assuming he was single, to meeting his . . . girlfriend? The mezcal had definitely started to turn everything fuzzy. I bid good night to everyone, careful not to catch my heel in the wooden planks.

Chapter 3

Celia

Six thousand people, and their dogs, seemed to be on Veterans Memorial Island over the Memorial Day weekend. Not that it was surprising at all, which was why I dragged Oscar out early on the Saturday morning, rather than on the holiday itself. In fact, we met at my house and ran two miles over, flags tucked in waistbands, cutting through Riverside Park and over the footbridge onto the island. Until Oscar lost Nate, I'd never put too much thought into this pedestrianized sanctuary in my hometown. Each entrance welcomed and bid farewell to visitors with a memorial to those lost in all wars.

Lest We Forget, a common memorial phrase for those who perished during World War I, though applicable to each life lost in battle. Walking through the tributes to each branch of the military, and each conflict and war, raised the hair on my arms. The Naval Memorial plaque was on the far side of the island, nestled outside the mangroves and trees that lined the banks of the Indian River Lagoon. The bronze memorial was simple: logo, crest, no fuss. But still Oscar stood staring at it. Despite the curl of his upper lip that came from the resentment of his fiancé dying in service to a country that spat on their union, he planted a small flag in the grass. With a hand over his heart, my beautiful brother mumbled a prayer for his lost love.

Boston was sleeting the day I'd gotten Oscar's call. In the basement of the museum I'd been working in sat an unmatched set of pre-Roman casks. It was unremarkable, and the casks were two a penny in the archaeological world. These, however, had been used to hide weapons, making them a part of the museum's military intelligence installation. A big-ticket aerospace mogul donated loads to the museum for the installation. It wasn't my area of interest or expertise, but it made for a diversion and had monopolized my time. Something to take my mind off the horrible weather at least. Everyone in the Northeast was moody when such a wet storm moved in, but for me, it meant unwelcome visitors tended to lurk in the dark corners. One such visitor had been standing behind the cask I had yet to examine. There was nothing distinguishing about him, and the apparition was so faded my peripheral vision didn't even pick up any notable manner of dress. When I looked that day in the museum basement, however, there was more of a familiar aura to who stood near. My attention snapped up, meeting the eyes before me. Anyone who had met Nate remembered his glacial blue eyes. Eyes that were always smiling. But not that day. They were pleading. And then they were gone.

I'd ignored a call from my mom and one from an unknown number, but when Oscar's name popped up, I answered without question. He was quiet in that dark way he got when we talked about Papi, or his scar. Or the time he'd been cornered in the locker room in high school and called a faggot. Before he'd learned to fight back. When all he knew to do was hold his elbows in front of his face and kick. It did the trick at the time, but we knew, Mom and I, that it was a turning point for him.

"What's up, Os?" The phone was clutched between my ear and shoulder while I stood from the cement floor of the basement and brushed off my jeans. It was a Saturday, and I didn't need to be dressed in work attire. Especially as I didn't get paid extra to be at work that day.

"Did I ever tell you that Nate was supposed to be a SEAL?" his raspy voice asked. There was a mechanic clunking sound in the background almost drowning him out.

I said yes, he had.

"He made it through BUDs. The big training week or whatever. I mean, you've seen him. He's so fucking fit. During Hell Week and some test in the water, he had a heart attack. It disqualified him."

I hadn't known that.

"He was still an officer, so he started with the weapons development team."

"That's how he ended up in Bahrain?" I asked, wondering where this was going and suspecting it was nowhere good. Oscar took in a breath that sounded almost like his wounded-animal laugh. The laugh we both shared.

"Yeah, the beautiful little shit was part of weapons testing and development with the Naval Support Activity station there. Went into Afghanistan last week, I guess."

My stomach dropped. I grabbed the doorframe to the stairwell, wishing I'd taken the call from Mom. From whoever called from that unknown number.

"Where are you, Os?" I asked, trying to control my voice. The ticking sounded again, and a muffled voice came over some sort of radio.

"It was an IED, Ce. Took out their convoy. They said . . . he was . . . that face. There's nothing left."

I stumbled back, my calves hitting the stairs, and I sat hard on the concrete. There was nothing I could begin to say. I stared back into his fiancé's eyes in front of me once more, the ghost of Nate fading before me.

"He's gone, Ce. And I don't know what to do. Like I literally can't figure out how to do anything."

"Tell me where you are."

"In a cop car," he laughed, sounding slightly insane. A voice in the background swore. "No, no. I mean, yes, I am. But it's a friend. I have to go."

"No. Os. Where are you? I can come home."

By the time we spoke again, he'd put on his capable hat. It wasn't often he spoke about Nate. The edges of that hurt were too raw still. But when he did, he shone a little brighter. Sometimes, I even thought Nate must be close by. He was his golden boy. His Apollo. I hadn't even believed in love until I saw them together. Love was as mythical as faeries and elves. Until I saw my brother and his Nate. That being taken away from him made me angry in a way I'd never been before. I'd stopped seeing friends. Stopped going out. Stopped doing anything but working. I'd known I wanted to come home long before Oscar called with the listing. I'd known I wanted to come home the minute I answered that call.

So, when he stood from placing the flag in the soft earth and said he was ready to go, I crossed myself like a good Catholic, as though we were in church, and took his hand to walk away. The sun shone a little brighter through the trees. The glow on Oscar's face a little more gilded.

CHAPTER 4

CELIA

IF LIGHTING A VIRGIN MARY CANDLE EVERY TIME I came home wasn't enough evidence of my discomfort in my house, I didn't know what was. Maybe the salt I kept handy or agreeing to have a full glass of water under my bed at all times, as per Abuela's insistence. The heat of summer wore on as I worked on parts of the house, transforming it onto fair representation of my style. By the end of June, the floors were laid in the living room. Cute accent rugs in cream and black were scattered around, and my new bone-colored linen sofa sat covered in plush cushions. I'd even made up the guest room. The house felt like home.

Darcy came over and lounged in the pool with me while we drank sangria. Oscar sat alongside us, his long legs dangling in the water. She chattered about the guy she'd been seeing and how he acted like he was still in school.

"I mean we're almost thirty. You don't need to drink beer in the bed of a truck every Friday night."

Oscar chuckled and said she should see his options.

"Is that why you've been driving forty-five minutes to

27

Melbourne every weekend?" I asked him, pulling on his toe in the water.

"That," he said, splashing me, "is exactly why." The side gate creaked, and a figure came alongside the house, followed by another. My heart sped up, but Oscar stood. "It's Adrian and Sarah."

For some reason, my whole body went rigid. My brother let them in the screened patio while I sneaked into the kitchen.

Seven types of fruit went into my sangria. Watermelon, peaches, lime, plums, and three types of berries. Each time I poured a glass, a good remuddle with a wooden spoon was required. I stood in the kitchen, dripping a bit on the floor in only a cheeky bikini. My fingers yanked Oscar back when he came in to grab a bag of chips.

"Why didn't you tell me you'd invited them?" I hissed and spooned some salsa into a bowl, thrusting it at him with more force than necessary.

"Dunno. Forgot. Why's it matter? We have plenty of food."

"Yeah, but it's nice to know when someone is coming over to *my* house. I may have made an effort to look nice or vacuumed or something." Oscar grinned and walked out. Of course, Adrian was standing in the door.

"You didn't know he'd asked us over."

"I . . ."

"We can leave. It's awkward."

"No, no. I'm sorry. I'm pissy for some reason. I just—you know when you have people over, you want to make sure the house looks nice, yada yada?"

He smiled at me. "Looks great to me." There was a millisecond there that I thought I saw his eyes flash over me, but as soon as I thought it, I felt like a shit. "Compared to last time."

"Oh! Come see the living room. Power tools are gone, and

there's actually a floor." I had him follow my dripping trail. I supposed I didn't need to vacuum, but all the Virgin Mary candles could have used a tuck into the closet.

We stood in the living room, both of us in swimsuits, chatting about the flooring material (tiles that looked like wood), the paint color (Foggy Morning), and why there was a salt barrier on the windowsill (ugh). He checked the lock on my door and the window latches, careful to not disturb the salt.

"Completely changed the look of the place. Nate's mom hadn't changed anything since like '89 I think." I shivered in the air conditioning and asked if he wanted to go back outside. He motioned me to go ahead of him, and I may have swished my hips a bit. Just a bit. I was an asshole.

"I remembered where I'd seen that painting—the one you showed me in the back room," he said. I had the pitcher of sangria in one hand and asked him to grab a couple of acrylic glasses. We set it all on the sidebar by the pool, and I poured glasses for the girls. "Judy had it. Nate's mom." I paused with the drink to my lips. "She had it in the hall outside her bedroom. Your bedroom."

"The one with the gator?" Oscar asked from his perch near the pool.

Adrian confirmed.

"I wondered where that went. As soon as she was moved to the facility, I don't remember seeing it. I wondered if it was stolen."

I set my drink down, not interested in it at the moment. Darcy hollered for me to come in the water, but I asked for a moment and went inside to my laptop to write some notes down. Oscar whistled at me from the kitchen door.

"Hey, sexy thang," Darcy called. "Your guests are out here, and you're preening for an Excel file." She laughed and called for me to get my pretty little tush back in the pool. In the file was a list of the paintings, the date of the donation, and the shipping receipt. They'd come from Fort Pierce, which didn't really tell us anything. I remember there was a hold put on our acquisition of the art. It was supposed to come in January, but it only arrived in late May. I'd never seen a print of Emil Cesar's, but that didn't mean they didn't exist.

Something crashed in the house. A sound like glass breaking. Adrian was by my side immediately. I began walking in the direction of my bedroom, but he put a hand out to stop me, his palm flat on my stomach.

"I'll go look. Bedroom?"

I nodded. Oscar followed Adrian.

"Christ!" my brother exclaimed. He popped his head out and told me to come in. Fragmented glass from a mirror was strewn over the whole room, across the white and gray makings on my bed. I was speechless. Sarah and Darcy came up behind me, wrapped in towels. Darcy swore. How did a mirror shatter when it was still hanging on the wall?

"Adrian," Sarah said. "Who did this?"

I went into automatic action, grabbing a dustpan and brush, sweeping up. Oscar moved everyone out, but Darcy grabbed the top layers of my bedding and shook them out, making sure there wasn't any glass left. A car pulled away from the house, and Oscar told me that Sarah and Adrian had gone.

"Come stay with me, Ce," he said. "Until we figure it out." But I'd made my decision. I stood in the middle of my room and said it was my house. I was staying here, and any spirit squatting in with me could get the hell out if they didn't like me.

Darcy looked pale and took out the wastebasket filled with glass.

"This is my house," I muttered again.

I KNEW I'd said I would have all the paintings unveiled the next week, but it took me another month. An insurance hold up kept us from being able to expose them to anything, which, honestly, suited me fine. I had enough to do with the ones we'd already opened and the mayhem in my home. Caroline was pushing me to get moving on all of it, so we could have a gala.

"They take at least eight weeks to plan, Celia. You know that. It's the slow season too, so we need to give people time to fly back into town if they want to come."

I was on my hands and knees in a Valentino pencil skirt I'd bought from a consignment shop on Newbury Street in Boston. If Caroline only knew. This skirt was my own curated piece. I pulled at a bit of packing shavings still stuck into the back of the frame and a folded, yellowed slip of paper caught on my finger. I pulled it out and unfolded it against my thigh. Caroline peered down, squinting through her readers. It was written in a hasty script. For some absurd reason, I didn't want her to know what it was yet.

"Looks like a packing slip. Inventory. Nothing special. I'll file it later." I stood and placed it on the table against the back wall. Caroline told me to finish up with this piece today and move on. Her sensible flats shuffled from the room, leaving me in the dim light. The paper read, *For Anton. I'm sorry to have left you.*

I wondered if Anton ever read it. If he knew Emil was sorry to have left. The title of the piece was *Naufrage*. Not incredibly original, as it means simply "shipwreck." I thought the name was interesting, since Cesar used such a simplistic name for a painting full of whimsy. I wanted to look up Cesar's life. From what I already knew, he was the only son of an American army nurse and French potter. The two had met in Brittany at the end of World War II. His mother died in childbirth while still-birthing his sister. Cesar and his wife,

Marie, had no children. Perhaps Anton was a lover? It was not unheard of in his generation to be married to a woman when your sexual orientation was otherwise. Maybe I'd find more clues to the mysterious Anton the further I delved into this collection.

The lights above me started flickering and went out completely for five seconds. I knew it was five seconds because I closed my eyes and counted to keep from screaming. Once they came back on, the backing paper on one of the frames had been torn open. I yipped and ran over to it, more concerned that I would be implicated in defacing the collection than I was with the fact that something had been in here with me. I pulled out my phone and text Barbara. She should be getting off soon, as the museum would be closing in a half hour, so no one would be allowed in. Not that Barbara would be any kind of physical help, since she was close to eighty years old. But at least it was someone else in here with me.

CHAPTER 5

CELIA

FLICKERS OF LIGHTS ON THE HORIZON WERE THE only breaks in the expanse of darkness in front of me. Though I awoke in my bed from the dream just before a wave came down on the beach, it wasn't the nightmare but the glimmer of a face hovering before mine in my darkened room that had me up and out the door. The face hadn't seemed as menacing as it had before. Not that I'd stuck around to find out. Coming to the ocean was the only thing I could think to do. Oscar was in Melbourne again. Plus, it was midnight. I texted Adrian from the car and immediately felt stupid. At least I knew he wasn't sleeping.

Tomorrow was going to be rough at work if I didn't get any sleep tonight. Only a few cars passed along the street by the boardwalk at that hour. Tires crunched into the parking spots lining the beach. I looked over my shoulder to see Adrian walk up the steps to the boardwalk. He hopped up and sat next to me on the railing.

"Did it hurt you?" he asked.

I shook my head and told him about the dream and the

face. His own face pinched like he was annoyed, and I apologized for calling.

"I told you to call. Don't apologize."

"This whole thing is making feel like a lunatic. I mean, look at me," I said, gesturing to myself. "I'm not even dressed. What would I have done in Boston? Run through the streets in my nightie?"

"It would be very Sylvia Plath," he said with a repressed chuckle.

I turned to him and put a hand on his shoulder. "You don't know art, but you know poetry? Dear God, man, whatever would the boys on the force think?"

"I was an English major."

"Can I ask you something?" I asked, my voice nearly a whisper.

"No, it doesn't look like a Victorian nightgown," he answered. I smiled despite myself. He was an interesting complexity of character.

"Do you think . . . Nate. Could he be angry?"

"No." The answer was quick and decisive. The strap on my white cotton nightie slipped down my shoulder. He reached over and lifted it up. Goosebumps ran up my arms. "Nate was never angry. That's why he was so good at his job. His patience with everyone made him a fantastic soldier. It made him a . . . great goddamned friend. And he loved Oscar, Celia. He did. What's . . . haunting you . . . isn't Nate. I would put money on it. Hell, I'd swear it."

Haunting. I hadn't said it out loud yet.

"What a mess."

We were silent, staring out to sea. The air was heavy and humid, no doubt making my wavy hair reminiscent of an eighties band. Surf crashed on the soft drop off. A police car slowed down behind us, window rolling down. The officer called over to ask what we were doing. Adrian hopped down and spoke to him. When he walked back over, he grabbed my hand and told me to follow. We descended the stairs to the beach and walked over to the shore. I slipped off my flip-flops and let the warm Atlantic water tiptoe over my feet. "Could I speak with Nate's mom, do you think?"

"Judy? You can try. She's not always lucid, but she loves visitors. Some days, though," he said with a heavy swallow, "she doesn't remember that Nate is gone."

I looked at him. Really looked for the first time. He was in workout shorts and a white T-shirt, standing tall and straight. Those dark eyes had a lot of pain behind them. His arms were tensed, veins protruding in the muscle. Even though I knew that to outside eyes it would look ridiculous, us standing there in the middle of the night, me in my nightgown, I reached out and squeezed his hand. He looked surprised but squeezed back.

"I've never had a best friend like that, or a great love like Oscar had. All I've had is Oscar. If something happened to him . . . I don't know what I'd do. So, I imagine that's how you feel, and my heart hurts for you."

He looked at me for a split second and gave me a small half smile, eyes still squinted, then looked out to sea.

"But honestly, what in the hell is going on in my house?"

He laughed and pulled me to his side, an arm going around me. It was friendly and not a romantic gesture, but my stomach argued with that.

"I can take you to see Judy on Tuesday when I'm off. Unless Oscar wants to go." The handkerchief cotton of my nightie made the press of his arm around me warm and inviting. It took me a minute to answer without feeling out of breath. Long enough that he turned to look at me, our faces inches apart.

"Yes, that would be good. Thanks." Damn. I was in trouble. "How's Sarah? She was freaked out at my house." I didn't want to bring up sweet Sarah but felt I had to. He dropped his arm as if realizing how it could seem.

"She wouldn't admit anything was wrong. So, I didn't say anything. She's very logical. Engineering mind and all."

Two in the morning was a real stupid time to be awake, I'd determined. My roommate at Boston College said her father would always say, "Nothing good happens after midnight."

That's how I felt standing on the beach with Adrian at two with no intention of going back to my house to sleep, but knowing I was dead tired.

"I'll take you to Oscar's." It was as if Adrian read my thoughts. "You can at least get some sleep," he said with a yawn.

Adrian walked me into Oscar's condo and looked around like a good officer. I was exhausted and braided my hair loosely while he looked around.

"Looks good," he said at last. "Good night, Celia." He kissed my cheek and walked out, leaving me standing like I'd been pinned to a post. Double damn.

CHAPTER 6

CELIA

SUNDAY BRUNCH AT RIVERSIDE CAFÉ WAS COMING to a close when I finally pulled off my rash guard after spending the day on a stand-up paddleboard. Music still played inside as people lingered over the last omelet and crab legs, but the midmorning rush had ended. I was dragging. Every noise in my house had woken me up. Every creak sent my heart racing, and I wasn't able to just relax in the way I needed. I took a small tour along the Indian River early this Sunday morning, and we stopped to watch a family of otters romp on the tiny river island across from the fire station. Getting out on the water more was on my list; I just needed more rest than I was getting.

Darcy sat on one of the high stools outside the restaurant and motioned me over as I shut the gate to the private dock. Her family was all gathered at the table, and it looked as though they were celebrating a birthday. My skin was sweaty, sticky, covered in sunscreen, and I just wanted to get home.

"Celia Sullivan," Darcy's mom stood and hugged me. She subconsciously tugged at her Lily Pulitzer sheath dress, and I winced. "I had lunch with your mama last week."

That reminded me, I needed to call my mom. Oscar was always telling me off for forgetting.

"Tell me. When will the museum gala invitations go out? I've had my tailor on standby for a month."

"They went out on Friday," I told her.

"Tell me. Who is doing the flowers? I hope it's not Bird Street. They put weeds into everything."

I assured her it wasn't.

"Celia has the most gorgeous pool, Mama," Darcy jumped in, saving me. "You would just die for the water feature." Her mom asked for photos, which I procured awkwardly from my phone after fishing it out of my backpack.

"Tell me," she said.

Darcy raised an eyebrow. We used to do impressions of her mother when we were in school. She always started with "Tell me" and it usually led to a compliment sandwich or an underhanded remark.

"I heard from Lara that Oscar isn't 'engaged' to that army man anymore." She air quoted *engaged*, and I saw Darcy mouth an apology. Her father grunted, which could have meant anything. I hiked my backpack farther up my shoulder and smiled.

"Nate was killed in Afghanistan about eighteen months ago."

"Oh dear. Tragic. I think I do remember reading that in the papers. His mother is a bit of a vegetable now, isn't she, poor dear. Does she even know he was killed in the army?"

"Navy. He was in the United States Navy. His death broke my brother's heart, and yes, his mother knows. If you'll excuse me, I must get home. I have dinner plans."

The air conditioning was blasting my face in my car before I checked the text that had immediately buzzed as I walked away.

Oh my God, Cece. She's a virus. I'm so sorry.

Oscar's car was on the crushed-shell driveway when I pulled up. I dumped my keys and walked straight outside and fell into the pool. My brother laughed and told me he'd made paleo enchiladas for us. I floated on the lounger and opened my mouth about twelve times before he told me to spit it out.

"I want to go see Judy." He twitched his mouth and nodded.

"Of course, Ce. She's . . . delicate. Sometimes she sees me and she bursts out crying, then forgets who I am altogether."

"Adrian said he'd go with me if you didn't want to."

"I can go. I haven't been since the beginning of July anyway."

We floated while the scent of enchiladas wafted out from the kitchen door. "So," Oscar began and smirked. "Aaaadrian said he'd go, did he?"

I groaned and flipped off the raft.

"Was this during one of your midnight rendezvous?"

"Okay, I'm done." I got out of the pool and made to go into the house.

"I'm glad he's looking out for you, Ce. He's a good guy. And he's hot."

"And he's with Sarah. He's been very kind. Now, are we eating?"

My brother got out and shimmied past me with a pointed look. "Mm-hmm," he said and snapped a towel around his hips.

I didn't know how one made paleo enchiladas, but Oscar's were phenomenal. We were dipping non-paleo tortilla chips into the remaining sauce, lapping it up like dogs.

"We were supposed to move to Spain," he muttered while I soaked a casserole pan. I stopped and turned to him; his head was hung, dark hair curling where it dried. In the golden light of afternoon, his raised scar caught the light. I stamped down the rush of anger I felt every time I thought about it. "Nate had bought a place. He thought I didn't know." He huffed and half smiled, pulling at his nose.

I set the casserole dish down and leaned over the counter to listen.

"Remember when I told you I'd met someone?"

I did. I was starting my last job in Boston. The sun hadn't shone in a month. When Oscar called, as I was getting on the Red Line train on the T, I swear the sun started to peek through. They met when Nate was on leave and was home to see his mom. She had just been moved to the facility, and the two men ran into each other at Home Depot. I laughed my ass off when he said that. My brother at Home Depot was like finding a polar bear in the jungle. Oscar said he had been staring at plumbing equipment for twenty minutes, trying to figure out what he needed to unclog the toilet in his condo. Nate caught him watching YouTube and finally walked over to help. According to my dashingly handsome older brother, he couldn't speak when Nate first approached him. Rendering Oscar speechless was a talent I never possessed, so I immediately commended the man.

"God, Ce," he'd gushed to me. "He was like fucking Apollo. Golden from top to toes and everywhere in between."

I'd pretended to barf.

Oscar hadn't wanted to admit to Nate what he was in Home Depot to buy, so he said he had an ant problem.

"Are you watching YouTube to see how to snake ants out of your toilet, or is that something else?"

My brother said he had never felt redder and more embarrassed in his life. Nate handed him a toilet auger, saying he hoped he was less full of shit when they met again.

I laughed myself hoarse, catching disapproving northeastern glances on the train.

"Swear to God, Ce. I held up my phone and asked for his number right there."

I didn't meet Nate until they were engaged. My boss didn't let me take the time off to come down to the party, so I arrived the weekend after. Really, I'd only seen Nate three times total. All I did know was that he made Oscar happier than I'd ever seen him. It must not have been easy for them. Bahrain was quite literally the other side of the world, and Nate was only on leave every few months.

"Remember when I met him in Costa Brava last spring? We got so lost trying to get to the beach from town that we ended up on someone's farm."

Nate pointed to the stone house and told Oscar he was going to buy that house, and they would have their fucking fairy tale. Or a fairy tale with fucking. It seems they were both really drunk. Oscar found the deed in a file on his computer a week before another officer called to tell him Nate had been killed. Now, in my kitchen, Oscar slammed his palm down on the marble counter and stood.

"Os," I said quietly. "It's okay to keep talking." He'd never told me this. He just shut down. I mean, three times a week or more I'd get phone calls giving me the most intimate details of their relationship, and now he just shut down. He kissed my cheek and left.

Chapter 7

Celia

Judy Cosgrove lived in a room dedicated to Nate. Oscar had only one photo of his fiancé in his condo. It was normally facedown on his dresser. I also knew he went through the pictures on his phone constantly. We brought Nate's mom lavender truffles, which Oscar ordered regularly for her. I'd never been good with illness. Being in this assisted-living home made me want to run. Like run for miles. My brother, on the other hand, sat next to Judy and immediately held her hand. She smiled at him and patted his cheek.

"Hello, handsome," she said, voice like wet paper.

"Hi, Mom." Oscar introduced me, motioning for me to step closer.

"You look just like Oscar. Come closer, sugar. Oh yes, just different eyes to those eyes my Nathan liked so much. Still so pretty. Like chocolate buttons."

Shades of mauve and celery decorated the room, just as they had in my house before I gutted it. A photo of my brother and Judy's son sat across from her bed. Their arms were around each other's backs. Though each had a cup of something in hand in front of them, their pinkies were linked as though needing to be in an infinite touch. Nate looked like his name had just been called, eyebrows high on his forehead, mouth slightly open in a smile. Oscar's head was just slightly turned to his partner, adoration written across every feature.

Being here made me angry that I had been stuck up north through most of what my brother went through. Happiness and emptiness both. I shouldn't have stayed. I should have moved back long ago. From the window, I could see McKee Botanical Gardens just up the road. It had been years since I'd been there. Years since I thought about what I liked doing.

Oscar asked Judy about the painting that hung outside her bedroom. She stiffened, but a small smile crept onto her fair face. I could see how she had once been beautiful, before grief wrung it from her, dulling her blue eyes.

"I'm going to tell you a bedtime story I used to tell my little boy," she began. "Come sit, sugar. Bless your heart, you could be twins. Here, move a little, Oscar love." We squeezed together on the love seat next to her recliner. "There once lived an orphan in a land far away . . .

"He made a living for himself writing poems for the townsfolk while he traveled through towns and villages. Sometimes he was taken in by kindly mothers whose hearts broke to see such a child so impoverished. Oftentimes, he was kicked out of town for being a nuisance. Ever since the boy could remember, his goal was to make his way to the sea: to get on a boat and travel far from the lands that claimed his parents. But that would have to wait. Over the years, he picked up a few travel companions. A rat named Stefan; a magpie he called Annie. Many legends say magpies warn of death. Well, our boy felt that was a load of ol' garbage, and he loved his feathered friend. The two companions, feathered and furred, followed the boy, who was slowly becoming a man, throughout the countryside. Annie and Stefan stayed hidden when they must but stayed close in the long, cold, dark hours when he slept alone.

"The boy turned seventeen the day he arrived at the sea. It was a sea that had seen years of war. Death beyond measure. Annie cawed somberly, no doubt seeing the tragedy of the beach with her magpie's second sight. The lives claimed by the shallow water. The boy's dream of seeing the sea dissolved like sugar. In his heart, the sea was not like this. In his heart, the sea was warm and bright and not interested in the lives of soldiers. So, the boy turned on a worn heel and made his way into town. He wrote poems that filled walls and rooms, barns and cafés. He met a girl and they married. The girl did not care for the boy's companions and tried many times to shoo them from the home they shared with her parents. The boy's poems were read around the world. Though the couple remained poor and childless, the boy traveled, bringing his poetry to different locations. He always looked for the sea that was the sea in his heart and not the sea that was the sea of dreams lost. He came home one day to find Stefan gone and Annie singing like a nightingale, mourning the loss of her friend. The boy's wife held no remorse for the lost companion and told him so. So the boy left. He went in search of the sea that was in his heart, and not the sea which crushed dreams and men.

"In time he found it. The boy, who was no longer a boy but a man just past his prime, walked along a trail by the coast and pulled aside a scrub of fat leaves, revealing the sea beyond. The turquoise sea that tumbled frantically and happily, as if it had been waiting for him his whole life. The boy, who was not a boy, sat and wrote a poem about the discovery. About the sea that was the sea of dreams and not the sea which consumed them. About the colors and magic in the sea he had finally found. And while he wrote this poem, coming back to it day after day, a girl watched him.

"She stumbled upon the poet the first day. Seeing the

wonder and awe on his face when he saw the sea, she fell in love. On the fourth day, she went to him. She was so colored by her love for him, she had no head for what he might say to her. He only stared and told her she was a siren. A siren sent from the sea of dreams; a siren who had shipwrecked him with her siren's light, allowing him to live a while near the sea in his heart before he returned to the sea which claimed dreams. And, for that, he was always grateful."

We sat in Judy's room, totally engrossed in her story. She looked up finally, meeting Oscar's eyes.

"Hello, handsome," she said. "Have you heard from my Nate today?"

Oscar's shoulders sagged. I saw a tear catch on the scar that ran in a crescent from his nose to temple.

"Not today, Mom," he said, voice shaking.

"Oh, I do miss him. If I hear from him today, I'll tell him to call you." She turned to me.

"Hello, sugar. I'm sorry. I'm being rude. I can see you are Oscar's sister. You look just like him."

Chapter 8

Celia

Sunset in July started late, allowing the early evening to bake in the relentless heat. After being with Judy, Oscar wanted to be on his own, and I needed to run. South Beach, just off Seventeenth Street, was the easiest place to park and there was always a police car in the parking lot.

Barefoot sprints along the shore took me past condos and houses, but few people. An oncoming storm loomed on the northern horizon, about a half hour away. I ran past the boardwalk, where I'd sat with Adrian, and turned around, picking up speed on the tail end, trying to beat the weather. The first rumblings of thunder chased me roughly a mile from the beach where I'd parked. The sun was very low at this point, the golden hour passed, water darkening. I slowed to a jog, staying away from the dusk shoreline, which always seemed treacherous to me. The portentous wind pushed at my back, a precursor to the storm behind me.

I thought of the paintings waiting for me at work the next day. About the tempest in the Kikumoto painting I'd shown Adrian. About his face as he studied the painting. Lightning flashed, and I had to get off the beach. People who aren't from

Florida, or aren't from the South, never understand the dangers of an electrical storm. My first roommate in Boston thought I was crazy for refusing to shower while it was lightning out.

The planked walkway presented itself. No one was around, after dinner walkers were long since back home; the lifeguards packed up hours ago. Wooden decking led through a mangrove and sea grape forest from the beach to the parking lot. I hurried, flashes of light pulling shadows from every round leaf. When I was about halfway through the trees, the cicadas stopped their keening song. The absence of song felt so loud in its void that I stumbled, my knee hitting the sandy wood. It was much darker than I'd anticipated. Sore and hobbling because of my bleeding knee, I did my best to hurry.

In the next flash that burst through the leaves like water in a sieve, a dark figure appeared on the path before me. I wished I'd taken the shorter path. Rapid heartbeats hammered in my chest while I contemplated whether to run back toward the beach or try to move past it. Thunder crashed around me, sea grape leaves trembling with the violence of sound. The darkened figure moved toward me. I screamed, hoping that might just fend it off. Because malevolent darkness shakes in its boots when a girl in booty shorts screams. I started reciting the Our Father in my head, even though I wasn't technically a Catholic. All the help I could get at that point. At least Abuela would be proud. Chaotic, half-formed thoughts ran directives in my mind.

I backed up, jumping at the flash that gave the dark shape more defined features. It was a man, angered and hateful. I fiddled with my phone until the emergency screen came up. If I called 911 again, I'd be labeled as crazy for sure.

"What do you want?" I screamed at the darkness slowly fading back into the shadows of the beachside forest. I looked at my phone, and as soon as it opened up, I instructed it to call

Adrian. Lightning flashed, and the figure was in my face. Icy hands wrapped around my biceps and shook me, freezing my body from the inside. I ran like a bat out of hell, as my mom would say. Cold pinpricks grabbed for me as I passed, nearly making me fall. I screamed again and yelled "South Beach!" into the phone, not even knowing if Adrian had picked up.

Lightning flashed again, and the form was once more in front of me, causing me to fall back, landing hard on the planked walkway. "What do you want?" I repeated, crab walking backward until I could hoist myself up using the guardrail.

Thunder rocked the wood, then darkness fell again. I had to run through it like that bear hunt book from my childhood. I couldn't go under, as there was jungle floor teeming with God knows what four or five feet below. I couldn't go over. Oh no! I had to go through it. I had to run my white-booty-short-covered ass through it as fast as all five foot five of me could run. When I got to the dark shape, I ducked down. Landing on my hands, my wrist barking with pain, I bear crawled until my legs picked up the slack again, allowing me to run more. How long was this mother-effing walkway?

A flash, brighter than any before, lit the entire forest but showed the blessed opening at the end. I sobbed with relief as the sound of lightning hitting something quite near shook the ground. Once in the open, I pushed for my car and wrenched the door open, slamming it hard enough that the glass rattled. The shape stood outside my window as I threw the car in reverse and pulled away from what was once my favorite beach.

REFUSING to eat the pork posole I was given at Tía's house was the primary indication that I was not okay. I drove straight out to Fellsmere, needing to know I wouldn't be alone. My phone had cracked when I fell, so Teresita told Oscar I was there. Each family member tried to get me to shower, but I refused to be alone in the bathroom. Both Teresita and Abuela were much larger than I was, so they pulled a plaid, western-style shirt from Abuelo's closet for me to wear. It snapped up the front and had a winged collar dating from the seventies. I put it on over my sports bra. The shirt hung below my running shorts, but I didn't care. Abuelo joked that if I had more clothes on, the fantasma might not be so interested in me. Abuela whacked him with her tabloid magazine while Tía let out a stream of virulent Spanish that had him pinch faced. It was close to midnight, and I knew they all wanted to get to bed. I'd told Oscar to stay home. He was emotionally spent as it was.

Headlights shone through the windows of my family's living room. Abuelo pulled himself from his chair and looked out, claiming it was just a man not a ghost. I smiled a little at that, and he winked at me. Seeing Adrian walk up, I opened the door and unlatched the screen door. The family stood in an expectant semicircle behind me. Adrian smiled at them, and I turned to see three toothy grins smiling back. Rolling my eyes, I led him to the back porch.

"I just finished my shift. As soon as I heard the message, I sent a unit over there. They found some blood, but nothing else. I called Oscar."

I was nodding, hugging my knees in tight, which made the skin split, blood seeping through the bandage. He asked me to recount what happened, and so I did. His hand pulled up my wrists, and he frowned at the bruises along my arms where icy fingers had latched on. I had this huge acquisition to prepare, the gala in a few weeks. A bar-fight aesthetic was not what I was going for.

"Can I ask you something?" he tried.

"I don't know. Can you?" I teased, but it came out so void of merriment it lost the joking edge.

"How did Oscar get his scar? I know it's none of my business, but Nate alluded to abuse."

Turning my head so my cheek rested on my good knee, I looked at him.

"You don't have to tell me. I'm just connecting dots here."

"Such a good cop."

"Just a friend," he corrected, pulling a piece of hair away from my eyes.

"When we were really little, we would come stay here to visit our family. Our parents were married for a year, I think. They had Oscar, and then when Mom was pregnant with me, they were pressured into getting married. Anyway, I don't remember ever seeing them together. Different people, you know?"

He hummed and sat back, his hands behind him. The story started coming out before I considered I'd never told anyone before.

"Papi slept on the pullout couch in the living room, claiming he needed to 'get back on his feet' after the divorce, basically taking advantage of his former in-laws." I rolled my eyes. "We always slept on piles of blankets and never minded. It was an adventure. I was ten and Oscar twelve when our father started drinking. Well, that was when it was obvious to us. He was so charming and likable. He was hired easily and always had a girlfriend.

"I mean, look at Oscar. He's gorgeous. Looks just like Papi when he was young. Only Oscar got Mom and Abuela's gray eyes. I was always jealous of that."

"What's wrong with brown eyes?" Adrian asked with a twinkle in his.

Not a damned thing, I thought.

"The problem with Papi was that he couldn't keep a job. We never knew why, but I suspect it was the drinking. He had friends over a lot. Men and women." I paused and swallowed.

"They'd sit out here"—I gestured to the patio—"drinking all night." Abuelo had gotten sick and couldn't work anymore. Teresita worked two jobs to keep up the household. One of Papi's friends, a "Jim" or "Rob" or something, always gave me the creeps. He never did or said anything to me, but he just kind of had that dumb look, and he made offensive remarks. Like making Mexican jokes, thinking he could get away with it since Papi was white. He'd say gross things about women. Then he started on the gay jokes. Oscar came out to me when he was almost fifteen. He had known forever, he said. It didn't surprise me. We were in a Catholic household though, so he worried about coming out to them.

"What about your mom?"

"I think she always knew. Oscar was closer to her than I was. I think I always felt she didn't quite get me. Mom heard from Teresita about the people Papi had over, and she started limiting how often we came here. So, things got strained between them. Mom hated that her family still allowed Papi to stay here." I yawned, shaking my head to wake up.

"Well, finally, Oscar came out to Papi. I encouraged it because I didn't want our father or anyone in the family to not see him fully. Papi didn't say anything. Like, he literally walked away, and we didn't see him until two weeks later." We came here after school on a Friday and dumped our stuff in Tía's bedroom. She told us to be careful and that, if we wanted, she would drive us home. I went to the kitchen for a snack before dinner, and Papi was already out there with Jim/Rob and two women I'd never seen. There were bottles of beer and God knows what else lying around like they'd been at it all day. Papi called me outside. Oscar followed.

"'Not you, maricón,' Papi said to Oscar. I remember being so stunned that he used that word to Oscar. It was like he wanted it to be as insulting as possible, so he used the Spanish slur."

Adrian breathed in deep and shook his head. I yawned again. A tentative hand touched my back. I had the horrible urge to be held and to cry, but I reined it in.

"What happened then?"

"I opened my big mouth. I yelled at my dad, and he just sat there. Then Jim, Rob, whatever his name, got up and looked at Oscar," I told him, continuing the story. "I whirled around and told him to back up. All five feet of me. He grabbed my chin, then Papi and Oscar both flanked me. Oscar pulled the guy's arm away from me.

"'Fucking faggot,' he said and spat in Oscar's face. Oscar lost it and pushed him hard, but he was fifteen and gangly; the guy was strong and full of alcohol. He pulled back and smashed the full bottle of beer on Oscar's face. It knocked him out. Concussion and like seventy stitches. He nearly lost his eye. My mom's cousin is an attorney. He made sure the guy was put in jail for attempted murder. He's still there, I think."

"Jesus," Adrian said and put his arm around me. "Jesus."

After a few minutes, I pulled away and was glad I hadn't cried.

"After that, we didn't come here. Until after Papi wrapped his car around a tree. So yeah. That's our tale. Pretty ugly, huh?"

"I can't believe your grandparents let him stay that long. They must have hearts of gold."

I nodded. "They do. I kind of wish we legally used Mom's last name. We've always been Cisneros, rather than Sullivan. It feels like we took away Abuelo's legacy." I shrugged.

He said it seemed like Abuelo was wise enough to not think it meant we were ashamed of him. We sat in silence for what seemed like hours.

"I'm afraid now. Of being alone." Admitting that really cost me. But it was true. When I'm alone, that thing comes after me. "I don't sleep. Why am I telling you all this?"

He reached over and traced the dark circles under my eyes.

"Come here," he said quietly, opening his arms and scooting so his back was against the wall. "You need to sleep." I leaned against him and breathed him in.

"I'm sorry. I probably smell," I said. His stomach rumbled under me. "I was afraid to shower on my own."

"I think if I helped you with that it might be breaking some rules."

I smiled against his chest and wished I could break every rule with him. Which made me an asshole. Again.

"I REFUSE to answer any questions beyond what I've told you, Os." He pestered me and pushed until I hung up on him.

Adrian followed me home in his car. I'd had to call in sick to work because I couldn't very well say I'd been attacked by a supernatural being. The story Caroline got was that of a stupid girl who fell running during a storm. The morning was already dark as sin, inky clouds converging from three different directions. Oscar had to be in Viera for a bank meeting, Darcy was working, my mom had a client meeting, and I really needed to shower. You know when you're a kid and you turn out the light in the kitchen, then run full speed to your room so the boogeyman won't get you? That was my life. Luckily, Adrian offered to be there, and he had the day off.

"I'm out of food," I announced, coming out of the shower

in my bathrobe, towel drying my hair. "I'd like to feed you, so either I need to grocery shop or go get something."

"We could get something. Do you like Jamaican food?"

"Oh! MoBay?"

He grinned in agreement. MoBay was one of my favorite restaurants, and it was just a bit up the road in Sebastian.

Turning to go get dressed, I made myself say something. "Do you want to see if Sarah can join us?"

"Do you *want* Sarah to join us?" He folded his arms across his chest. Well, obviously not, but . . .

"I just . . . didn't know if it's weird. For her."

"So, I'm going to say something, and I don't want you to take it the wrong way," he said.

I kept running my hands through my wet hair for something to do.

"I am a public servant. I took an oath to protect people. Maybe it's not the most conventional situation, but I don't feel like protecting you—especially since I am friends with your brother—is out of line."

Everything he said was true. Undeniably, glaringly obvious truth.

"Do you?" he asked.

"No," I said, and it was a whisper, so I cleared my throat and said it again.

And sometimes, the truth is the right thing, and it's the best thing, and it's the damnedest thing too.

COCONUT-CRUSTED SNAPPER and fried plantains certainly took my mind off everything for a short time. Adrian's eyes kept straying to his phone, responding to texts. From our booth was a view of the Indian River and the islands in the middle. I'd been so wrapped up in work and the house that I'd barely gotten any sun. Not that I was a fair English rose, but my skin was a bit sallower than it used to be. I decided to spend the following weekend at the beach—another beach. I looked at the bracelet on my arm, remembering Oscar being so excited when he bought it for me in Spain last year. The gold twisted into a thick rope on which a tear-shaped opal hung.

"How's the wrist?" Adrian asked. I'd nearly forgotten about it. It was swollen and sore, but less annoying than not knowing when I would be able to be alone again.

"Fine," I lied, shrugging my shoulders and looking back out across the street and toward the water.

He sniffed a laugh at my expense.

"Doesn't really matter. I have so much to get done. I can't worry about a boo-boo."

"The gala?"

"Yeah, and I've located a Kikumoto, but it doesn't have a certificate of ownership, so I'm trying to sort that out. It would be amazing to have it before the gala, but it's looking less and less possible. Anyway, I don't suppose you plan to come? I'm forcing Oscar to come as my plus one."

"Galas aren't really in my budget. Or, honestly, on my list of things I'd ever care about doing." He laughed. I agreed with him there.

The skies opened up just as we pulled into my driveway. Great. He checked the house while I lit the stupid candles and smudged the air, feeling ridiculous. Wind was blowing the shutters as rain lashed the windows and the screens.

"Look," we both said at the same time, then laughed. I motioned for him to go first.

"It's my day off," he began. "I'm supposed to see Sarah. If I stay—"

"I get it," I said, putting a hand up. "Thank you so much.

For everything. I'll be fine." Mental note to not call him every time something says boo.

Slow footsteps took him to the front door where he paused, opening his mouth as if to say something. I had a hand in the bottom of my white T-shirt, twisting and untwisting it. Instead, he leaned over and pressed a light kiss to my cheek before slipping out the door.

Chapter 9

Celia

An antique shop on Ocean Drive had a contract with my mother. Normally I shied away from antique dealers, secondhand shops, anywhere there might still be someone hanging around postmortem. As I said, un pie en el otro lado was my call sign. I'd always had one foot on the other side. Instead of being near death itself, though, I saw those who hadn't let go of this side. Artwork, sculpture, and things I dealt with in curator life didn't have the same pull to spirits. Of course, there was always an exception. Just as you could get a spirit hanging around on a county bus. However, the antiquities people had in homes, jewelry, even favorite clothing were the things that carried spiritual weight. When I entered the mix of object and spirit, the ghosts took notice. A week after the South Beach incident, I was a bit more confident in my stronghold on my home. Connie from the antique shop reached out to me saying she had an odd painting that reminded her of something she'd seen in the museum.

So, on a Wednesday afternoon, I rushed over after work to check on this strange painting. Connie was wholly southern, with perfectly coiffed auburn hair and makeup that didn't dare misbehave. What I hadn't expected was for my mom to be there when I arrived. She immediately noted my new Sézane pin-tucked white button-down I wore with the Valentino skirt. It wasn't buttoned high enough for her liking, but she approved of the ensemble. Mom herself was looking sleek in a Michael Kors suit, her highlighted brown hair pulled into a low chignon. Watchful eyes from the corner of the store bore into me while I spoke to the two older women. Each time I shifted my gaze to meet the presence, it would duck behind a large urn. Mom caught my looks and led Connie away, so I could note who was watching me. I figured one spirit on my side couldn't be a bad thing. The presence was female and less corporeal than I expected. Her features weren't discernible, dissolving completely when I neared.

"Here it is, doll," Connie called. "Came in just the other day, and I knew I'd seen something like it. Put two and two together, and four was that I'd seen the artist at the museum."

My hands went to my mouth as I gasped. In the painting was a street lined with brightly lit lanterns, though the scene was overall more muted. Fish danced along the street, while a child holding the hand of a rabbit sauntered down the center. If you looked closely, you could see that the bottom edges were rounded using light techniques, and there was an opalescent line toward the top. The scene was set in a fishbowl, the little girl trapped, but happy. The hand that did not hold the bunny's was holding a chrysanthemum; her feet stood in ballet first position over the open leaves of a book.

I walked to the back of the piece, and sure enough, it was signed by Taiko Kikumoto himself, dated 2019. Shaking hands took my phone from the black embossed-monogram bag on my shoulder and took photos. This wasn't the one I'd been playing cat and mouse with. Somehow there were two Kikumotos floating around Florida's Treasure Coast. Not to dangle from the thread of the fishbowl painting, but something fishy was afoot. The museum board had approved funds only for one additional Kikumoto, and there was a low cap on that as it was. There was no way I could get approval for this one. As sweet tea as Connie was, she was a shark in the market, and surely the scent of my blood was all over the place on this one. I had to strike before she had time to wiggle out.

"I'm very impressed, Celia," Mom admitted, sipping her pinot grigio. I smiled onto my own glass.

"Thank you. It's been a favorite summer wine of mine for about a year now." She narrowed her eyes but laughed.

"You know I meant about the painting."

"It's what I do, Mom. You've just never seen me in action." She was quiet for a time. Cars drove by the small off-shoot street in the beach area frequented by tourists; the bougie district Oscar called it. This wine bar had become a favorite since I'd been back, despite everyone telling me there were seldom locals here. Plus, they had my favorite organic dry Italian white, so what's not to love? "I'd like to see you in action more. I feel like I haven't seen you at all lately."

Though the fans whirring under the overhang kept the air moving, it was still August and approximately a million degrees out. I rolled my sleeves one more time and undid another button on my shirt to get some air. Mom tutted.

"It's effing hot and I'm hardly exposing anything," I retorted.

"I can see your bra!" The waiter came by just then and brought a plate of marcona almonds and a goat cheese torte. I snickered, but Mom looked mortified. Oscar would have peed his pants laughing. Where was he? He was on his way a half hour ago. Once the waiter left, I pulled the collar aside, showing more of my bra, pointing out the white eyelet cotton.

"It's Aubade. Anyone worth his salt would know it's meant to be seen a little bit."

She huffed but peeked over. "It's just not professional."

"I'm having a glass of wine outside. At the beach. With my mother. I punched my time clock on my profession an hour ago. Admit it. It's a gorgeous bra and you're 100 percent going to go online tonight and look at Aubade's latest collection." She giggled, making me feel lighter.

"Is it a little blue bow on the strap?" she asked. I leaned forward to show her. Cornflower blue bows graced the middle of the wide strap. It was perfect with the Sézane shirt because both deserved a bit of airtime.

"Oh hey, y'all," a soft voice called. Mom and I looked up to see Sarah and Adrian with that Jacob Wentworth and another friend standing at the table. And I still had my shirt pulled open. Oscar ran up behind them, apologizing for being late. He leaned down and kissed our cheeks and straightened my collar.

"Ce, you're showing your bits. Nice Aubade." And I died. Mom shot me an "I told you so" look.

"Latest collection. Curator through and through," I answered, pretending to be nonchalant and praying that no one caught the waver in my voice. Adrian smirked and shook Oscar's hand, then introduced us to their friends. Our small family-of-three drinks night became a party of seven. After she finished her glass, Mom took her leave, claiming it was too hot for her outside. The men all stood as she left, and I walked her to her car at the end of the block, hoping no one could see how horribly sweaty my poor Valentino skirt was.

"Your mama is lovely," Sarah chimed when I sat back down. "Beautiful lady. You don't look anything like her though." Oscar and Adrian both coughed on their drinks. It made me laugh because I did look quite a bit like her, just more olive skin and darker eyes. It seemed like everyone waited a beat for her to amend the comment, but it was there to stay.

"Yes, well, Oscar got all the beauty in the gene pool, I'm afraid."

"Oh, I wouldn't say that," Jacob said. "No offense, Oscar, but I think your sister is the prettier one." Oscar put a hand to his chest and flung his head back in mock indignation. I was embarrassed by the whole thing and didn't know what to do with myself. Under the metal table, I was rapidly dangling my clearance Jimmy Choo from the ball of my foot, and it flung off and into the street. And I died. Again. Adrian and Jacob both jumped up to get it.

"Here you go, Cinderella," Jacob teased. I took the shoe and was sure I was twelve shades of crimson.

"Did you get those at the outlet in Orlando?" Sarah asked. "I thought I saw a pair there. Your feet are far bigger than mine though. They didn't have my size."

Adrian looked at her with knitted brows. Oscar sucked in his cheeks, trying to not laugh.

"Got my monster feet from my mama," I answered, lifting my bare leg straight out, showing my toes, which were decidedly not monstrous. I always had them pedicured. "At least they keep me from falling over."

The boys chuckled.

Sarah pointed to the scabbed mess on my knee. "Adrian said you took a fall last week."

Jacob pulled out his phone and handed it to me. "Text me your number."

We all knew he did it to break up the tension, for which I was grateful and immediately obliged.

"Now you don't have to call the police when you trip at the beach," Sarah said in that sweet voice that now sounded saccharine and cancerous. She drank her wine with a mischievous gleam in her green eyes.

"I'm out, ya'll." I stood, slung my monogram bag over a shoulder, and kissed my brother's cheek.

"Ce," Oscar said. "Stay."

"Pleased to meet you," I intoned to both new boys, though I had of course met Jacob twice. "Sarah. Sergeant."

"Let me drive you," Adrian said. I didn't turn around but heard a female huff.

"It's like three blocks. Good night." I walked briskly, knowing I'd have a damned blister by the time I got home. Which was at least five blocks away. Texts buzzed the entire walk, but I refused to pull out my phone, mainly because I would've had to stop, and the walk was utter hell. I didn't even care if there was an angry ghost in my house at this point. I was so glad to see the bougainvillea-covered front stoop. Once inside, lights all on, I opened up the texts. Oscar, of course. One after the other.

You should have stayed. Claimed your territory and all that.

What a horrendous bitch. She won't shut up. Adrian isn't even speaking to her.

Jacob's kind of hot.

I mean, a bit more Jake Owen than your usual type, but I'd do him.

Then Jacob: *No idea what that was about, but your feet aren't that big. Can I take you out this weekend?*

I text back a quick *Sure* because why the hell not.

THE BLISTERS HURT like the devil when the water hit them, and the open sores on my ankles were screaming demons at me. The night was the kind of heat the air conditioning doesn't quite hold the upper hand over. Every window was fogged over with moisture. A 2019 Kikumoto painting with no title was a rare find indeed. If I could only get the release for the other piece I'd found, I could bet the gala would draw art dealers and patrons from much farther than our usual guests. Strange that the Cesar acquisition had come from Fort Pierce. While it had a small arts community, the town just south of us wasn't known for the careful upper-middle-class and bourgeois lifestyle of Vero Beach. Maybe I was tired, but it felt like I was missing vital puzzle pieces here. An anonymous donation of a huge Cesar collection, Kikumotos appearing out of nowhere, seemingly belonging to no one, and a Cesar having once been in my house but now missing.

Cabinet doors slammed in the kitchen, and a thump preceded the sound of running water. I jumped in my seat, leaving my laptop open on the small writing desk, which sat facing the front window. Goosebumps ran a race up my legs and arms, chilling every inch of me. Clenched fingers opened and closed over my phone. Screw it. I texted Oscar.

Something is in here. Don't call Adrian. If you're already home, no worries. Just letting you know.

As I raised my eyes from the phone screen, a reflection caught in the fogged window. Silhouetted against the arcing bougainvillea was a man, standing directly behind me. The chair crashed to the floor as I stood like a jack-in-the-box. An icy touch reached out. I grabbed at the salt from the windowsill and tossed it at the shape, watching as the aberration in the room broke apart momentarily. A Spode Blue Italian salt bowl sat on the corner of the black spindle-legged desk. I cupped my fingers into the salt granules, pulled a handful, and spun in a quick circle, entrapping myself within the purported protection circle. I chanted an old Wiccan protection spell I'd found in an eighteenth-century grimoire in Boston and watched the spirit come closer and closer to the circle.

"Elements of Day,
Rays of Sun,
Hear what I say,
Gather as One,
Goddess of Night,
Strength of Other,
Goddess of Light,
Protection of Mother."

God only knows why I had that memorized when I'd only seen the piece a handful of times. The Catholic side of the family would be appalled by my use of a Wiccan spell, but La Madre María hadn't been working so far. Over and over, I chanted the spell, like thumbing down the length of rosary beads. Sweat covered my body, despite the iciness in the room and my state of semi-undress.

Two sets of headlights shone through the window. Still, I stood, salt clenched in my hand, chanting the spell. A second shape moved against the first. Inhuman screaming sounded when the looming malevolence lurched toward me but stopped inches away, where the salt line held. Moth-black features seemed to press along the invisible barrier between me and the entity. Footsteps crashed through the front door. Dark, incensed eyes bore into me where I stood terrified and unable to breathe. The shape looked as though it were being pulled back, that high keening scream following its retreat. The room fell silent, and I collapsed in the ward I'd cast myself. Strong hands lifted me up, pulling me to the couch. Oscar wrapped a cream-and-black throw blanket from the sofa around my bare shoulders. No one was speaking. A bright flashing on my computer screen drew my eyes across the room past Adrian, whom I hadn't even registered as being there. Great. Standing on shaky legs had Oscar telling me to sit back down, but I crossed to the desk. Cursor blinking in the center of a blank screen hovered at the end of an affiance:

His anger is consumptive. I will not leave you alone in his sea of vengeance.

CANS OF BEANS, bags of organic coffee, and vitamins all spilled onto the counters and into the sink where I'd had to shut off the water. Stacking the foods and supplements gave me something to do while I processed what had happened. What *had* happened? Music turned on. My brother's voice told Adrian I relaxed with the sound of lo-fi male singing. Something told me Adrian was laughing about that, though the room was relatively silent. Coffee grounds and bits of oatmeal covered the white marble, waiting for my rhythmic wipe with a dishcloth.

"You can go," I muttered, my back still to them.

"Not a chance, Ce," Oscar said, pulling the trash from the bin and tying it.

"I had it under control. I told you not to bother." I shot a look toward the stupidly good-looking police officer standing against my refrigerator.

"You told me not to tell him. I technically didn't. We were grabbing tacos together."

"Tía would be appalled," I retorted haughtily.

"And the fact that you were calling on pagan gods?" Oscar asked, a wide grin on his face. I lived for making him smile like that. His gray eyes creased, lighting up his face. I had to smile, rinsing the sink for the last time.

"Well, I never got that part in Macbeth I wanted in high school."

"Macbeth is a cursed play," Adrian chimed in. "People are always dying during productions. Better you didn't get the part."

Oscar and I burst out laughing. They'd seen the ghosts. I knew they had, but they both confirmed it, making me feel far less crazy. The fact that there seemed to be one spirit in my corner relaxed me a bit. Bins rumbled on the side of the house as Oscar took out the trash and did me the favor of rolling out the cans.

"Sorry," Adrian said to the floor, kicking his foot back and forth. I scrubbed at my face, aware we were alone and I was once again in my PJs. "Sarah was . . ."

"She's your girlfriend, Sergeant. Just leave it." He was quiet for a long time. No way were the trash cans taking this long. Note to self to throttle my brother later.

"She's not. I mean we aren't . . ."

"Just stop."

"Celia, let me apologize."

"You don't need to." Each word was ground through my teeth.

"Fine," he bit back and walked out of the kitchen. Oscar came in the front door, and I heard them talking before the door shut with a resounding click.

A long-suffering sigh came from the hall.

"Do I need to kick his ass? I mean, it would be a real pain in *my* ass, especially since he's twice my size, but I've been in Krav Maga for like six years now."

I growled and stormed off to my bedroom, slamming the door.

CHAPTER 10

CELIA

Sculpture from an artist who almost exclusively did oil painting was like seeing another side to the artist. Vulnerability ran through the veins of an artist's marginal work, revealing a side or nuances we may not get to see from something polished in their typical medium. As a rule, I preferred paintings. The depths involved in capturing the mood of a piece impressed me.

L'habit ne fait pas le moine. Though it was the fourth Cesar we had unveiled, once insurance gave us the go ahead, it still made me sit and stare. "The habit does not make the monk" was the title's meaning. Gray clouds covered the small, fourteen-inch square canvas. In the bottom left corner stood a man in a navy pin-striped suit, his back to us. Images of the same man projected outward, like carbon copies, multiplying diagonally from the original image to the faintest ghost of one in the upper right corner. A flume of water ran down the center from the top as though a fountain spilled from inside of the frame. In the water, which pooled at the bottom, were animals and flora. Lavender blooms and palm fronds—an odd pairing, I thought—reached from the puddle, like they were trying to stay above the water. It almost reminded me of the Kikumoto with the girl in the fishbowl.

The sculpture was titled *Perte*. "Loss." Twenty-four inches high with a fourteen-inch diameter, the work stood on a small pedestal. It was noted the pedestal was not a part of the work itself. Cesar was not known to be a master sculptor, so the fact that this piece became available signified to me that either the anonymous benefactor knew him personally, or it was found separate from any others in his collection. Cesar died in 1990, having outlived his wife. There was no known date on the piece, but his later pieces tended to contain the lavender vines, sometimes surmised as alluding to his inability to ever leave France. Initially, it was listed as a pigeon sculpture. As soon as I'd seen it, I knew it was not a pigeon but something statelier. Running soft-gloved fingers along the cement-gray body and head of the bird, I found striations, both intentional and seemingly unintentional, covering the animal. Something struck me as feminine about the bird, though there was no way for me to have known. Its head leaned down, no space having been cast between the neck and chest. A long, sharp beak had the slightest nick of a curve at its point, tucked tightly into the crook of its chest and flank. The eyes were onyx black and held sadness in their downcast gaze. Vines of lavender crept up the short legs, entangling the bird's body, binding it in place. I squatted down, a slight grunt escaping me as I was incredibly sore from my morning workout. Under the bird's body, as though she were shielding her nest, was another small body. Pointed face and tiny legs. I began to note that it was a baby bird, but closer inspection revealed it was a mouse, its tail curved, becoming one with the lavender. Such an odd piece. What looked like the flower of the lavender under the bird's claw was in fact a ladder-horned seashell.

"What story do you have to tell, friend?" I asked aloud, sitting back to look from a short distance. Lights flickered, but

I wasn't nervous. It was almost like an acknowledgment, like a brief batting of eyelashes. "Okay then. I'll try to figure it out. It's not like I have anything else to do." Christ above. I was actually speaking into the ether.

"IT'S INCREDIBLE. Someone just listed it as a pigeon. Just a throwaway dirty bird," I said excitedly to Jacob that same night.

"Pigeons are dirty birds, that's for damn sure." He reached for my hand that was drawing a horrible rendition of the *Perte* sculpture on a cocktail napkin. Fingers stroked mine, tickling and making me smile. "Have you finished, Cece?" he asked pointing to my plate.

Internally, the nickname Cece made me cringe. Darcy had used it since we were little, just to tease me, and it became her regular moniker for me. Hearing it from anyone else, however, left a bad taste in my mouth. Low lights hung in exposed bulbs, casting retro warmth in the heavily wood-paneled restaurant. It was a new gastropub in downtown, a block from the library. When we left, the Friday night crowd was huddled against the outside wall waiting for tables. Sticky heat left a sheen on my skin, making me feel self-conscious. After work I'd changed into an ivory maxi dress, accessorizing with a gold cuff and Tía's Cuban chain necklace.

We walked toward the street on which his high-end electric sports coupe was parked. Jacob slipped an arm around my bare back. I stiffened at the contact, but he didn't seem to notice. Buildings of every color and varying architecture rose and fell in this area of the city. From hundred-year-old structures to fairly modern, soulless ones, indicating the exact lineage and passage of time the city had taken. Every parking meter was occupied, likely due to the opening of the new pub and the two other restaurants in the area. Considering it was the slow season, the Friday night was alive, and it made me happy to see the businesses doing well. Just as we turned the corner onto the street where we'd parked, a couple came from the opposite direction. I jumped aside, grabbing on to a meter to keep from falling into the street. Jacob palmed my elbow, pulling me back.

"Jacob!" Sarah's diet soda voice chimed. "How are you? Hi, Celia. I've never seen you covering your legs before."

I stood, not knowing whether to laugh or spit venom at her.

Adrian's eyes closed briefly while he scrubbed a hand over his face.

"Sergeant," I said, reaching down toward my feet. "I would have thought you'd have been working tonight." Now finished, I stood.

"My days off changed to Friday and Saturday. First time in a year." He looked at me quizzically, then smirked, covering his mouth. I'd tied the hem of my split-skirt dress so that it was now knee-length. Holding out a tanned leg, I ran a hand over my knee like a game show host.

"There, Sarah. Now you don't have to feel so baffled by my change in appearance. Is that enough leg for you?" I started walking off, grabbing Jacob's hand to tug him behind me.

"I should've thought your mama would have schooled you better," she called. I swore I heard a muttered "Mexican ho" follow, because Adrian also barked, "What in the hell, Sarah?"

One of my greatest accomplishments in life was not rising to that bigoted remark. There was a pause in the air around us when she said it. Jacob whispered a curse and put his arm back around me, pulling me to his side, which is exactly what I needed in that moment. Something to tether me to the ground and humanity. We could hear Adrian hissing something to her, but our footsteps were quick, and the roaring in my ears drowned out what he might have said. When we got to the car, I must have looked like a wild animal, because my date turned me to him, my back pressed against the white door.

"Hey, beautiful," he said. "She has nothin' on you."

"Do you think I care?" I spat. "She could be a damned supermodel-fucking-fairy-queen and the only thing that would get me is the uneducated, fucking racist, vitriolic bull-shit she just admitted."

"Damn, girl. That's a mouth on you."

I laughed, the pinpricks of adrenaline ebbing away. He leaned in slowly and brushed a slow kiss to my bottom lip. I responded, meeting his mouth with mine.

"I never finished telling you about the sculpture," I said when we had pulled apart.

"Not to be a dick, but I don't really care about the painting right now, Cece." He pressed his lips to me again, a hand pulling me closer.

He hadn't even listened to the type of art I'd told him about, which really bugged me. My phone buzzed from my handbag, interrupting us. Then kept buzzing.

Ce, I'm having a bad day. I hope you're not with Jake Owen right now. If you are, it's fine. I just think I need to talk. The bottle I've been chatting up isn't talking back.

WHATEVER SET Oscar off this week had done a fine job of it. His usually tidy modern condo had empty glasses everywhere, T-shirts on the sofa, and blankets and pillows on the living room floor. Jacob dropped me at the front of Oscar's condo building within minutes of the text. My brother hadn't changed out of his suit, apart from missing his jacket, but he was rumpled, looking like he hadn't slept in ages. We sat on the edge of the tufted gray sofa. Really, I had been waiting for the other shoe to drop with him. Adrian said he'd been in a state after Nate's death, but there hadn't been the fallout I thought would happen.

"I don't know that I can go to the gala, Ce. I'm in a bad place."

Shaking my head, I told him to hell with the gala. I didn't care. I cared about what was going on with my brother. "I met someone," he said and choked on a sob. My arms were around him. "The client in Melbourne. I don't know how it happened. We just clicked, you know?"

I nodded against his messy hair.

"He's so different to Nate. I hadn't considered him at first. I hadn't considered anyone. I didn't want anyone else." He was openly crying, chest shaking against me. "Since I had to keep going up there, I was seeing him a lot. We had dinners and lunches.

"Last week I finished his account. So, technically I wasn't working for him anymore. We had dinner. You know that place on Main Street that looks like a hippy hot mess but has the best damned blackened mahimahi?"

I said I did.

"After dinner we walked, like a date. It felt good. I felt butterflies. Shit, Ce. It had been so long. I was standing there in my suit, all G-fucking-Q, and he was in these hot Lulu shorts. We looked ridiculous."

I laughed, soft and hopeful, still holding his head against me.

"No one was around. There was a space between two buildings. Not quite an alley but just room enough for crates and shit. And us. We just stood there, staring at each other like we didn't know what to do next. I sure as shit didn't. My hands were shaking, but he took them and kissed my palms. I pulled him closer, and I swear to Christ, Ce, it was one of the best kisses of my life.

"A few days ago, he came down to see me. We had a bottle of wine on the balcony, and he gave me a gift. One thing led to another, and we were in my bed getting six kinds of hot. Sorry. Is it okay to tell you this?"

"Os. Honestly. Of course, it is."

"When he left, I felt empty. I'd betrayed Nate," he sobbed. "It's like, he buys us a fucking house in Spain and dies serving our country. A country that did everything in its power to say we shouldn't have been together. So instead of honoring him, I just fucked another guy. In the bed we'd shared." The blankets and pillows made sense now. He hadn't slept in his bed since.

"Have you spoken to him?" I asked.

He made a so-so shake of his head.

"You did nothing wrong, Os. You're allowed to kiss and fuck and love anyone you want. It's not a betrayal."

His fist lodged between his teeth as he sobbed. I pulled it away and put my hands on his face, forcing his eyes to mine.

"I'm serious. You are justified in grieving. You are justified in living. If you like this guy, don't give him up out of guilt. Nate loved you. He would want you to love again. Or at least have a good seeing to."

He sniffed a laugh. "Why is your dress tied up?" he asked, wiping his face. I laughed and told him to wash his face, and I would clean up the condo and tell him.

The bedroom was worse. Sheets were torn from the mattress, shades drawn tight, the one photo of Nate facedown, a hat on top. Sounds of running water told me Oscar was showering. I gathered all the linen and put on a load of washing, then moved to getting the glasses picked up. He walked out of the bathroom, drying his hair, eyes swollen and red.

"You like this guy?"

He nodded, tears rolling down his face. "He's a few years older. Doesn't look it. Totally your type—hands off."

"Call him. Introduce me."

"Should we double date with Jake Owen?"

I groaned that he kept calling him that. Especially since there was a Jake Owen song that reminded me of another guy I wasn't dating. "Hard no."

"You're not even into him, are you?"

"We aren't discussing me. Show me the gift."

In the spare bedroom, which he had set up as a gym, a framed painting sat against the wall, facing away from the room. I crossed, stepping over a line of dumbbells. Oscar turned the frame to face me. At first, I couldn't comprehend what I was seeing. Oscar smirked.

A traditional Japanese tea service was depicted in the center of the canvas surrounded by sea horses. Impressionistic droplets of water made up almost the entire background. Japanese characters filled the teacups, spilling over and splashing onto a polished plank table. I bent to look at the detail on the teacups. One had a man's face, shadowed with large gray eyes lined with dark lashes and a scar under them. I covered my mouth with my hand. The rest of the cup looked almost like gingham, but it was tiny chrysanthemums making up the pattern. One seahorse had a minuscule book in hand.

"Turn it around," I whispered. On the canvas back was an inscription:

You have bewitched me
Sleet-gray eyes like distant storms
You have drowned me whole
Kisses like sugared ginger
You have enthralled my being
For Oscar. Taiko. 2020

This changed everything. Everything and nothing. Taiko Kikumoto was not missing. He certainly was not dead. The key point was that he was dating my brother. And my brother had an original Kikumoto—why did it seem as if no matter where I turned in my life, there was a Kikumoto of varying lineage waiting in a corner?—sitting in his oceanfront condo. It was hurricane season. I kept panicking that Oscar's impact-resistant glass would blow in, and the priceless piece—literally priceless as it wasn't insured yet (plus, you know, it was a heartfelt, priceless gift to my brother)—would be swept into the oblivion of the storm. I stared at the intricacies of the painting for hours, noting my observations, taking photos of it. Oscar joked that I could take the painting to bed if I wanted.

It hadn't occurred to me previously just how alike Cesar and Kikumoto were. Not in their respective styles, per se, but there was a subcurrent of feeling in every work, which spoke of an emotion felt at the time of the painting. Yes, it could be said that was the case with most, if not all, artists. But with these two . . . I felt like I could reach out and grab a line of prose from the atmosphere above the paint. Almost like synesthesia, where a person sees colors when listening to music, I thought that these two artists seemed to evoke words, sounds, diction in their brushstrokes. Could that be a sensory gift? Was I making it up? Excitement bubbled in me at the prospective opportunity I would have to ask Taiko Kikumoto whether this was the case with him. Could he, and possibly Emil Cesar, be a type of synesthete? Did I hit on a nuance in their personalities or intellect that blurred the lines of artist and poet? It annoyed me that Jacob didn't give a hoot when I was telling him about *Perte*. I wanted to dissect this theory with someone. It really felt like I'd hit a piñata filled with tokens of knowledge waiting to be scooped up.

CHAPTER 11

CELIA

SLINGING MYSELF ACROSS THE GREEN FELT OF A POOL table was not a normal Saturday night for me. This was game five, the game that would determine who would win and who would be buying drinks for all of us. Just before I took my shot, aiming to sink the eight ball in the corner pocket, a herd of Harleys rumbled along the street, pulling into the packed front lot. I readjusted my fingers, flexing slightly and leaning my hip farther over.

"Did you call 'Uno,' Ce?" Oscar yelled.

I peeked at him over my shoulder and mouthed "Uno" followed by an air kiss.

"Damn girl, those long legs are distracting," Darcy yelled into her red cup.

"Then look away, Darcy, because I'm about to shake what's attached to these legs when I win this game." Collective laughter rang out. The crowd was a fair mix of aging bikers and the rest of us, with quite a few cops too, based on everyone who kept coming up to Adrian.

"The suspense is killing us, Cece," Jacob said, chalking his cue.

I shot Oscar a glance which he returned with a lopsided smirk. I told Jacob he wouldn't be needing the cue, leaned over, and took the shot, sinking it and winning three out of five games. I flung myself back over the table and kicked my flip-flopped feet, laughing. Jacob helped me hop from the table, and I bowed for the crowd. Another round of drinks was on Jacob, and we all made our way out front, where the bulk of tables were. Everyone was picking at fries and burgers, but all I could think about was the food just down the road at MoBay. Darcy had convinced me to take a shot of something strong and awful before we started on the well drinks. It had been ages since we'd all been out together. The distraction was needed in the weeks before the gala. I described to Adrian the epiphany I'd had about the two artists. He looked like a fire had been lit behind his eyes.

"I wonder if that's really a thing. I mean to say, I wonder if it's a documented ability," he mused.

"Well, it very well could be," Darcy answered. She explained that many people were visual learners. Instead of memorizing text, they memorized pictures. Pictures of objects interact with our brains when they flow across our retina. "It gets neurons firing and makes associations. It's much quicker in visual learners. There's a term called hyperphantasia, which refers to people who can create super detailed images in their minds." This was why Darcy and I were friends. Well, that and we could both spend an entire day singing country music together and doing absolutely nothing of consequence.

"I did a course last year," Adrian added, sipping a beer. "It was an add-on to my master's. There were case studies on this in adults with autism, plus neurotypical adults with artistic abilities. Hyperphantasia ran in both sets of adults. It almost sounds like your theory on the artists is the counter side to that, Sullivan." He smiled at me, which did about eight drop-kicks to my tummy.

"Where's Sarah?" Darcy asked, and I kicked her under the table.

"Home in South Carolina for the weekend. I think," Adrian answered and took a swig of his beer.

He thinks she's in South Carolina, or he thinks she's there for the weekend? Or maybe I should just shut that line of questioning out of my brain.

"Not eating, Celia?"

I looked down at the fries and deliberately shoved a few into my mouth. He laughed around his beer bottle, eyes sliding to mine. "I bet you're thinking about the plantains you devoured next door."

Yeah, that too. My stomach was all kinds of sloshing then, and I made a mental note to either start drinking harder or stop altogether. The latter seemed a better idea. Jacob pressed in close behind me, resting his chin on my shoulder. I closed my eyes a brief second. When I opened them, Adrian was looking at me. He shook his head. I excused myself to the toilet, Darcy in tow. When we came back out, Adrian had left.

Every night that Jacob took me home, I made up an excuse to not invite him in, or a reason he needed to leave. The excuses were getting stale, and we both knew it. Driving through my neighborhood, I was looking at his profile and even reached out to touch his face. Stubble -lined jaw and side-burns met, scruffing up his preppy appearance. Other girls were always following him with their eyes. Yet he was always attentive to me. Under my touch, he turned to look at me in the dark car, then back to the road.

Bougainvillea was a fiery bloom from the front stoop to the large front window. I was told it had been planted when the house was built in the 1950s. My date kissed me good night, giving me a flash of Adrian's lips around his beer bottle. I was dizzy with the thought and kissed Jacob back harder. He took the encouragement and pressed us against the unlocked door, both of us falling into the house. The lights were out, and the more he kissed me the more I saw Adrian.

I stepped back and shook my head. Every single girl in the bar tonight was watching Jacob when we played pool. Eyes were on him when we were at the beach. Tanned with floppy hair that only the trust fund boys could pull off without looking like a stoner. I reached for his T-shirt, tugging him closer, and he was on me again, hands under my white tank top and in the waistband of my cutoffs. The feeling of his heat against my skin sent me memories of standing on the beach in the middle of the night, Adrian's arm around me. We crashed to the couch, shoes kicking off.

Coming to my senses, I stopped and put a hand on him to stop as well. All the lights came on one by one, like dominoes. Pulling apart, I scooted back away from him. Even my laptop lit up. There was so much light in the house, it was like a hospital.

"Timer?" he asked, out of breath.

"Ghost," I answered.

He chuckled but saw that I was serious.

"Hey, I'm not really, um . . ."

"Into me?" The cockiness he always wore was pulled down a bit, and I could see I'd hurt him. Probably every time I stayed just out of reach. Every time I'd shot him down.

"No, I'm just . . . There's a lot going on in my head."

He nodded, standing up. "Ghost? Really?"

As if in answer, the lamp in the corner turned off, which I thought was quite funny.

"Friendly I take it?"

"One of them."

He paled a bit and reached for our shirts, tossing mine over. "So, I'm not wrong. This was all pretty one-sided?" His having to ask the question made me feel like trash. I mean, I was just attached to his mouth, thinking of someone else. God, Celia.

"I'm a mess, Jacob. I don't know what's wrong with me. You're really hot."

He chuckled and shook his head.

"And you've been so sweet. I can't keep my head on straight lately."

"Well, you'll change your mind." He winked. "Call me when you do. I like you. I really do."

I walked him to the door and pulled him back before he stepped through, but he nodded again and walked out.

Well, I suppose I continued my how-to-lose-a-guy track record. After falling on top of my duvet, I called Darcy so she could tell me what an asshole I was.

CHAPTER 12

CELIA

As a home, this would have been cramped and midcentury small. As a mom-and-pop Thai restaurant, it was one of the coziest places to eat in town. Also, the most private with curtains around the booths and not a huge lunch crowd. I didn't even know they were open on Mondays, and so it wasn't surprising that, when I arrived, Adrian was the only one seated, waiting for me. He stood from the booth as I walked up, the badge on his uniform flashing in the dim lantern light. My hand went to my hair, smoothing it as I sat, then lay the napkin across the lap of my pants. It was chilly inside; goosebumps broke out on my upper arms.

The waitress brought some appetizers he had ordered and an iced green tea for me. Adrian didn't look up while I ordered a green papaya salad with shrimp. Once she'd retreated to the kitchen, he pulled out his phone.

"Sorry, I know you're busy this week." He fumbled through the device, and I tried to not think about how I'd pictured him in Jacob's place on Saturday night. "Something was sent to me. I think you should take a look, and we can proceed from there." The clinical manner in which he spoke had me sitting up straighter. This was not my friend, Adrian —this was Sergeant Kikumoto.

A video started on his phone. It was dark and shadowy, probably taken on an earlier model phone as the quality was terrible. There were flashes of light and thunder. Then a woman screamed and yelled, "What do you want?" My arm was pressing into my stomach, trying to quell the nerves because I knew this was me in the video. Then I was in the frame, visible mostly by my white shorts and sneakers. On screen, I fell and swore, but there was nothing there. I was screaming at dead air. A nut job having a fit on her own in the middle of the night on a beach trail. Nausea ripped into me.

"Stop, please," I said, so low I wasn't sure if he heard.

He paused it and looked at me.

"I don't . . . I don't know if I can watch this." The fact that someone sent this to him meant that someone else had been there and hadn't helped me. I didn't know if it upset me more that someone would silently film me being attacked, or if it was the fact that it looked, to outside eyes, that I was certifiably whacko. "It wasn't . . . It wasn't in my head, Adrian." Meeting his eyes was difficult. His own went wide, and he grabbed my hand.

"No, no. Keep watching. I didn't even think that would be what you'd assume. Shit. Here," he said quickly and withdrew his hand to unpause the video. Where my hand had been warm, it felt like ice now. We watched again.

Something *did* move in the dark, grabbing my shoulders. I fell back and crab walked away, the shadowy thing moving toward me. Whoever was filming stumbled, the video going wonky. That must have been what gave me time to get up. When I fell again, you can see my sneaker lift in the air, the only bright spot in the darkness. An underbreath swear from the cameraman was what presumably made the shadow release me. That was when I was bear crawling until I could launch back into a run. The camera ran with me, through an indistinguishable thicket of subtropical plants. The camera burst through the trees. It didn't have me in its sights, but after a moment, you could see the side of my car pulling out. A layer of extra darkness stood in the parking lot, lit up with a flash of lightning.

Turning my attention from Adrian's phone, I cleared my throat and sat back. Twice my brain tried to form words, and twice it failed. For a moment I held my face in my hands.

"He said he heard you yell my name into the phone to call me, so he looked me up. He seemed to have no idea who you were and didn't catch your plate number." Adrian sat back as our food was brought over. I picked the wrapper off a spring roll until all that was left of it was the exposed innards. Not unlike how I felt in that particular moment.

"What does he want?"

"He wants to expose it. To send it in to some ghost hunters or some bullshit. It would lead to them looking for you, interfering with your life, your job."

"Interfering with your job," I amended.

"Yes, but I wasn't in the video. Regardless, I'm not worried about myself. I'll stand by you, however you want to move forward."

"What can I do?" I muttered.

"He's transient. Ex-con. He has a record. We've had him in before when he accosted a grandmother once while she waited for her family at the beach. He's stolen bikes, peeping tom stuff. I could get a statement from you saying he was blackmailing you. The truth. Go that route. The video may get released. You did nothing wrong. You don't look crazy. The thing is that you might get media attention. They could say you set the whole thing up."

This year just kept getting better. I looked away.

"I am not letting this ruin my life," I said with a ferocity that surprised me. Adrian's mouth turned up at the corners.

"No, I expect you won't. So, shall we play a bit of a game?"

I was staring at the wood carving on the wall. Willing the tears to stay behind closed doors, I tucked my chin once but stayed turned as there was a traitorous wobble to my lip.

"Eat. please."

I rubbed at my nose, working out whether I would be able to keep the food down if I were to eat. In the end, it looked too good to pass up.

"THANK YOU," I said as we stood at our cars in the driveway of the restaurant. "For looking out for me. You've been a friend. Thanks." I turned to my car door and stopped at the hand on my bare arm.

"I'm sorry."

That could have been a hundred apologies. I'm sorry about what you're going through. I'm sorry my girlfriend called you, and every Mexican woman, a ho. I'm sorry you were attacked by a ghost. Sorry you live with ghosts. Sorry I can see you clearly have a thing for me, but I just don't return the feelings, and please leave me and my racist girlfriend alone.

So, I opened my car door and said, "I know."

CHAPTER 13

CELIA

CESAR HAD A HEAVY TOUCH ON ALL HIS WORK. THE darkness reminded me of Rembrandt, but the subject matter was so different. This last was as dark as *Naufrage*, the shipwreck picture, but a female nude. I'd never been a huge fan of nudes, but I could, of course, appreciate them for their talent and often hidden meanings.

Quand on a pas ce que l'on aime, il faut aimer ce que l'on a. "When one doesn't have what one loves, one must love what one has": the title of the Cesar nude we had. The woman was on her side, presumably asleep. One hand was clutched in a sheet beneath her. Her belly sloped in the lower section, shifting its weight to the side due to the angle at which she slept. Each rib exposed was carefully shaded, the structure of her chest so precise I felt I should look away. He had painted her breasts larger and rounder than her frame would suggest she would have, which could be for a number of reasons. Top reason, artistic liberty. Reason two, it was the late 1980s, so she could have had implants, but that would have suggested a different society. She seemed to me, though, from this painting alone, to be less self-aware. Reason three, she was just well-endowed. I wasn't small chested, but my chest was proportionate to my frame, which was overall thin but rounded where I liked it to be.

The woman in the picture was thin all-around. Bony thin and long limbed. So, my guess was that she was pregnant. Her belly was not large, but gently rounded beneath the belly button where it met her pubic line. Flaxen hair lay over her shoulder and cheek. I had the urge to push it back out of her face to see it more clearly. Despite this, I felt a sense of déjà vu, as though I knew her. Or had met her. She wasn't young by any means, the lines in the corners of her eyes were pronounced even in sleep. Freckles covered her face and chest. Her mouth puckered in a small bow, a tiny scar just above it. He knew every detail of her. Even a violet smudge inside her upper arm, suggesting a bruise, was deliberately added.

In the background of the fair model were lines upon lines of lavender blooms, faint and almost haphazardly brushed on. The canvas was the largest of the lot. She was close to life-size in the center, the outer edges solid black vignette. I wondered if "For Anton" was this woman. Antonette? A nickname? The seed he'd planted in her belly?

Honestly, I'd expected there to be lights flickering when I thought about it, like there had been before, but there was nothing. Disappointing. The paintings were now hanging in their semipermanent location in the gallery. I had the idea that the walls behind should be darker than the green they'd been. The work, I felt, would be complemented appropriately by the void of color. Plus, the gala was a black-and-white affair. In the center of the gallery was *Perte*, the sculpture. Two weeks and three days until the opening gala. A couple museum docents and I used the pulleys to hoist the sailcloth in front of each piece. Shutting off the lights on this gallery for the evening let me breathe a sigh of relief. One huge task down.

Mom was having us over for dinner, and I was running

late. Everyone but the security guard had left for the evening by the time I stepped from my office. They knew I was on my way, but I still felt bad since the three of us hadn't had dinner together in months. I made a mental note to go out and see the Cisneros side of the family as soon as the gala was over.

After Adrian and I had lunch the day before, he'd arranged for me to meet with a friend of his from the University of Miami Film School. Through whatever magic Adrian possessed, he'd had the guy—Ted—meet me this morning to take still shots of me in my stupid white booty shorts standing near the sea grapes. We also snagged a couple selfies with the "director." He hadn't minded driving up the three hours to do Adrian a favor. Ted tweeted before we'd left the parking lot that his short film was done with production and would be released later in the year. The simplicity of it blew my mind, taking that burden off me. Needless to say, it had been a busy day, coming into work late and having to stay late. The glass of chilled Beaujolais I knew Mom had waiting for me would be cherished. It wasn't quite dark, but there were so many trees heavy with Spanish moss around the museum and park that any light still around was dappled and unreliable. I came out from the building and made it only a few steps before someone stepped into my path and swung at me. One hit glanced off my arm, but another followed. Everything went black.

HOWEVER LONG I was out was time enough for the dappled light to flee as well. My eyes struggled to open, pressure in my head kept me from lifting myself up too much or too fast. I patted the ground looking for my phone or handbag, which obviously weren't there. So, I lay back down, the fuzziness claiming me. Once again, I looked up through half-closed lids and decided I needed to try to move. Some primal, self-preserving instinct told me I couldn't go back to sleep. Luckily, I'd had the good sense to keep my jacket on, which kept my arms from getting scratched up, but my poor Balenciaga pumps were getting the beating of a lifetime. Though, I suppose so had I. The fact that my mind automatically went to the fate of my designer accessories told me that not only was I alive, but I was as shallow as a kiddie pool. It seemed to take ages, but after a few moments, my knees were firmly on the pine-needle-covered ground, hands planted flat in a quadruped position. Yoga tabletop, my brain managed to say. There was a lamppost doing absolutely no good whatsoever, flickering in and out with bugs flying into it. I grabbed it and pulled to standing, immediately throwing up and falling back down, where I stayed. I started yelling. Yelling for help, for the security guard, anyone. There was blood on the side of my head above my ear, and I was fairly sure my shoulder was dislocated based on the amount of pain I was in. As a child, my shoulder always popped out if I fell or was pulled. It hadn't happened since I was eight, but I remembered the feeling. The world, as I could see it then, was cut on the diagonal. Nothing was in its normal upright position, which had me throwing up more.

Eventually a car drove by, and though I was slumped against the streetlamp, I waved at it with my good arm. Headlights froze on me. Someone ran out, and I realized it was a police officer. He radioed dispatch and asked me what had happened. I said I didn't know. Someone got in my path, swung at me, and that was it. Whether I was able to make the words come from my brain to my mouth, was a mystery.

"Can you tell me your name, ma'am?" he asked. I'd be lying if I said it didn't take me a minute to get it out.

"Celia Sullivan. Can you . . . I'm late for dinner. Call my mom? Please."

His radio was going, and sirens were distantly sounding.

The world was flashing red while I was loaded on a fire rescue truck. I know I asked if they had my shoes. My Goddamn Balenciagas. They assured me they did and had me hooked up to all sorts of gadgets. Somehow, I missed the transition from truck to hospital, but I woke in a brightly lit room, a massive headache pounding, my mom and Oscar beside me.

Gingerly, I tapped my shoulder. Better. I knew it was just dislocated, and a bit bruised. They held me overnight to assess the head injury. There was no subdural hematoma, but I had a decent concussion.

"I was really looking forward to dinner, Mom," I said. She squeezed my hand.

"Christ, Ce, you scared the shit out of us. I called Adrian and had him tell Jacob." Ugh. I closed my eyes.

"I'm not seeing him anymore, Os. Doesn't matter. I need to sleep."

"No!" they yelled at the same time. Mom covered me in essential oils, telling me to breathe this one, and this goes on my feet, and this one on the brainstem area. They just kept chattering. It must have been after midnight that Adrian came through the door in his white T-shirt and black shorts. My family conspicuously left us alone. Adrian had seen me in every state of disarray. It made me angry, and I had to count backward to not allow the anger to lash out at him. It obviously wasn't his fault that I was a disaster.

"I let Jacob know," he told me. I just waved my hand and looked down, muttering that I wasn't seeing him anymore. "You'll hear more in the morning, but we traced your phone and the suspect tried to use your credit card at Denny's. So, we have him on camera."

"Was it the guy who filmed me?" He shook his head no, two fingers to his lips. "Oh. Fabulous."

"You can't catch a break, huh?" he asked, looking remorseful. I just shrugged and sank farther into the scratchy pillow.

"Don't sleep, Celia," he said touching my chin. "The concussion." I must have whimpered because he laughed.

"Thank you for not calling me Cece," I muttered.

"Ha. Doesn't take a genius to see you hate it coming from anyone but Darcy. I know when to push my luck." Oscar came in with a small speaker and turned it on for me.

"I'm still going to the gala. It's mine. I've worked my ass off for it."

"There wasn't a question in my mind, Ce."

"I thought I was hearing things on the radio, when they said your name," Adrian remarked with a yawn. "It wasn't clear how you were. Thompson said you were covered in blood and not holding on to consciousness. Had a hard time finishing my shift, I'm not going to lie."

"Well, all's well that ends well, and all that nonsense. You must need to sleep. Didn't you work a double shift today?" I asked him.

He huffed, looking down.

I wanted to touch his face, but I knew I couldn't because he wasn't mine. Plus, I looked like hell. "Go home, Sergeant," I said.

Adrian's head tipped toward mine. He kissed my cheek, hovering for a smidgen of a second, and left me with Oscar, who chuckled but pointedly said nothing.

Tía moved in with me while I healed. Though she worked most of the day, it was someone with me at night—which was more a necessity for paranormal reasons than medical. An angry ghostie simply would not do at the moment. I had an event to get ready for, and I'd wager there wasn't a ghost in any realm who would dare to mess with Tía Teresita.

The bruising set in on the side of my face, though it was fairly faint. My hair covered where I was bashed up on that same side. Ugly, but it hadn't required stitches. Thank God. Where I'd hit the ground there were scratches along my cheek and ear. Mom swore her makeup artist could cover them.

The headache finally let up on Thursday afternoon. I'd been lying on the lounger in the pool while Tía sat at the outdoor table stuffing poblano peppers. Each time I tried to help she slapped my hand and yelled "Vete!" for me to get out. Which is how I came to being a "lady who leisures" in her pool lounger. She scraped the insides of the pepper, discarding the seeds and membranes. Chicken and tomatillos had gone in the slow cooker at the crack of dawn before Tía left for work. A bowl of the tender meat sat waiting, shredded floss thin. Once the peppers were stuffed and ready for the oven, Tía cleared the kitchen, again refusing my help, and started on the tortillas. I slipped away to shower, remembering I needed to arrange pickup of the last Kikumoto.

Maybe my brain was damaged because it was just days before the gala, and I had forgotten all about it. In my room, I sat perched on my bed in a towel, furiously emailing the dealer who'd tipped me off about the painting. Caroline didn't know about it, so it wouldn't be a letdown in that respect. Still, I didn't want to let go of the trail, and it would look brilliant having both the Cesar collection and the Kikumotos up on Saturday night. Plus, I might have let the cat out of the bag to colleagues that I already had these paintings.

CHAPTER 14

CELIA

CELADON IMPORTS AND SHIPPING CALLED ME BACK Thursday night saying the painting was ready to be picked up for a six-month loan to the gallery. The owners claimed distant relation to Kikumoto himself, which was likely not true, but people collected art for all sorts of reasons. As I'd not booked it ahead of time, our normal transport company wasn't available to do the pickup in Fort Pierce for me. I was scrambling.

Steeling myself to put another favor in her pocket, I called Connie and asked if her delivery guy, who was dropping off the painting she had tomorrow, could do the Fort Pierce run for me. Even Mom said they were the best in the business, and she wouldn't trust anyone else. An hour before I left the house to head to Fort Pierce to sign the mountain of paperwork involved in an art transaction, a text came through on my new phone from my friendly, absurdly good-looking neighborhood police officer.

I'm off today if you need anything.

I think I'm good, but thanks, I texted back, wondering what Sarah thought of him offering to help me. If she knew at all.

You're not driving, right? Because you aren't supposed to be with that head injury.

I rolled my eyes. *Yes, sir. I understand, sir.*

A photo came through. Just his face with a skeptical eyebrow raised at me, lips pursed. My whole body went hot and cold at the same time. Damn. So, I quickly finished putting on mascara and fiddled around in the room until I had half-decent lighting and shot a photo back of my own eyebrow raised.

Nice lighting. Take care of yourself.

Well, I try. After a minute I sent him the code to my door lock and said, if he wanted, there was a fridge full of Mexican food I would never be able to get through and to help himself.

. . . Any of that pork your aunt made me take when I was at her house?

That, and much more. Help yourself.

Now I'm already hungry for lunch. Thank you.

Because I was in a rush, I sent back a heart and felt like an ass. Everyone used hearts though. Right? Damn.

I knew you'd be driving somewhere.

Am I?

If you were home, you wouldn't have sent the lock code. You'd be there to feed me.

Rollercoaster-level stomach drops were taking place inside me. Did I even need to go get this painting? I mean, what was my career anyway? With my luck, though, he'd show up with Sarah. And she'd eat Tía's food and insult me.

I have a delivery company picking up a painting. Half-truth? I kept looking at his stupid photo. Gold spires topped the mirror Mom had given me to replace the one that my ghostie smashed. In it, my reflection showed a casual Friday manner of professional dress with my silky ivory skirt and plain white tank top. Before looking down at the buzz on my phone, I slipped on a pair of sandals.

Another photo of his head tilted to the side, dark eyes narrowed to slits. I laughed as I left the house and locked the door. Just in front of the bougainvillea, I took a selfie showing where I was. *Waiting for my ride*. Well, it was waiting for me. Like five feet away. But still. I really had to be going.

Navigation was spotty, but after winding through an industrial area, I found the warehouse where Celadon was. Connie's transport guy hadn't arrived, which was just as well since I first needed to view the painting myself and sign the loan. There really weren't many parking places. Though I had a small car, it was still a juggle to squeeze between a truck and a desert-tan Rubicon with huge wheels and an extended bed. Adrian had a Jeep like that, and it always made me think of WWII vehicles, not anything on the streets now. Mainly because they were bulky in weird spots and took up too much room. Tamping down on my driving aggression, I checked that my mascara hadn't melted off during the brief period between getting into the oven-like car and the air conditioning kicking in.

Inside Celadon were two desks facing the tinted-glass front doors, a door to the back room behind them. I was shown to the owner's office, which looked out over a space vastly larger than it seemed from outside. From behind her desk, a woman stood and beckoned me in, her hand extended. She was likely in her early sixties, tall and elfin looking with glossy chocolate-brown hair, golden skin, and brown eyes. Something about her made me think she was always in a good mood, which was a strange thing to think. In any case, her dark eyes were smiling when we made our introductions. Julianne Kestler bade me sit and turned the papers for me to sign while she called for someone to bring in the Kikumoto. She had photos everywhere of vacations and graduations, grandchildren, and dogs. Maybe I should get a dog. I'd always wanted one and was never allowed. Footsteps sounded. Julianne stood.

"See, I knew you'd be driving," Adrian said behind me. I whirled around and stood, catching myself on the chair arm before I toppled over. "Whoa, careful." I turned to Julianne, confused, and she had her lips pressed together trying to keep from laughing. Right behind her, where I somehow missed it thirty seconds ago, was a photo of Adrian in uniform, having his badge pinned by his parents.

"You're right. I shouldn't have driven. My head's all fuzzy, and I'm feeling totally discombobulated. When she said to bring in the Kikumoto, I wasn't expecting you."

He set the painting on an easel and lifted the cloth from it, revealing the most whimsical Kikumoto I'd yet seen. It was a kraken. One tentacle wrapped around the crescent moon, stars and flowers raining over the scene, his colors catching the light as though lit from behind. The water surrounding the animal was effervescent like Champagne, bubbles rising to meet the fallen stars and chrysanthemums. I looked all around the piece.

"It's here. I think." Adrian pointed, his arm reaching across. The scent of his cologne or soap or whatever coming off him made me even dizzier. Hidden under a group of stars was a tiny book, the pages turning into a flower. The mere fact that Adrian knew what I was looking for gave me a little palpitation.

Stopping to arrange my headspace, I drew up my professional mask. "So that I, nor the museum, can be implicated in anything untoward, I must have a document signed attesting to the acquisition of this piece being legal and consensual to both parties."

Julianne tapped the paper. "Certificates of authentication as well as the estate benefactors release are all here. Feel free to take your time. I'll get us some coffee." I looked at my phone for the time. Only two hours to get it back and into the museum.

"Long story short?" he asked.

"Until the long story can be long. I don't have that much time, but you definitely owe me an explanation."

He sucked in one cheek, lips pursed in amusement. "When I was in the navy, I was on a ship off Bahrain," he began. "There was this other kid I worked with. I was his superior because I went in as an officer, just like Nate."

The boy took to Adrian because they shared the same last name—not an uncommon one in Japan. He was fresh out of high school and scared to death, even though they hadn't seen any action whatsoever. Ronnie, the younger Kikumoto, didn't get into his top choice schools, so his parents told him he should join the military and go to school on the GI Bill to make up for the disappointment. If he did that, they would pay for grad school and unfreeze his college fund.

"So, no pressure," I said snarkily. He huffed.

Ronnie's family had shares in a major hotel chain, and his father was on the board for one of the big oil companies. There was no shortage of funds. Ronnie liked art. He had planned to be prelaw but minor in fine arts. An amateur collector, he sought art and trinkets with chrysanthemums on it.

"I didn't think about him right away when we were talking in your kitchen that first night. I don't know, it's been a while since I thought about him. But days after, it occurred to me that he used to talk—the kid talked a lot—about an artist who was considered young and shared our last name. Like I said, it's a pretty common name outside of here." He grinned, eyes creasing. I think a small sigh came out of me, and I looked down at my lap. Gather thy self, Celia.

Once they were both discharged after a full tour, Ronnie would send random texts saying he found another painting, or his dad didn't realize he was the one who procured a Kiku-moto for their private collection. He'd been building a small collection for years.

"So, the night after you were attacked at the beach. When I stayed with you in Fellsmere"—I nodded, saying I remembered. Like it wasn't something I thought about all the time. Internal eye roll—"I texted him. I said you were looking for one that was missing and to let me know if he finds anything. I thought I could just pass the information on to you. But a few weeks ago, he asks me where to ship it and to say it was loaned from the personal collection of Mr. Ron Kikumoto."

"Why didn't you say anything?"

"Well, I toyed with this surprise bullshit I just pulled." He ran a hand through his short black hair and scrubbed it over his jaw. "I had decided against it and asked my mom what she thought. So, she reached out to you. I honestly wasn't even going to be a part of the whole thing, because, I don't know. I don't know. But Mom and I agreed it would be even weirder if you found out later. Is it weird?"

"Totally."

He laughed. "Well, just pretend I wasn't involved."

"I'd rather not, if that's okay." Our eyes met and held.

"I've got coffee in the conference room, next door, hon." Julianne peeked her head in. A whoosh of breath left me. Considering my brain needed as much oxygen as possible right now, I needed to control my breathing. As we exited, I turned, saying "Thanks" at the same time, but ended up with my hand pressed against his chest.

"You're welcome," he said, voice low and hoarse. He cleared his throat. "Sorry for the cloak-and-dagger business."

I turned away quickly and joined his mother.

CHAPTER 15

CELIA

ONLINE CONSIGNMENT SHOPPING AT TWO IN THE morning was never a good idea. Those Balenciagas that were destroyed were my cornerstone pair of shoes. They made my legs look a mile long, went with everything, and took me months to save up for. The black Vuitton Monogram handbag I couldn't even think about. Oscar said he removed the shoes before I could see how decimated they were, but the handbag had been stolen.

Not sleeping the night before the gala was going to bite me in the ass. A message blipped in that the bid I put on a Chloé dress was accepted. It was different from what I typically bought, but given the circumstances lately, maybe that was a good thing. Maybe I could wear it on my birthday. It was more an autumnal color anyway.

Notifications popped up on all my social media accounts at the very same time as a text came through from an unknown number. Someone had been through and trolled all my photos, reposting everything onto a fake page. One picture of me lying on the beach in Nantucket had been edited, knife emojis placed all over my head, and posted. I opened the text message: *The dead aren't the only ones after you now, bitch.* My hands shook. The window started rattling in its frame, the glass of water Tía left under my bed slid out and spilled over the rug. Darkness crept in from the hall, and my bedroom door slammed shut. I pulled my salt out, but before I used it, the room settled.

"Thank you," I whispered.

It was far too late to call Adrian; Oscar was asleep in the guest room. This guy was hell-bent on ruining my life. He very nearly succeeded in killing me the first time. I'm quite sure, given the opportunity, he wouldn't leave me alive next time.

I hope this doesn't wake you. I texted Adrian, not able to help reaching out. I really hoped it didn't wake him as it was his night off. I sent screenshots of the text, the social media trolling, all of it.

I was awake . . . Christ. Report it to the media outlets. Block his account and make yours private. I'll take you in to make a statement tomorrow.

I can't tomorrow. Like, I really, really can't.

You really, really need this to stop.

No shit, Sergeant. I will be in hair and makeup all day trying to make myself look presentable and not like I was beaten and left for dead a week ago. Which, you know, I actually was.

Okay.

Sunday. I can go Sunday.

Is Oscar there?

Yes. Sleeping.

So, you feel safe enough?

Not in the least, but sure.

Need me to come over?

I wished in the moment that I were drunk and could say yes, for every reason I shouldn't. Like that Lady A song, I could skew the subjectivity of "need" inebriated. Sober, however, I couldn't justify asking someone else's boyfriend to come over. Even if I hated her insipid fake sweetness. Even if I wanted to feel him against me. Damn, damn, damn. My bleary eyes stared at the phone for a long time.

I'll be okay. Adrian?

Celia? The snarky tone came through in that one word, and a smile escaped me.

I appreciate you. The ellipsis on the text screen blinked for a while then stopped. Blinked, then stopped.

Just doing my job, ma'am.

I know. That's why it hurts.

The covers were slightly chilled when I slipped into the bed, my head spinning and stomach churning wildly. I really needed to sort myself out.

As a hairstylist blew out my long waves, pulling my hair tight and winding it up, the wound on the side of my face stretched and throbbed, the acetaminophen I'd taken earlier not touching the pain. Mom placed a hydrocodone pill in my scabbed hand, but I didn't do well on medication. I curled her fingers back over it, shutting my eyes once to say no. With a concussion, I didn't want to risk anything causing more bleeding. But this was torture.

Blessed reprieve came at lunchtime. Darcy ran out for sushi to bring back to us at Mom's house. She'd been such a star, picking things up for me so that I didn't have to drive around doing stupid things. Like picking up secret paintings. It had been very quiet in my house recently. To the point where I couldn't decide if I was relaxing a bit with the situation, or if I was tensing for a bigger shoe to drop. The calm before the storm. Or rather the eye of the storm.

Oscar was bringing Taiko. I hadn't met him yet because of all that had been happening, but my brother seemed better. Good days and bad days, but better. I couldn't wait to meet Taiko and probably fangirl over him a bit. Which, considering he'd dropped off the map for a few years, he would hate.

When I came into this job, the board of directors was giving me an opportunity. I had been an assistant curator at the previous two museums I worked, and before that, an intern. This gala and its acquisitions would be my academic journaling, so to speak. This would give me the clout and background to do anything. As long as it went well.

"She's panicking, Mom. Where's your Bluetooth speaker?" Mom had him follow her out to the pool, where I was sure they would have words about me. Oscar came back in, his hotel-style bathrobe tied tight, and hit play on his phone. I didn't know how it started, but he insisted that I calmed with lo-fi male singing voices. At this point, it was conditioning. I calmed because Oscar said so. I couldn't imagine not being near him again. Ten years away was necessary careerwise, but I was apart from my favorite person, and that just wouldn't do anymore. Feeling sentimental, I held my hand out for my brother. He took it and kissed my knuckles.

"I love you, Os."

"Love you too, Ce. But I can't believe you broke up with Jake Owen before the gala. He would have looked F-I-N-E tonight."

"Yeah, he would have. Are there any more spicy tuna on crispy rice? I'm starving."

The final head count on the guest list was made Monday, but I hadn't looked after my accident. I say *accident* like someone wasn't at fault. Attack. After my attack. It looked to be somewhere around three hundred people. Repeating to myself the short introduction speech I'd written kept my mind off the sequel to hair torture. God, I hoped my dress was okay, and I hadn't eaten too many enchiladas this week. I hoped the makeup covered my bruises, and my hair didn't look debutante. I hoped the last two paintings were hung properly as I hadn't been able to personally check. Music came through the speaker, and I focused on the guitar, the deep voice.

Once hair and makeup were done, I stepped into my dress. Mom zipped it up, and we stood looking in her freestanding bronze mirror. Oscar knocked and entered behind us. We made a pretty family. He was sleek and handsome in his black-on-black tux, hair slicked to the side. Mom's black silk fanned off her shoulders, dropping behind her like a summer capelet. The skirts descended straight to a soft pool above her pointed mule shoes. She wore no necklace, opting for diamond chandelier earrings that met her jawline.

"You look stunning, Mom," Oscar said, planting a loud kiss on her cheek. We all laughed.

"Careful, son, or I'll take a brush to your perfect hair."

I leaned forward to check there was no crimson lipstick on my teeth. Barrel curls folded the layers of my chocolate-brown hair inward, pulling attention from the bruising. A black barrette secured the opposite side. Hair spilled on top of my shoulders where ebony bows tied, holding up the snowy bodice of my dress. Corset-style boning ran up and down and along the cups. Just past the ribs, tight pleats of the moon-white satin that made up the whole dress dropped to floor length. One side split at midthigh, a single pleat on either side of the split a shock of black. Shoes were five inches of black satin straps. The diamond studs I'd received for my graduation from Boston College adorned my earlobes, but I decided to forgo any other jewelry.

"Ce is like old Hollywood and Aphrodite's lesbian love child."

"How would that be biologically possible?" Mom asked, grabbing her clutch.

"Aphrodite is a goddess. It's magic."

"Sometimes I can't even with you, Oscar," Mom said and broke up our mirrored portrait. Oscar and I barked a laugh. Our laughter was so similar we sounded like hyenas when we got going. Speaking of getting going. Our car had arrived.

CHAPTER 16

EMIL

Thirty-Five Years Ago

IT WASN'T THE FIRST FLIGHT HE'D TAKEN. IT WASN'T the farthest he'd flown. He knew, somewhere deep in him, beyond the place the light shines, that it was the only flight that mattered. Painting after painting appeared by his hand, one more mediocre than the next. Yet they sold. He scarcely had the time to work the menial jobs he'd started out doing. The jobs he took to eat and support a wife.

On a summer's day in August, he had taken to a café in Juan-les-Pins, working in tandem with a duo who sang cover songs to the tourists. They sang; he painted. His paintings were traditional and provincial, turned out quickly and soullessly. He'd never signed them—they were trinkets, souvenirs of seascapes and lavender fields. Fields that appeared serene, but were in fact, haunted battlefields, lost in time. At some point, he'd had enough. His wife had sent him south. Away from their flat in Brittany that was perpetually suspended in gray fog. They'd grown tired of one another. If either were honest, they were tired of one another after the first night when they'd been caught by her father and forced to marry. No children came from their union and neither truly complained as there was rarely any money to spare. What there was, she drank.

Privilege doesn't understand the animosity of those who struggle. The ones who spend their lives from cradle to grave clawing for purchase on some semblance of the life so often romanticized. "Why are they angry?" they ask. Why? Because we see ease and luxury, uncomplicated love, and comfort in the distance. Like a shore in sight, yet blockaded by treacherous waves. Emil painted in the cafés and on the shoreline, selling shit paintings to tourists and falling into bed with any girl he came across.

A woman stood behind him, staring at his work with her arms crossed. The scrutiny of her gaze made him set his brush down, a pause in the idyllic poppies and lavender on his reused canvas. He turned, coming within inches of her freckled face.

"Do you consider yourself an artist?" she asked in flawless French, though too educated, a slight up tilt to her accent.

"I have a brush and paints and my heart on my sleeve," he replied.

She doubled over laughing, sun-streaked blonde hair touching him like phantom fingers.

"Have I made a joke?"

She raised her index finger to catch her breath. "Your heart is on your sleeve, and yet you paint the same rubbish as the artist two blocks down, and the one after him?"

He looked at her like she had slapped him. Crossing one ankle over the other, he watched her bowed mouth as she spoke. The way her freckles moved like stardust across her bronzed cheeks.

"And what shall I paint, madam?" he asked her, noting the rings on her finger, the gold hoops in her ears. "The strife of the underclass? The lingerie of the rich? Tell me."

A full flush swept up, and he could see she was excited to have been engaged in her challenge. He pulled a blank canvas from his satchel and motioned for her to get on with it.

"Who do you see when you sit here all day? Surely you hear conversations. Different languages and cultures. You hear fights and innuendo, mothers singing songs to restless children. Can you not paint that?"

"I can paint it all, madam," he said through gritted teeth. "I must make a living with this rubbish, as you say."

He watched her consider him a long moment, her face a tide of emotions he didn't know if he wanted to figure out. He glared at her, resenting her gold earrings and her holiday attire. He wanted to have a drink and a cigarette, and not think about paint.

"Paint me something," she said. "Make it real. From the heart in your chest." She placed her hand over his color-splotched polo.

His breath caught unexpectedly.

"Whatever you paint, I will buy. Tell me where and when to come. I am in town until Friday."

He pulled a napkin from the table beside them and wrote an address on it. He said he would have her painting ready by the next day. Whether Emil could produce a painting to her standards in such a short amount of time was a matter of debate. He knew he wanted to see her again and soon. As she walked away, he started sketching.

All the following day, he sat painting things in his heart. What he'd dreamed of since he was young. He mixed colors and stories. Everything he'd been afraid to put on his precious canvas. While he painted, he imagined she walked the town, even wandering twenty minutes up into Antibes, if rich women could be bothered to walk that far. The old town market, the hidden coves, he wanted all the places he frequented to see her foot traffic. He wanted the town to bear her mark as he himself felt marked. As the sun was setting, she knocked on the door to his flat in Juan-les-Pins. He had tried to tidy. Really, he had, but the enthusiasm with which he wielded his brush left splatter of color everywhere. He presented the commission to her, next to the small window. He watched her move toward it, her legs more golden than the day before, her hair blonder. Emil couldn't take his eyes off her, though he felt she must be much younger.

She traced the lines of the work, keeping her fingers from the canvas itself, hovering them just before it.

"Will it do?" he asked her, standing closer.

"Oh yes," she answered, her voice like the movement of tides over rocks.

Emil watched her stare through the curtain of greenery painted on either side of the canvas, looking out to sea. He saw her eyes flicker as they moved to the shipwreck offshore, the alligator who seemed to be winking at her, the mouse hidden in the corner. She commented on the color of the sky and the texture of the sand.

"How much do I owe you?" she asked, biting her lip like she felt foolish for not asking ahead of time.

"Nothing," he said. "It allowed me to express what I have held back. It's yours. I hope that, perhaps, you can think of me when you look at it."

She stood on her toes to kiss his cheeks in the French manner. Something in it was slow and burning. He touched her back in response, and she tilted her head up to him to kiss properly.

The woman left Juan-les-Pins a couple of days later, having told him where she lived and to come to see her.

She carried her painting with her on each leg of her flight from Nice to Paris, Paris to New York, New York to Orlando.

CHAPTER 17

CELIA

CAROLINE WAS ALREADY CLUCKING ABOUT LIKE A mad mother hen and grabbed me as soon as I entered. We were the first to arrive of course, but cars were pulling up directly after.

"You didn't tell me there were two more Kikumotos!" she hissed. "We didn't get funding approval from the board."

"There wasn't time, and I managed them without funds. One belongs to family, the other is a personal loan." She asked how I'd managed to procure three lost pieces of art in the space of a couple of weeks but was interrupted by Connie walking in. The antique dealer glittered and shone from head to toe, thanking me for the opportunity to be there. I winked at Caroline and slipped away. The lobby filled, people shoulder to shoulder under the black glass chandelier. Photographers swam through the crowd, pulling some of us aside for posed shots.

I caught sight of my brother and another man. I kept trying to make my way to him but was waylaid each time by patrons commenting on the event.

It may have taken a half hour of crowd surfing, but I made

it to Oscar. Seeing him next to a classically beautiful Japanese man, I couldn't help the wide grin I gave them.

"Don't fangirl, Ce. It's not your style. Taiko, this is my sister, Celia. Ignore her gushing, she's had a head injury." I took his hand and held it between mine, thanking him for coming. Oscar was wiggling his eyebrows at me, having me barely controlling my giggle, but I noticed his sneaky smirk and tried to read it.

"Oh, hello, Adrian," my brother said in an affected voice I wanted to rip out of him. Taiko held out his hand to our friend, and when he introduced himself, Adrian looked at me with wide eyes.

"Long story," I said with a shrug that made the black bows on my shoulders bounce. Good God. I was secretly hoping he looked terrible in a suit, but that was not the case. "I thought galas weren't your thing?" In a panic, I shot my eyes around to see if Sarah was there.

"They're not. I thought it might be wise to keep an eye on you, in light of what happened last night."

"What happened last night, Ce?"

I closed my eyes briefly, and Adrian apologized.

"I didn't know there were still tickets available," I said in a rush.

He touched the black silk bow, his thumb brushing my shoulder.

"I took my mom's." He spoke to my shoulder, watching his own fingers stroke the bow. Each featherlight brush against my skin seared through my whole body. People pushed past, making me wish we were alone. I always wished we were alone. Once in a while, his dark eyes met mine, and I could swear his thoughts were running a parallel race with my own. It was as if we were spinning on an axis holding up only the two of us. "I don't even know how to tell you how you look tonight." His hands shoved into his pockets; I didn't know what to do with mine. I wished I'd had a glass of Champagne, but I couldn't drink for a couple of weeks after the concussion. So, I stupidly smoothed the lapel of his tuxedo jacket. His hand came up and held my wrist where it lay against his tux.

"You don't look bad yourself," I told him, voice shaky.

He closed the distance between us and said into my ear, "You're the most beautiful thing in this place. And I really do like that chandelier." The slightest brush of his lips scorched the skin on the side of my neck.

My fingers bent into the fold of his lapel, my body off-kilter. The clean sandalwood and lime scent of him overpowered me, making me forget momentarily that I was working.

Caroline's keen eyes locked on me while she waved to me from the doorway, and I excused myself. A look of umbrage sat on her birdlike features.

This was the first speech I'd given outside of school. I'd been shoving the thought of it to the back burner for weeks. When it was time to stand in front of these three hundred people and get it over with, I had to find a mark to focus on. Locking onto Oscar's face, I opened.

"Good evening and thank you all for coming tonight. For those who do not know me, I am Celia Cisneros Sullivan, curator here at the Vero Beach Art Museum. It is only with the support of our patrons and friends here in Vero that not only does this museum exist, but also we can bring you the talents and imaginings of artists like Emil Cesar and Taiko Kikumoto.

"One element flows through the works of both artists: water. They both bring the viewer into souls both lightened and drowned by the sea. In the pieces you will see tonight, emotions flow through and between worlds and whimsy, carrying your senses on a journey through the artists' lives. It has been my great pleasure to put together this opening for you tonight. I bid you open your hearts to the genius of both

Taiko Kikumoto and Emil Cesar. Without further ado, as they say." I half turned and waved to the gallery behind me. The pulleys moved sailcloth from all the pieces. "Please enjoy."

I stepped down and sought out a glass of water before joining the crowd in the gallery. Many faces smiled at me; many hands were shaken.

In the gallery, groups gathered around the individual pieces, pointing out things here and there. I found Adrian in front of *Perte*, talking to my brother and Taiko.

"Ce, doesn't this remind you of Annie and Stefan?" I twisted my mouth in thought. "The magpie and the rat in Judy's story?" he prompted.

I walked around it as though I hadn't done so a hundred times already. From *Perte*, I crossed to *Naufrage*, waiting until a space was clear for me to look closely at the bird and mouse in the curtains of foliage. I motioned for Oscar to come over, the other two men following. They stared at the painting too. We circled the other Cesar pieces and settled before the nude, *Quand on a pas ce que l'on aime, il faut aimer ce que l'on a.*

"When one does not have what one loves, one must love what one has," Adrian translated quietly to himself.

I turned to him. "'I am profoundly enchanted by the flowing complexity in you,'" I said to him before I could cover my mouth in embarrassment.

"Keats," he said, recognizing the words. "Don't always look so surprised. I'm not as dumb as I look." He nudged my shoulder, his fingertips slipping against mine.

"Oh, I've never thought you were dumb. You just impress me." He stared straight ahead as I wondered whether I should regret having said that.

"So," Oscar began, "do we think the woman in the painting is the one he must contend with, or the one who got away?"

"The one who got away," the remaining three of us said

simultaneously. Electricity buzzed in the hair's breadth between Adrian's fingers and mine.

"Unless he is painting her to convince himself he is happy with her," Taiko commented. "The detail and nuances suggest to me he is cataloging everything he will miss."

I had the horrible urge to cry, but the two hours this makeup took would not be ruined by my emotional state.

"I agree," Adrian said, looking closer. "I don't know anything about art, but every freckle and reflection of light on the hairs of her arms is captured."

"I think she's pregnant in this painting," I added and told them why I thought so. Oscar kept staring at it like he was focusing and unfocusing his eyes. "Does she look familiar to you too?"

"It's Judy," he said in awe. "It's Nate's mother."

"Sorry I'm late. Damn, girl, you look pretty tonight."

Four of us turned from the painting and the implications in Oscar's observation to see Jacob standing behind us, polished and perfect in an Armani tux. Adrian's hand, which had been so close to mine, dropped, leaving a tangible pocket of cool air. Jacob's eyes darted to my hand where it was now clenched at my side. I had no words but did have the absurd desire to grab Adrian's hand and walk away. But that would be rude—not to mention unprofessional—so I implored Jacob with my eyes.

"I didn't know you were coming tonight, Jacob," Oscar said, saving me as I'd apparently gone mute.

"I wasn't sure if you had forgotten that you'd invited me, Cece," he said, running a hand down my arm. I saw red, my eyes shooting to his face. "What with the noggin injury and all that." He mimed getting hit in the head.

"There is nothing wrong with my memory, Jacob," I said. "I did not invite anyone here as my date. I am working."

This was not the time or place to cause a scene. Adrian was

trying to meet my eyes, and I found I couldn't. If I looked at him and he saw what I was thinking, like he always seemed to, I might cause a scene, and this was neither the time nor place for one. Jacob chuckled, once again knocking his head with splayed fingers.

"If you'll excuse me. I need to speak with my director." Caroline was laughing with a group of older ladies. I insinuated myself into their huddle, accepting praise on the opening. Once I thought Jacob wasn't ogling me, I darted to an adjacent hall as fast as razor-thin five-inch heels would allow. There was a small alcove where I stood against the wall, trying to figure out how to turn this night around.

"You okay?" Adrian came around the corner with his hands in his pockets.

I nodded, closing my eyes.

"You sure?"

"I didn't invite him."

"Kinda figured that by your reaction."

"Here, I thought I'd kept my poker face."

"Maybe I can read your poker face."

"If so, that's dangerous." Oh shit. I actually said that out loud. He stood in front of me. Close enough that I could feel warmth and the comfort of his presence.

"Why's that?" he asked, his voice like tires on gravel.

I lifted my eyes to see his on me, and my breathing caught. I made to fiddle with his bow tie, plumping the ends. I felt his hands over the silk covering my hips. "You tell me, if you can read my poker face."

"I just don't see how I'm not supposed to want to kiss you right now."

Not a single part of me was willing to cooperate with movement. My hands stayed on his chest, atop his jacket.

"I need to get back out there. I just needed a moment." The words came out calmer than I felt. He started to say something, but Jacob walked behind him, Caroline in tow. I dropped my hands and stepped away from Adrian like I'd been caught by the principal.

"Ah, there she is Ms. Unger. My date all over Vero Beach's finest. She just hasn't been the same since the head bop."

Oh, you have got to be kidding me.

"Celia," Caroline scolded. Actually scolded. "This is your workplace." I walked to her and filed us out of the hallway.

We exited with smiles for the guests, but my director said for me alone to hear, "This kind of display will not be tolerated. I would like for you to see me first thing Monday."

Closing the night meant a long train of stragglers staying behind to chat. Exhaustion pulled at me hard. The dregs of adrenaline left my battered body feeling like a rag doll. Yet, I kept my shoulders back, my heavy head high. Mom and Oscar kept urging me to call it a night, but with Caroline's hawk eye on me, I couldn't leave until the last guest vacated the museum. Adrian was gone, yet Jacob remained. By midnight I was done and ready to quit if she didn't stop talking to the city manager.

Once we were finally able to leave, I ignored Jacob and walked straight out the door, headed to where the car was waiting. Sliding into the back seat, I checked my phone for the first time all night. Texts from Oscar, Mom, Darcy. Jacob.

I can't believe you humiliated me like that, he wrote. The temptation to say something really nasty back made my fingers itch.

I did no such thing. Though I hope you had a good time at the gala, you were not there at my invitation. We are no longer seeing each other.

That's not the way I see it.

I screenshotted the conversation and sent it to Oscar. Where was Adrian? The hired car pulled up to my house where Jacob's car was waiting too. Shit. His headlights shone straight at my front door. I asked the driver to turn away. Mom didn't pick up when I called. It was too late to call Tía. Shit, shit, shit. Giving up and giving in, I shot a message to Adrian.

I'm in the car outside my house, and Jacob is waiting.

If I come to your house, there will be an altercation.

Never mind then. Sorry. I'm sure I'll be fine.

Come here. My heart was going a thousand miles a minute. *I'll take you to the station first thing tomorrow.*

Oh, that's right.

The driver plugged the address into his navigation, and we pulled away from my drive, heading over the Barber Bridge, and up the highway. I had no idea where Adrian lived, but we seemed to be headed up near Sebastian. A figure waved from a house on the water side of the street. To my credit, I held it together walking into the house.

Everything was open plan with minimal furniture and a bright kitchen at the back where the doors opened to a slope of lawn and dock behind.

"You're sure he didn't follow me?" I asked, my voice strained to the breaking point.

"There wasn't anyone else out there."

Lights blinked on the water, reflecting bubbles and splashes from fish. Warmth shone from the houses along the water on either side. I walked to the doors, and he opened them so I could step out. He had removed his jacket and tie, shirt buttons half undone. Painful lances racked my back from being in heels all night. Everything hurt, from my head to my toes.

"I'm so tired, Adrian." Arms closed around me, shutting out anything intrusive. Gentle hands held my head against his chest as he pressed a small kiss to the top of my head. He led us inside and told me where to find a toothbrush and towels. A clean T-shirt and boxers were set on the guest bed. With every wipe of my face, more of the yellow bruising was revealed. An exhausted, irate bitterness sat solid in my stomach. The shirt smelled like Adrian. The scent enveloped me as I fell asleep in his house, too tired to even wish more of Adrian were on me than his shirt.

GOOD GOD ALMIGHTY. Following the scent of coffee brought me to the kitchen, which was bathed in the early morning light coming off the river. What made me twist my hand in the borrowed University of Miami tee was not the sunshine but my host. There was no amount of running and planking that would give me abs like that. I was very aware of my messy morning hair and lack of makeup. Dark, raised eyebrows looked up as I walked in.

"Coffee's there," Adrian said, interrupting my shameless appraisal. "There's only oat milk creamer." I gave a faint smile. "Lactose intolerance and all that."

We drank a few minutes in silence, but my eyes found his, and I couldn't help but giggle. "It's no wonder I thought you and Oscar were more than friends."

"What the hell does that mean, Sullivan?" He set his coffee cup down on the poured concrete counter, eyes lit up and twinkling.

"Just that he's all gorgeous and you're . . . you." Umm. Damn it, Celia.

His phone rang, breaking the tension for a millisecond. While he spoke, I walked outside to finish my coffee. A few boats were already out, cruising upriver, their wake beating at the dock. Brine from the brackish water sat heavily in the humid summer air. When he came out to where I was sitting in a white Adirondack chair, Adrian had a T-shirt on and more substantial shorts. To cover my disappointment, I drank deeply from my nearly empty coffee cup. His tanned legs stretched out in front of him as he lowered himself into the chair beside mine.

"A buddy of mine is on shift today and said he'd come by in a few minutes to take your statement if you'd rather not go in. Up to you."

I looked down at myself in his T-shirt and boxers and twitched my mouth, gesturing to the ensemble.

"Like I said, up to you. But I think you look fine. I told him you were followed home, and that's why you're here. No walk of shame." Though the sunrise coming at us masked it, I could swear his cheeks reddened after he said that. I knew mine did.

"I'm not even wearing a bra." Speaking of blushing, but it was true. I had just enough up top for it to look a bit rude.

"I'll give you a hoodie."

I followed him back into the house to get more coffee. Standing in the kitchen, I pulled my mass of hair on top of my head and started to tie it in a knot. Adrian fumbled through a drawer. I heard a soft snap and he handed me a disposable chopstick. Using it, I speared the messy bun on my crown.

"You may be able to read my poker face, but I sure can't read yours," I said, realizing I'd stepped us right back into our interrupted conversation from last night. He stared at me for a long minute, sipping from his cup, his other arm braced on the countertop.

"Probably a good thing," was his final answer. Well, what did that mean? Without meeting my eyes, he started pulling stuff from the fridge and cabinets, then switched on the stove.

"Adrian?"

He stopped and half turned to me, cracking an egg into an oiled pan.

"Why did you leave last night?" I asked while looking

down at my hands in my lap. The sounds of a wooden spoon moving the eggs in a pan and crunching noises were my only answer for a long time. I switched up my gaze to look out the window. A plate slid in front of me on the counter. Eggs and tortilla chips covered in beans, salsa, and cheese. I looked up at him.

"For spring break one year, I went to Cancún. Big mistake, by the way. The most hungover I've ever been in my life. Had this for breakfast, and it was like magic. So, I learned to make it."

"Chilaquiles are a favorite of mine." I didn't say that it was what Tía made us every time Papi was so drunk the night before that Oscar and I went to bed crying. Or that it was what I ordered even in Boston at Border Café when I was hungover. Or that I'd never had a guy make me breakfast. Or any kind of food. Or do anything for me that Adrian had done. "So do you make breakfast for all the sad cases of girls who have to crash at your house?"

"I left because I fucked up. I was unprofessional and it cost you." I set my fork down, already halfway through this plate of heaven. "Oscar and I told the driver to make sure you got in the car and home. I was there to keep you safe, and I overstepped my boundaries. And I'm sorry."

The roiling in my gut wiped my appetite. Our conversation from weeks ago came back to me. *I don't want you to take it the wrong way . . . I am a public servant. I took an oath to protect people . . . I don't feel like protecting you is out of line.* Oh, I understood now. Each bite was an effort after that, forcing it down and wanting to be away. He wouldn't let me wash my plate, so I went back to the guest room to wash my face. Rather than a hoodie, I put on my dress from last night and popped his T-shirt over top, tying it in a knot at the waist before coming back out to meet the officer now standing in the living room. Adrian and I both gave our statements. I sent screenshots of the texts and social media threats. It was a fairly quick and painless process, made so much better since I hadn't been required to go to the station.

"The house is sharp, Kikumoto," Officer Thompson said, turning in a circle. "I think the last time I saw it was when you had that barbecue, and we smashed through a wall to kickstart construction."

"Slowly coming along," Adrian replied. Slowly? It looked polished to me. I started to excuse myself to call an Uber.

"It's good to see you up and healthy, Miss Sullivan," the officer said.

I looked at him.

"I was the one who found you last week."

"Oh." Brilliantly articulated response, Celia, I thought to myself. "Thank you. I think if you hadn't been there at that time . . . I was told I wouldn't have made it."

Adrian had a sharp intake of breath.

"I'll get this plugged in for you today," he said with a sad smile before turning to his friend. "You on later, man?" I walked off, hearing Adrian respond that he'd be in for his shift that evening.

Not that I had anything with me, but I took my shoes from the guest room and stripped the bed, attempting to sneak the sheets into the washing machine outside of the kitchen.

"You didn't have to do that," came a voice from behind me.

"I don't mind."

"I was going to ask if you needed to stay another night. I'm working, but—"

"It's okay. I'll go home. I'm a big girl. All appearances to the contrary."

A notice popped up that my car was five minutes away.

"I would have taken you home," he said, a sliver of hurt in his voice.

"I don't want to inconvenience you anymore." I hit the start button on the washer. "Public service extends only so far." The tone was supposed to be joking, but the waver in my voice made it anything but. Thankfully the car arrived before the conversation could embarrass me further. At the door, I raised up on tiptoes and kissed his cheek, feeling like I could die right there.

"I really do appreciate you."

Chapter 18

Celia

Distracting myself became a priority once I got home. Oscar hadn't texted, so I assumed he and Taiko were making a weekend of it. I didn't really want to see anyone anyway. Triple checking my locks and alarm felt paranoid, but the reality was that I had been attacked and harassed. Emails came in from colleagues in Boston, New York, and LA. Congratulations on the acquisitions and a successful opening. What should have been a celebratory weekend turned into a nightmare. No amount of chilaquiles, enchiladas, or sopes would make this better. Running might help, but I wasn't allowed any physical activity for a month. Signing into my work laptop, I copied and downloaded the files, images, and research I'd done on all the Cesars and Kikumotos.

With the wake of the gala turning into a detention for me, I hadn't revisited the reality that Cesar's nude was Judy Cosgrove. The painting was dated 1987. Were she pregnant in this picture, and I was fairly sure she was, then was she pregnant with Nate? The cursor blinked at me as though it were hesitating to write the thought down. When I did, the lights flickered. The weather was fine outside, and I attributed that to the lack of "companionship" in my house.

Could the story Judy told us have been true? Embellished, of course, but could it have been a story of Emil Cesar? The course of his life and love with Nate's mother? Running footsteps sounded in the hall, headed toward the living room. And me. I picked up the salt and tossed it in a circle around me. Darkness reached out, but as calmly as I'd acted today when Adrian shut me down, I chanted the Wiccan chant.

"Elements of Day,
Rays of Sun,
Hear what I say,
Gather as One,
Goddess of Night,
Strength of Other,
Goddess of Light,
Protection of Mother."

For good measure, I recited the Our Father and a few Hail Marys. Couldn't hurt. For a full hour, I sat in my circle, reciting prayers I'd grown up with. Eventually, it was clear the entity had gone, and I was once again alone. A dozen emails lit up my laptop. Two were from Caroline. An official reprimand for "behavior unbefitting of a museum official," which could have been contested had there not been another email terminating my employment. I was to pick up my belongings on Monday. This didn't add up. I had done nothing wrong. I engineered the most successful opening the museum had seen, gained attention from colleagues and media outside of Florida, and had the entire night go off without a visible hitch. Think, Celia. Hanging my head in my hands, I gave up and did the only thing I could think of.

"Tía?" I asked when she answered her phone.

"Sí, mama, what's wrong? You sound like you're trying to not cry, hija."

I told her. All of it. She said to tell my mom as she had weight to throw around in this town. I would. I knew that. I just needed to be able to think.

"Y your guapo police officer?"

"He's not *my* anything."

She was quiet, which was always a bad sign. "I'll call you back, hija. I'm driving home from work."

Setting the phone down, I hung my head back over the chair and saw a face near the wall behind me. Too fast. I moved my head too fast, and the world started spinning. Looking back, the face was still there. Dusty brown hair and wintery blue eyes peered over. It wasn't frightening like the darkness that came for me. Nor did it seem the way we often think of or see ghosts. The man I saw could have been a snapshot on the wall. A perfectly preserved memory in my mind. Insubstantial, yet not lacking in detail. I risked a greeting; he tipped his head to me. From all the research I'd done, I was 100 percent positive the man I was now in the presence of was Emil Cesar. He walked from the room, beckoning me with his hand. I followed, more curious than scared. God, I hoped I wasn't having repercussions from the head trauma.

We left the main part of the house and went into the garage. He stood near the water heater and moved a hand in its direction. The apparition was fading, so I hurried to where he pointed. All the renovations the house had gone through this past year, I hadn't had to replace the water heater or the roof because Nate had done it as soon as he started preparing to sell the place. I reached behind, feeling nothing. The apparition stood closer to me. Against the wall, at the back of the cubby where the water heater sat, was a booklet taped up. I peeled it from the drywall, and it dropped. Still fumbling, I felt the object and pulled it out.

It was a journal, bound in forest-green leather, the initials EAC embossed on the bottom right corner. Mildew colored the edges of the paper because nothing in Florida could escape mildew in a garage. I swiveled to show my incorporeal companion what I'd found, but he was gone.

THE JOURNAL WAS IN FRENCH. Not shocking, but it would take me some time to get through it. Fortunately, without a job, I had time. Also in the "without a job" category was the fact that I had both house and car payments with minimal savings at this point. For hours, I read the journal, taking notes on the side, trying to piece together a shoddy translation. My French was far from fluent. Manageable with clients and in travel, however, a journal written in a colloquial hand was proving I had much more to learn. What's more, as it got further into the evening, my French and Spanish were beginning to hit a crossroads, rendering my attempt useless.

By seven the next morning, there was a knocking on my door and five texts from Oscar. I read the texts as I put a light silk robe over my nightie.

Got your text late last night. Shit. Sorry about your job. Tía called me at five this morning. Caroline seems super sketch. I have an idea. Give me time.

Come to dinner with Taiko and me. I'm taking him to Mulligan's, because it's a rite of passage. No tourist shall go un-Mulliganed. We're even going to get the cheeseball photo on the giant beach chair. 6 pm.

Ce, honestly. You should have told me about Jake Owen being a dick.

I heretofore shall stop calling him Jake Owen, because the real Jake Owen is not a dick, and Jacob is. You should've told me. I thought maybe you were staying at Adrian's because, you know . . .

Fuck my life.

Love you, Ce.

Rapid chatter in Spanish on the other side of the door clued me in as to who was there. I opened to find my aunt and both grandparents standing on my porch, each holding a Publix bag filled with who knows what.

COFFEE PERCOLATED while Tía ran around the kitchen, pulling things from cabinets and plastic shopping bags. It took me a sleepy minute to realize she was making the same thing I'd had yesterday. Only today I felt a bit sick at the thought of it. When I didn't annihilate the plate in the first few bites, she turned to Abuela, and asked, in Spanish, what was wrong with me as though I wasn't sitting right there. A conversation ensued regarding my mental state, sleep habits, lack of nutrition, stress, and perhaps a spirit stealing my appetite.

"Okay!" I said. "Enough." I told them about yesterday's chilaquiles. Both women were quiet, Abuela strumming her fingers on the handle of her hot-pink, zebra-striped cane. Abuelo casually made his way out to the patio and sat in a lounge chair to read his paper.

"Maybe it won't taste the same. Of course it won't. Mine are more authentic. Cancún! Pshaw!" I walked out and sat next to my grandfather to escape the female diagnostics inside. He placed a gnarled brown hand over mine and patted it, making the loose stone in his gold ring click.

"Estás bien?" he asked me.

"I'm okay," I answered.

He looked at me, his smiling eyes narrowed to slits. "The truth, Celia?" I loved how my name sounded when pronounced in the proper Spanish way: a soft *e* and singsong *ia*. It was so much nicer than the standard anglicized *Ceel-ya* Americans said.

"The truth? No me siento muy bien," I told him. I don't feel so great.

"Muy pesado?" he asked.

Very heavy indeed, I agreed.

His fingers curled in mine, and though my eyes were pricking, no tears came. No real tears had come since that day Oscar was hit. Nothing was as painful to me as that day. "The top problem solvers the world over are working on a solution in your kitchen, so fear not," he assured me in Spanglish.

Together we sat watching the sun glint on the pool. Tía came out and thrust a serving of flan at me, saying she knew the "handsome police officer" hadn't made me flan. Abuelo told her he would wager the police officer would, if he knew it was a test of loyalty. I waved him off, saying his loyalty to me was solely based on his public service oath and loyalty to Oscar. As he so often did, Abuelo remained quiet and thoughtful, pointing out the iguana who still lived on the palm tree.

Running was out of the question, but a good long walk was probably exactly what I needed. It was hotter than hell at five when I left my house. Most of the streets were shaded until I got close to the beachside shopping area, where the afternoon heat was held in the walls of the buildings I passed. I had to sneak past Connie's antique shop on Ocean, which felt ridiculous. Traffic didn't clog the street on a Sunday evening in August. Families were packing up picnics and beach supplies. I dashed across Ocean and walked through Humiston Park, where children ran and squealed on the covered play equipment.

As I neared the lifeguard station, I took off my sandals, then descended the stairs onto the beach. Bathtub-warm foam licked at my feet. Even as an adult, I couldn't help picking up shells or stones that caught my eye. Each one I pilfered from the cradle of the shore got shoved into the pocket on my denim shorts. Oscar wouldn't let me live it down if I met him with sand or saltwater on my camisole. The thought made me smile and hurry to see my brother.

Timing the T trains in Boston for ten years made me quite efficient at estimating my arrival at places via walking. At 5:58 I was taking the steps up from the beach at Sexton Plaza straight to Mulligan's. There couldn't possibly be any better-looking couple, I thought when Taiko strutted to the table in what must have been the Lulu shorts Oscar had told me about. My brother's head stood higher than Taiko's, so I could see both of them walking in, golden faced. Fanning myself dramatically, I sat back against the outdoor chair.

"Aye Dios," I mimicked Teresita. "Hello, Taiko." I stood and kissed his cheek. Oscar looked so damn chuffed, I wanted to dance like a crazy woman. We fell into easy chatter that soothed my nerves further. Oscar said Taiko was nearly ten years older, but he didn't look a day over thirty. Soft cheek-bones rose when he smiled, smooth skin creasing gently. He spoke about leaving Japan and working with an English marketing firm. The move to Melbourne happened as a means to further separate himself from his father once the elder Kiku-moto passed away. Oscar tried to seem blasé, picking at his food while Taiko spoke, but his gray eyes smoked over like a stormy sea when Taiko turned to him. Without missing a beat in his story, the other man hooked a pinky around Oscar's and folded their fingers under. Rosy patches bloomed high on my brother's sun-kissed brown cheeks. He looked down at his watch, and I could see him suppressing a smile. He met my glance with a wink.

"So, chilaquiles?" he asked me, shit-stirring like it was his profession.

"So, my *job*," I retorted.

"Give me a week. I have an idea. Until then, tell me why our dear friend made you—"

"Hey ya'll." All three of us looked up to see Sarah standing next to the table, dressed like she had just come from work. Fleeting fantasies about flinging popcorn shrimp at her silk top ran through my mind. The grease stains it would leave on the material . . .

"Sarah," Oscar intoned dryly.

I didn't want to seem like a jealous bitch because she was Adrian's girlfriend. I wanted to seem like a pissed off bitch because she called me a ho.

"It's really quite Mexican at this table. Oh, and a bit Japanese. Sorry, babe, not sure it would suit your racist sensibilities." I fucking loved my brother.

"I'd like to apologize."

"To whom?" I spat.

She shifted in her kitten heels, running a hand down her shiny brown hair. "You. Sorry. I'll leave it at that." She clicked her heels away from the table. Oscar and I burst out laughing, the hyenas having been released. Taiko looked momentarily alarmed at the ruckus.

"That"—I pointed to the empty space where Sarah had been—"is one of the many reasons I refuse to talk about chilaquiles."

Taiko rose from his chair and bent down, his lips inches from Oscar's ear. My brother's hand lifted to Taiko's hair like the response was programmed into his nerve endings. I looked away until the other man left the table. Oscar cleared his throat.

"What does Sarah have to do with breakfast?"

I rolled my eyes at him and took a long sip of iced tea.

"They've been broken up for like a month now. Longer. I personally don't think they were much of a thing to begin with."

I literally could not swallow my tea. A lump the size of a ping pong ball lodged itself in my throat. "Os," I whispered. "He said multiple times that he was a public servant, and his interest in me was merely out of an oath he took to protect. And his friendship with you. Please don't drone on about it suggestively. It makes me feel worse."

Oscar gave me a raised eyebrow look that told me he wanted to argue but wouldn't. To change the subject, I asked Taiko about his creative process. Poor thing was barely back in his seat before I pounced.

Upon my questioning, Taiko explained that when he painted, he indeed saw words along with the illustrations in his mind. He explained it felt like reading closed captioning on a movie. He saw the images as clearly as the words that represented them. Sometimes, however, when he was overcome with emotion, the two separated. The thoughts expressed themselves in a pictorial manner, then the words came after. Like a first-spoken language, painting was dominant. Fascinated by the explanation, I kept asking questions, but eventually, Oscar called me off. Taiko laughed and said he had never spoken about it. He never realized anyone would pick up on it, and he didn't know what it truly meant or was. Taiko understood my comparison with Cesar, and how the two artists complimented each other. Academically, I felt both fulfilled and more curious. How many artists worked in such a riptide of senses?

I hugged them both before leaving, opting to walk back home rather than have them drive me. It hadn't cooled down, but the sun was setting, allowing the tree canopy to be a little more laissez-faire.

But he did make you chilaquiles, Oscar texted.

I shoved the phone back into the side pocket of my outlet center handbag. I missed my Vuitton. On the front stoop was a large vase of flowers, a florist's tag poking out from the depths of red roses and irises. Quickly glancing around, I unlocked the door and lifted the flowers in with me. The note was signed by Jacob. It was an ugly arrangement. I dumped the whole thing, vase and all, into the trash.

Asshole.

CHAPTER 19

CELIA

EMIL'S JOURNAL WAS PUT ON THE BACK BURNER FOR the time being. Oh sure, I skimmed it and translated lines here and there. By Tuesday, I'd had several job offers. Regardless of Oscar's "idea," a week was still a long while to wait, jobless and financially insecure. Mom asked me to work for her in the interim, which was all well and good, but not a long-term plan. Wednesday and Thursday held back-to-back online interviews for institutions in Sarasota, Lake Wales, St. Augustine, Miami, and Winter Park. The Ringling Museum of Art in Sarasota was a dream location. It had all the architecture, the art, and the feel of a renaissance villa in Italy. I worried about what a referral from Caroline would be like at this point. There seemed to be nothing at all she could pin on me. Not a damned thing. So why the fuss? Sitting ramrod straight, I texted Oscar just before the meeting was about to begin Thursday morning.

Can we check donations to the museum? I asked him.

I can do anything.

I want to know exactly what was donated, and by whom, in the last week.

I know you do. I've been looking into it already. Waiting on some favors.

Whether I had to take a job elsewhere or not, I wanted my name cleared. After three interviews that day, I was beat. Reaching out to Darcy for some girl time just led to her asking if I was up for a beach day tomorrow, because she was taking off to celebrate a huge deal. A beach day, I decided, was exactly what I needed.

Lamenting all my recent purchases because I was out of a job was getting me nowhere but down. The swimsuit I'd bought last month looked fab, and I needed to just suck it up, buttercup, and wear the damned thing.

Darcy picked me up with two other girls in the car just like she did in high school. Oscar and I had shared a car, since we were only two years apart. As he's older, he had it most often, so I always rode with Darcy. The music was turned up, blaring out of the open windows of Darcy's Range Rover as we tooled up the coast to a lesser-known beach where we could be fairly alone.

Topaz-blue skies met the crystalline water in a fever of summer perfection. With our umbrellas up and blanket down, our claim on the day was made. Scorching sand had us running to the shoreline to wet our feet, but I wanted a full dip right off the bat. Though my two-piece swimsuit was high waisted, the sides laced up at the hips, drawing the coverage on the bum to next to nothing. Emerging from the water required a quick readjustment of the yellow fabric.

Trudging up the sand embankment, I saw a few others added to our party. He didn't need to turn for me to see who it was. As he did, I sent a quick prayer to whoever might be watching me today that I could get through this day without losing my cool. Adrian stood with Darcy's beau (her word, not mine) and another guy I hadn't met.

"You okay?" Adrian asked, pulling off his shirt. I squeezed some water from my soaked hair and shrugged. A very girly squeal fueled by a second can of hard sparkling water preceded the raising of the speaker's volume. Luke Bryan played, so Darcy grabbed me and Maddie to dance and sing. I pointed to my head. Who knew if dancing was allowed, but I'd rather not risk it. Or the ensuing humiliation in front of Sergeant Kikumoto.

The girls sang at full volume, making me laugh. Through my sunglasses and past my tipped-down hat, I pretended to not be watching Adrian wade in and out of the surf. Jesus, I was in trouble, and it wasn't getting better.

"What are you reading?" he asked, running a towel over his hair. I looked up fully, as though I hadn't been staring. I was smooth.

"A journal. Well, I'm trying to. It's in French, so I'm taking forever getting through it."

"Can I help?" He sat, laying his towel on the blanket next to me. It was extremely hot today. He cracked a can and drank from it. "Whose journal?"

"Funny story," I began and quietly described the events after I'd left his house on Sunday. We sat facing the water, knees bent, but our heads were discerningly close so no one else could hear us. Darcy danced behind me and smacked us each with a kiss on the cheek.

"So cute," she said with an air kiss. I rolled my eyes at her, but somehow it was hard to get as close to him again. He took the phone from me where I'd photographed ten pages of the journal, so I could look it over while I was out. The journal was far too delicate to risk bringing to the beach, but I had a notebook along to jot down my translations. He read, resting the phone on his knees, elbows braced. Waves lapped in the near distance where I stared off as I lay on my back, knees still bent. Big tough police officers weren't supposed to subconsciously bite their lips while reading. It shouldn't be allowed.

"Here," he said and looked over, eyes following me to where I'd lain back. He scooted back to me and lay on his stomach, showing me a line on the phone. "You annotated here that it says, 'that was the night I was sick.'" I turned to see, our heads once again close, looking at the screen. "Based in the context and his dialect, I think it means more, 'In that night, a sickness grew in me,' which I know sounds like semantics. But I think he refers to her. The Woman. I think he means heartsick."

I rolled farther onto my side, so I was inches from him, looking at the subject of his correction and the surrounding lines. Despite having an umbrella overhead, the sun was wickedly hot on my legs, the heat coming off him, unsteadying. I asked what made him think so.

"He says . . . here." He pointed down a few lines, his arm lying across mine. Thank the good Lord for sunglasses, because my eyes were wholly unfocused. "You have, 'exquisite pain' marked, which is right. But, there's a saying in French, 'la douleur exquise,' which is a phrase manifesting the physical pain of wanting someone you can't have."

Fuck. My. Life. Pardon my French.

"You are quite the scholar," I said, knowing my voice sounded like a caged rabbit. Though he had Wayfarers over those dark eyes, I felt them on me. "Would your public service extend to translating a French journal from the 1980s?"

His hand lifted and touched my waist, just above where my bottoms hit. Yellowed bruising and scratches remained, though mostly unnoticeable under my tan unless you were really looking.

"I didn't know you were bruised here too." A note of anger was laced in the statement.

Twangs of a guitar played from the speaker a blanket over from us. The first few lines started up, a Jake Owen song about a guy who wanted a girl despite her always keeping him at arm's length.

I growled and yelled at Darcy to skip the song. She laughed and turned it up. Adrian was chuckling softly beside me.

The song sang over and over how he just couldn't let himself be alone with the girl. And here we have it, ladies and gentlemen. That was the damned Jake Owen song that replayed in my head when I thought of the guy next to me correcting my French.

"Of course I'll help with the journal. Later?"

I agreed, and he hopped up.

"I need to cool off." A hand reached down to me and pulled me up until I was nearly pressed against him. He ran into the water while I walked along with Darcy, arm in arm. Truly, I didn't want to move away from Vero. My field of expertise was art. I had no desire to run an antiques shop, so that left me with museums. Unless I wanted to work in a pirate treasure museum in Sebastian, which was not quite my niche, I couldn't stay. Not without a job.

Rather than dwell on it, I swam, my head above water, floating over the sparkle of the sea. Four of our group were playing chicken, getting knocked over continuously by wave after wave, all of us laughing. Adrian had hoisted Maddie onto his shoulders, Darcy was on Logan's, and they were pulling each other until another wave swept them apart. Underwater, a solid arm wrapped around my waist. I screeched, erupting in giggles as Adrian surfaced, dragging me against him as he swam backward. When he dropped again, I searched the water for his shape under the rolling surf. Cutting through the water like a dolphin, he dove over the next wave. We were face-to-face again, my cheeks near painful from grinning.

"I've never seen you smile so much," he said.

"You've seen me at my worst, I think. I'm not always so awful." He sank under the water again, coming up behind me and towing me toward our friends.

"You're not awful," he said into my ear before swimming off.

They say you get deadly cramps from eating before swimming. However, the havoc wreaking about in my stomach was not from eating. It was la douleur exquise.

THE TALE of moonrise in the South was told in the chirping of cicadas in the trees outside. Adrian's long fingers held the cup of coffee high while he read through the journal. We had the laptop open to check our translations, however, the overall nuances in Emil's writing—especially in the shorthand— needed our analog translation. As I'd said, my French fell far short compared to my companion's academic insight. We'd gotten through most of Emil meeting the tourist in Juan-les-Pins. Descriptions Emil wrote of the painting he created for her were self-deprecating, yet the emotion in them came through. I pointed to a line that confused me as the contractions seemed to switch, nullifying the statement. Adrian peered closer, his tooth catching his bottom lip, my focus zeroing on that small detail.

"'The sea that wasn't the sea of the death of dreams, but the sea that was the dreams he dreamed, when dreams could never be, but unless was met the paradise of death,'" he translated thoughtfully. Because *that* wasn't complicated. I asked him to repeat it so I could write it down. On the laptop, I pulled up *Naufrage* for us to compare. Based on the description, this was the painting for her. Judy's story played back to me. The repetition of the story's depiction of each sea. I closed my eyes, trying to remember her tale, then recounting it to Adrian. Opening my eyes, I saw his on me. The look on his face was one I couldn't decipher.

Folded into the next page was a letter. It was dated 26 September 1985, Vero Beach, Florida. Skimming to the bottom, it was signed by Judy Monroe. Though short, within Judy told him, in a practiced French hand, how she had carried the painting on her lap on each flight home. She included a photo of the ocean, slightly hazy and out of focus.

"'Perhaps,'" Adrian read aloud, "'I can never be yours in name, but my heart will always wait for you, in your sea of dreams. Meet me where the night begs the day to roll away like the tide.'" We both exhaled at the same time, not even bothering to remark on how heartbreaking their story was.

It was a good time to stop and refill our drinks. My water and his coffee. A favorite part of the new kitchen was that it didn't have glaring, overhead lighting. I'd installed three drop pendants over the island instead. When the undercabinet lights weren't on, the kitchen was bathed in a warm glow. Adrian under the lights felt like he was meant to be in there. As though under these lights, in my kitchen, messy and worn out from a day in the sun, he was home. I blinked several times, not knowing if I was blinking away the image or feeling the saltwater.

"I was offered a job in St. Augustine," I told him. "I'm fairly sure the interview I had today for a job in Sarasota went well too." He took the refilled MFA Boston mug and quirked his head at me.

"You think you'll take it?" He sipped the black coffee and leaned back, feet crossed at the ankles.

"Not sure what to do. I need a job."

He nodded.

"One less troublesome citizen for you to deal with here." The cup clicked when it met the marble counter. "I know I've been a pain in your ass. It's okay, I get it. You've been clear about why you go out of your way to help me, and I respect that."

Silence killed me. I almost wished a ghost would start banging around to break it up. I knew the friendly one— Emil—was probably quietly watching. Which wasn't creepy at all.

"Do you think I would do this for anyone?" he asked, eyes on the floor. "Do you think I would *want* to do this for anyone?"

"I don't know," I said barely above the sound of the cicadas. "But that's kind of what you alluded to. Quite a few times."

"I also said I wanted to kiss you. Which is why you got fired."

"No. Something else is going on there. We're figuring it out. It wasn't you." We were two feet apart, but it felt like we were simultaneously closer and miles away. From the other room, my phone buzzed. "You didn't say you wanted to kiss me," I clarified. "You said you didn't know how you were not supposed to, or something." I waved my hand in the air, my cheeks feverish.

A slow, mischievous smile spread across his golden-brown face. "Or something."

Time slowed, watching him push off the kitchen island, closing the short distance between us. We were both still in our beach clothes, salty and coated in sunscreen. His gray T-shirt tickled my bare midriff. He brushed his thumb across my bottom lip, then traced a line to my hair, so he could tuck it behind my ear. Fingers slipped into my salty hair. "To be clear, I do want to kiss you. I've wanted to kiss you since you opened the door that first night here. Though I wasn't sure, at the time, if you were crazy."

"At least now you know for sure I am."

He chuckled, the sound rocking his chest against me. I brought my hand to his hair, touching the ebony strands. That ache in my stomach tried to pull me closer to him.

"I'm crazy about you," he breathed and met my lips with his. That bottom lip I'd watched molded itself to mine. Both his hands cradled my head, and I had my hands on his neck and back, wanting to feel all of him against me. He pulled back; his hands still held my face. I moved forward again, claiming his mouth. His phone vibrated against me where it sat in his pocket. We ignored it, not pulling apart an inch. Only a faint shadow of stubble lined his jaw, and I nearly growled at the feeling of it against my neck where he kissed me. The damned phone kept going. And going. He pulled it out of his pocket and dumped it on the counter without looking, but my eyes caught the name: Oscar.

"It's my brother," I said, hardly any breath left. He backed up, lips bright red. I tugged his hips toward mine and told him to check it quickly. Before he called back, it rang again. He swiped it on.

"I was hoping it would be you, Officer Kikumoto." I was close enough I heard the voice. Adrian put it on speaker and walked to the living room, instantly in a different mode. He picked up my phone and handed it to me to unlock before switching on the voice recorder.

"Do I know you?"

"We've been acquainted. I reckon you're with the girl. Your car is at her house."

Adrian moved to the bag he'd brought with him and reached in, unclipping a gun from its holster.

"These two." The sound on the other end was of a dull thud, like slapping a watermelon. A muffled yell came through. I looked at Adrian in horror. "I found this one saying some faggot shit to his homo sweetheart."

Jesus Christ.

Adrian switched on my laptop and logged into a website, quickly typing while he spoke into the phone.

"What is it you want and where are you?"

A laugh. "These two ruined my life. I've a mind to do the same. Seems the way I cut 'im up last time didn't keep him from his sinnin' shit."

Adrian hung his head but recovered and kept typing. He pulled his phone away and went into messaging, shooting texts to multiple people. Uncontrollable shaking took over my body.

"Really I just want to talk," the voice said, forced laziness in the tone.

"Then let's talk. I'm listening. Just us here."

Adrian motioned to my clothes. It took me a second, but he meant for me to change. I was still in a swimsuit and shorts.

He followed me to my bedroom but turned his back, giving me privacy to change. Cold shaking set in, so I sat on the side of my bed, twisting and untwisting the throw blanket which hung off the headboard.

"That girl is the devil's child," came the voice on the phone. "I've seen that demon after her. I have that proof."

I must have squeaked because Adrian whirled to me. We both realized what he meant.

"Now I know, Officer Ki-ku-mo-to—that a Jap name? You're as bad as the Mexican scum—I know you would be callin' your heat on me. I ain't too stupid though. Bring the girl here if she wants to see her fairy-ass brother again. He's alive now, but not for long. And not if I hear sirens."

I was nodding, Adrian shaking his head back.

"Tell me where."

"There's an old tool shed out in Fellsmere, off the farm

their daddy worked. It's a building ain't been used in years. Hell, it wasn't used for years before I's in prison. You have one hour." The line went dead. Immediately, Adrian called his station and reiterated the details, sending the recording as well.

"It's a different police department," I said in a panic. "Adrian, we need to tell Fellsmere Police or we won't—"

"I did. Everyone knows. The phone was traced to just outside of Fellsmere. The Indian River Sheriff is close by."

"I have to go. Whatever he wants. I— He'll kill Oscar." The hands that had so recently held my face while he kissed me, smoothed my wild beach hair and hugged me to him.

"We are going to stop him. I don't want you near this."

"It's him. Jim, Rob, whatever. Avery. That was his last name. I didn't pay attention when he was put away. I'm so stupid. He was the one filming me." He must have paid off the other transient to contact Adrian.

There was a brief knock at the door. Two Vero Beach Police cars sat outside, no lights on. Thompson stood on my stoop with a few others looking around the property. They wanted to take me to the station to make sure I was safe. I argued to stay home. The tires on Adrian's Jeep had been slashed. My phone was going, Tía started yammering about Fellsmere Police surrounding the house. I breathed a sigh of relief that they were okay but told her I'd explain later.

"Adrian," I said as we stepped back into my house. "I need to go. Please don't tell me to sit here while my brother is tortured."

Flashes from childhood came to me. When my father, and all his charm, couldn't keep a job. Early mornings just before Oscar was hurt, he went to work on a farm. But it wasn't in Fellsmere.

"I know where he is. It's not where he said. He . . . maybe he told us Fellsmere to keep you guys away. I know where it is! Please, I can get there. Have them follow or whatever needs to be done. But if I can keep him from hurting Oscar . . ." I lost it. The tears that had stayed dry for seventeen years rushed out like floodgates. "I don't care what happens to me. Please," I begged him.

"I care what happens to you. In case that wasn't obvious. I really, really care, Celia."

"Just let me go there. Please." My hands were bunched in his shirt. He inhaled like he had before diving into the ocean.

"Okay." It came out as a whisper. "Okay. Fuck. Okay. Let's go."

He grabbed the keys to my car, and we pulled out. There was chaos on his phone with his captain calling in, Thompson complaining that we sped off without letting him know where we were going.

"Will you be in trouble?" I asked as we drove over the bridge and onto Indian River Boulevard. He turned right, saying there would be less traffic this way.

"Probably."

"I'm sorry." I reached over and covered his free hand with mine. We crossed over the railroad tracks, the street darkening.

"He's my friend too."

We flew past the Indian River County Sheriff's office, going far faster than I'd ever dare to drive. Streets and houses out this way were spaced farther apart, interspersed with small farms. We hung a left onto Sixty-Sixth Avenue, and I yelled that it was up ahead. Just past a tiny taxidermy shop was a slip road. My small, German-made car bumped along the dirt until I noticed the farm. Papi was set on working there because they allowed farmworkers to live in campers on the land. Hippies and vagabonds came from all over, and my father thought it was his answer "until he got back on his feet." As far as I knew, it hadn't been used in years. The lack of viable crops confirmed my suspicion. Adrian called someone, telling them exactly where we were. Dilapidated clusters of buildings sat maybe a quarter of a mile back from the slip road. We pulled to the side of one, the car still visible from the road.

"Celia," Adrian said, stopping me when we got out of the car. He looked like he was wrestling with what to say, finally settling on "Slowly."

I nodded once.

The phone was back at his ear. "We're here. Alone. Tell me what building."

Chapter 20

Oscar

Three Hours Earlier

Painted streaks of burnt orange and rose gold lined the sky, colors cast by the sunset behind us. Though the balcony faced due east and out across the Atlantic, none could argue that the day's end here wasn't majestic. A couple of years ago, just after I'd bought this place, Nate and I sat out here drinking a sweating bottle of Veuve Clicquot, just happy to be with one another. He was shipping back out in a week, and I always worried. I hated it in fact. It pissed me off that this beautiful, brilliant man chose to use his intelligence to analyze weapons development and testing. Or whatever the hell he really did over there.

I'd begged him to get out and go into aerospace or something. Or anything that wasn't in the ass-end of the world. He would always smile and say not to worry. That one night on this balcony, he pulled long and hard from the Veuve bottle, and I watched his cheeks hollow on the pull, throat bobbing as he swallowed. Holy Mary, it was getting too hot to stay outside. Nate tipped the bottle back from his mouth with a pop and smirked at me, passing the Champagne. I couldn't break that eye contact, even if I'd tried. Not that I tried. He seemed to watch me drink, as I'd observed him, and before I knew it, all six foot two of him was leaning over me in the lounge chair, pinning me with knees and torso.

Shirts came off, our heated chests slipping against each other while we kissed. The chair under us creaked and shifted. He laughed against my mouth, and I pulled him fully onto my lap, groaning at the feel of him. Thank God there was a wall on either side of the balcony, and nothing but the horizon to see us.

"Oscar," Nate said quietly against my neck. I hummed in answer, pushing up into the hard line of him. He snickered and repeated my name.

"Sorry, I'm unavailable at the moment, please continue to seduce me and leave your message."

"God, you're a cheeky little shit."

I reached into his pants and yanked his ass toward me while I bit his earlobe.

He growled, holding my face in both calloused hands. "Will you marry me?"

A thousand thoughts and emotions ran riot in my mind and body at that question. A thousand ways to tell him yes. "Are . . . are you sure?" I asked instead, and there was all this hurt across his sun-god face. I immediately kissed him repeatedly to wipe that pain away.

"I've been sure for a very long time. Are you not?" he asked, trying to escape my lips. His fight was totally half-assed though because I was five foot eleven on a good day. Like, after Pilates.

"I would have married you in Home Depot that first day," I said.

His smile was slow, shy, and the most incredible thing I'd

ever seen. My hands smoothed his cheeks and thick, ruddy eyebrows.

"Yes. Yes, I'm sure. Yes, I'll marry you. Yes, to all of it."

He stood and pulled me up and pushed me against the wall. "I didn't think you would want a ring yet. Adrian said an engagement ring would be kind of cheesy."

I laughed. Of course, Adrian knew. I told him I wanted a ring when he had a ring. He got down on one knee anyway.

"You've made my world the place I fight for it to be. I love you."

I pressed his head against me, feeling his short blond locks caress my stomach. "Then don't fight anymore. Just stay with me."

His face upturned, he looked at me, cerulean eyes glazed. My weak knees barely held me up. He slipped my pants from my hips, taking any further response from me with his ministrations.

So, here I was, years later, sitting on the same balcony with Taiko. I was in love. I knew I was. A different love to what I'd felt for Nate, but in love nonetheless. I'd been worried that Adrian would judge me for it. Nate being his best friend, I wasn't sure he would be on board with being my friend after Nate. Especially if I was with someone new. At the gala, he'd clapped me on the shoulder and said he was happy for me. I remembered thinking, I wished he'd just tell my sister how he felt about her. They were so tenuous with one another. I wanted to tell him she wouldn't break. I wanted to tell *her* she wouldn't break. Instead, I teased them both.

I hope you enjoy the beach today with MY SISTER, I'd texted him earlier. *Wear the black trunks. You look hot in those.*

Surely you have a painting to pose for, Oscar?

No, just a multimillion-dollar account to settle. I'm still impressed you made her chilaquiles. Don't think it didn't matter to her, Mr. Public Servant.

Which black trunks?

I'd smiled to myself and sent him a photo from the last time he, Nate, and I had gone out on the boat with everyone.

She told you about the chilaquiles?

God, you're such a guy.

Yes.

Of course she told me. Now stop bugging me. I have work to do.

Taiko was looking at me funny as I checked my phone to see if Ce had texted. He understood what haunted me. Not unlike what haunted Celia. Her ghosts were in her house; mine were in my head. Mine were everywhere I'd ever been with Nate. Taiko understood, and still he stuck around. We all had our demons. His centered around his father's abusiveness. His mother's suicide. I put my phone away and turned to him. That halo of golden hour sun lit him up in gilded silhouette.

"I'm pretty sure I'm in love with you," I said to him.

"I'm fairly sure you are too."

We both laughed. An embarrassing laugh. I looked down, still smiling, feeling the raised scar on my cheek press into my eye. It made me self-conscious, but I never looked into getting it fixed. There was a reason I got this blasted thing. Even if the world didn't know my story, it showed I survived; that I was a survivor and would keep living.

Taiko's fingers lifted my chin. He looked at me like he was seeing the stars for the first time. All of them glittered in his nearly black, up-tilted eyes. Every angle on his smooth-skinned face was sharp and daring. "Let me know when you know for sure. I'm pretty sure I will return the sentiment."

His voice and accent sent tinges of electricity through me. Just the slightest hint of Japanese under a carefully cultivated English accent. He had to head back to England in the morning and was leaving my place tonight. It was only a week's trip, but I found myself dreading it. PTSD from Nate's last bon voyage.

WE STOOD in the parking garage saying good night far longer than we needed to. His car was parked in the guest spot, where we leaned against it. Shadows trolled the dimly lit garage where no one was around. Few cars were even home, so I made out with Taiko like we were sixteen and feeling invincible.

"Come back to me," I said, feeling just a little too vulnerable.

"Always," he said, confirming it with a fucking glorious kiss. Watching him get in his car and leave had me talking myself down from the panic. Blue light shone on the elevator button where I waited. There was a click and pressure in the small of my back where something pressed.

"Hey there, faggot," a voice I would never forget said to my back. My eyes closed briefly. "Come with me, now." He yanked my arm back behind me and kept the gun on my spine.

I knew I should be doing something, but everything I'd been taught about fighting someone off who had a weapon on you, fled. I just kept thinking that, if I moved, the bullet would go through my spine. So, I went with him, knowing that when an attacker took you to a secondary location, you were fucked. He smelled like cigarettes and cheap alcohol. Though I suppose that the stench of any alcohol on him would smell cheap. He shoved me into the trunk of a late-nineties-model Ford Taurus and knocked the side of my head with the gun, then he tied my hands and feet.

While he drove, I tried to pay attention to how many turns we took, but it was useless. I rammed my head into the back seat, tried to stick my fingers through the lock, but they were bound so tight behind me, all it did was put me in a worse position. Thank God Taiko left when he did. We must have been going for twenty minutes before the car slowed, turning onto a road that had the sedan bouncing, and my shoulder screaming from the torque.

The car skidded and stopped, rolling me into the metal trunk side, smarting the spot he'd hit with the gun. As soon as the trunk opened, I used all my strength to kip up, bringing my bound feet into his jaw. It cracked and he swore, falling back onto the dusty ground. I scrambled to lift myself over the lip of the trunk, tearing my arm open on the latch. He was standing, rubbing his face, as I fell and hit the gravel. I'd trained for this. I'd had my arms and legs tied in class. But I hadn't felt the pressure I felt in that moment: the dancing spots in my vision, the weakness. Still, I flipped onto my knees, nailing my head on the car bumper. When he came forward, I realized he'd lost the gun. Not that I could use it with my hands laced behind me, but it gave me a hint of leverage. If only I could just run.

He came at me and swung, missing my face, but his fist rammed into my shoulder. I spun with the impact and was back on the ground. Back to my knees, I readied, feeling him come closer in the dark. I turned and used all my weight to knock into him. He went down but grabbed my hair in the process, taking me with him. From there he stood, dragging me by my hair as I kicked uselessly. Somewhere in the dirt, he managed to find the gun. Fucking great.

"Suck on this," he spat, shoving a bandanna in my mouth, and dropped me on the floor. Gagging, I tried to calm myself so as to not hyperventilate. The room was dark and smelled like an old garage: rusted metal, fertilizer, wood, mildew, and rat shit. Slowly, my eyes adjusted. He had my phone and was calling someone but kept slapping the phone on his leg in frustration.

"Your little whore of a sister isn't picking up. I saw the

cop's car outside her house before I came to get you. Slashed his tires."

I screamed through the bandanna, choking on the fabric. Bile rose from the bandanna touching the back of my throat, and tears stung my eyes. At least I knew Adrian wouldn't let Celia do anything stupid. Think, Oscar. I shifted on the floor, groaning from the shoulder pain. Last week I'd bought myself a new pair of running shoes. In this cesspool, they were getting as trashed and destroyed as the rest of me. Why was I thinking about my running shoes? In all the terror I'd felt, it hadn't occurred to me that this piece of shit redneck, Robert Avery, was the one who had attacked Ce. Rage, quick, bottomless, and unchecked, rose in me. Seventeen years of rage. I waited for him to come closer.

The tie around my wrists was pulling my shoulders back, reminding me why I did Pilates. My shoulder mobility was crap, yet my wrists were slimmer than the long sleeves he'd fastened the ties over, so I had some movement in my wrists and hands. But without a way to cut my feet free, I was shit out of luck on that front. In the dark, I watched him calling over and over, then scratching his head with the barrel of the gun, which seemed like a really stupid idea, and I wished he'd keep doing it. I slid closer to him, trying to make as little noise as possible. He smiled at the phone and spoke.

"I was hoping it would be you, Officer Kikumoto," he said. I squeezed my eyes tight. He was talking to Adrian as I tried to yell through the gag. Avery turned to me suddenly and kicked me in the ribs, then backhanded my face. Sheer will kept me from throwing up. He chatted, pacing in the dark. God, I wished the gag was out, it was getting truly difficult to breathe.

He'd hung up and gone to look out, standing, a dark outline in the moonlit doorway. No sirens, no lights. No one coming. We weren't exactly where he'd told Adrian. We hadn't driven far enough for it to have been Fellsmere, but surely, they can trace phone calls? I always kept location services on as I was always losing my phone. Avery came back, shutting the door. I closed my eyes and counted to thirty so my vision could adjust. He kicked my legs, then my groin once for good measure. I coughed, choking on the bandanna, then started gasping for air. It was wholly unpleasant, and a really shitty way to die.

My shoulders lifted from the ground and slammed back again, rolling me on my side.

"The fuck's wrong with you, asshole?" he yelled, but there was a nervous sliver in his voice. He toed at my feet.

I made low, moaning noises in my throat, desperate for air, thrashing on the ground.

"You fucking dying, kid? You better not fucking die. I need that fucking money."

Flashbulbs were going off in my mind, my body vellicating on the filthy ground. I was facedown, my head turned to the side trying to catch air, my legs jerking until I just stopped. Every limb and movement stopped in that shithole shed in God-fucking-knows where. Thoughts of Ce, of Taiko, of my mom, my family, filtered in. Thoughts came of Nate, who I thought would be proud of me.

"Oh fuck, you stupid piece of shit." He squatted down.

Yes, Nate would be proud. Because I fucking missed him, and he taught me just how much love I was capable of. And just how much shit I was capable of not taking. Avery bent over me, nudging my still cheek with his gun. He ripped the gag from my mouth, yet still I didn't move. Didn't breathe.

"Awwww, shiiiit. Now I'm gonna be fucked." He tried to roll me by using one hand to push right near the ribs he'd kicked. And because I'm a goddamned survivor, I threw my head back into his and grappled with my bound hands for the gun he'd had just above my back.

"Jesus, motherfucker," he yelled, stumbling but keeping hold of the gun. He tried to kick me, but I wouldn't let go, yanking him sideways. My fingers found the trigger and pulled, shooting in the only direction I could tell wasn't mine. The shot went through the wall. I pulled again, angling us differently. He sent an elbow just under my shoulder blade, which had me scream and release the gun. He was unsteady enough that I could still flip and kick both feet up into his hand, knocking the gun across the room. I didn't care that my head was feeling like there was a balloon inflating inside it. As soon as I kicked him, I kipped myself up, onto my feet. Nearly falling straight forward, I became a battering ram and head-butted him flat in the chest. Avery went down, smacking his head on the hard ground, and stilled.

Scampering off, I tried to shuffle outside, but blacked out just past the door. The last thought in my head was that I should've found the gun first.

CHAPTER 21

CELIA

NO SOUND AT ALL CAME FROM ANY OF THE outbuildings. Adrian's mouth pressed to the shell of my ear.

"Tire tracks on the ground," he said. "Someone's here."

He'd gotten no response from Avery when he asked which building, and I began to worry. Arms and legs shook from nerves. We went around the side of the larger shed and saw an older Ford parked, the trunk open, and blood in the middle of the rusted green paint. Lines in the grit beneath us revealed what looked like something or someone had been dragged, and I knew then that I couldn't do this. Adrian had his gun trained ahead of him, turning methodically to scan the area. He caught my expression and lowered the weapon. I shook my head, my body starting to rock back and forth. He pulled me to him and kissed the side of my head.

"It's okay. Sit behind the car. Don't make a sound. I'll find him." It sounded like a great idea until I spotted a shape on the ground against the shed, hidden in a pocket of darkness. Both of us moved quickly, seeing Oscar's new sneakers glowing white in the moonlit night. There was a crunch of tires on gravel in the distance, and I hoped it was the police.

Oscar was unconscious. I touched his face. His arm was bleeding, an interminate stream of life escaping him. His wrists were blistered and bloody from the zip tie around them. Adrian pulled his phone out and started calling rescue. There was a shuffle just inside and a gunshot, followed by Adrian's gun firing three times.

I didn't know what had happened until Adrian was thrown back, almost falling on Oscar. I grabbed for him, keeping them from hurting one another. Doors slammed and feet were running, but my world was at a standstill. No sounds made sense. Nothing processed. Four more shots fired, and I hadn't even the sense to move or duck.

All I could think was that he wouldn't have been shot if I hadn't insisted on coming. It was my fault. My fault he felt compelled to protect me. My fault he came out here. All of it. Every ounce of blame was mine. He wouldn't have even been with me had I not asked him to help with the stupid journal. I. Did. This.

Indian River Deputies arrived first, their guns trained on Adrian. Voices were yelling, someone was asking me questions, and all I saw was blood and flashing lights.

"Issarright," Adrian slurred. "I'm 'nofficer. My badge. Pocket." A deputy had kicked the gun away and was reaching into Adrian's black swim trunks to find the badge. He radioed in, and there was more commotion, the other department showing up.

"Ma'am," someone said firmly. "Ma'am, we have to move you. Are you hurt?"

Rescue moved in, and someone was pulling me from between the two men who meant so much to me. Oscar was groaning, and I sobbed, looking at him.

"Nn-no. My brother." I indicated to the stretcher being loaded into the truck.

"I can take her," a male voice chimed in. "Miss Sullivan.

Celia. Remember me? I'm Officer Thompson. Jarrod, Adrian's friend. Will you come with me?" I think I nodded. He lifted me, but I was still holding Adrian's hand.

"I'm so sorry," I said to him. "I'm so sorry."

"'Sokay, Sullivan," Adrian slurred.

Law enforcement cars from three or four different jurisdictions covered the once-open space, their lights a wicked spectacle, taking me further from the here and now. Vaguely aware of being settled into the car with a blanket, I thanked Officer Thompson. It could have been thirty seconds; it could have been a year. We arrived at the station and I panicked, asking to be taken to the hospital. Mom met us inside, and she took me in her arms. She was crying and holding me, telling me she was going to the hospital to be there for Oscar. I had to stay and answer questions. Voices carried in the loud din of the station.

"My girlfriend," a male voice was saying. "Let me see her. Celia!"

Shaking my head no, I backed up. Officer Thompson stepped in, blocking Jacob from coming toward me. "She had an accident a couple weeks ago. Sometimes she can't remember things. Come on, man. She's obviously in shock. Let me comfort her."

"No thank you, Jacob," I said, my voice surprisingly strong. "How did you know what happened?"

"Your mom told me. It's okay, I know you were with Adrian. I'm not mad."

My head whipped around wildly looking for eyes with which to plead. A female officer came to my side and told him to "Fuck. Off."

They escorted him out, and I pulled out my phone, showing Officer Thompson and Officer Kriss the text thread where I'd said in no uncertain terms that I didn't want to see him. Thompson told me he knew from Adrian telling him why I'd been at his house. I broke down, sobbing at the mention of his name. They gently asked me a ton of questions, most of which I couldn't answer. Finally, I was free to go.

"My mom doesn't know him. Jacob Wentworth. She wouldn't have told him anything." It felt important to let them know that.

Officer Thompson drove me to the hospital.

No INFORMATION WAS RELEASED to us that night. Mom had been told that Oscar was being assessed for brain and internal damage. I didn't get any updates about Adrian. Desperate for information, I called the station and eventually left a message on his mother's work voice mail.

Darcy drove me home to change, since my clothes were covered in blood and dirt. I insisted on going straight back, though my entire being protested at the lack of sleep. Tía was there, talking to Mom, hugging her, and praying. I ran to them, fearing the worst.

"He's awake," Mom said, her voice like dry leaves.

Tubes were covering him, patches fed from his shaved head to a monitor. His arm had so many stitches in it I couldn't count them all. But he was awake. Neither of us tried to smile. Neither feigned that strength. I curled onto the edge of his bed, fitting myself against his side without disrupting the machinery. Two officers, two deputies, and two FBI agents entered the room.

They all introduced themselves and asked Oscar as many questions as they could fit in. There was footage from the parking garage showing when he was accosted. It was indeed Robert Avery, who had cut my brother all those years ago. He was dead. They asked if anyone else had been in there with him. Oscar said there wasn't.

"You put up a hell of a fight," the FBI agent said.

And so, Oscar told them what had occurred.

"He kept saying that if I died or if Celia didn't come, he wouldn't get his money," Oscar explained, fading in his concentration. "At the time, I didn't care. But it seems weird now. Especially with what happened with Ce's job." His eyes were closing as I stroked his face.

That was how I ended up five cups of coffee in, describing all the events of late to the FBI—minus the ghosts, no one needed to hear that.

"YOU LOOK LIKE HELL, SULLIVAN."

There was not a question in my mind about my appearance. Though I'd showered, changing my clothes meant switching into the softest leggings I owned and a tissue-thin Boston College T-shirt. Deep circles marred his undereye area. Where his beautiful face was normally a golden bronze, it was now faintly yellow. Perhaps there was a forcefield over the doorway as I couldn't seem to make myself move past it. Straddling the room and hallway, I stood chewing my lip.

"You can come in," he rasped. Darcy gave me a little shove from behind and closed the door. "But," he said carefully, "you don't have to."

I looked at him in his bed, the stupid hospital gown covering what the sheet didn't, and made myself walk to him. He took my hand with his untethered one. That feeling of his rough hand in mine made me want to fall into him. But I didn't. It wasn't appropriate, and I was to blame for where he was.

"Oscar's okay? I mean, I heard he was. But is he okay according to you?"

"He will be," I answered with my head hung.

"Thompson said it looked like he fought like a beast."

I was nodding without taking a break. Clouds were pushing in from the coast, the sky beyond his window darkening.

"It's not your fault."

Sick, humorless laughter came out of me. It was ugly and cruel. "It's all my fault. All of it. Even fucking Jacob coming to the station and humiliating me. Dragging your name through the mud."

"I heard about that."

"Yeah," I said and pulled my hand from his to get my hair out of my face. "If I hadn't been insistent on going, you wouldn't have been there. You would be fine. If I hadn't kept calling and texting you, you wouldn't have been anywhere near me. Now look."

"Oscar's my friend." He'd said that before too. "I would have gone after him."

"Things would have been different. If I'd left you alone."

He shrugged and winced from the pain in his side where the bullet had gone straight through the very little body fat he had.

"I've accepted the job in St. Augustine. I'll be starting in two weeks." It had been a hasty three a.m. decision.

"Oh." He looked out the window and nodded. "I guess it's what you want."

What I wanted was him. I wanted my job back here. I wanted to not be haunted. Or to not be haunted by an evil spirit at least. I'd take the benevolent one. I wanted to not have an ex-con and a jealous former not-even-boyfriend after me. But what he needed was to not have me turning his life into a living nightmare. So, I just said, "I guess."

"I hope you . . . I guess, I hope that you're happy."

Walking out of that room was the hardest thing I'd ever done. I didn't know what that meant, or how to handle it, but there was no way to pinpoint the spot where the pain settled. No way to show where to direct some light, because everything in me, body and soul, was dark and empty. All I'd done was steal and absorb any light offered. The price of that was the pain I felt.

CHAPTER 22

OSCAR

OCTOBER WAS NEVER MY FAVORITE MONTH. Everywhere online and in movies portrayed the midfall month in rich color and blustery days. In Florida, it was still hot as all hell, and maybe the sky was a bit bluer, but nothing really changed. I didn't complain about the weather, though. No, I'd never wanted to live somewhere cold.

When Ce lived in Boston, I'd visited regularly, getting to wear a smart coat and scarf, but God I was always happy to be home. Although, every time I left my sister, the hole in my heart I tried to ignore most of the time tore right back open again. So, this time, I'd had her back for almost a year. Almost. I thought she'd stay. But life had other plans I suppose. It had been a month since she'd been gone. St. Augustine? I mean really, Ce. Not your scene, but hey, what do I know? Maybe you'll get recognition on that sexy Chloé dress you bought and never got to wear here. I'm not saying Vero was the pinnacle of fashion. It was truly not. But at least I'd be here to appreciate her Chloé dress.

Another few weeks and I would get the green light to work out again. Swim. Be together with Taiko. Adrian said he was already running. Bastard. I hadn't asked him what was said between them. I hadn't asked her. I knew my sister, and I understood. So, we were all sad little people stuck without one another. Life, I guess. It was a Friday afternoon when Taiko and I decided to drive up and see her. It was my chance to nerd out and show him around St. Augustine. On a quiet street that backed up to marshland, we found the blue building she called home. It was a cute little place inside but . . . yeah.

Both Taiko and I had to stifle gasps when she opened the door. It was the thinnest I'd ever seen her, and she'd never been even just a bit chubby. I pushed the aluminum pan covered in a Publix bag at her.

"Christ. Eat something, Ce."

"Hello, dearest brother. Good to see you too. Taiko." She gave us each a kiss and led the way through the small two-story apartment. Can you call it an apartment when it's two stories?

"Tía has a list of groceries for me to give you. She said she knows you won't be eating well."

She rolled her eyes, offering us drinks. Mom sent a bottle of Beaujolais, which Taiko passed to her.

"Adrian is healing, told me he went running this week. It's a couple weeks ahead of schedule."

I couldn't get her to bite. Taiko pulled out his phone and showed her pictures of a painting he was working on. She was interested in that, and I was able to sit back a little. I knew she had to disassociate from everything. From Vero. I got it. But damn if it didn't kill me.

MORNING BROUGHT MORE of those impossibly blue skies, so we told Taiko we were taking him on the full St. Augustine tour, starting at Castillo de San Marcos, the fort. Ce kept letting her eyes wander, indicating to me that she was seeing people the rest of us couldn't.

"Have you seen Cesar lately?" I asked, trying for nonchalance.

"No. I haven't translated the rest of the journal yet though. There's no point."

"I think there is," I said, toeing the ground. We looked out across the water while Taiko roamed up and down, inspecting the old canons. "I mean, you seem to think he might be Nate's real father. That's important to me."

"Then you translate it," she snapped. I put my hands up. I knew she and Adrian were doing that together the night everything happened.

Tradition had us visiting the Fountain of Youth, and just before dinner, Celia walked us by the museum where she now worked. It was impressive. Once a hotel, when the town was a magnet for people like Henry Ford and that crowd, it now stood proud and glamorous. And Celia was unhappy as fuck.

Just inside the old town, we had dinner at a small Italian place with bistro tables on the deck. She ate her gnocchi, mopping up the creamy pesto with a torn piece of rosemary bread. So, she either didn't eat at home or never sat still. It seemed as good a time as any, so I opened Pandora's bloody box. I cleared my throat and spoke up.

"There were several donations made to the museum two weeks before the gala."

She sat back in her seat and checked the buttons on her white sundress. Mental note to remember to tell her how cute it was. Very Palermo, 1965.

"On the Wednesday, two separate sums of money came in. For the same amount. Both respectable, yet not overly large, sums. I found it curious, so I traced it back." I took a sip of wine.

Celia didn't seem to realize the wine was there. Her chocolate bunny eyes just stared at me. Taiko put a hand on my knee, knowing it was difficult seeing her like this. He kept reminding me that though she hadn't been injured that night, she'd been attacked weeks before. And, more importantly to Ce, I was a mess when she found me. And she witnessed Adrian get shot. I knew she was seeing a therapist. Sometimes she let it slip she was at her session. Hell, I went twice a week. Mind fuck did not begin to describe what we'd been through.

"How did you get this information?" she asked me.

"I have a couple of friends who owed me favors."

Her eyebrows shot up.

"No, nothing illegal. I also looked into Caroline. She's super above board. Real Girl Scout, Anne Taylor and Olive Garden sensible. Really, not a lick of artistry there. Anyway, curiously, on that Friday, a direct deposit was made to her personal account for ten thousand. By Monday morning, another fifteen was there. That sum was from the same account that donated to the museum."

"And I don't suppose you can tell who made the contribution?"

I strummed my fingers on the table and took my time drinking the rest of my glass. Taiko snorted.

"Os," she warned.

"Jacob fucking Wentworth."

She sat forward like her chair had been tipped.

"He's very proud of himself. At least give him a little credit or his ego will never recover," Taiko teased.

She stood and walked off.

I was confused.

"Does she often do that?" he asked me.

I shrugged and ran a hand through my dark shoot of what will soon be waves. Five minutes or so later, my sister returned to the table. I did compliment her dress so I wouldn't forget, but she ignored me. That was pointless. I explained how we tailed the funds.

"But why?" she asked. "Surely it's not just to get me fired."

Taiko suggested Jacob had really liked Celia. And that he was likely certifiably insane. Sounded about right to me, though still extreme. Night came on quickly, fairy lights twinkling over cafés, the old town looking quite charming. Not Chloé-dress charming. Not Balenciaga-pumps charming. But charming. In the humid cover of darkness, I slung my arm around my sister. Her head tipped onto my shoulder. No, it wasn't Celia charming.

"I sure miss you, Ce."

She squeezed my middle, making me grunt; my ribs were still tender.

"I wish you'd come home." The sentiment I had never voiced when she was in Boston.

She stiffened beside me. It wasn't just Adrian she had run from. No, my sister had come home only to have home betray her. I knew she had to get away. I also knew it was time to come back. We walked in silence, a curious trio of quiet companions.

Her attention drifted to the alleyway we passed, making her pause and stare. My sister's fingers laced through mine, tugging me forward. None of us spoke, but she smiled, tears running down her face, and I couldn't fathom why that would be. She looked at Taiko and nodded, but he seemed as clueless as I was. If she wanted to tell me, she would. Eventually.

Before we left the following morning, I found Emil Cesar's journal sitting on the bottom shelf of the ugly-ass coffee table that came with the furnished rental apartment. If she wasn't reading it, I could take it home. Right?

CHAPTER 23

CELIA

WHEN WHAT WAS FORMERLY THE WORLD'S LARGEST swimming pool was turned into a restaurant, it attracted scores of brides looking for the perfect wedding venue. It really hadn't been part of my job description to show newly engaged couples around in the interest of nuptial planning. One exhibit, which had been planned before I was onboarded, got canceled. There was a customs hold up, and it would have run into the exhibit to follow. So, I cataloged and tweaked a new collection: fashion from the Edwardian era, as depicted in film and television. While not my usual forte, I did find a kind of tabloid fun in being among the gowns and breeches of yesteryear.

As a hotel, the museum had been a spectacle. An American castle in the oldest city in the United States, once inhabited by Henry Flagler, among many other well-known American tycoons. Historically, it was engrossing. Odd bits of eclectic collections covered the polished halls, but I missed the kind of art I specialized in. There were two Emil Cesar paintings on loan here from a gallery in Bruges. Often, I found myself standing and staring at them. A kinship had grown between me and the artist who still haunted my house. I found myself missing his quirky presence. When Oscar left last week, I felt like a hole had been punched in my chest. I always felt like that when he left. He was my best friend. Truly, I had never been happier than I was when I moved back and got to see him all the time. I knew he had Taiko now, which made it easier for me to be away. I knew he saw Adrian often, and that made it harder.

Most days I kept occupied with work and anything else I could do to get out of my own headspace. Anything to not think about hauntings and nefarious bosses, kidnappings, and violence. Anything to not think about Adrian. I wasn't the girl who mooned over boys. I wasn't the one who lay down and cried. I was never the one to fall for someone. Never. So, this time I was caught off guard. And I didn't know how to handle it. And I thought that maybe . . . maybe I handled it poorly.

The office I shared with another junior-level curator faced out behind the museum. The day had come to a close. Nothing remained to be seen in our acquisitions. No more bridezillas needed walking. My fingers tapped along the perimeter of my desk, trying to figure out dinner. Tía's sopes were long gone, and I would have committed a crime for her albondigas soup. October made me crave soup, though the weather was still overly warm and there were still three tropical systems out in the Atlantic we were keeping an eye on.

Carson, my boss, popped his head round the open doorframe, calling me into his office. On his desk sat a plastic box, which he unlatched and opened.

"Care for a game?" he asked me, gesturing to Battleship.

I laughed and said why not, taking my seat across his desk. We took a of couple minutes to configure our boards.

"B3." He began the game.

"Miss. E5."

"Hit. B4."

We plugged the pieces in, and I said it was a miss.

"You're not happy here."

"Pardon?" I asked. He gestured to the board, and I called F5, which was a hit, sinking his patrol boat.

"B7," he said, and I confirmed a hit and called H3. "Hit. I can see that though you've been wonderful—truly an asset to this museum—you aren't happy here. It's not hands-on enough for you. B6." Hit.

My call of H2 was also a hit.

"B5."

He'd sunk my submarine, and I called H1. Another hit.

"E5." Miss.

I called H4, with a hit. "You have to say it," I teased.

"You sunk my battleship," he said, humoring me with a grin. Carson was probably the nicest boss I'd had. Wouldn't it be just typical that it was the job I enjoyed least? "F4. Ha! Gotcha. Now I'd like to tell you something in confidence. If you are uncomfortable with that, we can skip it. But I think you'd like to hear this."

I said of course and called C6.

"Damn. Hit. Your opening at the Vero Museum was like the Shot Heard 'Round the World. The art world. F5."

It was a miss.

"Shoot. Anyway. You can write your own ticket now." We plugged in our hits and misses.

I called one.

"Miss on C7. E4." Hit.

"I'm not sure I understand," I admitted. "C5."

"Hit. I mean that I'm fairly sure that anywhere you applied at the moment would take you on and make a spot for you in some capacity. I mean like Getty to Guggenheim. We were lucky to get you. D4."

"It was a fantastic opportunity," I said honestly, confirming the hit and calling C4.

"You sunk my destroyer. Perhaps it was, but I believe you would have been happier not having to move. Am I wrong? G4." We played the next few turns without chatter, my aircraft carrier sinking. "Your former director, Caroline Unger, called me."

I was so surprised, I dropped the peg I was holding.

"She asked for my discretion, but she was remiss for letting you go. Said it was due to circumstances 'out of her control.'"

Yeah, I bet it was. Like twenty-five grand.

"Her recommendation for you had been quite gleaming to begin with. However, she wanted to be sure we—and you— knew that your dismissal was a mistake. She is stepping down from her position." He took a breath before continuing. "There is also a rumor that a certain Japanese artist has put pressure on the board to investigate Unger for extortion should she not step down. You didn't hear that from me."

Holy Mother of God. My patrol boat was sunk, and I had two pegs weighing down his carrier. "I'm not sure why you're telling me this, other than to maybe keep me from—E8— winning the game."

"The position for director will be reviewed by the board next week. I am happy to speak with them and give you a glowing review. A1."

"D9. I don't know what to say. Like, I really don't. That's very generous of you, Carson. I'm just a bit thrown." He called the second hit on my destroyer, and I sank his carrier, winning the game.

"Would you be interested in taking over Ms. Unger's position in Vero Beach?"

"I would, yes."

"Then I shall be in your corner. If you ever do leave there, look me up. I may not be here forever, and I'd be pleased to work with you again. Clear your desk and go home. Good match," he said with a final wink.

FOUR DAYS OF SCRUTINY. Four days of phone interviews and written statements. It took less than three hours to pack up my apartment in St. Augustine. I dropped the keys in the mailbox and drove home. To my house. The local taco dive just over the bridge had a Thursday night meal deal, and everyone piled in for margaritas and micheladas. Luckily, I was there past the rush, walking up to the counter, shaky with hunger. I'd driven the three hours in denim shorts and slides, both of which were starting to chafe. While waiting for the food to be done, I turned to grab some napkins and hot sauce.

There was a table of maybe six police officers finishing up their meals. Adrian was staring at me, taco held midair. It seemed like no part of my body was inclined to move as I held his stare. Thompson and Kriss noticed me too and stood to walk over. I shook myself from the stupidity and greeted them. Officer Kriss had kind eyes and a lovely smile on her dark skin. She'd had my back with Jacob, and I was forever grateful for that. Adrian finally came over, looking uncomfortable. The two others peeled away, leaving us to talk. He seemed like he would rather have been anywhere, with anyone, other than standing with me in a taco shop. The suck fest of the whole thing was that I realized I didn't care where I was, I would have wanted to be with him. So, in my realization, I steeled myself to walk away.

"Oscar said you were coming back."

"Yeah. Thanks," I responded like an idiot, though he hadn't asked me anything. "Are you . . . all healed?" God, Celia. My voice caught in my throat.

"Yeah, yeah. I'm good. Can't lift super heavy yet, but no other restrictions. Finally off desk duty."

"I'm glad." Brilliant discourse, Ce. My order was called.

"I have the journal. I've gotten through some of it. I think you should read it."

"*You* have it?" I was confused but made the connection that the last time I saw it was before Oscar left the previous week. "Sorry. I didn't realize he'd given it to you." I turned to take my bag, holding it against me like a protective device.

"Kikumoto," one of the officers called to him. "Let's go."

We said a hasty goodbye, but he turned at the door, nearly smacking into me. Even in uniform, his clean sandalwood and citrusy scent assaulted me.

"St. Augustine wasn't what you wanted?" It was so abrupt, I wasn't at all sure how to answer.

"No," I answered quietly. "No, it really wasn't."

"I'll drop the journal off. I can leave it if you're not home." He dashed off, and I tried to remember how to breathe. I didn't even want tacos anymore. Okay, that was a lie. I did want tacos. But still . . .

CHAPTER 24

EMIL

FOR SIX LONG MINUTES HE STOOD ON THE boulevard, watching The Woman's taxi drive away until he was watching nothing at all. He looked at his secondhand Swatch watch, marking in his head when the taxi would arrive in Nice. How long it would take to unload. When she would be on the flight. When the plane would land in Paris. He drove himself mad.

So, he holed himself up in his flat and painted all the paintings from his heart. He walked into galleries and shops, showing his works. As Emil had not sold his tourist pictures in some weeks since The Woman left, he was dangerously close to hungry. After strapping a load of canvases onto his back and onto the rack of his bicycle, the artist peddled up the hill to Mougins, an affluent village oozing bourgeoisie art. Once through the village entrance, where cars were not permitted, he slipped off his bike, sweating and hopeless. Cobbled streets ran a maze around the village with tiny cafés and galleries hidden in stone construction.

Coins littered the sunken depth of the fountain he sat upon. A small child walked to him, asking what was strapped on his bike and back. The mother scolded the child, but he remained, haughty and commanding. Emil smiled, impressed at the precociousness, so he pulled from the stack a relative copy, though far larger, of the painting he'd done for The Woman.

"What do you call this?" the child asked.

Emil wasn't quite sure if the boy asked to learn the name of the piece, or if he asked in the manner one does as if to say, "This is rubbish." So, he answered, "It is called *Naufrage*."

"Obviously," the child added.

Emil laughed.

"How much is it, monsieur?"

Emil looked at the mother, and she shrugged as though her child regularly dealt in art on village squares. He told him it was three hundred francs, expecting the mother to pull him away. Instead, the child turned to his mother and said he wanted to purchase it for two hundred fifty. The mother agreed, and Emil couldn't contain himself. He laughed until his sides hurt. He followed the family through the town until they arrived at a small villa just across from the old cemetery. Emil was told to wait there and was soon met by a man.

"My son tells me he purchased your art."

Emil presented the piece to the father, noting the white, pressed trousers and perfectly tucked cravat.

"Very well. Have you no gallery?"

Emil nearly laughed in his face, as he wasn't sure he even had a flat anymore. So, the man told him to bring his collection to his gallery in the village center, and they would see about selling the lot of them. For a wild moment, Emil thought he'd been played a fool. Money was pressed into his hand, and he was told where to bring the collection.

The paintings sold immediately. There had been nothing like his art there, turning it into a status symbol. He was commissioned by heads of state, film stars, and owners of wineries. Emil traveled Europe, appearing at openings, amassing a nest egg. He wrote in his diary about his wish to see a distant shore. A sea that was the sea of dreams. Each sale brought him closer to that dream. To that woman he knew so briefly, but to whom he owed his success. His heart. He'd had affairs, of course; women he met on his travels. For he knew The Woman he always thought of was far away, someone else's bride. Just as he was someone else's husband, though he'd been estranged from Marie for several years now.

For four long months spanning winter into spring, he unofficially lived with another woman in Amsterdam. A socialite who came to the art scene when she fell from the graces of her society. By April they parted ways.

The following summer, Emil had a showing in New York. He had risen quickly in his field, spanning the globe with his works. He rented a car and drove the Eastern Seaboard, determined to find the sea that was, and not the sea that wasn't. When he arrived along the shores of her hometown, he felt the completion of his soul. She had sent a photograph of her favorite spot by the ocean. Emil wandered for days to find just that spot.

It was early morning when he saw her, sitting on a patchwork quilt, bare feet in the sand. She was just as he'd remembered her, down to the freckle under her eye. He walked to her and sat, not knowing what he could say after all this time. She looked at him sidelong and said in her textbook French, "Your shorts are rather shorter than what is worn here."

He chuckled into his hands, saying she was impossible.

"I've kept up with your success. I am so very pleased."

"And are you pleased I've come?" he asked, looking at the majesty of the sea he had seen in his dreams.

She turned to him fully. "So very pleased. I must tell you, though. I am married. He . . . is not very kind but is seldom home."

Emil thought about whether he cared. He had told her from the beginning that he was married as well. And so, he stayed there, in that place where dreams of the sea manifested. He stayed there, painting. He stayed there, watching as her belly swelled with his child inside. The child he could never admit to fathering. He stayed even when the child, his son, was born into the world, his mother's golden looks, his father's glacial blue eyes.

And as the child grew, Emil knew he could no longer stay. So, he said his goodbye as though he were not saying goodbye. He slipped a note behind the original *Naufrage* and made to leave. The Woman's husband came home and found her distraught. He beat her until her lip bled and the second child she carried became just another dream lost. And when she cramped and bled and cried, she raged. She grabbed the vase that was always kept filled with flowers and smashed it over his head. Shards of painted porcelain exploded, stems and blooms showering the room. With that one act of self-defense, The Woman killed her husband before he struck her again.

And so, Emil left and chased the bottom of a bottle until it finally let him catch it. He died not knowing his son. Not knowing The Woman had killed her husband and was free of his abuse. He died, however, in possession of a legacy.

Chapter 25

Celia

Truth be told, the journal was much more difficult for me to translate than I'd anticipated. Especially as many of the things Adrian annotated would have gone well over my head. Psychometry is the gift of being able to glean information by touching an object or person. I often wished I had that gift. If not for my own profession, then for this life I've managed to cannonball into. Instead, I saw ghosts. Wholly unhelpful. When my security light and motion notifications popped on at midnight that Friday, I rushed to the door. The journal was placed on my mat, wrapped in a plastic bag, and the faint glow of taillights moved down my street. Behind me, standing within the darkened hallway, was Emil, a faint impression of a man, his arms crossed. I shook my head, still not comfortable. His mouth quirked up in a teasing sort of look. I nearly smiled back.

The note Cesar had left on the back of *Naufrage* still bothered me. Who was Anton? Perhaps I'd find out in the journal. Also, if I could somehow figure out who the anonymous donation to the museum was from, it may shed some light. I sighed and, after a half hour, finally gave in and texted Adrian, feeling my heart race.

Thank you for the journal.

You're welcome. Immediate response.

Can I ask you a quick question?

Dunno, he responded. *Can you?* I rolled my eyes but smiled. Damn.

I haven't read through the rest yet, but I'm wondering if you came across the name "Anton."

No. Why?

On the back of "Naufrage," there was a slip of paper which read, "For Anton. I'm sorry to have left you." Just wondering.

I don't recall seeing it, but I only got through a couple pages because I haven't had any time off.

Why not? Not that I should be snooping, but I was curious.

Just been working overtime. This weekend will be my first couple of consecutive days off since I was shot.

Those words rang through me, causing a ripple of emotion I wasn't ready to handle.

It's not your fault, Celia. Don't go there.

You read my poker face through text. That's cheating. A beat of silence.

It's not. It's knowing you.

I'm sorry.

Me too.

It was that la douleur exquise feeling again. Heavy, crushing pain sat in my chest. *I know it's last minute, and don't feel like you have to come*—I really shouldn't have been texting this—*but I'm having a small party for Oscar's birthday tomorrow afternoon at like 3ish. Nothing fancy. Just drinks by the pool.*

He mentioned it. I have plans in the morning. I may not be back in time.

Okay. Well, I'll see you around then.
Yeah, okay.

As it was my second phone in the last few months, I shouldn't have thrown it. At least it only hit my pillow. He was better off without me. I felt eyes on me from the corner of the living room where the journal sat. Emil rolled his eyes and shook his head at me. I glared back and stomped to my room.

Seeing a ghost, no matter how pleasant its face was, is not the best way to wake up. Emil's face leaned over my bed so that as soon as I opened my eyes he was there. In the interest of full disclosure, I pulled the covers over my head before I thought that maybe running would serve me better. After a time, I peeked out, and he was standing on the other side of my bedroom, casually leaning against my dresser. I mumbled something about his needing to wait until after I'd had coffee if he wanted me to read the journal. But first, I needed to get out and run.

From my house, it was just over a mile to Riverside Park, wending through shaded neighboring streets. It did not escape me how fortunate I was to live where I did. Minus the haunting business. Entering through the back of the park behind the museum, I took the narrow paths, which had stations on which you could do things like step-ups, balance, push-ups, and the like. Normally, I'd run a couple of miles, then sprint the Barber Bridge.

As I came to the bottom of the bridge, I spotted Adrian about a hundred meters ahead of me, running with a dark-haired girl. I stopped so suddenly someone bumped into me from behind. If I ran behind them on the bridge, at some point they'd turn around. Then I'd be running face-to-face with him and this new girl, and I wasn't ready for that. New Girl. The thought did terrible things to my mood. So, I turned and headed for the entrance to Veterans Memorial Island. It was peaceful there, and I'd not been since Memorial Day when I'd accompanied Oscar.

Coming out into the park, I went straight, cutting through the grass to get to the street I'd take home. It was four miles in, and I was starting to wear down. On the pull-up bar was the dark-haired girl, Adrian's hands on her waist, assisting her. I remembered the feeling of his hands on my hips at the gala, his hands on my back when we'd kissed that fateful night. His hand in mine when I pulled away and left him alone in his hospital room, a storm on the horizon. Now those hands were on someone new.

As I passed, he caught my eye. I waved. The wave of passing a fellow runner: elbow tucked, quick flick of the wrist to acknowledge another's presence on the road. Then I kept running, picking up speed and arriving home having completed my fastest mile time since college. Even more impressive since it was my fifth mile of the day.

ROSETTES MADE OF THE LIGHTEST, fluffiest frosting covered the entire cake I'd bought from the Mexican grocery in Fellsmere. Tía gave me a platter of carnitas and tortillas, pinto beans, and Spanish rice. I had been planning on ordering pizza, but this was so much better. Oscar and Taiko lounged in the floats, sangrias in hand. There was a good crowd of people. Darcy and I sat on the edge of the pool, leaning back on our elbows.

"Remember in high school," she started. "When I said I wanted to be a doctor, and you said you wanted to be a journalist covering the war in the Middle East?"

I smiled at the memory. I'd switched majors in my first semester.

"I'm really glad neither of us did that shit."

I laughed then.

"I mean seriously, I could have. But I make more money now and have more freedom. You would have been fine, but can you imagine poor Oscar?" It was a sobering thought. "Hi, Adrian," Darcy said, looking up past my shoulder. Luckily my swimsuit was black because I dumped the entire glass of sangria onto my lap. Before any fruit fell in the pool, I scooped it up and made a run for the kitchen.

"I didn't mean to sneak up on you," he said.

I waved him off and blotted at my stomach with wet paper towels.

"Did you have a good run this morning?"

I said I did and turned to the sink to wet the paper more, squeezing my eyes shut for the teensiest of seconds, so I wouldn't wreck my mascara.

"Okay, chica, I am starving," Oscar whined.

WE ALL HAD little food babies by the time we'd finished the tacos, and it was getting dark as Oscar blew out his candles. I knew he didn't celebrate his birthday last year. I was still in Boston, and Nate's death was too fresh. Looking like the Cheshire cat while making a wish, Oscar then turned and kissed Taiko in front of all of us. We all cheered and whooped, and the world felt a little more hopeful.

Most of the guests left after cake, leaving Darcy and her Logan to hang out with us. I liked him. He was a calming opposite to Darcy's level-ten energy. Adrian hung over a pool noodle, floating next to me. The birthday king refused to give up the float, so we were all mere subjects bobbing around him.

"Need help with the journal?" Adrian asked, floating at my side, water droplets on his eyebrows. I felt the urge to brush them off.

"You don't have to. I know you're busy."

"I'm not. I have less overtime now. I only had plans this morning."

I deliberately looked away.

"I've been trying to get him out and doing something for a month. Suddenly he has plans this morning. What did you do this morning, *Adrian*?" Oscar asked him.

"My little cousin applied to the Brevard Sheriff's Department and asked if I'd help her get ready for the physical test. We ran and I helped her get her first pull-up. That's when I saw Celia running a three-minute mile," he said with a lopsided grin that sent my stomach on a wild ride. More like a six-and-a-half-minute mile, but whatever.

"Wait," Oscar barked, flipping out of the float, splashing us all. Darcy grabbed for it yelling, "Huzzah!"

"You were helping your cousin, who is a girl, work out this morning? And you saw Ce?" He turned to me, and I knew the little shit was about to drop me in it.

"Hope you're having a lovely birthday, Os," I said with forced sweetness.

"And Ce, you ran a three-minute mile? Impressive. Don't do too much cardio, though, you'll lose your ass."

I sent a wave of water into his face, which he shook off like a dog.

"Did you get to meet his cousin?" he asked.

My whole face was in my fishbowl-shaped sangria glass, likely giving me a red wine mustache. There was a quiet hum of discomfort.

"Oh," Adrian said. "Oh."

"You are such a guy, Kikumoto. I'm going to get a beer," Oscar said with a snicker. Setting the glass on the side of the pool, I sank underwater, mascara be damned.

We were alone in the pool, apart from Darcy, who I believe was asleep on the float.

"She wants to be able to run a mile and a half in twelve minutes and get some pull-ups."

"I understand that," I said with a laugh. "I was at the end of my run. Totally worn out."

"Did you know that when you feel like you have nothing left in you, you're only 40 percent to your max? It's an old navy rule."

I was thinking that I didn't know if I could face 60 percent more heartache.

"Don't look at me like that." His face was on its side, cheek pressed to the pool noodle.

"Like what?"

"Like I broke your heart." It was getting colder in the water, making me shiver. "I have the time if you need help with the journal."

"Okay." That was all I could manage.

Surely, I'm at like 80 percent.

CHAPTER 26

CELIA

As a child, I took horseback riding lessons near the Vero Beach Municipal Airport. I didn't spend as much time out that way as an adult, but there was a coffee shop I liked to go to, tucked into a warehouse block of businesses. Truthfully, it wasn't far from where Robert Avery held Oscar. Where he shot Adrian.

The drive out was probably the hardest part; I went the way we had driven that night to find my brother. Adrian was sitting at the back of the shop at a scuffed dark wood table, surrounded by students and people on laptops. The place was run by an organization which took no profit from their sales but used the money to support impoverished people overseas. It was the kind of place I could get behind. So, it seemed like a good place for meeting Adrian in public. On the table in front of him, he had both a steaming cup of coffee and what looked like an iced latte. I decided to feel out whether the iced one was indeed mine before ordering at the counter, so I walked over to dump my bag first.

"It's yours. Coconut milk latte, right?" he asked, flicking his long fingers at the glass.

"Thank you, it's perfect." He looked exhausted, and I said as much.

"Thanks, Sullivan."

There was no point in adding that he didn't look bad. He never looked bad. He just looked tired. We opened the journal to where he and I had left off that infamous night. He'd translated the next two pages, and we went over them, seeing how Emil wrote about watching The Woman leave and about distracting himself. We laughed at how he sold the *Naufrage* remake—presumably the one hanging in the museum a few miles away—to the child. Emil described, sometimes in great detail, the people he met as he showed his art. He spoke of the women he took back to his rented flats and how he always thought of The Woman he could never have, thousands of miles away.

Caffeine in large amounts made me a bit shaky, so I pushed the latte to the side for the time being. Cesar's first show in America was in New York a year after he'd met The Woman, whose name he never mentioned. Out of respect to both, at least for now, we never said her name either. In his journal, he wrote that he might have told her how she captured him, enthralled him. I told Adrian about the inscription on the painting Taiko painted for Oscar. The one that was loaned to the museum. Showed him a photo of it.

You have bewitched me
Sleet-gray eyes like distant storms
You have drowned me whole
Kisses like sugared ginger
You have enthralled my being

Adrian pointed out that it was a tanka, a Japanese poem structured with five lines and thirty-one syllables. I hadn't noticed before and called him Professor Kikumoto under my breath.

"And your brother didn't think Taiko loved him?" he asked with amusement.

I shrugged, saying Oscar was haunted by as many ghosts as I was, but at least mine were outside of my head.

"Are they though?" he asked. I pursed my lips and looked back down at the journal. We were not talking about me. It seemed Emil was ready, once he set foot in New York, to find The Woman by her sea of dreams. He wrote that he should have told her how he felt. Adrian cut in, annoyance coating his features.

"I believe it was Victor Hugo who said, 'Aimer c'est savoir dire je t'aime sans parler.' To love is to know how to say I love you without speaking. He painted for her. He drove down for her. So, I mean, really, why go on about not saying it?"

"One, impressive pulling Victor Hugo out of your ass. I would reiterate my Keats quote, but I think your ego is inflated enough, Sergeant. Or is it Professor? Two, she may not have known he painted for her. For all we know, she hadn't heard from him at all. He didn't have her address. She may have believed all she was to him was an opportunity. Nine times out of ten, that would be the harsh reality. Three," I said, ticking off on my fingers, "they didn't know each other very long. Less than a week? I'm not saying it's impossible—"

"Impossible n'est pas français," he interjected smugly.

I sighed and continued. "Yes, perhaps impossible is not the French way, but maybe Emil was running with a single emotion. He'd become obsessed with something he couldn't have. Maybe neither was in love with the other but only with the heat of the moment."

Next to our table, a young man pulled his earbuds out and leaned over to us.

"What book are you annotating? I'm an English Lit major." A trickle of relief came from his question. Adrian told him it was a random old family journal. I got up to get a snack, coming back with two flaky pastries.

"You're very cynical," Adrian said quietly.

I gave him a look that said I wasn't arguing. Heat prickled up my spine, making me pull my hair on top of my head and into a loose bun. He'd gotten as far as Emil finding The Woman on the beach. Once Cesar was in Vero Beach to stay a while, he spoke of an old fishing cottage he rented on the Indian River. It had a single bed and a wide dock on which to paint. According to his journal, they fought about that place. She urged him to get somewhere nicer. He argued it suited him. She said it wasn't fit for her to visit, especially in the way she normally did visit. He called her an elitist. She didn't disagree. In the heat of that argument, she returned to her own home. When they next met, Emil apologized, promising to worship her, and found her body covered in bruises where her clothes normally hid.

"Shit," I said. "That's why she was afraid to leave."

Adrian said they saw it all the time with domestic violence victims. Most of the time it was a financial issue. The woman was threatened with destitution, so she stayed. In the next pages, Cesar wrote about finding out she was pregnant. His mix of emotions. He and Marie never cared for the idea of having children. They had not had a relationship which lent itself toward starting a family. This had been different though. He urged The Woman to leave her husband, and she refused. Her husband had tied up her trust fund, and she had no money to raise the child on her own.

Adrian sat back on the wooden chair and stretched, his arms reaching across his body, muscles defined and strong. I tried not to look and failed miserably. He rubbed at his side unconsciously, catching me looking.

"Is that where"—I swallowed—"you were hit? Does it still hurt?" I'd seen it in parts while he was swimming yesterday, but as soon as he was out of the water, his shirt was on, so I never saw the whole scar.

"It's kind of numb. In a weird way. It doesn't hurt anymore. It's just ugly."

"Nothing about you is ugly," I blurted before I could stop myself. Christ, Celia. I owned it though. It was true. It was true and he was shot because of me, so I could tell him he wasn't ugly. I wanted to tell him that he was the most beautiful man I'd ever seen, but we weren't there. "May I see it?"

"What? Here?"

I twitched my mouth as if to say why not. English Lit guy was gone, and it was early afternoon then, so there was really no one else in the café. He lifted his shirt on the left side. I went round to his side of the table to look, sitting on the chair next to him. I didn't know what I was expecting, never having seen a gunshot wound before. Just below his ribs, where people who weren't Adrian Kikumoto had love handles, was a puckered lump that ran about two inches in length. The skin around it was slightly paler than the golden skin on the rest of his torso. I touched his side, feeling the skin just around the scar, then stopped myself. Goosebumps broke out on his skin, making me shiver as well.

"Sorry," I mumbled as he dropped his shirt. We both took a breath and went back to the journal.

SHE HAD the baby and named him Nathan, after her husband, at his insistence. Emil raged about that. Nathan Cosgrove went exclusively by Kip, so Emil felt it doubly authoritarian of the husband to insist the child take his legal name.

"He may think he is the father, but I know better. There is no hint of that bastard in my son. He is made of her and of me and the magic we create together," Cesar wrote in French shorthand, as though too angry to write it all out.

"*L'habit ne fait pas le moine*," I said, touching the journal as though it would give me an image. Cesar's painting of the carbon copy man and the water flume.

"The habit does not make the monk," Adrian chimed in. "Do you think he's saying that the elder Nathan may play the part of father, but he really isn't?"

I did and said so, indicating the artwork.

The baby spent time with his real father. Emil wrote of sketching him and throwing out the sketches because he could never capture the beauty of the child. Then in that same year, when the baby started looking very much like his father and mother, and nothing of the husband, The Woman fell pregnant again. Again, she asked Emil to move, and again he refused.

Emil wrote that he was followed home from a meeting with the mother of his children, which they had both left in a tremendous state of discontent. Her husband forced himself into Emil's cottage and belittled his poor accommodations. After hitting Emil, the husband said if Cesar didn't leave, the wife would be killed. On the outside of his cottage, sticking halfway out from his mailbox, Emil placed his journal.

She must have found the journal, which was why it was in my house. A note was written in her own hand at the end.

I would have named him Anton after your own father. He was taken by the Lord through the violence of the man who once promised to love and care for me. It was by my own hand he met his end, and surely I will go to hell for it. You gave me love. You gave me my son. So though you too are no longer with us, I will not forget that I once had a great love.

Yours forever,

Judy

.   .   .

THE NATURAL TRANSITION from coffee and pastries to drinks was inescapable. Both of us were ready to have real food, and something strong. I dropped off my car at home, and we drove to Riverside Café together. Over our first round of drinks—a mezcal and soda for me, a beer for him—we were quiet. Someone was playing guitar inside, a leftover of the live music they had for Sunday brunch. When our waitress placed the plate of tuna nachos down with our second round, both of us switching to iced tea, the live guitar stopped, turning instead to piped-in music. The Jake Owen song that haunted me came on, and I tried my damnedest to keep my most pokerish poker face. Adrian toed my leg under the table.

"What is it with you and this song?" he asked, grinning, and I was convinced he knew.

"It bugs me." Even though it used to be a favorite, before it felt like a hot, twisting knife in my core.

"Liar." There was a challenge in his eyes, and I backed down from it. I hated that I'd done it, but I wasn't ready to risk that last 20 percent of me.

"I'm more upset over the journal than I thought I'd be. I mean, poor Judy. She marries this horrible man, is beaten, finds love, loses it, loses a child in utero, Emil dies overseas never knowing the husband is dead, then Nate is killed." I swiped at my eyes where they'd become wet. Adrian grabbed a hold of my hand and squeezed, not letting go. We ate the ahi nachos with one hand each, keeping hold of each other.

"Is it because Oscar used to call Wentworth 'Jake Owen'?" Adrian asked after a time.

Oh, he was still on that one. I shook my head and thanked our waitress as we walked out along the side of the building, feet crunching over sand and a few cigarette butts. Sliding into his Jeep and buckling up, I looked down to my hands. He was driving on the road toward my house when I finally got the nerve to say it.

"The song reminds me of you."

Though his eyes were covered by his Ray-Bans, I felt them pierce me. My house was close enough that the torture I felt after admitting that was mercifully short-lived. I thanked him for everything, holding up the journal, and went inside. Kicking off my sandals, I slid against the back of my front door. I guessed the discomfort I'd felt after my admission was just as bad for him because it seemed he couldn't wait for me to be out of the car. And that didn't sit well. I held my phone in my hand, shooting off a text to Oscar.

If you need me, I'll be living under a rock for the next hundred years.

What did you do now?

I told Adrian why the song bugs me.

He sent a laughing emoji.

It's not funny. He couldn't wait for me to be of his car and locked safely behind my door. God, Os.

Another crying laughing emoji popped up, and I chucked the phone into the couch on the other side of the room.

There was rapping on the door where my head leaned, scaring the hell out of me. Peeking out, I saw Adrian scrubbing a hand through his black hair. Oh man. I opened the door. He held up his phone where there was a picture of the album cover on his music app.

"I know the song. But I just listened to it, to understand."

Oh, sweet baby Jesus, find me my rock.

"And I'm confused."

It doesn't even have to be a large rock. A modest rock is fine. Just for my head to hide under. The couch would do even. I walked toward it and saw there were about ten texts from my brother. Maybe he'd bring me a rock.

Clearing my throat, I asked, "What confuses you? It's a fairly simple country tune." Oh, that's good, Ce. Be an asshole. I readied for an Olympic-style dive into the couch.

"The perspective," he said, matter-of-fact.

Huh?

"Is it me or you? The narrative is convoluted." I let this process for a second so I didn't sound dumb.

"I, um, what? This is really humiliating, so—" Nope. Didn't work. Still dumb. Stray tassels on my gray-and-cream striped throw blanket wound in and out of my fingers.

"Well, I mean, it could be written from my perspective."

"No, it's . . . it's from my perspective." I shook my head. He smiled a little, and I had no idea what was going on.

"No, no. I think it's mine."

"Sergeant, I think you've listened to the wrong song because clearly I am the one who can't be around you without losing my cool."

"You're changing the narrative again, Sullivan."

What was he talking about? And why was I standing in my living room arguing about how I felt about him?

"And I told you not to look at me like I broke your heart."

"You did," I whispered, chewing on my lip.

"I didn't. You walked out on me. Quite literally, by the way. Pretty sure you broke mine. All I've wanted, since I met you, was to be with you."

There's a sensation felt in the aftermath of an adrenaline rush that leaves the body feeling as though everything was pulled out of it. That was about where I was in that moment.

"So, if we're jockeying for the position of the dude saying it might kill him if he falls, I claim that position. Because I fell really damn hard for you."

"It kills *me*. You're just saying it would kill you because you were shot. It's an unfair metaphorical advantage."

"Sullivan."

"Sergeant."

"Will you shut up and let me kiss you?"

His hands tangled in my hair as we came together. His lips

met mine, much more demanding than last time, and I echoed his demand, pulling him closer to me, wanting to feel everything. His mouth traveled my jaw, small kisses trailing the length. I sent my hands up under his shirt and, with a pause for courage, lifted it over his head. Mine was next, our hands all over each other. He lifted me easily onto the back of the couch, so I could wrap my legs around his waist. Air constricted in my lungs while I looked at him and ran my hands along his chest. He leaned farther into my touch, close enough that I could kiss just over his heart, my breathing a ragged sound.

When I looked up at him, my chest bouncing against his with the rhythm of our lungs, he held my face and started to say something, but instead claimed my mouth once again. From the couch, he lifted me and turned to walk down the hall but stopped short when the front door opened.

"Oh my God," Oscar said then started laughing his hyena cackle. "I should say thank God." Adrian lowered me from where I was pressed against his body, keeping me pulled tightly to himself.

"Oscar," Adrian greeted my brother, sounding just slightly unnerved.

"Sorry, Ce. When you text me about the song, you sounded upset, so I thought I'd come to check on you." He held up a bottle of cava.

"Thanks, Os. Bye now." I leaned my head against Adrian, still drunk on his scent, the feeling of him on me. Featherlight strokes moved up and down my arm, keeping me close.

"One thing before I forget"—we groaned—"Jacob Wentworth's mother is Dutch."

"Jesus, I don't care right now."

Adrian chuckled beside me.

"She was in the art scene like thirty years ago. Was known to share a bed with an artist. I'm sure it's nothing. I'll leave you to it." He opened the door but doubled back for effect. "Oh, and Jacob's trust fund is dangerously low. The company that has his holdings is about to drop him because the funds are anemic. Tata!"

"Wait. Hold on." I walked to my brother, and he shut the door. "What are you suggesting?"

"You're the one standing here in undies," he pointed out, eyebrows wiggling. He peered behind me to say to Adrian in a sitcom whisper, "It's Aubade."

"I know," Adrian growled. "I remember from the last time I saw it."

I whipped my head around and stared at him. That was the day Sarah was rude to me after Mom had left. He smirked, eyes smoky and intense.

"I really need to get out of here and find Taiko. But if it seems like a lead, then maybe we can look into Cesar's illegitimate children."

Shit. We hadn't actually told him. I led Oscar to the couch and pulled on the first shirt I found which happened to be Adrian's. God, it smelled good. My guest took the bottle from Oscar and disappeared to open it. The journal was in my bag where I'd dropped it. I handed the leather-bound diary to my brother.

"Feel free to read it all. We finished translating it today. It is what I suspected. Nate was Cesar's child. Not Nathan Cosgrove's. Did you—" I accepted a glass from a shirtless Adrian and addressed the question to both. "Did you know Judy killed her husband in self-defense?" Both men nodded. Nate had told Adrian when they were overseas. He had zero patience for men who were disrespectful to their wives.

"Nate told me," Oscar began but stopped, saying he wasn't sure he should betray their intimacy. "The day he told me was the first time he really opened up to me."

"I saw Nate," I blurted. Both men looked at me, stunned.

"In St. Augustine. When we were walking with Taiko. Os, remember? You said you missed me and wanted me home. Then I saw him."

He stood in the shadow of a building, almost totally corporeal. A beautiful, golden man, wearing a smile that crinkled his whole face up to his eyes. Just like Emil's. He had gestured between Taiko and Oscar, then placed his hands over his heart. I knew Oscar and Taiko didn't know who I was seeing. Nate never spoke, but emotions trailed from him to me. I could feel his love for my brother. His relief that Oscar had found someone. His pain too. Though he was the one gone, he still hurt. That, I would never tell Oscar. I mouthed thank you at Nate, and he was gone. Telling my brother this was so delicate, I'd been afraid to do it for the past couple of weeks.

"He liked Taiko?" Oscar asked, sounding just as he had when we were little. I hugged him to me, feeling my shoulder dampen from his tears.

"We all like Taiko," Adrian said, and I wanted to kiss him just for that. I led Oscar to the kitchen, keeping him close to me.

"Let's get you fed," I said to my brother. The three of us moved around the kitchen, grabbing bowls and glasses. A synchronicity we all noticed but didn't voice.

The cava was nice and dry and went down easily with the pasta I made us all. Adrian kept eyeing me over his glass, making my toes curl under me. Oscar left after ten, apologizing for interrupting.

"Stay," I said to Adrian at the door. "The night I mean."

He leaned over me, pressing my back to the wall. Slowly, he twisted the hem of his T-shirt up my stomach, his thumb brushing my navel, until I had to duck out of it. Good God Almighty. Then he kissed me so thoroughly there was nothing in my head but him.

"I can't stay."

Not the answer I was hoping for.

"I work a double shift tomorrow and need to be up in like three hours."

Pouting was childish. Pouting was ugly. My lip jutted out, and he caught it between his teeth, making me purr as I slid my hands into the back of his waistband. "I'll see you in a couple of days though." His forehead pressed into mine. Those were going to be long days. I watched as he pulled his shirt over his own head, readying to leave.

"When you were gone. When you'd left," he said, running a hand through his hair. "Tu me manques."

"You were missing from me too," I replied, because in French, it is not I miss you. Tu me manques means "you are missing from me." What was once a part of me is now gone. Nothing was truer than that.

Chapter 27

Celia

Over three hundred fabric samples fanned across the steel-top worktable in the back of Mom's office. Eight clients were coming back to town for the winter months, expecting updated details on their homes, and Mom was in a frenzy. Which was to say, she was in her element. Completely engrossed in work, spinning in catch-tail circles, and rarely coming up for air. Through my education and work experience, I could differentiate between deliberate and accidental brushstrokes, the youth or maturity of an artist's particular painting, or the era of a piece which, to others, would simply be clumped in with a movement. Looking at these three hundred upholstery samples, I could not truly distinguish the twill from denim from broadcloth. They all looked sensibly *beige*. Rubbing my eyes, I called to Mom that it was lunchtime.

"It's eleven," she responded, keyboard keys clicking furiously.

"Then it's time for elevenses, and I'm starving."

"You're not a hobbit, Celia. Take an hour and bring me back something."

In the interest of not wanting to seem like I wasn't fully committed to earning my interim pay, I waited to go until I'd separated every taupe, "I gave up on life" colored fabric from the pile. At least I knew Mom was a wizard at taking people's boring style sensibilities and lending her chic magic to them. The afternoon would have me pulling embroidered silks and calling antique stores for mercury glass mirrors.

The office was close enough to home that I could have just gone there and made something to eat, yet I chose to grab a sandwich just across from the beach. Red and purple flags flew from the lifeguard station, letting beachgoers know that it wasn't safe to go into the water: dangerous marine life and possible rip currents. I sat under the covered awning to eat my caprese sandwich and watched the school of giant tarpon sail across the gray-flannel shoreline. Winds picked up, sending my napkins flying. I jumped to chase them before they blew down onto the beach. The paper caught just under the bench at the far side of the awning. As I grabbed them, there was a piece of heavy sketch paper stuck just under a bolt in the wood. It seemed to be a pen-and-ink drawing of a baby. I pulled it out, and I knew it was Nate. The rest of my sandwich forgotten, I sat on the wood, my jeans-covered leg out in front of me, and studied it. A trickle of a breeze pushed at my back, letting me know Emil stood behind me, watching me, his usual smirk absent.

The backside of the portrait had frustrated sketches across the paper, as though he couldn't take the drawing where it needed to go. Like a word on the tip of your tongue, demanding yet unwilling to cooperate. In Emil's journal, he spoke of never capturing Nate's beauty when he sketched him. We are always our own worst critics. Even each of the sketches on the back were painfully accurate. The main portrait on the front showed the softness in the child's cheek, subtle shading indicating a ruddiness. His eyes were round, and though no color accompanied the ink, reflections in the light of his eyes showed how clear the blue would have been. Those eyes were something no one ever forgot about Nate. Cesar took each eyebrow hair and the down of sunlight on the child's head and made it seem as though the portrait would be incomplete without that detail. A slight depression above the bow of his lip made his mouth just as Judy's was in her portrait hanging in the gallery. Even the single freckle next to the little boy's eye matched his mama's. No one was around, apart from the lifeguards who weren't paying attention to me. So I said quietly to the ghost of a father standing near me, "You captured his beauty. Make peace with it. Find each other."

The spirit moved beside me, effectively standing within the bench, which looked kind of grotesque. He shook his head and pointed to me. Darkness swelled a bit behind me. My chest constricted. I gasped, realizing that somehow, even here in broad daylight, the malevolent specter from my home was able to harm me. Had Emil stayed to protect me?

"You okay, ma'am?" the lifeguard called from the doorway of the booth. I stood, stumbling, my hand at my throat, struggling for air. He came over and asked if I could breathe, then stood behind me, about to do the Heimlich maneuver.

I coughed, and a great gulp of air found its way into my lungs.

"You all right?"

I nodded, saying I swallowed wrong. The dark smudge of malevolence faded toward the stormy sea, while Emil's phantom touch on my shoulder remained. Well, that was embarrassing.

TIME REALLY ESCAPED me in the midst of finding the sketch. I'd nearly forgotten to grab something for Mom to eat. I rushed back into the office, and she took the salad and plopped down a list of places to call before the end of the day. I tapped my pen on the side of the list, half focusing on the job at hand and half replaying my experience at the beach. What wasn't making sense was why the other spirit was trying to hurt me. My phone buzzed at four, making me jump.

I think this has to be the longest day ever.

I smiled, feeling a drop in my stomach seeing Adrian's text. *It's possible.* I didn't know what to say next. Ugh.

Lunch tomorrow?

I tapped my foot impatiently, itching to tell him to just come over after work.

I'll be totally useless tonight. Don't get off until 11.

Damn it. How did he do it every time? *Tomorrow sounds good.* Today sounds better.

Pick you up at your mom's office?

Just come over tonight, I thought to myself. Okay, shut it down, Celia. *I'll be here under an army of beige fabric samples, begging to be rescued.*

Ellipses blinked on and off the screen.

See you tomorrow, Sullivan.

Longest day ever.

A commotion sounded from the front of the showroom. Mom pulled up her mean-teacher voice, which still made me a bit nervous. There were several other voices. I walked out, almost tripping when I saw Jacob standing there with two police officers.

"There she is," Jacob said with a delighted smile I wanted to kick off his face. "God, I was so worried, babe."

The skin on my arms raised at his calling me *babe.*

"Celia?" Mom asked. I gave her a look saying I had no idea what he was going on about.

"When you didn't show up for our lunch, I panicked that you had another 'episode.'" He made air quotes. "Then a lifeguard at Humiston said you'd been choking. Sorry, darlin'. I called the police to make sure you were okay."

I looked at the officers, opting to address them first rather than dignify Jacob with a response. "I have a few complaints filed on him," I told them. "If I have to get a restraining order, I will, but this is private property, and he needs to leave."

"It's okay, babe. They know that you forget things, with the head injury and all." Jacob motioned a knock to the head, a pantomime which had gotten stale after the first time he had done it.

Mom stepped up behind me, her hands on my shoulders.

"Here's the plans we made," he said, showing me and everyone his phone messages. On it was a text string, saying my name and that we would be meeting for lunch at noon. Immediately, he put the phone back in his pocket. Before anyone could see that it was not my number from which that thread came.

"You have got to be kidding me," I said. "This is insane. Get the hell out of here."

He reached out and ran a finger down my arm.

I jerked backward. It took every bit of self-restraint I had to not hit him. I wanted to have my job back, and I knew, without any shadow of a doubt, if I hit him that would be out the window. The officers looked like they didn't care either way. "Officers Kriss, Thompson, and Sergeant Kikumoto know that this man has been harassing me. Please. Get him out," I practically begged.

"Mrs. Sullivan," Jacob pleaded to Mom, that slick southern smile on his face. "You—"

"I have nothing to lose if I punch that schoolboy grin off your face," Mom said, officially becoming my hero. "Remove yourself from my workplace."

211

He threw up his hands in submission and backed out.

"Damn, girl. If I didn't love you so much, I would say that head injury has become more trouble than it's worth."

I ran back for my phone and started texting Oscar and Adrian.

"Honey, you're sure you didn't make plans with that boy?" Mom asked delicately from the door.

I looked at her and sucked in my cheeks, incensed.

"I'm just making sure. You did have quite a bop to the head."

"I'm honestly so insulted you're asking this."

"Were you at Humiston?"

I said I was, and that I did swallow a bite of my sandwich wrong. No big deal. The big deal was that he was there and saw me. Followed me even. Oscar started texting me back. I told him what Mom asked, and her phone started ringing. He always did know how to run interference for me. I closed the door and went back to the lists of people to call before they closed for the day, determined to not shirk duties at Mom's company.

Believing that Jacob was simply jealous was hard to swallow. He could have anyone. Between his looks and his money, girls were in no short supply. So why me? In all honesty, I could understand a challenge, the thrill of the chase. But this was something altogether different—sinister even. I wasn't stupid enough to think I would get through it alone. Jacob's gaslighting had become a dangerous game he had no intention of losing.

Oscar met me at home where there was a florist's bunch of the same stupid red roses, this time filled with baby's breath like it was 1976 or something. I kicked it over into the bromeliads which lined my house, ornamental pineapple bushes stabbing their bayonet leaves through the wilted rose petals. When we walked straight to the kitchen, there was an envelope taped to my back door. Oscar pulled it off.

Cece,

I'm sorry for the fuss today. I was so worried about you when you didn't show up for lunch. It's a good thing I can find your car wherever you go. Who knows what might happen to you if you were on your own? I do find it insulting that you keep seeing Adrian while we are together. It may be time to start thinking about some meds to help with the amnesia. I'll see you tomorrow for dinner. Don't forget. I've left a bottle of wine in your fridge for you.

I Love You,

Jacob

It was closer to throw up in the kitchen sink, but I managed to make it to my bathroom. This game Jacob was playing was not only sick, but he trespassed onto my property. He came through my screened-in patio, which should have been locked. He came into my house. My security cameras picked up his stupid face and his asshat little wave as he stuck the note to the glass. The implied threat in being able to find my car anywhere was obvious. And I was absolutely done with the mental health implications.

Adrian hadn't responded when I'd texted earlier, so I figured he was busy. Not wanting to bother him further, I called Officer Kriss and told her the story. She said she would see what could be done. So far, though, since there had been no violence, they couldn't entertain the idea of an injunction against Jacob. I wanted to keep Adrian's name out of the whole thing for his sake, but it was in writing in the letter. Kriss said she would do all she could and that she would be my champion.

Oscar ran to Lowe's to get a new lock for my screen while I put up extra sensors that came with my home security system. We spent most of the evening tweaking the house, so I'd feel safer from Jacob. So, I had ghosts inside and monsters outside. Just fucking fabulous.

I lay in my bed, any hope of rest evading me, while trying to figure out a clever way to get Jacob off my back. That meant sorting out what he expected to gain from all this nonsense. Without sleep, I wouldn't be able to even distinguish beige from aquamarine tomorrow. I rolled to the side and folded the pillow over my head. When a soft knocking sounded, every light in my room, on my phone, and in the house came on, scaring me half to death. The doorbell notifications were chiming on my phone, vibrating the glass dish on my nightstand. I looked at the phone, my heart pounding because it was the middle of the damned night. The bedroom overhead light flicked on and off, courtesy of a mischievous French artist who liked to play along with my technological shortcomings.

"Very funny, Emil," I grunted, stumbling into the hall, walking straight through a patch of icy air.

The extra latch was stiff to unhinge, but I swiped it back and opened the door to Adrian.

"It was a mess tonight. I didn't get a chance to look at my phone until just before I left."

I opened the door wider for him to come in. He looked amused at the number of lights that were on. I said I needed to adjust the security settings and went around switching things off. The letter sat on my small desk in the living room, and he asked to read it as Oscar had taken the liberty of filling him in on the rest of the bullshit that'd happened since I'd texted.

"Why don't I crash on the couch or guest bed so you can get some sleep?"

I looked at him a long minute, seeing how tired he was, and said "okay." It didn't keep me from reaching on tiptoes to kiss him. Not a prolonged kiss, because I wasn't sure I would be able to back away from that again. I wanted him like nothing and no one I'd ever wanted in my almost thirty years.

He took my hand and kissed it, then held it to his chest. In his face I could see there was something he wanted to say. Instead, he tipped my chin up, our hands still folded together, and kissed me once, before saying he needed to clean up.

"I'm not rushing with you," he said from the top of the hallway. His back was to me. "Tonight, I just want you to feel safe in your own home." He disappeared into the bathroom, and I switched off the last lamp in the living room, trying to forget the way each word washed through me. A slow current I had no hope of outswimming.

My traitorous ears trained on the sounds of the shower and his movements in the guest room. For an hour or so I stayed staring at the ceiling, watching my fan spin in a frustrated whirl. Without overthinking it, I made my way to the room next door and slipped inside. Poor thing was totally out, the white linen tucked up under his arms. Still, I carefully lifted the opposite side of the duvet and got in, shifting over to him. Without a sound, he pulled me against him, my back to his chest, arms circling me. Our legs tangled together, a braiding of bodies. A sigh escaped me, feeling his slow breathing. Nothing in the world had ever made me feel like that.

Finally, I was able to sleep.

CHAPTER 28

CELIA

BOXES NEEDING IMMEDIATE OPENING CAME IN JUST as we opened the design office. I kept rubbing at phantom dirt on my white dress, making Mom roll her eyes at me.

"Would you stop?"

"I just probably should have worn something different."

"It's a cute dress. Reminds me of Portofino many years ago."

The dress was an easy decision in the morning when my eyes popped at six to get up, but I was still lying against Adrian in my guest bed. I'd wanted to get out of bed less than when my Boston apartment was frozen over. Especially when his hands started running up and down my legs and sides. Not a single nerve ending in my body wasn't on fire then. Good God Almighty. With a resentful groan, I'd pushed away and tucked him back in, thinking to press a kiss to his forehead. Those arms pulled me back down on top of him, and he kissed me silly.

I shook my head to make the light jump back to reality, then helped Mom haul out new wallpaper sample books and swatches. She had me pull all the old ones from her meticu-lously organized wall cupboards and file new ones in.

"Hello, Adrian. Aren't you a sight for sore eyes," Mom greeted him in the front of the showroom. I checked my phone, confirming he was early. Of course. Before either could come back and catch me, I dashed to the bathroom and checked my makeup and hair. It was so stupid being this nervous when I had literally woken up in his arms. With my pinky, I pressed a bit more poppy-colored stain onto my full lips and called it good. Mom embarrassed me by snapping a photo when I kissed his cheek. What was this, prom?

"I think it's cute, and you know Oscar would've done the same thing," Adrian said, opening the passenger door for me.

I said he didn't have to open my door.

"I know," he purred, pushing up onto his hands and meeting my mouth. "I just really wanted to kiss you."

Lunch. Lunch. Lunch. Lunch, I thought to myself. There's time.

"Lunch," he said to himself aloud, pulling back. Had I read his poker face or had he read mine? Or did it just not matter? Damn, I was in trouble.

Stay out. I'm all set for the rest of the day, Mom texted.

Smiling to myself, I put the phone away to concentrate only on the atmosphere around me and my date. Date. Oh my God. This was actually our first date. Great. I was back to being nervous.

WHERE HE HAD BEEN LOOKING DOWN at his menu, Adrian's face turned up, eyebrow raised in question. I bit my lip, totally dumbstruck. He gave me a lopsided smile that, I was convinced, had a direct button to my gut and the thou-sand butterflies living within. Overhead, the sky was bright and impossibly blue as only November in Florida could create.

The restaurant sat between the pool and beach of a fairly new boutique hotel in Vero.

"Have you been here before?" I asked him because I hadn't. He pressed his lips into a fine line.

"Yeah, once for drinks a couple of months ago." His eyes were focused on the menu, though we had already ordered. "Also got called out for work once."

"Can I ask you a question?"

"Of course."

"When did you stop seeing Sarah?" It had been bothering me. I wish it hadn't been, but I didn't like the idea of being a boyfriend stealer. It wasn't my style.

He ran a hand through his hair and looked up at me, pausing.

Dread filled my stomach. "Wait. You aren't still . . . Oscar said—"

"No. No, no. Sorry." I felt his foot hook around mine under the table. "We were never exclusive. It wasn't like—" There was a catch in his voice. "So, I had told her I didn't want to see her that day we all ran into you and your mom at the wine bar. I was going to say something earlier that night, but she invited Jacob and that other guy from work. I told her that day. Like, just after you left."

"But?"

"She apologized a few days later about how she'd acted with you. And I'd heard you were seeing Jacob."

Oh. He was turning all sorts of shades of red.

"She asked me to go to that new gastropub with her, just to talk. That was the night we ran into both of you. We didn't make it to the pub. After that comment she made, I was done. I turned around and took her home. Saw you and Jacob against his car. But yeah, that was the last of it."

I closed my eyes. All this mess with Jacob could have been avoided. Adrian's hand reached across the table and grabbed mine like he had at Riverside Café last Sunday. It had felt so natural then, which killed me at the time because I was convinced it was one-sided. Opening my eyes, I couldn't help but smile at him. His eyes lit up when he smiled back. I could watch that smile my whole life, and I knew it would never stop making my stomach flip. And I also knew that was a world of trouble.

"What are you thinking, Sullivan?"

"I thought you could read my poker face?"

"I don't always know if I'm right."

Every table around us dissolved to oblivion. There was only the two of us, and the persistence of the surf.

"Have you been wrong yet?"

"I haven't always asked. And I have to say, the song threw me."

I snorted. That damned song. "I'm thinking I wish you didn't have to go to work tonight."

"You aren't the only one thinking that." His dark eyes seemed to smoke over a bit.

"What are you thinking, Sergeant?" My voice dropped to a lower octave.

"I'm thinking that I hate that Jacob won't leave you alone. I hate that I was so stubborn, that I never told you I wanted to see you, and you went out with him. I hate that he kissed you before I did because since I met you, all I could think about was kissing you." He swallowed audibly. "And I'm thinking that I'd like to know what other Aubade-type things you have, and whether that's what's under that dress. And I feel like a cad for saying that."

My heart was racing; my eyes locked on his mouth as he spoke. "Have you ever used the word 'cad' before?" I managed.

"Never."

"I'd think you'd be more a rake. Dashing and seductive and all that."

"Cad connotes the disreputable things I may or may not be insinuating by the previous comment I made."

"Yes, but I see a cad as a bumbling sort of ne'er-do-well who lucks out with women. A rake, however, has the looks and the demeanor to turn what might be a proposition into something the other party practically begs for."

His eyes danced at my nervous chatter, lips twitching to the side.

I cleared my throat, knowing the prickle of sweat on my forehead was starting to show.

"Either way, I'm thinking I was hoping that's what that look meant." His fingers squeezed mine where I knew they were shaking a bit.

"I look forward to showing you every piece of Aubade I have, one at a time. I also hate that I kissed Jacob because all I ever thought about was you."

Miso-glazed black grouper slid in front of me, effectively stopping our volley of admissions. As soon as the waiter left, I lifted my leg over his knee under the table, immediately feeling his hand on my thigh. Roaring sounded in my ears, not unlike the crash of the sea.

Though the food was fabulous, we ate faster than was socially acceptable. His shift started in a couple of hours, but that was a couple of hours that needn't be wasted. We drove north a bit, turning back over the Wabasso Bridge where he pulled to the side along the river. An older man sat fishing a few hundred yards away, his back to us. Otherwise, only the wind on the brackish water was our company. It didn't matter to me why we were there, only that we were together for a while. Rocks crunched under my sandals as I hopped down from his oversized Matchbox car of a Jeep. Wind was coming in from the north, whipping my hair and dress around. I tried to straighten it but found my hands enveloped by strong, gentle ones. If he really could read my face, as he seemed to always be able to, surely, he could see just how hard I'd fallen for him. That possibility sent a surge of panic through me.

"I wasn't the one who walked out of that hospital room," he murmured, fingers tracing the sides of my face.

"I was the reason you got shot. I didn't want to hurt you more."

He sniffed a laugh, leaning in to brush a featherlight kiss to my cheek, just beside my ear. In invitation, I tilted my head to the side. His mouth accepted and ran slow lines along the exposed skin of my neck, while his hands slid up my ribs just under my chest. It could have been full dark because stars were blinking in my vision, feeling Adrian's hands through my dress, his mouth on my skin.

"Then don't walk out," he breathed against my collarbone. "Just stay."

I lifted his chin with a finger and placed my lips on his, as gentle as he'd been with me. "Okay then. I'll stay if you stay."

"Done."

And our kiss crashed together like every moment we'd been forced apart had to fit within this one. His thumbs ran over the swell of my chest, my hands pulled his backside to me, the line of our bodies pressed into one.

"This," he said, pulling away and pressing his forehead to mine, "is going to be a very long work night."

No breath was left in me to answer that. Every atom of my being was begging to pull into him. We stood for moments, arms encircling one another, faces pressed cheek to cheek, while the sun sank lower, ticking our minutes away.

CHAPTER 29

OSCAR

IT WORRIED ME A LITTLE WHEN I DIDN'T HEAR FROM Celia all day. Last I'd heard, she and Adrian had a real date. I guess I expected her to call me after and gush or something. I didn't know. She had always been careful about who she went out with, so it was a rare occasion anyone had her this hot and bothered. I knew the feeling, so I figured she was processing. Plus, that Wentworth mofo was still a hair in her ass.

By the morning after her date, I texted to see how it went. Mom said she was at work and quiet, so I didn't know why she wasn't answering me. In my head, I did a rerun to see whether I had pissed her off or not. It was likely, so I backed off and shot a text to Adrian because I was nosy as all hell. He hadn't heard from Ce since they spoke late the previous night, but he was working a double shift.

When another full day passed, and she didn't reach out, I started to worry that I really had done something. At times like these I regretted the pranks I pulled on her when we were kids. Like the time I put a harmless grasshopper in her bed when I knew she was sneaking a date into her room. The shrieks and screams were epically fulfilling from an older-brother standpoint, and it wasn't like Mom had been home to catch them. I wondered if she tallied up all those and would one day pay me back. Knowing Ce, it would be something like replacing all my artwork with that painter who does the light pictures and sold his soul to get shops in every mall in middle America.

Taiko poured me a glass of pinot noir and carried our charcuterie board over to the table. The sky outside was shot through with veins of copper as the sun went down ahead of an incoming storm. Every few minutes I checked my phone, but nothing from Ce. Taiko finally plucked the thing from my hands and put it facedown on the chair beside him while he popped a piece of prosciutto into his mouth.

"She'll call you when she's ready."

I blew out a dramatic breath and flipped my hair off my forehead. I needed a haircut. Truthfully, since they'd shaved my head after my abduction, I'd just let it grow. It was time to shape it back up again. Taiko rolled his eyes at me, draining his glass and refilling both of ours. "You've been texting Adrian or Darcy all evening. I'm a tad put out by your lack of attention."

I gave him my best smile, which made him roll those dark eyes at me again. He had started painting in a small studio near his place in Melbourne, and this was the first I'd seen him in a few days. There was paint under his nails, which normally wasn't there. I joked that his hygiene suffered when we were apart, and that clearly, he needed help in the shower. He got up and walked out, wine glass in hand.

"Wait. Where are you going?" I called from the table.

"You're deflecting. I'm going to clean the paint. Apologies for my failure. I was in a rush to get down here and see you." He shut the bathroom door. I hung my head over the back of my midcentury modern dining chair. Of course I was deflecting. Now he was going to put it into a painting or some shit. From the seat across, I heard the buzz of my phone.

Not sure what's with Celia, but she took the rest of the week off. Said she wanted to get ready for the museum next week. She doesn't seem like herself. Maybe check in with her?

Gee, Mom, hadn't thought of that. I started to text Adrian, *Hey*—but I heard the door open to the bathroom, and I guiltily put the phone under me, text unfinished. The door clicked shut again. Pulling it back out, I saw that he was texting back anyway. I wondered if he had been watching his phone too, which made me worry even more.

Have you heard from her?

I said I hadn't.

Neither have I. I'll go by after work unless you can head over.

Shit, Kikumoto, I just drank a half bottle of wine.

Kind of worried here, Oscar.

I wanted to hear how your date was.

Yeah. It was good. Like really good. So you can see how it's weird neither of us has heard from her.

Thank God Mom had seen her, or I'd have been out of my mind. The bathroom did open then, and I didn't care that Taiko saw me texting away on my phone.

"Don't give me shit. I'm worried about my sister," I rambled out loud, still looking at the phone. "If you love me, you have to deal. Just like I deal with your personal baggage."

After a while, I realized he was just standing there staring at me, a bemused look on his angled features. "I think I deal quite well, actually."

The flat tone didn't immediately register with me while I was still texting Mom and Adrian. I punched Tía's number to call her.

"Sí?" she answered. We started speaking rapidly in Spanish. Taiko shook his head and walked to his bag just inside my bedroom. He had it in hand, heading for the front door, while I hung up with Teresita. I tripped over my own stupid feet, then hopped, one-legged, in front of him, trying to downplay how fucking hard I just stubbed my toe on the leg of the table.

"What the fuck, Taiko?" I said, my voice strained over the screaming pain in my big toe. "I'm worried about my damned sister, and you're all royal highness about it?"

"We shall speak tomorrow, Oscar," he said with forced patience.

I knew that tone. When I was being a little too much to handle, and he was toeing a line of being pissed and thinking it was funny. Or maybe more pissed.

"Let me know if you hear from Celia." He lightly pushed on my shoulder to get me to move out of the doorway. I grabbed his hand and widened my legs to block it more.

"You're really pissed at me because I was ignoring you? Don't you think that's a little, I don't know, demanding?"

He sighed and squeezed the bridge of his nose. For a moment he looked at me like he wanted to say something, and I had this ski slope drop feeling in my stomach. Like I'd done with Celia, I tried to think of what I'd said or done in the past few days to upset him. What I did know was that if I let him walk out of the door, it meant we were breaking up. Not sure how I knew it, but I did. While I didn't understand the variables, the product of the equation would be a breakup. The numbers matched up with the tone and the expression. I was a numbers guy.

"Why?" I asked through a swallow that hurt as bad as when I sprained my ankle playing soccer and had to take a giant naproxen tablet without water—the damn tablet got lodged in my throat for an hour.

His fine-lipped mouth pursed, eyes sliding away from me.

"Taiko," I said softly, trying to turn his face toward mine. My phone buzzed in my hand again.

"You should get that," he said. I closed my eyes before

glancing at it. Once I saw it wasn't Ce, I tossed the infernal thing onto the wingback chair near us.

"I just wanted to make sure she's all right," I said, thinking I sounded a bit pathetic.

"And I understand that. I have no problem with your concern."

"So, what then? You just wanted me to put a time cap on my concern. I can show outward fucking worry for my sister between the hours of nine and five but not during cocktail hour?"

"You know that's not what it is, Oscar." He said it with such a long drawl of the accent that normally stayed hidden in the nooks and crannies of his speech. The British, with the Japanese undercurrent.

"Then tell me, Your Highness. What have I done? You're walking out on me. So far as I can see, you're just annoyed that I was on my phone and not paying enough mind to you. Unless something happened in the time since we last saw each other, I'll have to go with that."

I was getting angry then. Hurt and angry and freaked out about Celia since we all knew Wentworth was still messing with her. Plus, the toe.

"You said that if I were to love you, I'd have to deal," he said, voice soft.

"Well, then I guess you made the choice to not fucking deal."

"No, Oscar," he said, hanging his head when I stepped aside for him. "You throw around the word 'love' like bait. Always hanging it in front of me, but never saying it to me."

"Yes, I have." I shifted, thinking back. "You have never said it to me. So, I figured—"

"I sympathize with your apprehension. I do. I know you loved Nate. Love him still. I won't try to replace him. But if you can't find room for me, for a different love, then I don't think we can continue. Especially when your focus is otherwise engaged."

I was shaking my head. How had this gone so wrong?

"I don't want to be just someone who unloads his personal baggage on to you."

Fuckity fuck. "Look at me," I said, with more command than I felt. "Taiko, for fuck's sake. Look at me."

He brought his head up, eyes level with mine. Somewhere against the wood and leather panels of the wingback chair, my phone was buzzing. He started to look toward it.

"Me. Look at me. I love you. I do. Different to Nate, yes, but I love you. Do you love me?" I was dangerously close to needing to throw up.

"Of course, I do," he whispered.

"Yes?"

"Yes."

I started toward him, pulling his bag away and dumping it on the floor. "Then say it. I'm very needy."

"I love you."

I put my hands on his face and smiled, asking if he was still planning on leaving. My phone was buzzing again.

"No, but perhaps you should sort out that mess?" I hummed in agreement but took the opportunity to push him against the door and kiss him. He grabbed me and spun me to press me against the door. The tip of his shoe touched my toe, and I yelped. We both looked down at it and I gasped. It was nearly all black and swollen. Just great.

CHAPTER 30

CELIA

Oscar was worried. I appreciated that, but I didn't feel like talking. When it became obvious everyone was siccing the hounds on me, I sent a blanket text to Mom, Os, and Tía saying I was fine and needed to be alone for a bit. Funny. I'd wanted to tell him about the date, about the morning, about everything.

"Just stay," Adrian had said. I'd never heard sweeter words in my life. When I'd gotten home, I took a bath and poured a glass of wine, getting ready to sit down and call Oscar to tell him. That's when the texts came through from an unknown number. Simultaneously, an envelope was dropped on my doorstep, Jacob waving, giving me his attempt at a sad smile on my security camera. Two days passed in my blur of disbelief. I'd never been good at processing how I felt. I was explosive one second and catatonic the next. My emotions embarrassed me; I always thought no one needed to hear the raw edges of my thoughts. So, for two days I went to work with Mom and ignored everyone else.

By Thursday, I knew I needed to take the last two days off. My position at the museum started on Monday, and I needed to be ready and not moping any longer. Thursday night I texted my family and resigned myself to preparing for the following week. Rumbles of thunder echoed in the distance. The sky had threatened all day and I ran, feeling the ozone and pressure on my back for six miles while I let the music in my ears drown any ulterior reasons for pounding the pavement. Once inside and showered, the text sent, I sat on my sofa and tried to watch TV. The night became a fireworks show beyond the windows, power flickering with each crash of thunder.

On the screen, a couple was remodeling a house, like I'd done. They told a story of how the lake house had belonged to his grandparents, and they wanted to remodel it so that their children and family could spend summers there. I found my eyes welling up in a manner unlike myself. I'd let myself fall for Adrian and look where it got me.

FFS, Ce. Talk to me, Oscar texted.

Adrian's texts I'd ignored, knowing if I read them—if I let him in—it would be game over for me. So, I ignored them. And they stopped coming. I guess when you worked in the field he did, it got easier lying to people. Misleading them. But it had felt so real.

I know you're watching HGTV because the weather sucks for running, so talk to me, Ce.

I scratched at the skin around my nails, half focusing on the couple on screen, who were tearing through floral wallpaper to reveal a wall with faulty wiring. Lightning flashed outside my windows, making me jump. The room felt heavier than moments before.

I can't really talk now, Os. Maybe in a few days, K?

What happened, Ce? I've been so worried about you; Taiko almost broke up with my ass for ignoring him (no joke).

What?!

Don't worry. We're good. He says "Hello, Celia" (with the accent). What about you, chica?

Not now, Os. I just can't.

Just letting you know that we are all worried about you. All of us. Adrian too.

Nite, Os.

I guessed I was just feeling stupid. Lured, played, and stupid. The envelope from Jacob sat on my desk, a red ledger of how Adrian had lied to me. Thunder exploded at the same time as the lightning flash, my whole house shaking. The power went out completely, leaving me in darkness. Swearing, I lit up my phone and hoisted myself from the couch to grab a flashlight. I should have kept one by the door as well, but the heavy one was always on the floor between my bed and nightstand. Just before I crossed the threshold to my room, the feeling of hands was on my chest, shoving me back against the hallway wall. The impact of my elbow against the plaster released my grip on my phone, sending it flying toward the guest room. Though the light remained on, it faced the corner, utterly useless.

Where the house had been dark before, the interior was then permeated by a void of color, of soul, of good. In the addled state I was in, I didn't know if the hands that shoved me were truly corporeal or other. If they were real, I had no hope. If they were other, which I had been fairly sure of, I needed to remember how to halt them. The weather was a conduit to the other, allowing that stain of black to become stronger. Thicker, like oil on water, suffocating the life beneath it. Considering it had been able to choke me in broad daylight on Monday, I wasn't keen on finding out what it could do with the veil between us lifted.

I spun along the wall, falling into my bedroom. Cold fingers scratched at my neck, the only exposed part of me at the moment. My hands and knees scrambled on the stone-tiled floor. The darkness was so complete, I only knew I was near the bed when my hands met the fluff of the bedside rug.

As soon as I had the flashlight in hand, I swung around and shined it at the void I knew was behind me. My back pressed into the leather pulls on my nightstand, feet kicking to corner myself more. The void moved toward me, a looming wave of ether, promising to fill me with its soulless breath. I could not remember the pagan chant, so I reverted to my Catholic roots and said the Our Father while I felt the top of the night table. The damnable flashlight blinked out, because, of course, I hadn't charged it in ages. I growled and threw it just as my finger felt the salt bowl. As the granules hit the void, it became less abstract and more humanoid, pixelating like an image losing signal.

"Get out of my house," I screamed, wishing I had been on the phone with Oscar when the lights went out. The figure seemed to lean into me. Its—his—face came right before mine.

"Miiiiinnne," it seethed, acrid hot air swirling from its mouth. I turned my head, the scent and heat making me sick.

"Emil, if you're around, this would be a fantastic time to help out, you artistic French fool." The ghost before me bared its teeth at the name, my throat constricting once more.

"My money. My house," it said through its teeth, barely a hiss on the hot wind of its breath. It clicked. If this ghost thought he owned this house, then it could very well be Judy's husband. The one she killed in self-defense.

"Kip?" I asked.

It came even closer, frigid hands on my throat.

"Is that you? I can help you," I said, really having no idea whether I could or whether I wanted to. But I'd seen movies with hostage negotiation, and I was a Goddamn hostage. The hands loosened, and I coughed. "I can help," I reiterated. "What is it you want?"

"My son."

I closed my eyes. When they opened, Emil was standing

232

behind Kip Cosgrove, gaining form every time the lightning flashed.

"My money. My house."

"Nate is gone," I said, thinking of Oscar. Thinking of Judy. Thinking of Adrian. Everyone who lost him. "He was killed. In Afghanistan two years ago."

My head rocked back from a slap that felt like being hit with frozen peas. Emil's form rushed forward, and there was a whirlwind of energy filling the room. I took the opportunity to breathe. A bag of frozen peas sounded lovely for my stinging face and neck. What went on in the power struggle of two ghosts who had, at one time, shared the same woman was lost to me. A surge of power pressurized the room, tipping my head back against my mattress, and I blacked out.

"Shit, Ce. Help me get her up." Voices carried to me in that foggy way that occurs when you're still half asleep. Hands were under my arms and supporting my head.

"I'm okay," I said, attempting for lucidity.

"Mm-hmm," Oscar mumbled. Even half asleep I knew the angry tone. The one that so rarely made an appearance in my brother.

"Os, I'm fine. They were both in here."

"I'll get some water and an ice pack." Taiko was there too. They laid me in my bed.

As I looked around the room, the power back on, I saw that the only real damage was that the flashlight was in pieces where I'd thrown it in my temper. The salt dish was also broken on the floor, which is likely why my hands were bloody. Taiko came back in and handed me the glass, then placed a bag of frozen peas on my neck, and a small boo-boo bunny I'd had since childhood, against my cheekbone.

"It's Kip Cosgrove," I said without waiting. "The other spirit." Then I launched into the tale of my evening, stopping only to ask why they'd come over.

"You called me. Your phone did. All I heard was you screaming 'What do you want?' and hissing. It took forever to get here because the storm knocked out all the lights and there was a tree down at the end of your street."

I supposed Emil had been helping the whole time if my phone dialed Oscar. A knock sounded, the bells of the security system letting me know someone was at the door. Taiko said he'd get it and patted my brother's shoulder as he left.

"Unless it's Tía or Mom, I don't want to see anyone."

"If I have to kick Adrian's ass, Ce, let me know. It'll have to be served cold, because he's ripped, and I want a solid two weeks of training to precede the revenge."

I laughed a little. He would do it too. "Sorry I didn't text back. I'm just kind of off."

Adrian's voice came from the front door, Taiko's countering him, saying I didn't want to see anyone. Knots and crosses strangled my stomach hearing his voice. "Her phone called me. I just wanted to see if she was okay."

"She is, mate," Taiko answered. "But she specifically said she won't see anyone but her mum or aunt.

"Okay," Adrian replied quietly. "Okay. Is Oscar here?"

Oscar looked at me, eyebrows raised in question. I nodded, and he ducked out of the room.

"Hey," Adrian greeted him. I could tell from his voice that he didn't know how to interact with him, and I immediately felt bad because they were friends. Whatever was between Adrian and me shouldn't have messed that up. Adrian was all Oscar had of Nate.

"I got the same call. She's okay now. Just a couple bruises."

"I don't know what's up, Oscar. Can you just tell her—" He cut off and cleared his throat. "I don't know, bro. I guess I'm such a guy, Oscar, but I don't know what the hell I've done." The lights from the driveway flashed again and the front door closed. Oscar came in, and I was chewing on my lip.

"Please not now, Os."

"Are you pregnant?"

"By whom?" I yelled. "No. I'm angry and sad. At least if *I* were pregnant, it would mean that I had gotten laid in the past year, for Christ's sake." A sick, sloshy feeling settled in me.

"What do you mean?"

"Well, see you have to have sex—"

"Fuck's sake, Ce. What do you mean 'if *I* were pregnant'? Is someone else pregnant?"

Ugh. Resigned to having the worst night ever, I had him follow me to the living room. From my desk drawer, I pulled the envelope Jacob had dropped off.

"He texted the photos first. More of them actually. From an unknown number because I've obviously blocked his old one. But he dropped these off himself Tuesday night."

Oscar and Taiko sat side by side on the sofa looking through the pictures.

"Was that the girl we saw at Mulligan's?" Taiko asked.

I nodded. "Sarah, yes."

Oscar's nostrils were flaring, a muscle ticking over and over in his cheek. Oscar suggested there was a reason she and Adrian were in the photos together. I snorted and said to keep going through them. He got to one in particular, threw them down, the black-and-white bean-like shape of a new life drifting to the floor, and stormed from the house, already on his phone.

"You have both had a crap year," Taiko said and grabbed

my hand. I squeezed his back and blew an overinflated breath from my cheeks.

"Is Oscar limping?"

Taiko laughed at the question and told me how Oscar had broken his toe. That was when my brother came back inside, the storm from earlier replaced in his expression. "I don't want to know," I said, holding up my hand. "In fact, thank you both for coming over. I'm showering and going to bed. If there is another ghost invasion, then so be it. I'm done."

Oscar looked at me for a long time, tugging on his hair, which was in dire need of a cut. "I just want to say one thing," he began, and I growled. "Just talk to him, Ce. Also . . . has it really been more than a year since you've been laid?"

I tossed a throw pillow at him. Then another for good measure.

CHAPTER 31

CELIA

EMPTY WALLS AND A FEW WINDOWS. THAT'S WHAT the house felt like. Now that I knew how it felt to wake up being held, the smell of Adrian around me, the feel of someone caring about me. Supposedly caring about me. The debilitating wanting. Now it was a clawing emptiness made worse by seeing those pictures of Adrian and Sarah together the morning he had picked me up for lunch. The morning I was in his arms. It was one thing, thinking I could never have him. It was quite another thinking I could and finding out I was played the fool. So, the house felt empty and awful, and I resented that he did that to me. To my house.

Saturday, I went for a run first thing in the morning, before I'd even had coffee. My phone tucked into the side pocket of my shorts, I closed the door behind me, locking it with the button, a fast run playlist already queued up in my ears. I turned to find Adrian directly behind me on my driveway. I doubled over.

"Sorry," he said, "I called over from the car."

I stopped the music. "I'm on my way out," I said as though it weren't obvious.

"Yeah." His hands dangled at his sides. "Can I just have a minute? Please?" He ran a hand through his short, night-dark hair. I knew how that hair felt between my fingers, and it took a great effort to tamp down the feeling. "Look, I realize what it looked like. What you thought—"

"Don't patronize me." A neighbor was out, washing his car and looking over at us. I rolled my eyes and opened the door again, ushering him inside.

"I'm not. I want to explain."

"Explain? You were with your ex-girlfriend the morning before our date, Adrian. The same morning—" I waved my hand in the air.

"Yes, but not the way it seems."

I walked to where the photos were and tossed them at him.

"I'd asked you when you stopped seeing her. You didn't say, 'Actually, I saw her this morning. We held hands, and she showed me the ultrasound pictures of our fucking baby.' That was never brought up." Saying it out loud was like someone took a melon baller to my insides and dumped them out.

His eyes were wild, mouth pinched in a way I'd never seen. He looked at me, breathing heavily. "And that's what you think?"

"What do you mean? These are photos. Of you. And Sarah. And a baby in utero. Oh, and both your hands holding the other's."

"You know what I think?" he asked with heat.

"Not really, no." My fingers turned the earbud over and over in my hand like a magic trick.

"I think you're always looking for a reason to walk away. Maybe it's me. Maybe it's your own issues. But I can't keep doing this."

"Me? This isn't about me."

"Really? Wouldn't the rational thing have been to ask me? Text me back? That's why I think this is an excuse for you.

Because when I woke up here on Tuesday, I thought that I never wanted to wake up without you again. That's how right it felt."

"That's a bit quick, don't you think?" I spat, wondering if he saw it for the utter bullshit it really was, because that was exactly how I'd felt. And now here we were.

He looked like someone had hit him. His head snapped back, and he rocked on his heels. As though it were in slow motion, I watched him walk backward toward the front door. "It's not mine," he said in that placid voice of his, pointing at the photo of the ultrasound. "It's Jacob's. Sarah confessed to me that they've had a thing for a while, and he manipulated her into this thing he's pulling with you. She was asking for help to get away. Back to South Carolina. The department is getting a restraining order for her as they had a relationship."

I snorted. I couldn't get one because I'd never shared a bed with him, yet he was terrorizing me. She boinks him, and she gets to have one. Classic.

"I held her hands because it seemed decent. She was hurting. Take that as you want it, Celia. I'm done. I can't do this anymore."

"Why didn't you tell me?" I asked, the earbud slipping from my fingers and hitting the tile.

"I just wanted one day with you. A few hours of only us." He opened the door while I stood like an idiot, wanting to scream. To fill the cracks in my world that were spreading faster than I could chase them. I wanted to call him back. But he was done. *Done.*

And I didn't blame him.

"Take care, Sullivan."

I ran thirteen miles that day and spent the next in bed.

CHAPTER 32

CELIA

BEING BACK AMONG THE ART IN THE MUSEUM GAVE me a new breath of life. From the old familiar pieces that were permanent installations, to the collection I had personally procured through my own blood and sweat. Seeing Emil's works daily was like having the journal come to life in a way it hadn't before. I understood the musings and the brushstrokes alike. At times I would see him in the corner, watching me or the museumgoers. The one piece I had a hard time looking at was the chandelier. Knowing Adrian's favorite piece hovered above me each time I walked into work and walked out for the day was a strange sort of biting of the thumb.

Oscar's Kikumoto was on loan for only another month. I knew he wanted it back. Who wouldn't? The inscription on the back was sexy as hell, and the painting was fabulous. *In Time*, the one from Adrian's friend Ronnie, would be leaving soon as well. So, I wasn't sure why Julianne Kestler from Celadon Imports had requested a meeting with me the Monday after I'd started back. It was closing in on the holidays, Thanksgiving rolling in quick, and the museum was set to have a small holiday party for its members. Seeing as the last museum event didn't end up as I'd hoped, I was a little nervous. Tía Teresita had been working for years to set up a catering business. She saved for ten years to establish herself and pay for a small business loan. I was so proud to be able to have her cater part of the holiday party. Tamales were a staple of Mexican Christmas Eve celebrations, so I asked her to make mini tamales con pollo for the party. The Vero Museum crowd was decidedly unadventurous as far as food was concerned. We needed to have the typical hors d'oeuvres and finger foods, but I knew the tamales would be a hit.

Oscar announced at dinner the previous evening that he was taking a trip to Amsterdam in the morning and would see us in a couple weeks. It wasn't uncommon for him to travel for work, but normally for a longer trip we heard ahead of time, so I was suspicious. Or maybe it was just kind of sketchy the way he brought it up. Taiko was smirking, and Tía and I looked at each other with the promise of a private chat later.

"Más rápido, Oscar." Abuela told him to spit it out. Apparently, we could all see he was hiding something.

"No, Abuela. Cálmate." He told her to calm down.

"Si fuera demasiado para él, disfrutaría bebiendo el agua." Taiko, in perfect Spanish, which none of us knew he spoke, told my family, "If he were in over his head, he would relish drinking the water."

I laughed a bit at that.

Then he added, to placate them, "No se preocupe Ud, yo cuido de él." Or "Don't worry. I'll look after him."

Oscar was looking at him like every star in the sky shone from his bum, even though Taiko had just thrown him in the mud. The look was so intimate, we all took a moment to find our dinner fascinating.

"Y your guapo police officer, Celia?" Tía asked. I swallowed hard.

"No vale la pena, Tía," I responded. It's not worth a damn thing.

"He thinks you are worth it, hija," she said, calling me her daughter as she always had, eyes on her bowl in mock innocence.

I asked how she could possibly know that.

"He came by last night. No, Thursday. Sí."

"Here?" Oscar and I both said together.

"Sí. Here." Abuela and Abuelo nodded their heads in confirmation, "He asked . . . Ah. No, if he isn't worth it to you, I won't say anything then. Más albondigas, Taiko?" she asked. It was not lost on us that she had made Mexican wedding soup the first time Taiko had come for a family dinner.

"Sí, gracias, Teresita," Taiko said, holding his bowl.

"What did he come here to say, Tía?" Oscar asked, so I wouldn't have to.

"He asked if you were okay, hija," she said to me.

I pushed the meatballs around in my soup.

Oscar made a hurry motion with his hand, and Tía shot him a glare.

"M'ija," she told me. "Quien bien te quiere, te hará llorar." He who loves you will make you cry.

I stood from the table and grabbed my handbag from the recliner by the door, leaving the house. I hadn't left the table like that since I was fifteen.

"Celia," Abuelo called. I paused on the porch, hearing his painstaking steps to me, and stopped my retreat. "She means well, my love," he said to me in Spanish. "I think he does too."

"I can't let my heart break again, Abuelo," I squeaked. Actually squeaked.

"Has the heart been broken?" he asked. "Or is the heart living in fear?"

CLINK, shuffle, shut. Smooth, adjust, check. For fifteen minutes before Julianne Kestler arrived, I busied myself with random tasks that had no meaning at all. Oscar was en route to Amsterdam for whatever clandestine reason. I mean, he could have lied and said it was business, so I knew it was something unrelated to work. To be honest, I was chomping at the bit to find out just what it was.

Julianne appeared at my office door, wearing a sheath dress, her hair pinned back showing the tiny diamond studs in her ears. In her face, I saw Adrian. He had the underlying Asian features from his dad's side, but the full mouth and eyebrows were from her. I came around the desk and held out my hand to her.

"Ms. Kestler," I said with a smile. She pulled me in and planted a kiss on my cheek.

"Julianne," she corrected. "Ah, I know that scent now," she said, "orange blossom."

I laughed and said she was right. We sat opposite one another, exchanging niceties, and I silently applauded myself for holding it together.

"The owner of the painting, Ronnie Kikumoto, Adrian's navy friend," she said, "would like to gift the painting to my son once the loan to the museum ends." As it was arranged by Celadon Imports, Julianne took the matter upon herself, and the exchange contract between the four of us was drawn.

"That's quite a gift," I said, going over the document. "Does he know?" I asked, not even bothering to hide that I didn't want to say her son's name.

"Adrian? Yes, of course."

I nodded, still looking at the copy.

"It is to be in my possession for the time being, so Adrian

signed, as you can see, and left it to me to deal with the rest."
As in, deal with me.

I tugged at the neckline of my jumpsuit, flicking my heels
in and out of my Choos under the table where she couldn't
see. I said I'd have our legal department go over the contract
and get it back to her and Ronnie Kikumoto as soon as
possible.

"Adrian says you know the artist? Taiko?"

I pulled my phone and showed her a picture of my brother
and Taiko, quickly scrolling past any of me, or the ones of
Adrian I told myself I had already deleted. Especially the one
I'd secretly taken of him walking up the beach that fateful day.

"Oh, he's very handsome," she said. "I do love putting a
face to an artist. Some people are harder to read than others,
and I've found Kikumoto to be a puzzle."

Was she always the queen of double entendre? I gave her
my professional smile. The one that didn't show the knot in
my gut and the multitude of feelings behind said knot.

"I won't take any more of your time, Celia," she said,
rising to her feet.

"Not at all. It was good to see you."

She looked me over, her eyes twinkling in that mischievous, yet altruistic way that Adrian had. "I'm sure our paths
will cross again soon."

When she left, I closed the door and pulled my low ponytail around my face, tugging it across like a mustache. "Get it
together, Sullivan," I said, then pushed the heels of my hands
into my eyes.

When I came out of my office for the day, Barbara was
walking up, waving her hands in apology behind Jacob.

Oh, honestly.

I made the turn around motion with my hands and pulled
my phone from the pocket of my black jumpsuit, calling
security.

"Hey, babe," he said, sticking his thumbs in the belt loops of his khakis.

"Thank you, Barbara, you can go. And remember I have a meeting in the morning." It was a phrase we'd decided on if this situation were to happen. That way, though I'd called security, all cameras would focus on me, and if need be, the police would be notified. She bounded off, quick and controlled, despite her age.

"You're not welcome here, Jacob. This is my workplace."

He countered with the fact that he was applying for the board.

I felt like losing my lunch, which I hadn't eaten anyway because I'd been too nervous about seeing Julianne. But still.

"So, you heard the good news," Jacob drawled.

I kept walking toward the front. Jacob's hand shot out and pulled me to him. The cameras likely wouldn't have caught that yet.

"At some point, darlin'," he said, lips wet on my ear. "You will come back to me. One way or another."

I yanked away, walking briskly.

"So, you and Officer Kikumoto gave up? Shame he was banging Sarah the whole time."

Don't say anything, Celia. Don't give him the satisfaction. I reached the front where our panting security guard usually stood. There should have been a police car in Riverside Park somewhere, and I hoped it happened to be sitting out front as they often did.

Jacob hijacked the distance between his face and mine, slipping his hand into my hair like a lover. So that only I could hear, he said, "This whole thing would be easier if you and I were to be together. Otherwise, the consequences for you and little Oscar are . . ." He nipped at my lip. "Tragic."

"Why's that?" I managed to whisper, hating every inch of

him near me, tasting blood on my lip, tears pricking behind my eyes.

"I wanted to marry you," he stated with his slick smile, lifting my hand to his lips. He traced the ring finger with his own fingers.

Marry me? We'd been on like three dates.

"I'm still willing. It's so much easier than . . . the alternative." With that, he snapped my ring finger back, breaking it. A wheezing lapse of breath came from me as I tried to not scream, but I managed to knee him hard in the groin. He left before the guard registered what had happened. Hell, I'd barely registered what had happened.

It was a good long while that I sat in my car, crying and screaming into a jacket from the pain. I couldn't even drive myself home with the finger as it was. Barbara came out to check on me. She had called the police after all, and two officers I didn't know knocked on my window. One looked at my finger and lip and radioed in that they needed to track Jacob and bring him in for questioning. Barbara said they had some of it on camera, but not all. I handed over my phone. The voice recorder was on the whole time. While it wasn't the clearest, closest recording, it got some of it. It got his threat. Barbara offered to drive me to urgent care, which I accepted. As the officers were leaving, I ventured a favor.

"Would you mind not telling Sergeant Kikumoto?"

They looked at one another, and I could see my request was going to be denied.

"I just don't want him to have to be involved when he's done nothing to ask for the trouble."

"He'll be fine, ma'am. Don't even think he's on today." Except that I knew he was. Probably started just as this all went down.

"Just, if you can avoid it, you know?"

"You're the one who was attacked out here last summer?" one of the two asked.

I nodded. "The one who was with Kikumoto when he got shot?"

I nodded again. "I'm a walking nightmare," I said, my forehead leaning on the steering wheel.

"This kid's been bugging you this whole time?"

I nodded again, accidentally making the horn blast.

"You want a unit outside tonight?"

"No, thank you." I have ghost sentries now, I thought to myself, realizing I had well and truly lost my mind. The finger was throbbing, and Barbara shooed the officers away so she could drive me.

Well, I had another tale for Oscar.

CHAPTER 33

CELIA

COMPARING A NOVEMBER SATURDAY MORNING IN Boston to one in Florida wasn't really fair. The autumnal shades blowing in the bluster along old streets in Back Bay and Beacon Hill were idyllic—if you went for that sort of thing. I never had. Darcy's house, like Adrian's, was along the Indian River, where we pulled away from her private dock and onto the glassine water. Though I was loath to get up early on a Saturday, when we dragged our stuff out to the boat in the quiet hours, there were two otters sunning on the end of the dock, holding hands, their spare hands clutching a rock each. It was pretty much the cutest thing I'd ever seen.

"They are out there every morning," Darcy told me. Once we got halfway down the dock, they barrel-rolled together into the brackish water and didn't surface until quite a way out. Otters held hands while they sleep. They kept their special rock in one hand and held their partner's hand with the other. That way, through rough water, kelp, and sea sludge, they would never drift apart. Why did humans have to complicate things so much?

I stood looking up and down the river, taking in the

houses that lined the shore, the tiny island in the middle, the sunrise.

"Adrian's house is just past that island up there," she said, pointing.

I'd only seen it the one time.

"See the double dock with the speed boat and two wave runners? It's the one next door. It's kind of blocked; you'll see it better when we pass."

I couldn't even bring myself to respond. She gave me her beauty queen smile and asked if we were ready. Logan was already checking the boat and storing the cooler.

If I was being honest, it surprised me that I hadn't heard from Adrian after the incident with Jacob. I knew the officers would have told him. It was a small department. For all I knew, Darcy or Oscar told him as well. God, I was ready for Oscar to be back. I supposed I just wasn't Adrian's concern anymore. It was fair enough. The low rumble of the motor purred to life, slipping from the dock and into the no-wake zone of the river. We glided along, fresh air caressing my face and hair. Once we broke into the open ocean, Darcy sped us through the break, the boat hopping waves until we found a spot near a sandbar and anchored.

Glowing morning rays reflected off our legs where they hung over the side of the watercraft. The fizz of open cider cans came from behind as Logan handed us our drinks.

"I have an early birthday present for you," Darcy said with a smirk. "Okay, not really. But I think it will be useful."

Intrigued, I turned to her.

"David Wentworth, Jacob's father, is about to file bankruptcy." She sipped from her can.

Sensing there had to be more, I sipped my own, trying to be patient.

"You know I wrote the loan for his corporation?"

I hadn't.

"Well, he hasn't been doing so hot lately."

Oscar had told me weeks ago that Jacob's trust fund was drying up.

"He's a bit of a smarmy guy, David. Like, super cringe. Always telling me how damn pretty I look and all that. So, I decided to use that to my advantage. Or your advantage, doll," she said, air-kissing me.

I shifted, bringing my knees up to fully face her. She let her head drop back, the sun on her face, a coy smile playing at her mouth. Logan walked by, brushing a hand over her cornsilk hair. My heart did a little jumping jack seeing the affection. She turned to me. I raised an eyebrow over my sunglasses frame.

She had asked David how his family was doing and told the elder Wentworth she hadn't seen his son in a while, and she hoped he was well. He smiled at her and said everyone was well enough, and that she should come by the house for drinks.

"I wanted to barf, Cece," she said with a giggle. "He spoke about his property in Curaçao and said I was welcome to use the house whenever I wanted. So, I asked about the property."

I sat up, ramrod straight, my cider forgotten.

He'd purchased it as an investment ten years ago, but kept his wife's name off it because she is a Dutch citizen. Slippery as a snake. He planned to retire there soon.

"Alone. He told me with a wink," Darcy said, miming an additional puke session. "I said, 'I bet you and Jacob could get into some trouble down there, a couple of good-looking boys like yourselves. Daddy-son lady-killin' team.'" She swigged from the can and swished it in her mouth like she was trying to get the taste of her improv out of it. She got really still, the lap of water against the sides of the boat and the movement of Logan along the port side, fishing was all the sound. I waited.

"So, he put his hand on my skirt," she continued,

explaining how she had been leaning against her desk while he sat in the chair in front of it. "He asked if I really thought so, about the good-looking part. I was a half sec away from braining him with my rose gold stapler, Cece, but I said 'of course' with a bimbo laugh."

I felt sick for her.

He'd run his hand on the hem of her skirt and asked if she wanted to know a secret. It was just between them.

"He asked me if I'd still think about them being a good team if they weren't father and son. I was hella confused, and I'm not good enough an actress to fake my confusion, Cece. So, I turned toward him, and of course, being the creep he is, he put his whole damned hand on my thigh. He said, 'The boy isn't my son, but my wife doesn't know I know. So, in case you thought it might be weird to be with both of us.' Girl, I was ten kinds of nauseous. Logan!" she called.

He turned to us.

"What did I tell you when I came home that day?"

"To make you the biggest margarita and to promise I wouldn't kill the fuckwad."

It would have been funny had I not felt like smashing something on her behalf. Namely David Wentworth's face. "What did you say, Darcy?"

"I asked him when he planned to leave."

"And?"

"He said it was dependent on whether his 'son'—and he did air quotes—came through on his end of the deal. They were waiting for a windfall of sorts. That's when I called Oscar."

"You what?"

"Seems we had both been looking into it. Birthday present part two I expect will come when he gets back."

"I'm not sure I understand, Darcy."

She smiled, drained her can, pulled the straps down from

her bikini top to avoid tan lines, and said it would all make sense soon. She hoped.

"Did you smash his hand?" I asked.

"If your boyfriend weren't a cop, Celia," Logan called over, "I'd tell you about the time I might have slashed the tires on a Mercedes in the driveway of a nice little house on Johns Island."

Darcy shrugged, smiling around her new can of cider.

All I could manage was "I don't have a boyfriend, Logan."

"In that case, there may have been the word *pervert* keyed into his paint job."

While I wasn't an advocate for the destruction of property, I felt a tug of satisfaction on Darcy's behalf. That was if these theoretical revenge tactics had happened. Which, of course, I had no proof nor knowledge.

"Why don't you stay with me for a bit. I have plenty of room. Just to be safe?"

Everyone kept asking me to stay with them, but not only did I refuse to give in to all the bullshit trying to keep me out of my own damned house, I didn't want to have to be around other people all the time.

She said she understood but made me promise to take advantage of her open-door policy with me.

Fiery orange streaks danced through the blue, the sky moving from afternoon to evening while the boat bumbled down the river back to Darcy's. We were all sun-kissed and the lazy tired you only get from a day on the water. When we cut in closer to Adrian's, Logan was driving, slowing further to say hello to the small group on the end of Adrian's dock. I panicked, looking for a hidey-hole to disappear into. Wafts of barbecue rolled down his lawn from the grill near the house. Adrian stood between a couple of guys and two girls, all holding beer bottles, looking at the small craft at his dock, which was rocking over the light wake we created in our approach. He raised his arm, beckoning Logan to pull closer and join them. He had a sleepy look on his face, and I realized I'd never seen him drinking. Under my Panama hat and over-sized sunglasses, he must not have recognized me immediately. Or maybe it was because I had curled up into the far corner of the bench, wrapped in a towel, brim tucked down.

Darcy jumped up saying she was starving and would kill for anything off the grill. Then she tugged me out from the towel and yelled, "Come on, Cece. You were just saying how hungry you were."

"Darcy," I said under my breath, "please."

She looked at me, hearing the true plea in my voice, and a repentant sort of "oh shit" look crossed her face. It was too awkward at that point to not stay, so I stood, adjusting my bikini bottoms before getting off the boat.

"Hey," I said to Adrian, my hands wringing the two sides of the white button-down I'd thrown over my swimsuit.

"Hey, Sullivan," he said, a lopsided smile flashing on his face. That smile made my insides turn to goo.

"I can walk to my car. Darcy's isn't far. You know, if it's weird."

He gestured to the lawn with his beer bottle, saying to get some food. I wanted to cry. I didn't want to be there, and I was trying to not be angry with Darcy about it. I could slip out shortly, I realized, once Darcy and Logan were occupied. Thompson and Kriss stood near the grill, and each gave me a half hug when I approached.

"I heard about that," Kriss said, pointing to my broken finger. "You call me directly next time. You hear me, girl?" she asked, making sure I called her Leila, her first name. "I want that little shit behind bars."

"I heard he had a good story," I answered, looking down. And he had. The angle when he broke my finger was blocked from the cameras; it just looked like he kissed me and left. He spun a story about my head injury and my refusing to go on meds. He said he just couldn't stay away because he loved me so much. But each time he came to me like I asked him to, he'd said, it ended like this. He said that I broke my own finger.

"No one believes him," Thompson said.

I was nodding, feeling stupid. Humiliated. "Surely someone must. Or someone is in his corner. Because I can't get a restraining order against him." I was dangerously close to tears. My lawyer hadn't been able to find a way around it.

"His dad is friends with some city council bigwig, but know that we have your back." Thompson was so sweet.

But as much as they had my back, I had a bitten lip I kept covered in lipstick and a broken finger. I had those damned photos and every breach on my house.

"Kikumoto just about lost it," he added.

My head snapped up at that.

"I've never seen his temper. Like, ever. Captain had to physically pull him away from going into the room where Wentworth was being questioned. Right, Sarge?" Thompson called over.

I closed my eyes and hated that there was wetness dragging tracks down my cheeks.

"What's right, Thompson?" Adrian asked, walking up. Thompson repeated himself, heedless of Kriss elbowing him in the side three times. She looked at me and mouthed an apology.

I knew Adrian was doing his best to not look at me, but his hand grabbed mine, looking at the splint on my finger. Even the casual touch of him looking at the splint made my breath hitch. I knew what it would feel like to put my hands on his chest over that T-shirt. The way he would smell if I were close enough to let it enthrall me.

"Yeah," he answered his friend. "It was a long day. Just doing my job."

I snorted and looked at him. I didn't know if I was amused or just annoyed. His face was goofy and relaxed, and in that brief moment, I saw him lying there, asleep in my guest bed in the early morning hours. And the pain I felt in my stomach told me it was an image I wouldn't be able to shake. Not for a long time. If ever. La douleur exquise.

With the back of my hand, I jabbed at my cheeks and stumbled away from the group, through his side gate. Darcy tried to catch up with me, but I said I was going home. Instead, I went to Fellsmere, where I stayed the night, curled up on the couch in my old pink plaid comforter, Tía stroking my hair.

CHAPTER 34

CELIA

ONE THING I USED TO BOAST ABOUT WAS BEING A power sleeper. I could nod off within minutes of being on a plane or in a car. I could sleep in broad daylight and always felt like a million dollars when I woke up. In high school, any trip we'd take, I was the one on the bus with straw wrappers in my ears because I conked out straight away. In the past six months, I could probably count on one hand the times I'd gotten a full night's rest.

In the week that followed the barbecue, I took to running or walking down to the beach to catch the sunrise. Every. Single. Morning. The days I walked, I brought my coffee. It was a meditation of sorts. I'd go over in my head all I was thankful for and begged for a bit of peace. I'd heard a lot of people saying they settled into themselves more once they turned thirty. The problem wasn't an unsettled self with me. It was a constant seismic event reoccurring in my life. No amount of consistency in my own routine could keep the destruction at bay.

Oscar got back late the previous evening, so it was a given we would have dinner that Friday. As I sat on the steps leading from the beach entrance at Sexton Plaza, I sipped my coffee, noticing there was a bit of a chill in the air. I pulled the clip from my hair, letting it fall over my shoulders in a morning tumble begging for a brush. Even in Florida, there were times when winter started to announce itself on the sea. Whispered warnings that she was an object in constant motion. A gravitational force that no man can tame or predict. The thought reminded me of Judy. The brightness of her eyes when she was lucid. The mirror of those eyes in Emil's portrait of her. She was a force of nature herself. I'd made a mental note to go see her next week. Gathering my phone and coffee cup, I stood to brush the sand from my leggings.

We saw each other at the same time. Adrian slowed to a jog and seemed to debate crossing the narrow stretch of packed sand to me. His shirt was off, giving me an unobstructed view of the gnarled skin just under his ribs where the bullet took an express path through him. Scarring that would forever be a reminder of how I put him in that situation. Such overwhelming sadness filled my chest seeing it. Considering what both he and Oscar had gone through that night.

Before he saw through my thoughts, I tried to rearrange my face into a neutral blandness. Which, of course, was useless because that naked torso made me feel anything but neutral. For the love of God, Celia.

"Hey," I said.

"Hey."

That was what we were reduced to now. A watered-down, casual acquaintance stood in the place of the conversations we used to have. Conversations that I would put money on him being spot on with reading my every thought.

"Early for you, isn't it?" I asked stupidly.

"Yeah." He pulled his hand through the damp, dark hair crested above him.

I nodded like a dashboard hula dancer.

"Couldn't sleep."

"It's a club," I muttered, looking at my sneakered feet.

"An all-hours club." His response startled both of us into looking up, and there was a slight twinkle in his eyes I'd missed lately. "How's your finger?"

"Still hurts." I shrugged, looking at the increasing tide moving up the shore. "I, uh, need to get home. Shower. Work." Lack of articulation.

"Yeah." He grinned at that. "I think I was articulate once upon a time." Jesus, he did it again.

I smiled a little.

"I was kind of drunk that day you guys came up on the boat. If it seemed like—"

"It's fine. You were fine. I have to go." Part of my discomfort that day was realizing my whole social network overlapped with his. Yet he had his own, which I'd never been a part of. Never would be. Much of his life I hadn't even stepped onto the threshold of, much less knocked on the door. And I knew it was because of me. Not him. I wanted to bang on the damned door of his life now, when I'd been told, without room for discussion, he was done, couldn't do this anymore. So, even if I let myself knock, my invitation was expired. And I understood. I did. I just hated it. Because at some point, maybe even in the very beginning, I'd fallen in love with Adrian Kikumoto.

So, because I couldn't have him anymore, because I'd tossed away every chance, I hugged him. Quickly, just wanting to feel him one last time as my heart died. His arms came around me instantly, sticky with sweat and salt spray, but he hugged me back.

"Bye, Sergeant," I said into his shoulder, shaking like the temperature had dropped to subzero. Then I pulled away, rushing up the steps and across the parking lot.

"Sullivan," he called from the top step, though I was nearly to the street.

I turned.

"Should we make T-shirts or bumper stickers?"

I knit my brows, about to ask what the hell he was talking about, when he smiled.

"For the club. Should it be T-shirts or bumper stickers?"

A surprised laugh escaped me, making him smile broader. "T-shirts. Obviously. No one is sticking shit on my bumper. I'm sure you feel the same about your cliché cop Jeep." I winked, though it was too far for him to see it.

"Cliché? What the hell, Sullivan? Go to work. Clearly you need to school yourself in art appreciation more."

I didn't know if he took the sting out of goodbye, or made it infinitely worse.

CHAPTER 35

OSCAR

TAIKO OPTED OUT OF DINNER WITH CELIA. WE WERE both jet-lagged, and he hadn't slept a wink on the flight back, so he was face first in the pillow once we got home. I was a snoring fool before we reached cruising altitude, despite my throbbing toe. Air travel with a broken toe was not something I wanted to do again; the damned digit looked like a homing beacon by the time we landed. Limping around Amsterdam did not exactly make me feel like the suave, chic counterpart to Taiko I wanted to be. One foot in Hugo Boss, the other in a giant walking boot. Sexy.

Regardless of my European fashion fail, I'd looked forward to dinner with Ce. And I had a fair amount to share with her. By the time I arrived at her house, she was a half bottle in to cooking the risotto. I groaned at the gorgeous smell of the rice and broth. She had this knack for browning the butter just before the wine went in, and the whole dish turned into divinity. The music was turned up, playing a mix of country and pop that hurt my head a bit. She was swishing her hips, wearing a cute black dress that seemed to hold her hips onto her body when she flung them side to side, singing along to

261

the music. Had she worn it to work, there must have been a blazer on top. Or a cardigan.

"Were you dressed as sexy librarian all day?" I asked, pulling the already chilled albariño from the wine carrier.

"Had a blazer on over it at work."

Ha. Knew it. Though if she had the same heels on all day, I doubt it was much more subdued. That reminded me. I had to ask Taiko how he was doing on her birthday gift.

"Like the dress. It's like late-nineties D & G."

"It is D & G. Poshmark find."

Well, that explained it. There was even the corset boning on the torso and the sculpted cups. I really hoped the blazer covered those.

"Relax, Os. I know my market." She kissed my cheek, likely getting a press of that poppy-red lipstick on my skin.

"I'm flattered I'm your market, chica."

She laughed and said to open the bottle I'd brought. A light Spanish white was used for the risotto, and she slowly drained the bottle herself while the rice did its patient soak in the pan. We chatted about the nothings in the past couple of weeks, not touching on what we both knew was coming. I'd spoken to Darcy and knew Ce was briefed on her end of things. I'd told Adrian too. He'd been involved in this since day one, so it was only fair. Also, I'd told him to come over tonight, for which I was going to get my ass kicked. Seeing as my sister was really hitting the wine tonight, well . . . what the hell. Their relationship wasn't my business really, but I hated how hurt she was. I hated that I could hear it in how she sang and drank the wine. How she didn't talk about it all. I knew that shut down too well. I knew why she did it, and I wished I knew how to get her out of it.

Cheese and olives were set out on a plate for us to pick at while she moved the wooden spoon, a gift from a cousin in Mexico, around the pan, making the fat grains of rice swim.

My eyes kept moving toward the splint on her finger. That piece of metal and sponge was a tiny monument to what my sister had been through, and I had a hard time hiding how angry it made me. When I'd found out last week, I had to drop in on a Krav Maga place in Amsterdam to get the aggression out. I wanted Jacob dead. It didn't even bother me that I thought that. He hurt my sister. He broke her fucking finger.

Then she told me about the barbecue. Based on the bottle that was empty, she used half for the risotto, and drank half, and was now on her third glass. Not too bad. There were some tears, and when I reached for her, she yanked away and swore about her mascara, which was still perfectly in place. The third glass went down while she rambled about otters, a threshold, and knocking on a door, and not only would no one answer the door, but he'd probably moved out of the house altogether. I was trying to follow and not seem thoroughly confused (something about otters?) when there was an actual knock at the door. It was then I realized she was rambling about fucking up with Adrian. I kind of wanted to say she did, but that would be really unbrotherly. I'd hate me too. She looked at me with poison darts in her big chocolate eyes, seeing on the camera that Adrian stood outside.

"You have to see the poetry in the timing, Ce."

"You could have arranged my life in fucking iambic pentameter and just because I see it doesn't mean for one minute I appreciate it," she snarled at me, clinking those heels to the front door.

"Now is the winter of our discontent," I called, feeling smug I remembered iambic pentameter. "I prefer haiku, myself."

"Repent thou anon, would but an ass you have been, stir of shit anon."

"Fuck me, you pulled a haiku out of your ass just to spite me."

Ce yanked open the door, and I saw Adrian's jaw drop. That dress.

"Adrian, my sister is a fucking genius."

"Christ," he muttered, eyes locked on my sister. It was such a hungry look. My first instinct was to cover her up, which was stupid, because, holy shit, it'd been over a year?

"I crashed your party; you crashed mine," she said, heading back to the kitchen, immediately taking up the spoon before the risotto stuck. The music switched to "Crash My Party" by Luke Bryan. "Very funny, Emil," Celia called, seeming downright batshit. But the volume raised when she said it, making us all smile a bit. Who knew dead French artists were schooled in 2000s country music?

All three of us stood awkward and prim in the kitchen, drinking a young garnacha. I commented about how all the wines were Spanish but the food Italian. No one said anything. Ce was half-turned, stirring in a constant figure eight, singing softly to the music, unaware that Adrian was watching each flick of her wrist and pout of her lips. I honestly felt like I should leave, but there was a reason we were all there.

We filled the shallow bowls and grated pecorino on top. All the while, Celia was clicking around the kitchen, fussing with things that didn't need fussing. I didn't think she even knew she was singing the whole time. Adrian shot me a look, and I upended my hands in a question. Once she was fishing in the fridge for a mystery item, singing "Just a Kiss" in her sweet, throaty voice, I turned the music off. It was like waking her up. Her face was so red, I felt guilty for calling her on it, but it was getting weird.

"Sorry," she murmured, taking a seat at the small dining table tucked against the window to the patio.

"Amsterdam," I began and went straight into it. "Last year, when Nate's estate cleared," I explained, "the house he'd bought in Spain went to me. It's sat there doing nothing because I couldn't bring myself to go back without him. Anyway, I was made the beneficiary of other holdings, which had belonged to Nate, and I was given power of attorney over Judy's estate."

"Pardon?" Celia asked, setting her fork down as she blotted her swollen mouth.

"I didn't want you to think I was incompetent, Ce. I made sure her estate was put into a trust, and you bought the house from a trust."

"Why though? I wouldn't have had a problem buying the house from you, Os." Ah, shit. She was hurt.

"It doesn't really matter. You're my beneficiary for my property anyway."

"But you lied to me, Oscar. And don't do some lie-of-omission bullshit."

"I didn't want to deal with it, Ce. I didn't want to confront it. I wanted you out of fucking arctic Boston and here with me, okay? Would you not have done it?" I asked her. "If you had known. Even if you had known about the ghosts, would you have still bought it?"

"No. I've been torn to shreds, physically and emotionally, this year!" She dared a look at Adrian, who was staring at me kind of like I was about to get hit.

"Ce." I swallowed and shut up. I knew that was my problem. I always ran my damned mouth.

"Maybe I would have," she amended. "I don't know. I am just so tired of being lied to." She scrubbed at her face and scowled when the splint scratched her cheekbone.

"The money you paid, and will pay, for the house goes into another trust for you, offshore. It's my thirtieth birthday gift to you. Sell the house. Move. Make it a fucking dog rescue kennel. I don't care. It's yours." She started to speak, but I shoved my fingers against her lips, trying to be funny, and she swatted them away. She asked what this has to do with Amsterdam.

"In 1986, Emil Cesar lived in Amsterdam and was a large part of the art circuit there." They looked at each other and burst out laughing, which would have pissed me off if it hadn't been a tension breaker between them.

"We know," Celia said.

"Yeah, but did you know he was shacked up with some socialite there?"

"Yes," they said in unison, and whatever was in the look they shared made my toes curl.

"Yeah, but did you know that when he left here, he moved back there—don't say yes, for fuck's sake. He died in 1990, after drinking himself to death."

Ce had her hands over her mouth, and Adrian's mouth was twitching too. I glared at them both, and they leaned into each other, laughing hysterically. I watched as they were struggling to breathe, not realizing their faces were like a finger's width away. God, what the hell was wrong with them that they couldn't see it? Well, Ce was fairly drunk at the moment, so I'd give her that one.

"So sorry, Os. Go on," she said, biting her hand to keep from laughing.

"In the few months it took for him to kick the bucket—sorry, Emil," I said, feeling super fucking strange about the fact that the dude I was talking about was still hanging out in here, clearly listening. "He had moved back in with the socialite. Who was married."

That sobered the little shits up.

She was loaded and snorted her way through old money from 1985 to 1989, around when she had her kid.

"Van Hoote family ring a bell?"

"The aerospace company?" Adrian asked, paling a bit under that golden tan of his.

The same, I said. I legitimately had business in Amsterdam last week. Taiko did too, but his was because I sort of forced it. One of my investors was moving from the Netherlands over here, and we were sorting his assets. I'd pushed for Taiko to do an opening. He wasn't keen on the idea, and I knew it was shitty of me to ask, but he agreed in the end. When I walked into his gallery opening, I was totally dumbstruck at how much energy was in the room. It was a club. Lights and food, people blasted, high as kites, dancing and fawning over Taiko. He hated every minute of it, and I couldn't wait to get him back to the hotel. Six of his paintings were purchased that night. Six. For sums I won't even get into. Damn, I was proud.

"'Is that your boyfriend?' a woman, maybe just under forty, dressed in scraps of Vivienne Westwood with a ring in her eyebrow, asked Taiko. He said I was. 'Can I join you in bed?'

"I'm not kidding when I tell you I dropped my drink on the ground. I mean, I'm a sheltered Florida boy. My sensible nature was not ready for that."

Celia snorted at me.

"We both refused, obviously. So, she said she would pay to watch us."

Ce started pretending to puke under the table. Adrian was laughing and covering his eyes like he could see it then. God, even I was embarrassed telling them, but I continued the tale.

She asked if we knew who she was. The night had died down, and some of the lights had come back on, patrons and fellow artists were walking around bleary-eyed. Taiko was stone-cold sober. He never drank at openings. I couldn't have gotten through the night without a drink. We said we really had no idea.

"'Elisabeth Van Hoote. Do you know my family?' Knowing Taiko was going to throttle me, I asked her to come to coffee with us in the morning. She invited us to her house for breakfast."

"I hope you wore a chastity belt," Celia remarked. Very funny.

"Ce, I honestly wished you were there. Like, if I had been able to retroactively bring you with me, I would have. The art in that house. It was a palatial townhouse along the Canal Belt, and every room was a museum."

She was leaning so far forward listening to me, her whole chest was on the table. I laughed at her wide eyes while I described the rest of the Amsterdam affair.

We waited for Elisabeth in a living room or library, I didn't know. They all had overstuffed furniture and things I would likely break simply by walking—even without the boot. Elisabeth breezed into the room like she hadn't been strung out on something four hours earlier. She brought Champagne out and said we'd be better friends if we had drinks.

I asked her about Nina Van Hoote.

"She is my favorite auntie. I haven't seen her in maybe ten years?" She poured coffee as well. "She married that American pig, and we all thought it was a bad idea. My grandfather hated him. But he was good at what he did for the company, so you know." She waved her hand in the air. "I used to go to her flat when she had artists live with her. My cousin, Jacob, we all know he isn't David's."

I sat forward on the squishy cushioned settee.

"Do you speak to Jacob?" I asked Elisabeth.

"We tried for years. He wasn't very nice. Always tormenting the little cousins when he didn't get what he wanted. Lots of kids are like that, I know. That's why I don't have kids," she said with a wink and smile.

"How do you know for certain Jacob isn't David's?" Taiko asked in his soft voice.

"Mmm," she said excitedly while swallowing a piece of

pastry. "We have paintings from Cesar. You know, the artist? One has an inscription to Nina. It's quite funny. Says something like, 'I don't love you, I never will, but I appreciate you still.'"

I laughed in an embarrassing hyena spurt. She said she liked me.

"Another has an inscription saying, 'If he is a boy, name him Jacob. If she is a girl, Genevieve.' Well, she had a boy."

She'd shown us the paintings after breakfast, and I had taken pictures of them. I handed my phone to Ce. She and Adrian leaned in, looking through the photos. She kept zooming in on details, no doubt cataloging things I wouldn't have noticed. Adrian looked at them, but again I could see that hungry look on his face when their heads were close. I wanted to say something so bad. But again, I was working on shutting the hell up when it wasn't my business.

"I also gave her your number and said you'd be in touch regarding the museum," I said to Ce, pointing in her face. "You're welcome." She was practically dancing in her seat.

"So, what am I missing?" Adrian cut in. "We know Jacob was actually Emil's son, and David knew, but thought the wife, Nina, did not know."

"Oh, she knew he knew. That's the main reason Van Hoote Aerospace went public ten years ago. She wanted Wentworth's sticky paws away from the family money."

"Wentworth moved all his funds to an offshore account where he has property that isn't in his wife's name. Wouldn't she still be taxable as they are still married?" Ce questioned, pinching between her dark brows.

"His property is under a separate corporation layered under a virtual firewall of privacy. It keeps his name well away from hers," I answered her. "And he really doesn't have much in any of his accounts. He was kicked out of Coots and Buuren—his bank—for not meeting the capital requirements.

All he really has is that property, significant as it is. The Johns Island place is owned by Van Hoote. Wentworth is pretty much a caretaker."

"And we know Jacob's trust fund is nearly empty."

"His mother was topping it off monthly until two years ago. According to everyone I've asked, they don't speak much."

Celia grabbed another bottle and filled our glasses. I gave her a look, and she bit back at me, saying she was just going to drink water, but with the couple of weeks she'd had, she had every right to drink all night, and to stick my nose in my own bum. I saw the cut on her lip then, and it dawned on me why her lips were painted so red. Once she'd eaten, the lipstick came off and her bottom lip was swollen with an almost-healed cut. Adrian noticed too, and his cheeks sucked in.

"Not to be narcissistic, but what does this all have to do with me?" she asked.

"When Jacob was three, they moved to South Carolina, where David is from. That's also where he took over the East Coast branch in Charleston. They lived there until Jacob went to college at the University of Florida. Then Van Hoote opened a private sector branch here in Vero. As our young shithead graduated with a degree in aerospace engineering, he moved here after school as well to work the family business."

"That's where he met Sarah," Adrian said.

"Incorrect, Kikumoto," I said, after making an obnoxious buzzing sound. "They met at UF. They were both South Carolina transplants and became friends. He got her the job here and they moved in together. Apparently, theirs has been an on-again, off-again thing since college."

"Jesus Christ," Celia said.

Adrian looked like he'd been kicked. He said it still didn't explain what Celia's involvement was unless Jacob was simply sociopathic.

"He's 100 percent sociopathic. However. Here's where shit gets weird. Actually, Ce, you might want to pour another glass after all." I got up and walked into the living room, just to be dramatic. Also, I was full and uncomfortable, so elevating my foot sounded better. When my sister walked in, she toed off her heels and sank into the corner of the couch, pulling her feet under her.

I WISHED I could film every moment Adrian watched her. His gaze caught the strap slipping from her shoulder. He watched her twist and untwist her hair. His throat bobbed so many times I could play a drinking game to it. Had Taiko been there with me, I think it actually would have been a good one to play: take a shot every time Adrian looked at Ce like he was lost in the desert and she was the only glass of water; take a shot when his Adam's apple bobbed looking at her. I would have been three sheets to the wind in five minutes flat.

All three of us clutched the glasses in our hands. Adrian asked me if we wanted to share an Uber home.

"Why don't you both stay here? Adrian, you can sleep in the guest room. Os, you can be in with me or out here. It's already late, and clearly, this night isn't over."

I said fine, knowing Adrian wouldn't stay if I didn't. He was looking at Celia while she thumbed a text to someone, probably Darcy. In my imaginary drinking game, I'd have taken a shot. A double.

"I'll just head home. It's okay," he said. Her thumbs stopped, and I could see a tremor in her hand, but she nodded and tossed the phone between the cushions.

"I'll stay, Ce." She looked up at my tone. I knew our topic of conversation could stir up unrest with the entities in the house and voiced my concern. We had all noticed the lights flickering all evening, and the opening and closing of doors. Celia swallowed each time, but I wondered how often it actually happened.

"Why are you still in this place?" Adrian asked her, scratching at his head.

"Because it's my house," she said with a flame of conviction he raised his eyebrow at. "What am I supposed to do? Run because someone says boo?"

"Yes." His dark, almond eyes were wide and determined. "You've been attacked here."

"I've been attacked here, and at the beach, and next to the lifeguards at Humiston. I've been attacked by a very human attacker at work. Twice. Where am I supposed to go, Adrian?"

"The account that transferred money to Caroline—the fifteen grand—is linked to David Wentworth's offshore corporation." I interrupted because I knew if we pushed her, she would walk away. Adrian must have known that too.

"So, I know how much deep shit to prepare to be in, Oscar, how legal are the channels you used to get this information?" Adrian asked.

"Perfectly legal. I'm just that fucking good, Kikumoto." I winked at him.

Celia excused herself to go to the bathroom. I typed a text to Taiko telling him I'd be staying with Ce, which didn't surprise him. Adrian kept sipping his wine, bouncing his foot on his knee. I smirked at him.

"Problem, Oscar?"

I cackled a little. My laugh was a deciding factor in people's opinion of me. Most folks either loved or hated me. After years of therapy, I found I was cool with that.

"So many. You go ahead and pretend you don't have one, though." He glared at me. I'd never seen him angry. Not that he was then, but there was a hair of it there in the set of his mouth. He was that even keel that I always envied. Like Nate. I sometimes forgot that he'd lost his best friend too.

"Whatever."

"You don't have a problem?" I prodded. It's really a wonder I haven't been knocked in the jaw more. He scrubbed a hand over his face and tipped his head onto the back of the sofa.

"I have a really big problem, Oscar. And you know that. So shut the hell up."

All right, I felt bad then that I'd pushed. Ce walked back in, having changed from her hot little dress to those super short sleep shorts she wears and a baggy BC sweatshirt. She saw his head back on the cushions just as his eyes followed her back to the living room. Shot.

One last tip into each of our glasses drained the bottle.

"Snooping around Amsterdam was honestly more fun than I thought it would be. It stopped being so amusing when I found out there might be a hit on me. Again."

Ce and Adrian both sat up at that.

Emil Cesar rose to artistic stardom quickly in a time of extravagance. The mid- to late-eighties had money and drugs, and the sort of social fuel to keep a continuum between both.

"When his paintings sold," I told them. "They sold for stupid amounts. Hundreds of thousands. A bidding war happened on two of them, the selling price on each well over a million. His wife, Marie, was dead. He had no head for business but tried investing in companies worldwide. Some investments were successful, some tanked."

"I remember reading that he went in on a fashion house after meeting a designer at a party in Stockholm. The line didn't do well, but his investment was solid in the house. He pulled the money out just before he left for New York." Celia said it with a far-off look. We were all going to have splitting headaches in the morning.

"There were a few ventures like that. Emil wasn't used to having money."

"He lived in squalor according to his journal," Adrian added. Celia turned to him and agreed, their glasses half-empty.

"Remember the fishing cottage he rented in Sebastian?" Ce asked him. She put her hand on Adrian's leg in an unconscious gesture like "hold the phone." She half turned to me.

His Adam's apple bobbed. Shot.

"It was their love shack." She giggled. "Judy hated it and they fought over his accommodation."

Her hand stayed on Adrian's leg, and I wondered if she knew. He didn't move an inch but drained his glass. Shot. This was so engrossing, I almost forgot that there was some very poignant stuff I had to tell them.

"A friend of David Wentworth's came to me a few weeks ago. He heard I was nosing around and called me to meet up in Amsterdam." I started the final bits of the whole story as far as I knew. "Levi Visser and I met in grad school. While not employed by Wentworth, I knew he was a friend and casual financial adviser. I also knew he was a snitch for the Department of Treasury."

"How could you possibly know this, Oscar?" Adrian asked, shifting, which made Ce realize her hand was on his thigh. She didn't snatch it back, like I thought she would, but rather dropped it to the side of him. I *pshaw*ed at his question and continued.

"Levi and I met for drinks two nights before I left the Venice of the North. He told me he had some dirt on Wentworth and to watch myself. Money was set to wire to Robert Avery back in August.

"It was never sent, but a record of the transaction was logged in the routing system. I still don't know how or why, because these things should time out." Lights blinked momentarily in the living room. I kind of felt like that was a sign from Emil, but I was also rather drunk.

"Jesus," Ce breathed.

"Christ," Adrian followed. He leaned forward, elbows on his knees. "Why?"

"Million-dollar question, Sergeant," I said, starting to hit that state of drunkenness when you pause a little longer than intended.

Ce set her empty glass down, and something like a sob went through her. She recovered before I could react, but Adrian caught it and threw an arm around her, pulling her in. Shot? Or maybe a point for him. I was losing the thread on how my imaginary drinking game worked.

"If we wanted to get super technical, it's a multimillion-dollar question. Take a breath, kids, because I have something to tell you." God, we should've made coffee, because I'd lost track of what I was saying like six times. However, the longer I took, the cozier those two got.

"Os." Ce sat up, causing Adrian's arm to drop, but she wordlessly moved into his side.

He looked like he might be sick. Shot.

"Os."

"Right. Emil Cesar had a will." The lights did flicker then, a bulb popped in the desk lamp. We all jumped. "He left his entire estate to Judy Monroe and her next of kin. In Judy's living will, she stated that in the event that she needed full-time care, her money—and she had her own family money remember—be used for her extended care and medical. Everything else was put in a trust for Nate, indicating his trust would transfer to his next of kin. Everything."

Celia bounced up onto her knees and started to ask me a question three times before Adrian pulled her by the hips. Down. Onto his lap. Hell, I'd do a shot to salute the bastard on that one.

"But Nate left his estate to you," she said.

I nodded, my eyes heavy.

"You said he just left the house in Costa Brava to you."

"Judy's estate doesn't go to me until she passes. God willing, that will be in many years." I made the sign of the cross on myself.

"How much are we talking, Oscar?"

I couldn't keep my eyes open any longer, so I answered with them shut. "Around fifteen million."

"Come again?" Adrian asked. "I thought you just said fifteen million, and that can't be right."

"You know what really sucks about this whole thing? Like, what really fucking sucks? Nate could have retired. I begged him to retire. Begged him, on my knees. I offered to support us. And he even knew. He knew about it; I saw his signature on the deeds. The trust. Everything."

"He wouldn't have quit, Oscar. He loved what he did. He loved serving." Adrian was right. Nate was a soldier through and through. Goddamned patriot. For what?

"I just always hoped he'd love me more." I shrugged. I'd never said that out loud, and thankfully, I was too drunk in that moment to care. What I did feel was guilty for voicing that when I had a new partner, sleeping in my condo a mile away. "Not that I don't love Taiko. I do. It's just that there are so many things I wish I could have said to Nate. So much I wanted him to know."

"He knew, Oscar. I promise you, he knew," Adrian said.

"Don't you start on your Victor Hugo shit again, Sergeant," Ce said to him, turning in his lap.

"Even you have to admit it's fitting in this moment."

"Have you seen *Les Mis*?" Ce yelled. "Everyone dies!"

He laughed, and his arms went around her. I smiled, closing my eyes again.

"Speaking of dying," I said, slurring a bit and hating it

because this was truly important. "Ce, you are my beneficiary. If I have kids ever, that may alter. But as it stands, if I kick it, you're rolling in it."

"Oh my God," she said.

"Wentworth knew that," Adrian cut in. "He followed the trail. Cesar to Judy, Judy to Nate, Nate to you, you to Celia."

"So that's why Jacob was so weird about marrying me? He knew?"

"It would have been easier than the alternative," Adrian said, his arms tightening around her.

"That's exactly what he said before he broke my finger. Something about still wanting to marry me because he'll have me one way or another, and marriage is easier than the alternative. I assume Jacob knows of his parentage?"

I nodded. Wentworth was in the States when Jacob was born. Nina had him in a hospital near the family's country house. The record of birth was filed there, Emil Cesar listed as his father. Emil never knew. Wentworth signed a christening certificate when he returned to the Netherlands.

"So, if we are both dead, Jacob is next of kin. And Wentworth?"

"Apart from Darcy's questionably legal video recording of their meeting, I have a string of emails between Levi, Jacob, and David."

"But what skin would David have in the game?" Adrian asked.

"That's what we need to find out. Or, rather, the FBI. My case is being reopened. Sorry, bro. You'll be pulled in too."

"Of course."

I had to sleep, and maybe it was a bit abrupt, but I said good night and went to bed in Ce's room.

Chapter 36

Celia

Somehow, I had ended up on Adrian's lap, and because of the wine in me, it didn't leave me as embarrassed as I would have thought. However, I still needed to get off.

"Don't get an Uber," I said to him, grabbing the glasses from the coffee table. He was looking out the dark window, a knuckle pressed to his top lip. He started to rise, seeing me with the remnants of our wine party, and I said to sit. All I was doing was depositing it all in the sink and worrying about it in the morning. I came back into the living room where he was still in the same position. I knew I would have a hell of a headache in the morning.

"Why?" he asked.

"It's late. Take the guest bed."

Adrian agreed, and we said good night while I pretended to tidy the living room. On my way from the kitchen, I passed my room, and Oscar was spread-eagle, facedown on my own bed, so I was going to sleep on the couch. Once Adrian was gone, I turned out the light and sneaked to my room to grab a pillow. A shadow stood in the hallway, and I yipped, dropping the pillow.

"You take the bed since Oscar commandeered yours," Adrian whispered. I walked to the couch.

"It's fine. I'm okay out here." I settled on the couch. In the dark, a shape moved toward me. Adrian sat on the end of the sofa. "What are you doing?"

"I won't sleep in the guest bed, knowing you're out here."

"Kind of childish don't you think?"

"I'm a younger sibling." That made me smile into my pillow.

"I appreciate your gallantry, Sergeant, but I'm settled here. Get some rest." My eyes were impossible to keep open, especially in the dark. Shuffling sounds came from next to me. It was quiet, but he was still sitting up, so I knew he was still awake. I stretched my feet to the end, and his hands brought them up onto his lap.

"Sorry I didn't call after the thing with Jacob," he whispered.

"Did your captain really have to hold you back?"

"Yeah, I guess he did."

Somehow that made my heart swell a little, regardless of our relationship.

"I didn't know if you wanted to hear from me. So, I didn't call. I'm sorry."

"I was more put out that you didn't invite me to your barbecue. You know I'm always hungry."

He squeezed my feet, his legs twitching with a chuckle. "It was a bunch of people from work and my cousin. I didn't think you'd want to be around a bunch of cops. Plus, you know, I didn't think you'd be interested . . . in seeing me."

His voice was swimming through the darkness while my body felt a loose spin from the wine. I was always interested in him. Didn't he know that by now?

"I heard a rumor," I said.

He stiffened a bit and made a questioning kind of grunt.

"That you were out in Fellsmere recently."

There was a whistle of breath, and I knew if the lights had been on that he would be blushing.

"Now I don't know why you may or may not have been there. I left the table when I heard. Which, yes, is immature."

"Let's just say I was given a tutorial on making flan worthy of Food Network."

"Oh. And . . . did you? Make flan?"

"I suck at custard, Sullivan. It was a cottage cheese and scrambled egg hybrid. Total failure."

"Bummer. That was a defining moment. Judgment must have been harsh."

"You win some, you lose some."

"Tell me about your house," I mumbled, trying for coherency and fluffing my pillow under me.

"My grandfather was in World War II," he began. Not exactly where I thought the story would start, but okay. "Enlisted with the navy out in Oregon as soon as war broke out. When they realized his Japanese was fluent, he was moved from being a line cook to the Allied Translator and Interpreter Section in Melbourne, Australia. He was born in the US to Japanese parents. I think I told you that."

I nodded in my pillow, which of course, as it was quite dark, he couldn't see.

"While he was away at war, his parents were put into an internment camp in Oregon. They ended up dying of flu."

"I'm sorry. That's awful." He squeezed my foot again.

"My grandfather met my grandmother in Melbourne. She was Japanese as well and worked for the Australian Women's Army Service as an intelligence officer."

"That's incredibly cool."

"It is," he agreed, and his fingers moved along my foot, tickling me. His thumb swirled around my ankle bone, circling slow. His voice dropped lower, thick and tired. "They married in Australia and had my uncle. Once the war was over, they moved back to the States and had my dad. He had a couple of buddies who were frogmen in the Pacific Theater in the war. They told him about where they trained in Fort Pierce. Since he had no one left in Oregon, the family moved here. Well, Fort Pierce originally. They started an import company and bought some land—where my house is."

Long fingers brushed along my foot and calf in languid strokes. The wine spin was becoming a cyclone. It was almost as if I needed to set one foot on the ground to keep me leashed to my senses, but there was no way I'd move either foot.

"You still awake?" he whispered. I flexed my toes and wordlessly asked for more attention on my feet. A low chuckle sounded. "At first it was only a tiny cottage on the river, like our artist friend's." A knuckle pressed into the arch of my foot, making me groan since it's always sore from running. I felt him take a breath under me. "Eventually they put a bigger house on it. The house was left to my dad. I bought it from them when I came back from Kuwait and have been fixing it up for the last few years. It was in a bad shape; I all but tore the whole thing down."

"You've done beautifully. It's an incredible house."

"Thanks, Sullivan." A hand ran along my shin and back down.

"Adrian?"

"Celia?"

I smiled into the pillow. "You know you're making chilaquiles in the morning, right?" My feet shook against him as he laughed.

"I knew there had to be a reason you asked me to stay," he answered, a smile in his voice.

"La razón es porque te quiero mucho," I slurred quietly in Spanish, more to myself. The last thing I remembered before drifting off was his hands stilling on my feet and not moving.

IF THE SMELL of coffee hadn't been flitting through the open guest room door, I wouldn't have bothered getting up. I lifted onto my elbows, and my head felt like a battering ram had done its worst with me. I stumbled to my own room, and while brushing my teeth, it occurred to me that I woke up in the guest bed. Then I remembered saying I loved Adrian in Spanish, and I hoped beyond hope that either he hadn't heard me or hadn't understood. God. Oscar was still snoring on my bed, oblivious to the clinking of pans and utensils in the kitchen. I padded barefoot toward the smell of food, clutching my head so it wouldn't bounce too much. Adrian snorted when he saw me.

"My head's just as bad," he said. I poured myself a coffee and topped up his. He plated chilaquiles and handed it to me. "As demanded," he said with a wink.

"You're the best."

Oscar walked in, shadowy scruff on his face, his shirt wrinkled. "Chilaquiles?" he asked, gray eyes bright. "Awe, Adrian, you must love me too."

I nearly choked on my chips and eggs, but swallowed, keeping my eyes down. What the hell, Os?

"But first, coffee."

We had our breakfast in silence, squinting into the sunlight coming through the window and patio door. After a while, we spoke about the revelations from the night before. Oscar and I were targets. The fact that my brother already brought the issue up with the FBI was somewhat comforting, but the stark reality of someone intending to kill us both was downright terrifying. Beyond the screened pool, the tree leaves danced in the turquoise sky, promising a clear day. One ray shone on the iguana as he lazed about on his favorite palm tree, his scales absorbing the sun.

A knee bopped mine under the counter, and I turned to the chef who had made my favorite breakfast. He was staring straight ahead, not acknowledging me at all. I narrowed my eyes, making my head hurt more.

"Oscar?" Adrian called, still looking ahead. "I have a question for you."

"Yes, I do take commissions."

"What?"

"Nothing. Your question?"

"I speak French and some Japanese, a bit of Farsi, but it's been a while. Unfortunately, the only Spanish I know is what I've learned on the job."

I had a really bad feeling rising in my already tenuous tummy.

"O . . . kay . . ." Oscar said.

My grip tightened on my fork. In my peripheral vision, I could see Adrian's cheek rise, the lines that showed his true smile spearing from the corners of his eyes.

"How would one translate"—I thought I was going to puke—"oh, hang on, what was it? La razón es porque te quiero? Mucho. Porque te quiero mucho."

Fuck my life. Jesus, Oscar, don't answer that. Oscar shot coffee through his nose and sat back, wiping his face. I started to scoot my chair back, but my brother's arm came around my shoulders, keeping me there. I closed my eyes, knowing my face had to be lobster colored.

"La razón es porque te quiero mucho means, 'The reason is because I want you so much,' or 'because I love you so much.' Sort of interchangeable, but the meaning is pretty much the same. Why do you need to know?" Oscar asked with a shit-eating grin in his voice. I elbowed him in the stomach. "Ow!"

"Just wondering," Adrian answered, lips pulled up at the corners, eyes straight ahead. Oscar let go of me, and I took my plate to the sink, belatedly realizing Adrian had cleaned up the mess from the night before.

"Thank you for cleaning up. That was nice of you."

"He's in public service," Oscar said. "People think he's stepping over the line all the time and say inappropriate things to him."

Chapter 37

Celia

Both my guests left after breakfast, wanting to get home and showered. Once I had luxuriated in my own hot shower for far too long, I dressed in jeans with a cute cropped black blouse that had Swiss dots along the bodice. Then I sat. On the couch, staring out the window. In the chair, staring at the mirror on the opposite wall. On the side of my bed, attempting to read. On the kitchen stool, drinking a sparkling water. On the lounge chair, watching the iguana.

The day fell away in tiles of sunshine until it was that golden hour where everything seemed the most beautiful. Did it matter that I'd said what I had out loud to Adrian? Surely, he didn't ask Oscar because he wanted to humiliate me. Right? He wasn't cruel. I didn't imagine him holding my feet last night and stroking my calves. And I didn't walk myself to the guest bed, so I assumed he'd carried me. God. Sitting in my final spot, just outside the house on my front porch, framed by curtains of bougainvillea, I decided I was going to tell him how I felt. We'd run around this thing for so long now, each time coming closer to being together, and each time having somehow been torn apart. At least if I was honest with him, as hard as it would be to hear, he could be honest back and tell me to get lost. And I was thoroughly sick of sitting around my house. I grabbed my bag and drove to his house, hoping he'd be home.

The street was along the river, and his Jeep took up the driveway, so I had to squeeze my car between a bunch of others on the street. In the mirror, I told myself I had this and retouched the stain on my lips, then ran a hand through my hair, which I'd taken the time to straighten and curl.

Julianne Kestler opened the door, looking radiant.

"Celia!" She leaned in for a kiss on my cheek. "Come in. Adrian's out back with his dad and Viola."

Well done, Ce. Came to pour your heart out, and his whole family is here.

"Can I get you something? We just made a batch of sangria. I heard you make it well."

"I'm okay for the moment, thanks. I won't stay long. I don't want to intrude."

She waved me off, walking me through the house and out the glass back doors. Adrian was standing by the small boat I'd seen last weekend, showing it to his dad and another man. A woman, presumably his sister Viola, was lounging on the Adirondack chair holding a baby on her lap. I felt so out of place and wanted to run away. Adrian caught my gaze and walked over. I was twisting the hem of my top between my fingers, thinking I should have worn something different. Should have texted first. Shouldn't have even bothered convincing myself to tell him. Oh God.

"You okay, Sullivan?" he asked. "Did something happen at home?" Concern clouded his features.

"No, no. Everything's fine. I wanted to take a minute of your time."

"How formal." He grinned. "Come here. You look like you've seen a ghost. Trust me, I've seen you when you've seen a ghost." He led me over near the house where there were a couple other seats. When I said I'd rather not sit, he went extremely still, face instantly serious.

"This is really shitty timing, Sergeant. I'm sorry."

"It's okay." It was his deadpan cop voice that said that. "What's the problem?"

Across the lawn, his family was doing their best to not look over at us. Adrian peered over his shoulder and angled himself farther in front of me, crossing his arms, then uncrossing them.

"I kept sitting in different places in my house today after you guys left. Like I was trying to find a spot to chill. This is a bad idea," I blurted and turned to leave.

He caught my arm. "Talk to me, Sullivan."

"I decided you needed to know something." I took a breath, which did nothing at all for my heart rate. "Please don't think you have to be all 'public servant,' keeping the peace."

"Celia."

"I know. It's just." I scrubbed at my face, the stupid splint on my finger catching in my hair. Adrian pulled it free and kept my hand in his. Something about that made my eyes well up, and he returned to that eerie stillness. "When you said the other day that you didn't want to wake up without me. What I said back . . ." I took another breath. "I didn't mean it. What I should have said is that I didn't either. That I'd never felt the way I felt with you holding me. Ever." The dam burst in my eyes, and tears were rolling out unchecked.

What was I thinking, telling him this stuff when his whole family was there? God, Celia. What a dumbass.

He pulled my hand and held it against his chest.

In a shaky voice, I continued. "This is the stupidest timing. The thing is, I know you can read me. I know you heard me say that thing in Spanish."

"You were drunk, Sullivan. It's okay."

"It's not okay. Because I meant it. A thousand times over. I know you said you're done with me. I know I messed things up, and you can't do it anymore. It's fair. I just wanted you to know how I felt. How I feel. Because I didn't want this to end and you to never know that I'm in love with you. How much I love you. Shit. I'm sorry." For a few seconds, minutes, hours, I didn't know, we stood there. He was looking at me, and I had these ridiculous tears galloping down my face, wrecking my makeup. "I can go. So you—"

He pulled my hand in and looped his other arm around my back. Dropping the hand between us, he held the side of my face and kissed my forehead. I wasn't sure what to do. It felt like the precursor to a letdown. I stood there, clutching the bottom of his T-shirt, taking in his scent, his warmth.

"You're right, your timing is terrible. I'm never going to hear the end of this." And his lips met mine. Every hungry moment between us yesterday joined in the kiss. Into my ear, he said, "Please say you'll stay because I fully intend to finish this later." We pulled apart, a bit breathless. "And now you have to meet my whole family. Entirely your fault."

IN THE ELEVEN years since I'd graduated from high school, I hadn't met the parents of anyone I dated. Either I didn't care enough, or he didn't care enough. Usually, it was me. There was no one whose parents I wanted to meet. No one I wanted enough to humiliate myself and cry in front of. No one I wanted to wake up beside. Until Adrian. And it had scared me more than the ghosts in my house. Because ghosts could scare me, but this love? This had the power to break me, and I just wasn't used to it. But I wanted it. More than anything I'd ever wanted.

The sun set fully, lights twinkling along the river. Viola

and her family were making their way home to get the baby to bed. Adrian's parents, Julianne and Spencer, kissed them goodbye and stayed with me while Adrian walked them out.

The evening felt unrushed and heavy with promise while we stood out on the patio, feeling the breeze off the river. Julianne told her husband about my acquisitions for the museum. Each time she spoke animatedly about the paintings I paired, she would touch his arm for emphasis and look skyward with those twinkling eyes.

"It was equal parts interest in the artists and luck I think," I told them. "The idea for grouping the two artists was only really executed because things kept falling into my lap. You had a big hand in that as well."

"I was just the loading bay," she said with a little laugh.

Spencer put his arm around her waist and said he was sure she was more than that.

"No, really. Adrian and his friend, Ronnie put that together. I only just signed off. Which does remind me. Someone came by my office the other day asking questions about you two. I wasn't in, so my assistant told me. I'll get the contact for you. I don't plan on speaking to anyone."

I wondered who it could have been. The FBI would likely have made themselves known. I hated the idea that Wentworth and Co. were anywhere near Adrian's family. The thought made me shiver.

"You're cold. We were just about to leave anyway, weren't we, Spence? I know you weren't feeling all that well earlier, Celia, love. So don't catch a cold out here."

Her concern made me smile even though I knew she might have been fishing for why I was a mess when I arrived. Both parents hugged me before leaving and walked through the house while I stayed standing against the exterior wall, looking out onto the water.

Footsteps sounded from inside. When he walked out,

Adrian looked at me and kind of half laughed, scrubbing at his face. It was a timid sort of approach, and my stomach was in a nonstop zip line drop. My back pressed to the wall, the warmth of the day soaking through my top, I stood, looking at him. Heat flooded my face, realizing again how I'd laid myself bare. A sort of panic tore through, but I tamped it down. Through his gray T-shirt, his chest moved, pulling at the shoulders of his sleeves while he walked over. My fingers itched to touch those arms. Instead, I pulled my hands through my own hair, twisting it unconsciously until he was standing in front of me, inches away.

"Weirdness level on a scale of one to ten?" he asked me, voice low and gravely.

"Seven? Your family was very nice. Despite the fact that I was some strange girl who showed up at a family party crying." God. I looked down.

"They knew who you were."

"Well, yeah, I'd met your mom." His hand cupped my waist, thumb sweeping from the bottom of my ribs to the waistband of my jeans. I tipped my hips forward, shoulders still against the wall.

"I told them about you a while ago. Told them I'd met Nate's sister-in-law. Sort of. Mom saw straight through me. She always does. So, I think every time she saw me, it was, 'How's Celia?'"

I placed my hands on his chest, smoothing them over his shoulders and down his arms. A spike of something electric rose from my toes to my face.

"Don't bother trying to hide anything from my mom. She has this superpower to see everything." His thumb brushed higher, under the cropped hem of my top where my bra hit. He swallowed, the light on the lawn behind him seemed to detail his striking features. Had he been a sketch, the planes of his jaw and cheeks would have heavier outlines and shading. He was art.

"A bit like someone else I know." I ran a hand over the back of his head and down his neck, swiping my thumb over his cheekbone. For a second those night-black eyes closed as he leaned into my hand. Fingertips danced along his jaw and cheeks. God above, I couldn't imagine a face more perfect. He opened his eyes, a half smile tugging his mouth to the side, while I felt his hands on my bare back and stomach.

"I'm not so sure I'm that good anymore. You confuse me, Sullivan," he rasped. Under his shirt I raked my nails down his spine, and tucked my hand under his waistband, pulling his body closer to mine.

"I think you see more than you realize."

"I don't know. According to Oscar, I'm such a guy. I need it spelled out for me."

"You know you could have used Google Translate on the Spanish."

He chuckled softly, pressing me fully against the wall. "My Spanish is fine, Sullivan."

"Stinker." I smiled, my lips against his. His full bottom lip met mine, and everything in my world slid into place.

"I want to be clear about something though." He ran his hands up over my top and held my face between them. "I've felt this way about you since the day I drove out to Fellsmere to check on you the first time. Before that. Probably when I met you on the beach in the middle of the night."

"And how is that?" I asked shakily, touching his lip with the tip of my tongue. He shuddered against me, our bodies almost rigid.

"That I'm so in love with you I can barely sleep or think."

Fortunately, the house was open plan, and there were few things to bang into as we crashed through the first floor toward the stairs. Before going up, he held me against his chest, my back a line that followed every press of him behind me. His lips moved down my neck while hands explored under my top and fingers dipped down into my jeans, making me arch my back. The stairs were too long, the room too far. It seemed to take forever to walk through the bedroom door to his room. Faced with the bed, a bit of shyness came over both of us. I tugged at his shirt, lifting it over his head, then started on my own top. The sheer mesh of my balconette bra was interrupted by black embroidery that looked like climbing vines that wound up the wide-set straps. Adrian's long fingers traced the embroidery, making my breath a quick ragged storm of sounds.

"Aubade?" he asked, voice just above a rumble.

"Of course." I pulled my jeans the rest of the way down, showing the matching bottoms.

"God, you're just . . . perfect." He pulled the straps over my shoulders and kissed where they'd been, making his way down over the mesh cups. Tickling strands of black hair teased the skin of my stomach and chest where his mouth moved over every part of me. He stood to kiss me properly, his fingers slipping the material aside and feeling every hidden place that ached for him. Our backs hit the bed, getting an *oof* from me.

"Your bed's too low, Sergeant." I laughed, pushing my hips up into him.

"Yours is too high. I'll add a box spring." His teeth caught my lip in his, gently pulling, and I winced. "Sorry. I forgot." I touched his face and reclaimed his mouth.

Skin to skin, our bodies moved together in a quiet rhythm I couldn't have anticipated making me feel as much as it did. Valleys and corners of the muscles that moved on me felt indulgent on the nerve endings of my fingers while I ran my hands over every part of his golden skin. Surging waves of ecstasy found me grabbing his arms and crying out. He stilled above me, lowering himself to kiss my eyelids, gentle and warm, before finding his own release.

Light shone from the hallway, casting us in puzzle pieces of shadow as we held each other for an indeterminate amount of time.

"Mind if I stay?" I asked with a smile.

"Hmm. I have a bunch of things to do tonight—"

I pulled the pillow from under me and whacked him with it.

He spun me so that I was over him, my hair falling in a thick sheet onto his chest. "Stay tonight. Stay tomorrow. Stay as long as you want."

Turning toward his hand that ran through my hair, I let my head rest on his palm while I swirled my fingertips along his collarbone. Half of the expression on his face was satisfied male. Half was a bit goofy, shining with wonder. "What are you thinking right now?" I asked, bending to kiss the hollow of his throat, breathing in the scent of him. With a slight scoot upward to look at me better, he put me in a position I didn't think he was ready for me to be in just yet, and I made a small sound of frustration. In a very male answer, he pushed up, letting me settle over him, rocking slowly.

"There are a hundred thousand things in my mind right now, and every one of them is centered on you." He ran a finger over the bridge of my nose and down my lip. "I am wondering, Sullivan, when you knew. Or why today felt like the day you had to say something."

Sitting up completely had my legs straddling him so I could look at him better. That face I knew I could stare at for the rest of my life, and always love.

"It hit me when we had lunch together at the Thai place. A realization that made me feel like I was drowning. Today it was like—" I swallowed, promising myself I wouldn't cry again. "I felt like I'd lost you. For good."

"Why?" he whispered, holding me flush against him. "Why today?"

"I don't know. A feeling. When we three were having dinner last night I wanted that to be a regular thing. I wanted you there. I wanted you. When you left this morning, the house was so empty. I felt like I had to say something. I needed you to know. Even if you didn't feel the same." A corner piece in the puzzle of light coming in illuminated where our chests met, a dove-gray splash of light in the darkened room. Adrian lifted one hand from around me to stroke the enlightened skin on my breasts, just atop my heart.

"I love you," he said, lifting my chin so my eyes met his eyes. "I love you and I wanted to say it so many times. I feel like I've known you my whole life. Last night I nearly shouted it at Oscar because he was being an asshole, and I was drunk. I nearly said it to you on the couch."

"Beat you to it," I joked in a tinny voice with no force behind it.

"You did, but it wasn't in my native tongue, so it doesn't count."

"Te quiero mucho, Adrian. Te amo."

"Je te veux, Celia. Je t'aime."

I leaned my forehead against him.

"If something comes up, if you're pissed at me or whatever, just talk to me, okay?"

"Copy that, Sergeant."

And I was flipped onto my back, Adrian's mouth traveling south, effectively stealing any further snarky retorts.

CHAPTER 38

CELIA

SMOKY-GRAY SHEETS BUNCHED UNDER WHERE HE slept on his stomach, face turned to the side. Easy Sunday morning sunlight poked its nosy fingers through the shades, reflecting off his sleep-softened features. My pillow was still wet from my hair after our shower the night before, but I lay still, mentally tracing his brow and lashes. Maybe it wouldn't always be like this. Maybe there would be a day when I looked at him and he wouldn't make my breathing hitch, but I knew without room for a doubt, that there wouldn't be a day I wouldn't love him this much. As for now, I was finally allowed to enjoy the sensation he evoked in me.

Shifting ever so slightly to pull my foot from a tangle of the sheet, I looked up to see Adrian's lashes fanned across his cheek, the corner of his mouth that wasn't lodged in the pillow lifted in a sleepy smile. I reached over and stroked his face, then ran my hand down his arm and exposed back. He didn't seem inclined to move but opened those intent eyes as I touched him with sensitive morning fingertips. The ceiling fan above whirred in a lumpy sort of loop, making me drowsy again, my body melting back into the mattress. If I listened, I could hear the caps of river waves tap along the dock, gulls crying in the sky. If I listened harder, I could hear my heartbeat and his breathing, drumming a song only the two of us could write.

Who knew how long I was smiling at him? I didn't realize I was until he turned to me and traced my mouth with his finger. I understood then. Emil and Judy. Oscar and Nate. Oscar's guilt in loving Taiko. I understood what it was like to have someone know that they possessed you completely. And to crave it. As I'd done to him, his fingertips skated along my arms and hips. Over the crease between my breasts where they sat just above the sheet. Around to my back and down my spine. His face was still rumpled and not quite awake, making me want him even more. There was something vulnerable and boyish in this sleep-softened Adrian.

"Come here, Sullivan." Oscar always said my voice sounded like sandpaper dipped in honey. Adrian's sleep-thick voice was like the tide at midnight. Scooting closer, we lifted the sheet, fitting ourselves flush against one another. Both of us kept running fingers and hands, even toes, along one another's skin. He kissed the tip of my nose, my cheeks, my shoulders. I thought I would burst from my skin with each contact. "I hope you didn't have plans today," he breathed in my ear, pushing against me in just the right way.

"Just to run," I said, my head bending back, exposing my throat while his mouth moved along it.

"Mind if I change them?" A slight push again, fitting against me.

"Don't you have to work later?"

He smiled, hovering over me, those corded arms pushing into the bed on either side of my body. Good God Almighty.

"I have the day off."

"By all means, change my life." Okay, so I didn't really mean to say that out loud. It made me blanch and stiffen under him, but he laughed and interlaced our fingers, pulling my hands overhead.

"Okay then."

I was all for the only plans being us staying in this bed all day. Although the shower racked up a few points as well. I brought my legs up and wrapped them around his hips. Then the doorbell went. At the same time, his phone started buzzing. He glanced at the phone on the side table and groaned, his head dropping onto the pillow next to mine, and his hair tickling my face.

"It's my mom." Oh. My. God. He texted her quickly.

"My car is still here." He nodded his head against mine. "Shit."

He said he'd go down and start the coffee and feel her out while I got dressed. In yesterday's clothes. Groan. Gathering my discarded garments while he pulled on shorts and a T-shirt, I asked if I could borrow a tee.

"You, uh, you want to keep some clothes here? Like, for—"

I grinned at him, really enjoying the embarrassment on his face.

He pulled a fresh white tee from the drawer and tossed it at me. "Your hair's still wet, Sullivan," he said, low and suggestive, doing six kinds of things to me I really didn't need to feel at that moment.

Brush your teeth, Celia, wash your face.

The outfit looked completely normal and cute, but there was no way of getting around the fact that it was eight o'clock and I was here with no makeup and wet hair. Own your shit, Celia, I told myself, slipping on my sandals and loosely side braiding my hair. Nerves throughout my body were short-circuiting until I realized it just did not matter. If what he'd said about her was true, then surely, she'd known how Adrian and I felt about each other. And unless I was totally off, she seemed nothing if not encouraging. So, being a goddamned adult, I walked into the kitchen with my head held high, a bright smile on my face that wasn't in the least bit forced because I saw Adrian.

"Good morning, Celia," she said, turning on the counter stool to face me. I returned the greeting, kissing her on the cheek before taking the offered coffee cup from her son and kissing him softly on the mouth. I didn't know which of their eyes were glittering more, but somehow, I felt like I passed her test, and that he might be about five minutes from deciding where to have me next. "I didn't mean to interrupt," she said. "But I was up far too early this morning and decided to make muffins. So, I brought some up." From Fort Pierce. At eight in the morning. Uh-huh.

Never one to say no to a muffin, I took Adrian's cue and began picking at them. Chocolate chip: I loved her too. I may have muttered that out loud. She chattered about Viola's baby and how it was nice all being together since they would be in Oregon for Thanksgiving. Adrian's arm was tight around me while we drank our coffees. She stopped talking after a while and just looked at us and sighed. It was a strange sort of reaction. Finally, she picked up her handbag and said, "Took you two long enough," and she kissed us both goodbye.

In the corner near the TV and gaming console, sat my handbag. We heard the buzzing after Julianne left, and I realized I hadn't looked at my phone since before I arrived yesterday.

Where are you? I've texted like 8 bazillion times.

Sorry, Os. Haven't checked my phone. You okay?

Haven't checked your phone since last night? Wait. No, really. Where are you, chica?

I sent a picture of the view from the back door. Adrian laughed behind me. FaceTime lit up my phone.

"Rip it off like a bandage, Sullivan," Adrian said, coming

up behind me. His hand lay flat against my stomach. I accepted the call, knowing Adrian's face was visible on the screen.

"Thank you, Lord, Baby Jesus," Oscar screamed, making me pull the phone farther away. Adrian was laughing behind me, his face leaning on my shoulder. "That is some public service, Kikumoto."

"Okay, Os. I'll stop you there. We are good. You?"

"I had a coworker tell me there was someone sniffing around on Friday, wanting to see me and asking questions about where I was. She said he was in a suit but looked a bit sketch. Be careful, okay?"

"Adrian's mom said someone was at her office asking about all of us too. Something is up."

"I hadn't heard that." Adrian pulled away from me and grabbed his phone.

"I'll leave you to it then," Oscar said with a waggle of his eyebrows. "Adrian?"

"Yeah, buddy?"

"You hurt her, I'll kill you. 'K?"

I hung my head and growled.

"Wouldn't expect otherwise," Adrian answered, setting his phone down.

"Cool. Love you guys." The screen went black.

"Sorry. That was bizarre."

"What was that growl you just did?" he asked, prowling closer.

I laughed, pulling him to me.

"I think I've developed a thing for you wearing my shirts." His hands went up under the shirt, kneading my chest. "Can we go back to ignoring the phones?"

I was nodding, my breath speeding up.

"You're beyond beautiful," he mumbled, kissing away any response from me.

Chapter 39

Oscar

IN THE BACK OF MY CLOSET THERE WAS A GARMENT bag from an old Brooks Brothers suit I bought the first time I visited Ce in college. It was the fall of her second year in Boston, and I was applying for grad school. It seemed the right time to buy a suit, and that trip gave me a very short-lived preppy bug.

The suit was consigned years ago, but the bag I kept. Inside the garment bag, zipped where I didn't have to come across them all the time, were some of Nate's things. Most of his stuff Adrian, Mom, and I went through ages ago. Some of the bits I kept were pieces of him I refused to part with. His dog tags, of course, hung on the hanger, tucked inside. The tie he wore for our engagement party. I had been so mad at Ce for not coming. Her boss wouldn't let her off that week-end. I knew she tried. She came down a couple weeks later though. The three of us shopped together for our wedding rings. Those sat in two tiny boxes, weighing the bag down just a bit more than everything else, like they were mocking the blatant disregard time showed us. I'd taken them out twice since he died. I wore them both to bed, thumbing the beveled metal and hoping to see Nate in my sleep. The T-shirt he'd been wearing in Home Depot that day I met him was balled up, a shot glass he'd bought me from the airport in Frankfurt on his way home from Bahrain wrapped up inside it. Just a hint of him remained in the scent clinging to the T-shirt.

His knives were scattered in there, Damascus steel floating with the Breitling Emergency watch I'd bought him for our engagement. He'd worn it on our trip to Spain. It pissed me off when I'd realized he hadn't worn it when he shipped out last. That was why I'd bought the damned thing. The watch had a dual-channel satellite transmitter connected to it. Originally intended for pilots, so that should they have an aviation emergency the Coast Guard or search parties would be notified of the person's location. I guess I tried to keep him safe, as best I could. I guess you never really can.

Judy has his medals, his flag. Adrian gave me a burial flag. He and his dad folded it thirteen times. They'd both dressed in suits and presented me the flag, knowing that our country never would.

"On behalf of the United States Navy and a grateful nation," Adrian said, his voice choked, "please accept this flag as a symbol of our appreciation for Nathan's honorable and faithful service." It was as unofficial as they come, but it was more heartfelt than I could have imagined. So, when Celia and Adrian finally got their hot little selves together, I knew I wanted to give Adrian the watch. I didn't need to keep it myself. I'd rather get a new one. One without the dragging weight of Nate's headstone attached to it. But if I gave it to Adrian, he'd understand it was because I approved. I appreciated him. We had coffee before his shift the Thursday after I found out about him and my sister. He knew the watch; Nate had shown it to him. The dumbass tried to refuse the gift. I told him it was his and I'd made up my mind. He kind of pawed at his eyes and hugged me, saying he loved Celia. He hoped I knew that.

"Yeah. I know you do. Knew before you did, asshole."

He laughed at me. It was true though. God, those two.

Taiko sat with me on the floor of my closet as I showed him Nate's things. There was some closure in it; it was a way of reconciling the me who Nate taught to love with the me who was able to love Taiko. He didn't ask about the desert boots in the corner, or the locked gun safe I never touched. I could shoot. Nate took me on one of our first dates. Just before he shipped out for the first time. He said he wouldn't leave me unarmed while he was on the other side of the world. I think it surprised him when I was nearly as accurate as he was. I'd been shooting since I was fifteen. My and Ce's uncle took us out after the night with Robert Avery. I said I refused to be a victim again, so I learned. We were both decent shots. I just hadn't wanted to pick up the gun since I lost Nate. Taiko reached into the garment bag and pulled out the burial flag in its black triangular case, setting it on our dresser. He didn't comment on it, or make a fuss, but the gesture was pure.

I'd spent the better part of the past week teasing Ce and begging for details. She told me to kiss her ass. But she did tell me to knock her upside the head if she ever walked away from Adrian without hearing him out. She was head over Balenci-aga-fucking-heels in love with him. And had been for like six months. And he was hers, body and soul. So, when my phone rang from his number late that same night we'd had coffee, I didn't think much of it.

"Kinda late, Kikumoto."

"Hey, cocksucker," a voice drawled from the other end.

I stopped on my way to bed, grabbing the bathroom door handles for support.

"Got a minute?"

I started flailing my arms like a mad fucking hatter, trying to get Taiko's attention. He was sitting in bed, a book propped on his knees. I dove headfirst onto him, clawing across him for his phone.

"What the fuck do you want?" I asked, trying to open Taiko's phone, but the keypad was in Japanese, which I was completely unamused by. He took it from me and opened it, letting me go to the voice recorder, putting mine on speaker.

"Your full attention. So, get your hand out of your pants and listen. You know who it is?"

"Jacob fucking Wentworth."

"Ding ding. Not as dumb as he looks."

Please, bitch. You probably bought your way through school; I was top of my fucking class.

"Pretty obvious I didn't lift the phone from the pocket of the illustrious Sergeant Kikumoto's pocket."

"Did you hurt him?" I asked, dreading the answer.

"Not too bad. He's a fighter. Aren't you, ass wipe?" Jacob said away from the phone.

There was a grunt and a growl. It sounded like there was a gag in Adrian's mouth. I started sweating, getting flashbacks to the gag that had been in my own mouth. The feel of slow suffocation.

"Now. The thing is, Oscar. I need your compliance. I never wanted to hurt Celia. She's fucking hot, man. I wanted to keep her. But this fucker had to get in the way."

The sound of something getting hit came through.

Taiko was writing in his book. *What do you want me to do? Call police?*

I was nodding my head. The number for the FBI agent I was dealing with was on my phone. "So, what's the plan, Wentworth?" I pulled a pair of joggers on and zipped a jacket over my T-shirt. Taiko threw clothes on as well while he dialed 911.

"Well, for starters, I need you to come here. Alone, obviously. And bring your sister." In the background, there was a hell of a commotion. "Shut the fuck up!" he yelled, presumably to Adrian.

"You're stupider than you look if you think I'll bring her to you, you sick motherfucker."

"Oh relax, Oscar. I'm not going to hurt her. But don't forget to tell her I have her booty call here with me." He told me the address, which was weird because it was his dad's place on John's Island. He told me to take the boat from Adrian's over to the dock at his dad's house. I hung up the phone and screamed. I hit the fucking bed and tore at my hair. I absolutely fucking raged. Taiko stood in the doorway, not knowing what to do.

"Give the recording to the police when they get here." I went into the closet, used my code on the safe, and pulled the gun out, loading it and slipping it into the holster I'd clipped on my waistband. I kissed him hard and didn't stop to think about what it might be like for him if I didn't come home. I was in the car on my way to pick up my sister when she called me.

"I assume you're on your way to me?" she asked, so stripped of emotion I knew she was in a different plain of thinking.

"Ce, I already called the cops."

"Get here quick, Os. It's pretty clear he plans to kill one or all of us before the cops get there. And if he hurts Adrian, I want to be the one who rips his fucking eyes out of his head."

I ran the last light on Club and Beachside, punching the gas to get to her house.

CHAPTER 40

CELIA

IT WAS ON THE THIRD RING I PICKED UP THE PHONE, having just finished showering. Adrian was coming over after work since it was his day off the next day and I had to work. I'd barely said hello before a nervous-sounding voice I never wanted to hear again came on.

"Hey, Cece," Jacob drawled, his voice kicking up a notch on the southern accent. I pulled the phone away, double-checking it was Adrian's number. "You there, baby girl?"

"What is this?" I regretted everything I'd eaten.

"I'll call your brother in a little while so he can pick you up. Wear something cute."

"What are you talking about?" I went to my laptop in the living room and opened up the messages app.

"So, obviously I have Adrian's phone. Which, if you're quick on the thinking, means I have Adrian here."

I started texting Officer Kriss.

"Why?"

"Ah. To the point. I did like that about you. Like when you said you weren't into me. Respectable."

"You never respected me."

"No? Well, see I really liked you. I still do. I *wanted* you. Girl, I would have given you everything."

"What do you want now?"

"It would ruin the surprise. But for starters, in one hour I'm going to shoot your boyfriend."

I choked. There was a sound in the background.

"Dress pretty, darlin'."

"Wait! Let me speak to him. I want to know he's okay."

He sighed, long and suffering.

"I guess there's probably some last words bullshit, I shouldn't have fucked Sarah, blah blah. Here." There was a deep intake of breath.

"Hey, Sullivan."

I sobbed a breath but gathered myself.

"How hurt are you?" I asked, my hands shaking as I typed to Kriss.

"I've been worse, Sullivan. Listen. I want to tell you a couple things, okay?" His voice sounded strained. Deep in my chest an ache twisted and tore.

"Okay."

"I'm glad I introduced Oscar and Ronnie. He's a good guy, Celia. Make sure he takes care of you."

"Adrian, don't," I squeaked.

"'Le suprême bonheur de la vie c'est la conviction qu'on est aimé.'"

"Don't you fucking dare quote Victor Hugo to me now, God damn it!"

"Don't be a cynic, Sullivan. This isn't *Les Mis*. 'Ce qui fait suit en nous peut laisser en nous les étoiles.'"

"Without you, there will be no stars," I replied, feeling my soul slip away.

"Hurry up. I don't have all night," Jacob said, bitterness coating his voice.

"Remember that night we had dinner, and you didn't know I was coming?"

"Yeah," I sniffed. "Of course I do."

"Remember that song that came on and you yelled at the dude who turned it on?"

"You mean—"

"I mean that dude has your back. He knows you and knows how I feel about you. Tía would agree. But whatever you do, don't come here."

"That's enough of this," Jacob said, grabbing the phone. "I'll be nice and start the clock now. Hope your brother's fast."

I wrote down the French that Adrian spoke to me. It was botched and horrible, but looking it up, the quote was clear.

Le suprême bonheur de la vie c'est la conviction qu'on est aimé means "the greatest happiness in life is the conviction that we are loved." I tore at my hair and bit the heel of my hand to keep from screaming. The other I knew well.

Ce qui fait nuit en nous peut laisser en nous les étoiles. Whatever causes night in our souls may leave stars. The prospect of Adrian being gone was so bleak, I could fathom no stars. If there were stars, they would exist to me only in the vacuum of space. Nothing like the beauty in the night sky.

In the back of my closet, I kept a locked gun safe. I hadn't touched it since Nate took us all to the range a couple of years ago. Jeans, boots, sweatshirt, gun belt. Like hell I'd let him be taken from me. I was done with being a victim.

In the mirror across from my bed, Emil's face looked back at me. For a brief second, I was suspended in realization. Adrian meant for me to have Emil's help. That's what he'd meant when he spoke about the dude having my back.

"Emil," I said carefully. "Your son, Jacob, has Adrian. He's hurt him. He's hurt me. He's hurt Oscar. Nate loved Oscar, Emil. Help me."

Darkness swarmed like hornets behind me, filling the mirror and my room. I didn't flinch. I no longer feared Kip Cosgrove and his anger. I had plenty of my own.

"You," I said to Kip, my own temper smog thick and rising in the heady permeance of soulless dark Kip caused. "You were a violent, abusive piece of shit in life. You killed your other son."

The darkness gained form. Kip Cosgrove became more corporeal.

"I am not afraid of you. Judy was. You scared her in life. You can be angry about Emil, you can be angry about Nate. But understand something, this house was purchased with Judy's own money. Nate grew up to be the best damned guy I've met. Your cruelty drove your wife to Emil's arms. You should be grateful that she knew that happiness. Because you beat her and made her miscarry; there's a special place in hell for men like you."

He was standing before me, looking just as he must have in life. Emil's form was just as detailed.

"Either help me or get the hell out of my house. Because I will no longer tolerate your presence. Soy una bruja con un pie en el otro lado." Static energy picked up in the room, pulling at threads on the bed and the hair on my head. "So, ask your dead-ass self if you really want to deal with a pissed off, lovesick witch with one foot on the other side."

Headlights shone and I ran out to Oscar's car.

"Who are you calling?" Oscar asked. My phone was attached to my ear as I got in the car and switched to speaker as soon as the door shut.

"Julianne, it's Celia. I need you to get in touch with Ronnie Kikumoto for me."

"I have to get to my computer. I was asleep." Her voice was sleep heavy but alert. She was definitely going to hate me now.

"I'm sorry it's late, it's just that—"

"I'm moving, love. I understand. Adrian prepped me." I swore under my breath, hoping she didn't hear me.

"I don't know why I need to do this, but Adrian is being held. He said he was glad he introduced Oscar and Ronnie, though he didn't. He also said Ronnie's a good guy and will take care of me. All I could think of was that he simply needed me to get in touch with Ronnie."

"I'm pulling up his file now. I'll send you his number. Be careful, Celia."

Oscar whistled a swear. We were going so fast it was more likely to get us pulled over.

"Slow down, Os." He let up a bit, still flying over surface roads. It felt like hours on US 1 until we got to Adrian's house.

Neither of us really knew how to drive a boat, but it was small enough, and there was no one on the lagoon at that time of night. We had less than half an hour before the time was up. I couldn't let myself think about that. What I turned over in my head was why we were going there. Adrian was obviously taken to lure us. But why did Jacob need us there? This wasn't some gothic novel where no one would find out. The police, FBI, and whoever the hell Ronnie Kikumoto really was, were all told. We were meeting Jacob at his father's house for Christ's sake. The current was trying to drag us farther north, Oscar's less-than-superior boating skills really making it a challenge to keep moving in the more southeasterly direction we needed to be. He slowed, seeing the inlet to drive toward.

"Keep your eyes open, Ce. I have no Goddamn clue how to find the place from this angle." It was a mess of little cuts and inlets along the lagoon. Even in the lagoon, nighttime waters held an eerie menace. Ahead was a long dock that seemed to trail quite far inland. On the end was a massive boat. Not like the yachts you see in Cannes or places like that, but it was large enough to know it was the kind of boat someone like David Wentworth would have taken for a holiday to the

Bahamas. As in, it was seaworthy. From even the few hundred yards away that we were, I could see the two guards standing on the dock, large guns trained on us. In the dark, their cargo pants and flannel shirts made them look like anything from Everglades lumberjacks to backcountry militia.

"Jesus Christ," Oscar muttered over the sound of our engine slowing. "We are outgunned, Ce. Let's not be stupid."

"No shit. I haven't even fired one in years." Before we were in view, I took off my belt and unclipped the gun, stashing it in the cooler of the boat. Oscar had me do the same with his.

"Oscar, go home." I began panicking. "Please. He only wants me. Really. Only needs me."

"Fuck off, Ce. You think I'd leave you?"

"I don't, but I'm asking you to. For Taiko's sake. For Mom and Tía."

"Don't pull that on me," he snapped, his anger lashing out at me. We knew each other well enough to recognize when to stop pushing.

It took three times before we could sidle the small boat up to the dock. Even then, we bumped rather harder than Adrian might appreciate his boat being treated. One of the hired muscles jumped onto the deck of Wentworth's boat and popped into the cabin before rejoining his partner. We were roughly pulled up, patted down, and shoved through into the cabin. Sitting, each with a foot crossed over his knee, were David and Jacob Wentworth.

CHAPTER 41

CELIA

"When I said, 'wear something cute,' I was thinking more like a short skirt. It's okay, we can get you something along the way."

I couldn't even bring myself to answer him.

"Shame you haven't been out on the boat before. Impressive, isn't it?"

Still, we both stayed silent.

"Oh, come on. Oscar can never normally shut his mouth. What's with you two?"

"Where's Adrian?" Oscar asked.

"In the supply room with the rest of the bait," David answered, slick as a seal.

"Let him and Oscar go," I said. "I'll stay. Whatever Jacob wants."

David laughed and motioned for the guards to pull us along. We walked past the galley, another smaller seating area, what looked to be a couple of sleeping cabins, and back to the supply room. Once inside, Jacob put his arm around me and pulled me from the guard. Oscar reached for me.

"Whatever I want, huh?" Jacob asked. "You know I could

have anyone I want? I mean, like really. I've never been turned down before. Never. And the one thing I ever really did want —you—rejected me."

My eyes locked on Adrian's as they pulled a shower curtain aside in the far corner. He had bruises on his face and a few cuts, but the rest of him was covered in his uniform and jacket as it was a chilly night. His eyes shot to Oscar, and I could swear he nodded before looking back to me. The gag in his mouth made me feel physically sick. They had him kneeling, arms bound behind him, and a weathered chain on a wall-mounted lobster trap held him in the corner.

"This seems to be extreme for a bruised ego, doesn't it, Jacob?" I asked.

His nostrils flared at me, and his cheeks sucked in. For someone so good-looking he'd become ugly. A monster.

"I mean, you could have let it go and stayed friends with me. Instead of stalking me and abusing me."

The elder Wentworth chuckled.

Adrian's eyes bore into me, widening. The greatest happiness in life is the conviction that we are loved, I thought to myself. What if I laid it on thick? What if I wasn't so combative?

"What do you want from me, Jacob?" I asked with an almost demure tone. I wanted to go to Adrian. Get my arms around him. Get him off his knees, for God's sake. "I just needed time. That's what I asked for." I dared reaching out to him. Tugged on the sleeve of his black jacket.

He looked up at me like he was trying to figure it out. He wasn't stupid, and I had to be so, so careful. The cabin was silent, bar the motor. I hadn't noticed our moving until then. Cold prickling tiptoed up my spine, threatening to dig its nails into me.

"We could have it all, babe," he said tentatively. Instead of looking at me, he was shifting his eyes around the room, settling on David. Searching for approval.

"Okay. Then let's do it." My teeth started chattering, an involuntary aversion.

He stood looking down at me, touching my fingers with his. A strange sort of look was on his face, like a computer function gone wrong. He leaned in to kiss me, like he had the first time, and I hadn't minded then. This time, though I saw the softness in it, everything in me revolted. But I let him kiss me. Adrian was quiet, his eyes closed, brow furrowed.

"Want to escape with me?" Jacob asked like we were the only ones in the room. He ran his fingers down the length of my braided hair.

"Why not? We seem to be on our way anyway." I tried to give him a smile. It was the one Julianne Kestler saw straight through; the one Adrian scoffed at that day I gave him a tour of the museum. Jacob smiled back and squeezed my hands.

"Yes, but what about when I do this?" David asked, and his fist met Adrian's cheek.

I brought my hands to my mouth, a strangled sound coming out of me.

"Don't let her play you, Jakey Boy."

Jacob looked between me and his father.

Oscar was uncharacteristically quiet behind me. I saw Adrian do that odd chin tuck toward my brother again. An unspoken conversation between them I didn't understand. What I did understand, however, was Jacob. It wasn't necessarily me who Adrian was alluding to with the Victor Hugo quote. Jacob, who was not a Wentworth really, but a Cesar, spent his life desperate for David's attention. David's approval. Maybe he wanted me. Maybe he wanted me to want him because of his need for acceptance. He needed the conviction of being loved. Wanted.

The motor picked up, making us all jerk. I knew where we were, sort of. The boat banked left, so I assumed we'd traveled down to the Fort Pierce inlet. The break between the river and the Atlantic would take us out to sea. There was always a speed up needed to plow through the rough seam where the two bodies of water met. It was a line of demarcation that we all seemed to recognize, taking us from the relative sanctuary of the lagoon to whatever awaited in the endless ocean. I was shivering now. A kind of shock I couldn't tell myself to snap out of. The harder I tried to not look toward Adrian, the more I shivered. Oscar tried moving to me, but the hired muscle yanked him back.

"She's cold, tired, and wet, bro." Oscar spoke up for the first time since initially asking about Adrian. I didn't know how long we'd been on the boat. A half hour? An hour? Was he still counting down to shoot Adrian? I was wet and cold. That had little to do with how hard I was shaking, though. I was scared. Jacob took off his jacket and draped it over my shoulders, pulling me to him. The motor slowed a bit, leveling out, like reaching cruising altitude on a plane. We were settling in for a long ride.

"I have to get something, okay, babe?" Jacob asked. "Be back in a sec. Hey, cocksucker, hold her." He pushed Oscar to me as he went out the door. It took everything in me to not fall apart when my brother held me. Wentworth spoke to one of the gunslingers, turning his eyes from us for a second. I looked at Adrian who gave me a quick wink and hint of a lopsided smile, though his cheek was swollen and shiny.

Jacob came, and I pulled his jacket farther up my shoulders. He stopped in front of me and grabbed my hand. "Sorry about the finger. I lost my temper." I wanted to scratch the splint down his pretty face and watch him bleed.

"It's okay," I said instead. He turned to Oscar.

"I want to thank you for coming so promptly. I know it wasn't easy based on the convoluted directions."

I whipped my head to Oscar. He didn't bat an eye before responding, "I know when to push my luck."

Jacob nodded at the elder Wentworth. I wasn't understanding. Oscar squeezed my hand subtly before letting go. We were given the address here. I risked a look at Adrian, knowing he must be miserable on his knees this long. His lips twitched. I couldn't help the sound caught in my throat that escaped when I saw as the two armed men moved toward him.

"Been to Curaçao, Celia?" David asked. I put my head in my hands and called to Emil, quieter than anyone could pick up. The guard bent to link an arm under Adrian's shoulder. The lights started flittering and went out. A separate generator kicked in instantly, but that made a nails-on-metal noise before spluttering out as well. As I'd dealt with six months of it, I knew the heavy feeling in the room when Kip Cosgrove arrived. I knew it in the way I'd imagine the split second before an explosion or tornado would be. An expectant breath. It lasted just a hair too long. Then, from the dark, the thud of bodies hitting the wall of the cabin.

"What the hell was that?" one of the men yelled. I felt Oscar move beside me, then heard Jacob's yell and a double thump. Chaos everywhere. Something knocked into me, and I jumped back. The lights came on. Adrian was still kneeling, though closer to the door, his hands still behind him, eyes taking in the scene. The two guards were swinging their weapons back and forth, assessing. Oscar was the only one who wasn't covering up what he'd done. Jacob was on the ground, nose bleeding, clutching his groin where I assumed my brother had kicked him. Wentworth had stepped back, out of any potential mayhem. The guards rushed Oscar, and I screamed, jumping between them. One lifted the butt of his gun to me. All three of the younger men yelled. Adrian tucked and rolled, kipping to standing, legs and hands bound.

"Do not touch her," Jacob said with a vein of malice in his

voice. Then he pulled back to hit Oscar but stopped himself and smiled. "Not worth it."

My anger became a tactile sense. The feeling of the wrath balled in my hands like dough I could mold to my own desire. With that feeling, I turned to Jacob. I knew no matter how nice I played, how compliant I pretended to be, Oscar and Adrian weren't getting off this boat alive. And it didn't matter to me if I did or not. Not if they were gone.

"What are we doing here, Jacob? What are you playing at?" He widened his blue eyes—Emil's eyes—at the change in me. Maybe something shone through my own eyes, but he tipped his head to the side. Behind Adrian was a darkness swelling. I felt Emil behind me, and there was a swear from the guards.

"What?" Jacob asked. He couldn't see them. The guards could.

"Your real father is standing behind me, Jacob," I said with a killing sort of calm. "He's been inhabiting my house, and if I may be so bold, Emil, I think he's disappointed in you."

Jacob swallowed and looked to the guards who nodded.

"Enough fairy tales for tonight. Get them outside." David shoved to the center of the room, motioning to the muscle. "It's past time. We are on a schedule."

Each of the guards grabbed one of my men and pushed through the door.

"You should stay in here, Celia," Jacob said soberly. I wanted to be sick. "You don't need to see this."

"No." I took off from a sprinter's stance and was out the door, knocking into David Wentworth. He hit the side of the boat and swore, backhanding me.

"Celia, don't," Jacob said, grabbing for me. As I twisted in his grip, I caught Oscar's eye. He was feral, barely above losing his control. Adrian's hands started moving against each other, pushing his sleeves up the wrist above the zip tie. His long fingers moved swiftly with ease. They twisted the knob on his watch, spinning it until it popped, a small wire piercing from the watch. Immediately, he moved to the other knob on the opposite side and twisted until it popped up. It took him two tries, but he snapped the cap off the knob, a long coil springing free. He tipped his body sideways, the wires stretching out. The guards shoved him upright. One looked down at his wrists, and it took a long minute for him to notice something was wrong.

"I'm sorry, Jakey Boy. I know it was supposed to go differently, but this just won't work with her alive." Wentworth stuck the muzzle of a gun into my back and held me by the hair. My eyes locked on Oscar's. I shook my head to tell him no. Adrian's mercenary started to say something, but Oscar tucked his shoulder down with the slightest conservative drop, before elbowing the guard in the ear. Taking his gun, Oscar then drove his knee into the other guard. They both pulled up their weapons, an impasse of a shot. Seeing Oscar's face with an assault rifle aimed at it pulled all the coherent thoughts from my brain.

"Aim the other way, you stupid fuck," Wentworth yelled. Oscar stood directly in front of us.

It gave Adrian the time to bend all the way forward from the waist. He raised his bound arms high as he could behind him and with wide elbows, brought the hands back down, driving his elbows out, the force snapping the zip tie. He pulled the gag out and kicked the guard down to the deck just as Oscar sent his foot into the guy's face.

"God damn it," Wentworth said, moving me forward. He pulled the gun from me long enough to shoot toward Adrian. I screamed, but Adrian dodged the shot, rolling down, and grappling with the other guard. Movement on the black water took Wentworth's and my attention. White caps streamed in two rows from our boat out to sea. Another two of Wentworth's personal guards came out of the supply room, guns aloft. He indicated for them to go to my brother and Adrian. Jacob stood stock-still next to us. He looked like there was a rod up his ass.

"Is this what you really wanted?" I asked him, voice wobbling. I hadn't realized I was sobbing. "You could have everything, and this is what you wanted?"

Over the railing of the boat's side, came a rush of black, like insects. People rolled onto the deck. People clad in black body armor, helmets, and moving with far more stealth than the henchmen Wentworth had aboard.

"Took you long enough," Adrian said, backing out of the way and catching a weapon tossed to him. He twitched an inch to the side and shot the guard who had been fighting him. Oscar took a boot to the hip and fell back, but someone popped a silent shot into the guard who had been close to butting me with his gun.

Snippets of what was happening flashed like driving through dappled sunlight. Adrian's quick maneuver with the gun he was tossed, Oscar's fall, the team that boarded the boat —all of it pierced my comprehension of the events with a disconnected sort of presence. My brother mouthed for me to run. I did. Past Jacob, who had moved only to creep away from the violence.

Passages to the front of the boat were blocked by fighting. The narrow way leading to the back was peppered with Wentworth, his men, Jacob. I dropped to my knees, crawling past my brother to the opposite side. I debated jumping ship. I really did. I could swim, and the water wasn't too bad. It was lunacy, though, I told myself. I kept crawling, like a rodent from a broom. Shots sounded behind me. There was the smell of sweat and blood that mingled on the ocean air.

The boat was still moving but didn't seem to be going anywhere fast. As I rounded the closest cabin, I saw my mistake. Two of Wentworth's men stepped into my path. I tried to dive between three legs, but they yanked me up by Jacob's jacket. I was dragged around the back and tossed at Wentworth Senior like a sack.

The elder backed us up along the side of the boat.

"Dad," Jacob said.

"Shut up, boy."

"Let her go."

I looked daggers at Jacob, shaking my head. Somehow, I'd known. Once we figured out what these two wanted, I'd known it would come to this.

"It wasn't supposed to be—Celia. I tried to change it." He stumbled on his words, contrite and frightened.

I closed my eyes. None of the paramilitary, or whatever they were, had a shot to take at Wentworth. His gun was at my head, his hands fisted in my hair. We were wedged in a skinny walkway along the starboard side. He wasn't going out without taking me down too. I was breathing with scalpel-sharp intakes through my nose.

"Celia," Adrian called. "Look at me."

I did. Not crying. Not screaming.

"Eyes on me."

"Dad," Jacob called. I felt David turn to Jacob, who had a handgun pointed at David. David took an inhale, moving the gun from my head to point at the boy he'd raised. In that split second, there was a pop, and Wentworth Senior was down, a shot coming from the gun behind me as well. I fell forward. Feet shuffled over the deck, everyone in battle black. Familiar hands were on me.

"Look at me, Sullivan."

I knew I must have looked crazed. "You're okay. Got it? You're okay. Oscar's fine. We're fine."

I started to turn.

"Eyes on me."

"Are you fine?" I whispered, stomach contents rising.

He chuckled. "I'm fine. We're all fine."

"Wentworth's kid is still alive," someone called over. I scampered toward Adrian.

"Wentworth's dead," the same voice said from behind me. "All clear."

We were moved from the narrow deck to the bow where a helicopter hovered overhead, lowering a rope to us. Someone took Oscar up, then Adrian secured me to him, and we were lifted. From the air, I could see Jacob being put onto a basket. Once we were on the helicopter, the stretcher was brought in. I couldn't look at him. I didn't want to see him or the damage.

"What the hell took you so long to send out the homing beacon, Lieutenant?" someone sitting beside us asked.

"I had to get outside. Everyone seemed to be standing on ceremony in there. It's not like you didn't have eyes on us. You could have been there quicker too."

"There were three similar vessels out on the water. Would've been a hell of a fuckup hopping on the wrong cruise."

Adrian sniffed.

"You knew?" I asked him. He looked down at me, a look unlike I'd seen on him before. He could have been a stranger. My shoulders still shook. It was probably shock.

"Yes. No. Well, not entirely."

"Who is cleaning up this shit?" Oscar asked, his head back against the wall of the helo. "Who are you people?" His patience was dried up. I knew the feeling. Now that the adrenaline was gone, I felt like a husk.

"We are the puppets who monitor the sad bastards setting off that nifty little watch you gave our friend here."

"That's bullshit." Oscar sighed. "No one monitors that satellite frequency anymore. The frequency is only pulled up once the person has been reported missing. So, you crazy fucks knew we were out here already."

"Smarter than he looks," the guy on Adrian's other side said. I put my head on Oscar's shoulder.

"I get that a lot."

It didn't seem like very long before we were hovering, readying to land. Adrian leaned into me.

"It's going to be a shit show within minutes of landing. There's nothing to hide. You did everything right. Don't feel like you can't tell the truth."

"Sergeant?"

"Sullivan?"

"Did you lie to me?" My eyes were closed.

"Not entirely." He was looking down at his boots when I looked at him.

Oscar's hand covered mine on the other side.

"Just tell me if I'm going home with a broken heart. I'll sort myself out from there."

"I can't tell you that," he said.

I started nodding, trying to remember how to breathe.

"But if you do, I hope it's not because of me. I never lied about anything to do with us. I just had to leave out a few things about my career."

"Jesus, are you like Blackwater?" I asked.

He laughed.

"Blackwater is scattered like roaches," someone commented, standing and grabbing a bar overhead. "And no, your boyfriend isn't. Blackwater wouldn't hire his ass."

I looked up at the man standing over me. The Asian features, and the fact that he'd been the only one on the boat and flight who had been talking. *The kid talked a lot.*

"Ronnie?" I asked.

He winked. "Head's up, kids. Time to scatter."

Like roaches my ass.

CHAPTER 42

CELIA

Rain was coming down delicate and misty, uncharacteristic of Florida. I amused myself thinking that perhaps it was because it felt sorry for us. Oscar and I stood in the open air next, the fluorescent lights from inside the Coast Guard station backlighting us. Most of the roaches were huddled in a loose circle on the helipad, unconcerned by the rain. Each of their faces shone with drops of water, their black clothing absorbing the helipad reflectors. Adrian stood with them, the gun no longer slung over his shoulder. He said not to lie about anything, but I wouldn't admit I saw him shoot the first hired muscle. Whether he told or not was up to him, but it made no difference in my story. I'd called myself a witch and had ghosts be my henchmen that evening. In the instance of far-fetched stories, I would say admitting those details was more significant than at which point private military contractors killed kidnappers.

We were abducted by pirates. Rich pirates. Hysterical giggles escaped me. I had my hands in front of my face, mortified at myself. Oscar turned incredulous thundercloud eyes on me, clearly wondering what I found funny in this.

I said, in broken attempts, that we had been taken by pirates, and we were the treasure. So we were, essentially, pirates' booty.

He let out a loud snort of laughter that had us both turning into hyenas. The others were looking at us like we were batshit crazy.

Adrian walked over, stiff and official, leading us out of the rain. Inside the station, we had coffee and waited for the FBI and someone who looked quite a bit like a state senator. The team who rescued us was debriefed. News vans and helicopters were already in a blockade outside the station. The truth, beyond what the police knew already, what the FBI already knew, what apparently a private military sector had records of already, was that I knew nothing. I didn't think Oscar did either, but from how he and Adrian had acted on the boat, my brother had a sense of something happening that I clearly had not.

From the agent's phone, I saw that it was four in the morning. There wasn't a part of my body that wasn't shaking. Unrelenting stabbing pains lanced behind my shoulder blades from the shaking. The blanket around me didn't change the wet clothes or the fact that I'd peed myself a bit when the gun went off near my head. Speaking of the gun, the high-pitched buzzing in my right ear was slightly disorienting.

Uncertainty clouded my feelings about how my world might be in the next few days, weeks, months, and doubled the cold shroud around me. They asked about the guns they found in Adrian's boat at the Wentworth place. I said they were ours. We brought them for our self-defense. It was Florida, for Christ's sake. My neighbor's dog walker carries. And unlike many people, both of our guns were registered.

"Why did you leave them?" the agent asked.

"Because it seemed a reasonable idea when there were two armed paramilitaries with assault rifles waiting for us on the dock. I'm a decent shot, but I knew it would only get me killed tonight."

"Understandable."

No shit.

Another hour went by, and I was free to go. Oscar was released at the same time. I didn't know what Adrian was doing. Whether he was being questioned as a victim, witness, a what. At the gates sat a government SUV, engines on and idling, waiting for us. I kept looking around for Adrian, an empty feeling in my stomach. I didn't have my phone, which was almost comical. Three phones in six months. Cameras were flashing, streetlights were flashing, headlights were flashing. Scores of light trails chased us home. Highways of optics streamed by in indistinguishable colors. The night dropped away in beads of sunrise and Friday morning traffic, leading to the day ahead.

Adrian and Mom stood outside my house when we pulled up. The last I had seen him at the Coast Guard station was well before I had been taken in for questioning. Mom walked forward to greet us, arms open wide. We both fell against her, spent. The car waited for Oscar. To take him home to Taiko. It took a while for me to see the Vero Beach Police car across the street, sitting under the live oak tree.

"Are you in trouble?" I asked Adrian.

"No. Just a hell of a lot of paperwork. I have to go back in because I was getting checked out at the hospital."

My face must have changed, but my body was too gone to have noticed.

"I'm fine, Sullivan." He was curt. Measured. Not how he normally acted with me.

I didn't want to be alone and wouldn't have said it out loud if I had any handle on my own damned movements and speech. He looped his arm around me, kissing my head.

"I'll be back as soon as I can. Your mom's going to stay."

As he walked toward the car, a feeling like the covers had been pulled off my bed stopped me from going inside. Because "as soon as I can" had a lot of wiggle room. There was quite a large room full of "not entirely" in that phrase. Especially when there was a pocket of his life and career that seemed pretty clandestine. And I would rather know from the get-go.

"Sergeant"—he turned around with a notable wince—"please be honest. Will you come back? For real?"

He swore and crossed the pavement to me again. Hands held my face. "I'll see you in a few hours. I promise. I'll stay if you stay, remember?"

"I know, but I messed that up, so I wasn't sure if it was negated, and I'm really, really tired."

Chuckling, he kissed my forehead and lips. "I love you."

THE TEARS STARTED in the shower. Shampoo and water washed over my face as I gasped through the sobs, sliding down the tiles to the puddled floor. The water was cold before I could get myself out. Through getting clothes on and combing out my hair, I kept it in check, silent streams coursing down my face. The bed was freezing, but Mom had tucked my old plush jaguar stuffed animal into the covers, the one Oscar bought me for Christmas when I was eight because I was a fast runner. Always outrunning the boys. It slept with me until I left for college. Once I pulled him to me, the vellicating sobs returned. I knew once I cried it out, I would be fine. It just had to come out. We were all safe. It was over. All of it. Oscar was going home to Taiko; Adrian was coming home to me.

We made it through it all, and I was turning thirty next week. I wasn't crying because I was sad or feeling sorry for myself. I was crying because I was fine, and my body needed to purge the events that could have ended so differently. Swollen, painful eyes refused to close, even after the tears had calmed. I lay there, still, clutching the jaguar, a box of tissues slowly emptying until the door clicked open and shut. The bed depressed, Adrian's warmth folding me into him. He smelled like shampoo and sandalwood and asked why I wasn't asleep.

"Are you still contracting?" I asked him.

"No." He hadn't taken a contract in two years but was still on the payroll. "I officially signed my resignation tonight."

I asked how he came to be on the boat.

Ronnie's team had been keeping an eye on Wentworth, working alongside the FBI. Adrian put in a call when he left my house the weekend before.

"Based on what they were seeing, it would be a matter of hours before whatever half-cocked plans Wentworth made would be in effect." So, when Adrian took a call from dispatch to respond to a break-in at a bait and tackle store, he went alone since it was where they'd seen Wentworth's meatheads moving in and out in the days prior.

"Why did you go alone? You could have been killed."

He pulled me a little closer. "Nah. They needed me. They weren't going to kill me until they had you guys. Though, I am fairly sure executing me was the final plan."

I shuddered.

"The funny thing is, I think Jacob was trying to get caught. He gave Oscar the address. I heard him. But his dad thought he'd led you on a treasure hunt to find them. Who knows? The guy wasn't as bright as I would have thought. Worked out better for us."

"How did he think he'd get away with any of it? This isn't the age of hiding the Stuart gold. Oscar told me Wentworth's accounts were being watched for any sign of him leaving the country."

Adrian said his best guess was that Jacob played a dangerous game of leading on his father so he'd get caught.

"But why?"

"Because David made Jacob's mom so unhappy. Family is complicated."

Speaking of . . . "Your mom—"

"Has been in the import-export business her whole life and knows how to keep her head above water when she needs to. I told you to never underestimate her. I have formidable women in my life."

I turned in his arms and wrapped myself around him like a koala, falling asleep.

CHAPTER 43

OSCAR

TWO AND A HALF YEARS AGO, NATE CONVINCED Adrian to stop taking contracts with the private military. The first time I'd met him, I thought my sister and Adrian would get along like gasoline and a house on fire. The reason I'd never introduced him to Celia was because I wouldn't put her in the position of potentially losing him because he was caught in some Benghazi shit. Poetic that I lost Nate. It was just before Nate was killed that Adrian told us he'd decided to concentrate on his career here. It was sweet money he made, because, let's face it, police officers aren't exactly top of the financial game. Still, it wasn't worth it, and he knew that. He'd grown up.

When all this started with Wentworth, I'd wondered if Adrian had put feelers out to his contacts. He gave me that smirk when I'd asked and said he was looking at all angles. The reality was that, in my own training, and from what I knew of Adrian-fucking-Kikumoto, when I heard my sister calling for some guy called Ronnie, I knew something was up. Seeing him on his knees with just a zip tie and lobster trap holding him, it didn't take a genius to see he was waiting for something. I tapped my wrist, and he had nodded. The watch. It was just pretty unexpected that Ce had a gun put to her head.

Taiko met me at the elevator, pulling me to him and holding on. I'd never seen him super emotional, so the controlled sob that went through him took me by surprise. I was okay. I could deal with this shit. I go to therapy all the time anyway. Ce was a little messed up. I think she felt a yo-yo of doubt over what the deal really was with Adrian. That was up to them to sort through, but I had a feeling it would be fine between them. House on fire and all that.

There was a cup of my sleep tea sitting next to the bed for me after my shower. I stood there, the covers pulled back, and found myself telling Taiko I wanted him to move in with me. There was no reason to be going back and forth between here and Melbourne. My job kept me here, but I was ready to open my doors to him. Because, on that Goddamn boat, I kept telling myself I had to get home to Taiko. There was no reason to wait for happiness. I'd had so much taken from me already. When he sank onto the bed with me, I turned to him, wrapping myself around him like a spider monkey, refusing to see any emotion other than the profound fucking gratitude I felt to be home.

CHAPTER 44

CELIA

THE MUSEUM OFFERED ME A WEEK OFF. I DIDN'T need it, and it was a short week anyway, being Thanksgiving. We had a police barricade on both mine and Oscar's streets for privacy from the press. Everyone wanted to know what happened. The scandal. The Van Hoote Aerospace involvement. I wondered how Nina Van Hoote was. I wondered what she was like, and how she was hurting with Jacob still in intensive care. I could see that, in the end, Jacob hadn't wanted what happened. He was a little boy still wanting his father's attention, and it went south, forcing him to grow up in the span of minutes. My own mind wasn't clear on how I felt about that, and I knew that was okay. That every feeling I had was valid.

We went to Adrian's after a late lunch. I was still so tired I couldn't decide what to bring, which is how I ended up with an entire weekend bag of clothes being hauled out of my car. A now-familiar smile greeted us at the front stoop. Ronnie Kikumoto was far shorter than Adrian, though still tightly built with carefully honed muscles. The weirdness of having three unrelated Kikumoto men in my life at the moment was not lost on me.

Staring across the lawn to the lagoon beyond, I searched myself to see if I had reservations about the water, the river, this house, anything. Nothing set off alarm bells.

"So where did the painting really come from?" I asked, sitting next to Adrian.

"*In Time?*" Ronnie asked. "Oh, it's mine. Or it was. It's yours now," he said pointing to us. "I tracked it down a few years ago. It's a good one, huh? Like a circus in it. There's so much energy."

"I thought you were a nervous sailor," I said with a yawn. "Why do all this black ops stuff after?"

"You told her?" he asked, hand to his chest. "I give you a painting, and you told her I was a nervous sailor?"

Adrian was laughing at him.

"Payback is hell, my friend." Ronnie pulled out his phone and scanned through until he found the text thread he'd been looking for. It was then he recited a text conversation between him and Adrian.

"*Hey, Little Kikumoto,*" he read, lifting an eyebrow.

Adrian was cringing, his head ducked into the couch cushion.

Wondering if you can help me with something in the art world.

Lieutenant! Shoot.

"I need a beer for this." Adrian got up and walked over to the kitchen. I watched him pad barefoot to the fridge, and my toes curled under me. Ronnie kept reading.

Wondering if you've come across any Kikumotos lately.

I may have . . .

Adrian handed Ronnie a beer, me a glass of wine from the bottle we'd opened a couple nights ago. His eyes were amused.

I know someone who is a curator at the museum here, and she's putting together an exhibit.

Isn't it her job to, like, curate?

You seemed like a good contact for her.

Ohhhh. You want to seem like a sugar daddy, and be all, "look, baby, I gotchu a Kikumoto."

I was dying, laughing into my wine, while Adrian had the neck of his T-shirt pulled up over his face.

If you ever say the words "sugar daddy" to me again, I will personally demonstrate to you the interrogation tactics I used in Kandahar.

So no?

I tossed my head back, the hyena cackle coming out. Ronnie stopped and raised both eyebrows at me, before looking back down and reading out loud. Adrian sank lower on the couch, holding his beer on the armrest.

I just thought it would be a nice gesture to put you two in touch. Don't be a dick.

I'll loan it to the museum.

Really?

Sure. But you have to tell me something.

Groan.

Girlfriend?

No.

Booty call?

You're going to die young.

It's a rare, late Kikumoto.

Fine, you total shithead. I'm like 60 feet of water over my head, without a regulator, in love with this girl.

60 feet? That's just under two atmospheres. Decompression setting in?

How have you not been killed yet?

I'll send it ASAP. You gonna tell her?

Probably not.

Why?

It's complicated, Ronnie. Thanks for the painting.

Make sure you say, "Loaned from the personal collection of Mr. Ron Kikumoto, Sugar Daddy Maker."

I used five-inch needles and a clamp. When he didn't talk right away, I pried open his mouth . . .

I get it. Good luck, LT.

Adrian was still flat backed on the bottom sofa cushion, face covered with his T-shirt and a pillow. We were laughing, but I was so butterflies-in-my-stomach touched that I pulled the pillow off and pried his shirt away. His eyes were closed comically, but he squinted, opening one eye at me.

"I'm sure Oscar could thoroughly embarrass me too." I kissed him until he must have forgotten Ronnie was there because I was pushed back into the couch, smiling against him when Ronnie cleared his throat.

"Come up for air, Lieutenant."

"Sorry. My fault," I admitted.

"I'm out, guys," Ronnie said, putting his half-drunk beer on the coffee table. "I expect to get the wedding invites soon. LT, it was fun being in the sandbox with you again." He showed himself to the door, and called, "See you at the wedding."

We were laughing at each other, but I snuggled up to Adrian, sipping my wine.

"He calls you LT?"

"Hm? Oh, I was his lieutenant in the navy."

Ah.

"Why'd he point at me when he said the painting belonged to you now?" I asked. Adrian did a nervous chuckle, running a hand through his black hair.

"You heard him. He's all matchmaker, shit stirrer just like someone else we know."

"What aren't you telling me?"

"You're getting better at this, I see. I knew it would be trouble for me."

I fiddled with the bottom of his shirt, strumming my fingers just above his waistband.

Adrian swallowed a gulp of his beer and cleared his throat. "Ronnie wrote it under a contract that the painting was a gift to *us* and would be mine conditionally until we, you know . . ."

"Oh."

The sun was going down, the sky beyond the glass back of the house turning shades of rose gold and scarlet. Nothing about the implications of that conversation bothered me, surprisingly. We cuddled up on the couch, content and tired, for a fair amount of time, neither of us speaking. A cozy, companionable silence. I looked up at him. Dark, straight lashes shielded the glimmer in his eyes. There was such a stark contrast between the hard lines of the Adrian on that helo early this morning and my Adrian sitting here, his fingers threaded through mine. His face turned, catching my lips with his.

"Have you thought about selling the house? Or renting it out?" he asked, running a knuckle along my jaw.

"I think the ghosts are under control now."

His hand moved up and down my arm. My fingers made circles on his stomach. "Yeah, I didn't mean for that reason. I meant, like, if you'd want . . . to, like . . ."

I turned to look at him.

"Here. With me."

"That wasn't even close to a full sentence, Sergeant."

"Hmm. Okay."

"What's that mean?"

"Oh nothing. Doesn't matter really. I think maybe my sentence structure is an issue we should work out between us."

I poked his stupidly hard stomach. Then I decided I wanted to feel that stomach skin to skin.

"You want me to live here?" I asked, running my hands over his skin. He kissed the side of my head.

"Yeah. I do. If you want to. No pressure. It's just that, with Nate, then last night, and everything that's happened . . . I just feel like, why not?"

I was quiet, stroking his stomach and face. "I'd like that." Grinning like a fool, I nestled closer. "So, Ronnie was the first person you told that you loved me?"

He was laughing. "I have some regrets in my life. But I have to say, that's not one."

CHAPTER 45

CELIA

THANKSGIVING DINNER AT THE ASSISTED-LIVING facility where Judy lived started about an hour after we arrived. I hadn't wanted to stay long anyway. As soon as Oscar and Adrian walked in, she lit up. Oscar wrapped her in a hug and sat next to her.

"Hello, handsome," she said, patting his cheek. "I get all of you today. Adrian. Ça fait un bail, darling." It's been too long. Her eyes settled on me. "I had almost convinced myself I made you up. Sometimes I forget things."

Oscar made small talk, telling her he'd brought the lavender truffles she loved.

"The first Thanksgiving I spent without my Nate was the hardest. It was before you both knew him, so I didn't have such lovely boys coming to see me. I bet it's hard for you too, handsome," she said to Oscar.

I pulled out the sketch I'd found at Humiston and handed it to her. She studied it, touching the lines, and turning it over and over.

"He said he could never capture him. Never let me see the

341

sketches. I think he captured him perfectly, don't you?" she asked Oscar.

"I do."

Her eyes met mine. A presence at my back told me Emil was along for the ride.

"I miss them both. So much," she said, her voice wobbling.

"I know." Oscar twitched his nose, scrubbing at his scar. "I miss Nate every day, Judy."

She patted his hand. "He told me."

The three of us were stunned. Emil stepped to my left where she would be able to see him, if it were possible. Adrian put his arm around me.

"Well," she said, with a girlish laugh. "The reason for all of us being here together. The reason for la douleur exquise." Her eyes were to my left, locked, I knew, on Emil's. "Find your son, old man. I'm not ready yet, but à tout de suite." She will see him soon. Emil bowed his head to her and disappeared. I knew, in my heart, it was the last I would see of him.

"Judy?" Oscar asked. "What happened to *Naufrage*? The painting." She pointed to where most of the photos of Nate were clustered on the rattan dresser. Her finger beckoned Oscar, and a secret was said into his ear. "May I?" he asked.

"It's yours, darling. It's always been yours."

Oscar walked to the dresser and touched the photo of him and Nate, then lifted the rectangular box with Nate's burial flag. In the back of my mind, when we'd first visited in July, I'd wondered why the flag wasn't in the traditional triangular shape. My brother pried the clips from the back of the frame and popped the backing off. He took a breath. It was almost as if his thoughts were broadcast to me, the gears of his mind audible. He was thinking he wished Taiko were with him. He didn't know whether he could unravel the flag. He doubted himself. He missed Nate in a feeling so swift and offensive it was brutal. I moved to him, Adrian with me. We both put our arms around him in a trifecta of support. The flag tipped, six times to the right, six to the left. Wrapped inside was *Naufrage* —the original. The same slip of paper I had found behind the *Naufrage* at the museum flittered to the linoleum. I picked it up and smirked at the place the ghost of Emil had stood. *For Anton. I'm sorry to have left you.* I handed it to Judy, and she looked for a moment like she would recess into her unaware state. Instead, she smiled, tucking the note into her pocket and muttering something about Emil being a trickster.

"Some boy and his daddy came sniffing around one day. Said they were old friends of my Nate's. They had a hawk's eye on my painting. It was your mama," she said, pointing to Adrian. "She helped me wrap it up in there. Fitting. Some might say it ruined the integrity of the flag." She *tsk*ed. "I say, without that painting, my boy wouldn't have been around to have fought for our great country." She walked over to us. I hadn't seen her up and mobile yet. "Take the flag, handsome. Take that painting. Let it remind you that love exists. Sans regret. And you deserve it."

Then, to Adrian she said, "Ça en vaut la peine." It's worth it. "All of it. Coup de foudre?"

I wasn't sure exactly what she meant by asking about a lightning strike, but Adrian pulled me a little closer and squeezed my waist before he answered.

"Je crois oui, Judy." He thinks so. "Entre tous et mois." Between you and me. "Well, maybe not at first sight," he laughed, speaking to Judy. "But pretty soon thereafter."

"Ce sera notre petit secret," she answered. It will be our little secret.

CHAPTER 46

CELIA

FOR WHATEVER REASON, OSCAR WANTED OUR Friendsgiving the next day to be dressy. I'd hoped it wasn't to do with my birthday, which was the following day. Not that I have a problem with birthdays. Any excuse to eat cake is a holiday worth celebrating. It just felt like so much had happened in the last year, I was ready to pause. Tía gave Adrian the third degree at Thanksgiving. She referred to him as the "flan killer," and it was funny the first three or four times.

In the end, Abuelo shared a beer with him, and said, so that everyone could hear, "If she didn't like you, you'd be out on your calabaza. Behind your back, it's all about Celia's guapo police officer."

Adrian hung his head, chuckling. "Gracias, Abuelo," he said, shaking his hand. Some amount of stress left Adrian's shoulders after that.

I WAS RUNNING LATE GETTING ready to go to Oscar's the next day because I couldn't find the bracelet which matched the evil eye necklace that Tía had given me. After searching for nearly an hour, I pulled it from the pocket of my handbag and clipped it on. I wasn't used to getting ready at Adrian's. My tail was spinning to get out on time. A quick mirror check showed that everything was more or less put together. That Chloé dress I'd bought on eBay months ago was a perfect slip of emerald-green silk satin. It had angel-hair-thin straps, and a bias cut that caught the curves of my hips, before descending to just below the knee. I'd added the black satin five-inch heels I'd worn at the gala and pulled my hair into a curling ponytail to show off my smoky eye makeup. Adrian was standing by the door waiting, looking heart-stopping in black slacks and a black French cuff dress shirt.

"Sorry. I couldn't find my bracelet."

He turned, and the air seemed to pull from the room. His eyes took me in from toes to ponytail, lingering on my hips and collarbones. "Jesus, Sullivan." He cuffed a hand over his mouth and kept staring.

"Am I okay?" I looked down. I'd thought it came together fairly well.

"You're incredible."

"Yeah?" I asked, still needing to reach on tiptoes to kiss him.

"Don't start that. I'm far too committed to not make it an all-nighter after seeing you like this." He pulled away, shaking his head, and led me from the house.

Knowing Oscar, he wouldn't be serving more autumnal belly-bursting party foods. I was looking forward to his famous charcuterie board and some Champagne. Two Christmases ago, my brother and Nate hosted a Christmas Eve cocktail party. On the way to Oscar's this year I asked Adrian if he had been there and we somehow hadn't connected. He'd been working abroad. When he got back, Nate told him he'd missed his chance.

"Chance at?" he'd asked his best friend.

"To act like gasoline to a house on fire."

Adrian told me he was totally confused by that, but Oscar patted his shoulder and told him he was relieved to hear he'd fulfilled his last contract.

"So, which of us were they referring to as a hot mess?" I asked, walking into Oscar's condo for Friendsgiving.

"Both of us, obviously."

Taiko noticed us first, and he waved us over to the bar cart set by the balcony door. We filled a flute with pomegranate seeds and Champagne. Oscar was in his element, chatting with friends and being able to finally introduce Taiko to his peers. I could tell the artist was still uncomfortable with all eyes on him, so I pulled him into a conversation until Darcy arrived, singing "Happy Birthday" as she walked in the door. I just about died. Searching the room for Oscar, my eyes landed on Adrian instead, where he spoke with two familiar faces. I pleaded to him with my eyes when the room took notice that the one-woman birthday train was on track to embarrass me. Adrian instead raised his glass and gave me that smirk that was like a servant's bell to my core.

Pink rosettes covered a towering quinceañera-worthy cake brought out by my brother. The thirty candles lit up his wide grin and gray eyes, which sparkled as bright as the flames. Resigned to accept the attention, I lowered into a deep curtsy, Champagne flute held high.

"La reina de cumpleaños," Oscar announced. "Finally thirty. And more beautiful than ever."

"You'll always be the prettier one," I told him with a kiss on the cheek. I blew out the ridiculous number of candles on the sugar bomb of a cake I knew to be from the Mexican supermarket in Fellsmere. I thought of all that we had been through this year. These past years. And how it truly made sense to seize the moment. Grasp on to every happiness with both hands. While my eyes were closed in that thought, Taiko brought out a black-lacquered wooden box tied with a wide gold ribbon.

"Happy birthday, darling," he said, stepping back to let Oscar hold court next to me.

I looked at them, seeing if I could read my brother's usually loud thoughts. He just urged me to hurry up. "Más rápido, chica."

The ribbon slipped away with a whisper, letting me open the hinged lid. The box then dropped open on three sides so the items in the center were on display. My hands went to my face in a gasp. Oscar's arms were around Taiko, keeping him close (and likely keeping him from escaping the attention). On the bottom of the box sat my old Balenciaga heels—the ones that were destroyed when I was attacked. The ones Oscar said he got rid of before I could see how bastardized they were. But now they were art. A true Kikumoto.

Water was painted to splash from the soles, up over the pointed toe caps. From the white-capped waves, spilled effervescence through which a mermaid tail swam, her head lost where the shoe opened. Her arms were made of Japanese characters that then flowed into tiny chrysanthemums, winding in and out of gold and turquoise waters. The heels of both shoes became an open book, more characters emptying from its pages. The characters drifted around to the insides of the shoes becoming particles building a little girl on one shoe, reaching out to a little boy on the other shoe. Both children, presumably Oscar and me, held a chrysanthemum in their respective left hands, a palmful of flame in their right. The insides of the shoe were painted black with gold stars in constellations on each. Flowering vines ran down the heels, to where a minuscule three-dimensional silver rat sat on one heel, long metallic tail wrapped around the cap. On the right heel was a lacquered onyx magpie, her beak curved around the heel.

I picked up the shoes and under them, the soles painted in a near-mirror-finish red, was written:

You are fire at great
Depths. Be not afraid to be
Volcanic Beauty
Happy Birthday, Celia—Oscar and Taiko

Someone pressed a fresh glass of Champagne into my hand. I wanted to study the gift for hours. The shoes? They were no longer coveted Balenciaga pumps. They were art. Priceless, personal, heartfelt art. Salvaged from a favorite personal item and recreated to be a story of myself. One which, I would wager, I didn't know how to tell.

"What do all the characters mean, Taiko?" I asked him quietly.

"I've written it all down for you. Some are your names. Yours, Oscar's, Nate's, Adrian's." He pointed to the characters coming out of the book. "You have a story to tell, Celia. A cast of characters who fill it. There are song lyrics, as supplied by your meddlesome older brother." He pointed to the characters from the waves.

"Something dramatic about dying if he fell," he read.

I laughed, a sniffle of tears too, looking for the man who flooded my mind each time I heard that Jake Owen song. He had twinkling eyes on me from the other side of the room. I reached a hand for him to come over.

"Here," Taiko read, "it says, 'Every time I close my eyes, I think of you.' Oscar suggested we needed to add, quothe he, 'lo-fi male voice lyrics'. So, this is from—"

"A song," Adrian supplied, "from my favorite band." I looked to him. He shrugged his shoulders, sipping his drink with a wry twist of his lips.

There was a delicate chain inside the shoe. I pulled it. On the end was a folded origami crane dipped in gold.

"This was how I first saw you." Taiko spoke with more

confidence. "At the gala, you were in white and black, with red lips. It reminded me of the red-crowned crane, the symbol of longevity, creativity, regality. Happy birthday. That's the last phrase on here." He was blushing fiercely.

"Thank you. That doesn't even begin to express my gratitude. This is . . . I don't even know what to say, Taiko. Oscar."

Oscar jumped up. "Oh! Not to be outdone." He presented me with a bag. Inside was a replacement for my heels. He winked. "I bought them for you when you were heartbroken over Kikumoto here," he said, jabbing a finger at Adrian. "I couldn't have you brokenhearted and shoeless. Salt in the wound."

"Hey, Os?"

"Yes, queen?" He leaned his smiling face on his hands, batting those big rain-cloud eyes at me.

"You're the absolute best fucking brother."

"I've heard that before."

The night stretched on, friends and colleagues mingling. Oscar's balcony spanned the length of his living room, around to his bedroom, a length of ocean view. I slipped outside to look out on it. The party had died down, only a few of us left, and we were readying to leave. In the quiet moments, Oscar told me that when the time came, the money from Cesar's estate was going to starting a foundation. He wanted to support LGBTQ+ adolescents as well as arts and academics in the community and give these kids, especially those without supportive families, a chance. He also had plans to use the money for full and partial scholarships for underprivileged youth, minorities, and LGBTQ+ people. He asked if I would help head the foundation with him. It would be my honor.

A slight chill danced on my shoulders from a passing breeze. Adrian slid the door closed behind me and stood close enough to touch but a companionable distance apart. It made me smile. He was so controlled and so respectful of my space.

All the times I thought my heart would set fire to my skin if we touched, he stayed just out of reach. Even when he may have felt the same. That military discipline. I said that out loud to him.

"A constant test of my self-control. You had me at the very end of my line many times."

"Did you know that when you think you're at the end of your line, you're really just 40 percent to your max?"

"Mmm. Heard that. The thing is, there were a few times I pushed well past that and was still at the end of my rope."

I laughed, not giving in to touch him.

"Can I take you home, Sullivan?"

WE MADE it through the door. Mostly. I had his shirt opened, my hands splayed on his chest, while he turned the handle. Backing up the steps in heels became nearly impossible. He lowered backward, and I straddled him where he lay over the middle of the staircase. His hand slipped under my dress and touched me. I gasped, biting his lip. He sat up and lifted me clean off the steps until I had my feet under me to follow him up. My dress was off before we stepped into the room. The heels were more complicated. Steady, disciplined fingers unbuckled them, Adrian's hair tickling my inner thighs. He stood, pulling off the rest of his clothes. I stepped closer, our bare chests touching.

"I haven't said it every time I wanted to," I told him through half-drawn breaths. "When we were having coffee that day. With the journal." I touched him as I spoke, his eyes closing at the contact, his hands shaky on me as well. "You're beautiful. I wanted to tell you that."

His response was a low groan as my hand moved on him.

"The most beautiful thing I've ever seen."

His hand slid under my backside, setting me onto the crisp shock of cool sheets. My back arched to meet him. I took him in with every beat my heart could muster, absorbed every flame we created together. And when the fire was banked for the time being, I lay on him still. His fingers drew lines on my face and arms.

"I have two birthday presents for you. One, I'm a bit annoyed that Taiko beat me to." He reached to the drawer on his bedside table. A box containing a little zippered silk bag was presented to me. I sat up a bit, the sheet slipping from me. From the silk bag, I pulled out a necklace. It was maybe twenty inches in length. Looking closely in the low lamp-lit room, I could see the shape of a tiny origami crane. Crane after layered crane. There must be—

"A thousand cranes. Well, not literally." He took the necklace from me and clasped it around my neck. "In Japan, if someone is presented with a thousand origami cranes, they are granted the favor of the gods." He touched where the necklace hit in the center of my chest, then leaned in and kissed my collarbone. "You don't have to wear it. You can just, you know, keep it, or whatever."

"I will wear it every day." I rose to kneeling, just above level with where he was propped on his elbow. "It's extraordinary." He had a shy, pleased smile. "Two?" I asked.

He inhaled deeply.

"I don't know what to do here, Sullivan."

I didn't understand the hesitation.

"This is yours. Regardless. It can be what it looks like. It can be just a gift. A shiny toy. You tell me what to do here."

My eyes were narrowed at him. He got up off the bed and walked to the closet. I could hear the beeping of the gun safe, and a resounding click before he walked back to the bed. Even in the silvery dark, I watched the plains of muscle on his naked body as he walked to me.

"So don't freak out on me, Sullivan. Promise?"

"Promise." He tossed me a box, which I caught like it was an apple. In the box was a ring. A straight, knife-edged platinum band and a single emerald-cut diamond set in the center. A shiny toy? I looked from the ring to the man uncharacteristically picking at his fingers. "So, by saying it can be what it looks like, you mean—"

"I mean I'm all in with you. I'd like to marry you. It doesn't have to be now. I'm just telling you that you're the future I want. But I don't want that to mean it messes up right now. Because right now, I'm just a guy out of his mind in love with a girl. I'm going to ask you to take the lead on this and tell me what to do."

"Come here," I whispered to him, handing him the box back.

He looked away, letting me drop the box with its heavy gift inside.

Though I was stark naked and kneeling on the edge of the bed in front of an equally naked man, I felt at ease. "Forget you preempted this. Put the ring on my finger and ask me a question."

His chest rose and fell, like a trapdoor. Those long fingers that drove me to the brink of insanity plucked the ring from its nest. Both our hands shook as he moved the ring onto my finger.

"When I lost my best friend, something died in me. Then I met you and not to quote Victor Hugo—because you'll definitely say no—but there were stars again. And I'll wait if you want. But in the interest of not feeling like I'm actually going die right now, Celia, will you marry me?"

"Yes." Any capacity I had for articulate speech was gone. I jumped on him and said yes again, my face buried in his neck.

A thousand cranes slipped to the side and onto the pillow, where a final puzzle piece of wintery Florida moonlight locked the shadows away. The shadows that had haunted us both, keeping the picture of us in disarray. In a final stanza to an infinite poem, our hands intertwined on the bed beside us, a beginning and ending on an ellipse of time and fortune.

ACKNOWLEDGMENTS

There have been scores of strange occurrences and coincidences during the inception and execution of this book. From stumbling upon a rental cottage (two summers in a row) that could have been Judy's/Celia's house, to an incident where I ended up running down the street in Celia's neighborhood in a white nightgown. *Stars Like Gasoline* is a story tattooed on my heart and has been ever since Oscar woke me up in the middle of the night like a teething toddler. All of the art and artists within *SLG* are made up, apart from the chandelier (*The Way the Moon's in Love With the Dark*, an exquisite piece by Fred Wilson, which was at the Vero Beach Museum of Art on loan from the Pace Gallery in New York).

Huge thanks to all who have been involved with *Stars*, from original betas, Heidi (who got it in unedited chapters), Meredith, India, Becca my CP, Margarita, and Damian, who said, "What's the point of this book?"

Thank you to MaryAnn and Sarah for helping me with the Spanish.

Huge thanks to the City of Vero Beach, Florida, (and all of Indian River County) for giving me the inspiration to set this book along its beautiful shores. If you get the chance to visit, dear reader, please go for a meal at MoBay (say I sent you) and Riverside Café! You too can feed the catfish.

Thank you, Anna, for being the best editor ever. A tip of the hat to Jake Owen for getting the song "Alone With You" stuck in my head during one of my cross-country drives from

LA to Vero whilst in the middle of writing this book, and thus, it became an intrinsic part of the story. Obviously.

Thank you to all my readers. I wish you a thousand cranes.

If you've enjoyed this book, please consider leaving a review online (Amazon, Goodreads, Barnes and Noble, etc). Reviews are big deal to authors!

ABOUT THE AUTHOR

Jessika Grewe Glover grew up along the humid shores of South Florida, eventually marrying her British husband and moving to Los Angeles, where they live with their two teenage children and rescue bulldog. Jessika writes multiple genres from literary to speculative fiction. When she is not writing or reading, she can be found traveling, creating art, making chocolate dragons, and bantering in song lyrics. She is the author of the *Another Beast's Skin* contemporary fantasy series. *Stars Like Gasoline* is her first contemporary fiction novel.

ALSO BY JESSIKA GREWE GLOVER

Another Beast's Skin

A Braiding of Darkness

Printed in Great Britain
by Amazon